In Death, As in Life

Sonny Kohet

ISBN: 978-0-9804324-5-9

Dead Man's Eyes

Judy sat on an old threadbare sofa. Comfortable despite its age and signs of wear, and one reason she enjoyed coming to this shabby, aging, but full-of-character café. Music—a mixture of slow, bluesy jazz and classics from a bygone era—resonated softly in the background.

Nina Simone singing *Feeling Good*, the wooden table with its chipped and faded varnish, and a lace tablecloth—once white—completed the picture. Sighing contentedly, Judy sipped her cappuccino and dug her fork into her New York style cheesecake. She belonged here.

Judy liked the sofa because, other than being comfortable, it was beside the full-length window, which provided natural light, important for writing. She could study people walking past, often interesting in their dress or mannerisms. People-watching inspired many ideas. Some she used, most she discarded or set aside for another day.

She took her iPad from her shoulder bag, which sat on the sofa next to her like a close friend. The iPad seemed strangely out of place; technology from the future transported through time. *Now that's an image I can use.*

She tapped on her Notepad app and began typing, 'buy an old-style notebook and fountain pen…'

A shadow cast across the table, caused her to glance up. A man had stepped into her light. A casual observer might describe him as a fat, angry man, and never give him another thought.

Judy wasn't a casual observer. A professional observer of life, she paid attention to detail. Like many observers, she seldom took part.

The man was facing the café inches from the window, shouting into his phone. Anger, which oozed out of every pore—along with sweat—enveloped him.

He wore a brown suit. *Why do men wear brown suits?* It was a size—probably two sizes—too small. *Not through vanity.* That was the realm of women who buy a dress a size too small, to delude themselves they're smaller than they are. *This man is not vain, misguided; or otherwise.* The dated brown suit suggested he'd simply outgrown it.

His jacket, pulled tight across his shoulders, was still a little crumpled. Fresh sweat soaked through the stiff, pale outlines of old stains. It had been a long time since the buttons reached the holes. The trousers were tight around his thighs, struggling to contain his bulk. *Must've been difficult to squeeze himself into them.*

His stomach hung below his waistline. A pale-yellow shirt, a size too small, drawn tightly across his chest, and tighter across his stomach. The buttons functioned under enormous strain; the buttonholes stretched to their limits. *Some strength in the thread holding those buttons on.* If the thread succumbed to the pressure, and a button launched against the window, Judy wouldn't be surprised.

His shoes, also brown—scuffed and worn at the heels—may not have seen polish in the last year. The color and cut of his attire may once have been fashionable—with minor celebrities—but not for a decade, maybe two.

His face was bloated and burning red with rage. *What made him react so strongly? Whatever, or whoever, sure has him pissed off.*

Sweat plastered his disheveled—apparently self-cut—brown hair across his forehead. She tried to imagine him younger, before his face filled out. *Once a little—perhaps more than a little—handsome, before he let himself go. Handsome and fashionable.*

She found herself drawn to the man's eyes. They were light brown and a little bloodshot. They say eyes are windows to the soul. If so, his soul was full of anger. They bulged out of his head like a telescope goldfish.

His eyes widened, irises contracted, and anger dissipated, replaced with surprise.

The man moved in slow motion. He dropped his phone and clutched his chest. It was only a sidebar to the story. The story was in his eyes, and they mesmerized her. Fear supplanted surprise and his eyes became furtive, moving from side to side in the manner of a man trapped, searching for a way out.

He slumped to his knees—in slow motion. Passers-by—also in slow motion—moved towards him. Judy's adrenaline kicked in, heightening her senses, allowing her to observe every detail.

As the man sank lower, the furtive eye movement ceased, giving way to realization. The look one gets in their eye when they've had an epiphany. Fascinated by the unfolding story, Judy watched as realization became acceptance, then resignation, or perhaps somewhere between the two, as he acknowledged and reconciled himself to his fate.

However, there was something more in the man's eyes, something Judy struggled to identify. He stared directly at her, pleading, as if asking her for help. *No not help, that isn't it. It's the look people have when they want you to do something, but know they have no right to ask. He's definitely directing it at me.*

He smiled; the weight of the world had lifted from his shoulders. Almost as soon as his moment of contentment appeared, it left, his eyes lost all expression. There was nothing left. Strangely, the pleading remained.

He slowly toppled over on his side, his eyes wide open, pleading with her. His angry soul gone, leaving nothing except an impression of pleading.

Judy stared at the man, crumpled on the sidewalk, and he stared back. She wanted to look away but couldn't. She sat transfixed, as if under a spell.

A voice, a woman's voice… shouting, broke the spell. Judy looked up. A woman stood just inside the door of the café. *The woman who tried to help that man. She seems angry. Why's she shouting at me?*

Frank

Frank caught his breath before knocking on Billy's door. Even a short walk left him breathless. He needed to lose weight. *Soon. It's nearly done. Won't be long now. Hope Billy's awake. Hard to wake him when he's sleeping off the previous day's session.* Frank knocked.

"Enter!"

He opened the door and stepped into Billy's room. "Jesus, Billy," he balked, "put some fucking clothes on!"

Billy picked up his pants. "What do you think I'm doing?"

He made no move to actually put them on.

Frank surveyed the room. The furniture, basic, perhaps thirty years old, but well maintained. A single bed, a small desk with a chair, a closet designed for overnight stays, all finished in the same woodgrain laminate worn in patches to a dull mustard color and—glimpsed through a partially open door—a bathroom. Everything Billy needed and more than he was used to.

The room was spotless, except for Billy's clothes strewn across the navy-blue carpeted floor, and reflected in the full-length mirror on the closet door.

"Come on, Billy," Frank gestured towards the pants hanging limply in Billy's hand. "Get dressed and I'll take you to lunch."

"Can't Frank, lunch is my busy time at work, when I make my money." Pants still in hand, Billy spread his arms, and nodded towards Frank's stomach. "Looks like you should give lunch a miss, too. You look like an overstuffed sausage."

"Wouldn't call giving blow jobs in a park restroom *work*."

"Got to earn money for living."

"For drinking, you mean."

"Didn't they tell us in college to find something we love doing and find someone who'll pay us to do it? I love sucking cock."

"Don't you have any shame?"

Billy thought for a moment, as if giving the question serious consideration. "No, I don't believe I do."

"Why don't you come and work with me again? It'd be better than this."

"I'd only fuck everything up for you again."

"Come on, let's have lunch."

"Can't, got to keep the customer satisfied, you told me that. My customers always go away satisfied."

"You remember that…"

"I remember everything when I'm sober."

Frank could hear the bitterness in Billy's voice.

"That's why I drink."

Billy hadn't made a move to get dressed.

"Came by to give you a little money, for rent, not for drinking."

Frank threw three hundred dollars on the bed.

"Don't need your money. Earn my *own* money."

"Yeah, but you drink it away as soon as you earn it. Pay the rent."

"You should use it to buy a new suit. How old is that suit, anyway?"

"You're right. I've nearly kept my promise." *Then I'll have time to think of myself.*

Billy didn't ask him what promise.

Frank knew Billy didn't want to know. He guessed it would be another reason for Billy to drink, and he already had more than enough reasons.

"Pay the rent, Billy," Frank repeated as he left.

***

"Oh… For fuck's sake!" Frank exclaimed, realizing the taxi had dropped him at the wrong bookstore. He turned to grab the taxi, but it was too late. "Fuck!"

He thought of flagging another, but the bookstore he wanted was only a couple of blocks away. "Might as well walk," he muttered.

He didn't feel like walking. It was hot. In the taxi, he'd been sweating.

Don't know why I wore this old suit. Billy's right, it's too fucking tight. Maybe he wanted Billy to see him at his best, when he'd been on top of the world, when everything had been different. *Why? Billy doesn't care. He only cares where his next drink is coming from.*

Walking by a café when his phone rang, he stopped to catch his breath. A woman—sitting on a sofa—looked at him. *She's pretty.*

He glanced at the screen. "Fucking Myriam. That's all I need," he muttered.

"What?"

"Frank, you fucking useless loser bastard!"

"What do you want, Myriam?" he asked, still trying to catch his breath.

"Joanne saw that fucking loser, Billy. Says you gave him money."

Fuck, that was less than an hour ago. "What if I did? Not your fucking business."

"That fucking loser destroyed our lives. What're you giving *him* money for? If you got money to throw away, you can give it to me. I'm your fucking wife."

"Ex-wife Myriam, you divorced me over ten years ago."

Why does she make me so angry? If anyone should've made him angry, it was Billy, but he never got angry with Billy.

"Of course I did, because you're a fucking loser bastard, but I'm still your wife."

"You've married twice since me. Don't know what…."

Frank felt pressure in his chest, like a steel band was tightening around it. He dropped the phone and grasped at his chest, trying to loosen the band.

What's happening? Heart attack! It's okay. Just my time. No... no not yet, I haven't finished. Can't you hold on a few more weeks, a couple of months... then I'll be... No, I can't go yet. I haven't kept my promise I... that woman's still looking at me.

He was past living now, and he knew it. He pleaded with his eyes; they were all he had to communicate with.

Please, please lady, help me keep my promise.

***

Judy focused on the woman's voice. "Don't sit there staring, you dumb bitch! Call a fucking ambulance!"

Startled by such an abrupt call to action and confused why the woman didn't call one herself, Judy picked up her mobile, and entered the number for Emergency Services. They answered almost immediately.

"Emergency Services, which service would you like?" the voice asked.

"Err um H-h-hello."

***

An ambulance arrived.

Judy watched the paramedics attempt to revive the man, but it was too late. She could've told them; she'd witnessed him accept and then welcome his death.

She couldn't get those pleading, dead eyes out of her mind.

Next, the police arrived. After talking with the paramedics, they took statements from witnesses, including the woman who'd tried to help him. The woman—glaring—gestured towards Judy. *She's still angry.*

A police officer approached Judy.

"Hello Ma'am, I understand you witnessed that man's death. I need to take a statement."

"Okay."

"Can you describe what you witnessed?"

Judy wanted to tell him how the man's eyes told her the story of his passing, but she didn't.

Instead, she told him the man shouted into his phone, then dropped it and clutched his chest, before falling to the sidewalk where he lay motionless. She confirmed she called Emergency Services. The officer made a note of what she said, took her details, thanked her and that was that.

***

The excitement was over. Everyone had left. The angry woman glared at Judy one last time through the window as she departed the scene.

Judy remained seated on the sofa, finishing neither her cappuccino nor her cheesecake. She did nothing except sit staring blankly, seeing only those pleading eyes.

She glanced at her watch. Late afternoon. She'd planned to leave the café much earlier. Rain forecast for late in the day and she didn't have an umbrella.

Judy gathered her belongings and returned them to her bag as she prepared to head home. She glanced out the window. *Getting dark. Hope I reach home before the rain starts.*

Heavy black clouds hung low in the sky. She shuddered and hurried across the road, turned right and immediately turned left down a laneway. Exiting the lane, she was halfway across the road when the clouds opened, releasing a torrent.

She stepped onto the sidewalk, her light blouse soaked through, her hair plastered across her face. Suddenly, she desperately needed to pee. She became concerned she might wet herself, otherwise she'd continue home. It wasn't far. *Should've gone before leaving the café.*

She glanced up. She was in front of a bookstore. Pulling the door towards her, she darted inside.

The store owner stood at the checkout counter just inside the door. Judy looked at her expectantly, but the woman just stared at her.

Judy said, "I'm wet, it's raining."

The woman gave her head a quick shake, snapping herself out of whatever had transfixed her. "What? Oh yes, sorry. Here."

She passed Judy a box of tissues.

"Do you have a restroom?"

"Straight down the first aisle, in the back. Can't miss it."

"Thank you."

Judy pushed open the door and stepped into the restroom. She looked at the mirror, pushed her hair back from her face, and shivered a little. Her drenched blouse had plastered tight against her lacy bra, clearly visible through the thin, wet material. She could see a hint, well, perhaps more than a hint of nipple color. *Oh, that's what she was staring at.*

She grabbed a handful of paper towels, entered a stall, dropped her slacks, and relieved herself. *Ahh... ecstasy.* She dried off the front of her blouse the best she could.

Judy didn't know how long she sat on the toilet, staring into those pleading eyes. She shook her head, bringing herself back to the present moment. *Will I ever get them out of my head?*

Although still wet, her blouse was no longer stuck to her body. She took a comb from her bag and ran it through her hair, combing it straight back, and once more shivering as the water ran down her back.

She wandered around the bookstore, killing time until the rain stopped. Hopefully, before the store closed. *These heavy showers seldom last long.*

In her mind, she saw only those pleading eyes staring at her. She didn't intend to buy anything but chose a spiral notebook and a fountain pen. Remembering their earlier encounter and not wanting to show any sign of having been embarrassed, she gave the woman a big, warm smile, paid for her purchases, and left.

It was evening now and would soon be dark. She shivered as the cool air reached her still wet clothes.

"It's certainly been a day," she muttered, and hurried home, taking the image of those pleading eyes with her.

In Search of Frank Farrington

Judy's sleep was erratic, haunted by the man's pleading eyes. *Will they ever go away?*

She woke late the next morning, skipped her exercise routine, had a light breakfast of coffee and buttered toast, then showered.

Feeling her mortality after the previous day's events, Judy examined herself in a full-length mirror. She didn't like the dark circles under her eyes, but liked her shoulder length hair, Ash Blond now, a colorist suggested it was closest to her natural color. She didn't want people to know she dyed her hair.

Happy with her slight frame and smallish breasts, when younger, she wished for larger breasts, but noticed gravity dragged other women's down. She didn't want sagging breasts.

A day for aphrodisiac lingerie—Judy categorized her lingerie, *Aphrodisiac*, *Fine Lines* and *Who Cares*—white panties and a matching bra. *I still look good.*

Vanity ensured she never let herself go. *Why do people let themselves go?* She wondered, remembering the man who died yesterday, and many of her friends who'd stopped caring about their appearance.

Looking at herself in her lingerie sparked a memory of her college roommate and lover Samantha, who introduced her to wearing matching bra and panties. *Whatever happened to Sam?* They lost contact at least fifteen years ago. *How can people, as inseparable as we were, lose contact?*

She shook her head. "It's not important," she declared.

Focusing on the present, she selected a white slip to wear as an extra layer of coverage to prevent a repeat of yesterday's encounter at the bookstore. Besides, she liked the way the satin gently caressed her body when she walked.

Makeup today, not too much. Don't Pink So lipstick, and *Starry-Eyed* eyeshadow. *Just enough to feel good about myself.* Judy doesn't like cosmetics, lotions, and creams. *Do more harm than good.*

A long, parchment Egyptian cotton dress, gathered at the waist to show her figure, and matching shoes, open-toed, raised heels but not too high. *Might have a lot of walking to do.* She inspected herself approvingly.

Am I ever going to get those eyes out of my head?

Judy glanced at her shoulder bag. It didn't match her outfit, never did. That isn't its purpose. Nor does it have a designer label. Judy has three criteria for purchases: practical, comfortable, and quality. Despite reputation and price, designer labels seldom met her criteria.

She grabbed the bag from the sofa and almost remembered a cliche her father used to say. *Something about getting back on the horse.*

Judy sighed, concerned she wouldn't be able to return to the café. She liked it there; a perfect place to work; quiet. The table, not too small for her stuff, with abundant light from the window, but the man's death unnerved her. She took a deep breath, sighed again, and left her apartment.

***

Arriving at the café, Judy hesitated, took a long look at the spot where the man died, pushed the door open, and stepped inside.

Dorothy, as tired and dated as her café, was standing behind the counter reading the *City Telegraph*. She glanced up as she heard the door brush against the bell that alerted her when the door opened.

"Oh, Hello Judy. Wondered if I'd see you today."

"Good morning, Dot. You know, back in the saddle and all that. How're you doing after yesterday's excitement?"

"Not too bad. We got a mention in the paper today… associated with that poor man's death, unfortunately. Still, might bring in some customers, you know… lookie-loos."

"They say there's a little good in everything."

"Suppose. Want your usual?"

"Please. Oh, in the excitement, I forgot to pay yesterday."

"Don't worry about it." She turned away to prepare Judy's order.

Judy surveyed the room, trying to decide where to sit. As usual, there were few customers and many vacant tables. She sighed, as she often did, but was unaware of it. Her eyes settled on the reserved sign on her table.

Being her best customer, Dorothy left Judy's place reserved. Judy resolved to return to *her* sofa. Its position by the window made it perfect for her work.

She placed her shoulder bag—ever her companion—on the sofa beside her. She sighed again and gazed out the window. All she could see was that man, laying crumpled on his side, dead. His lifeless, pleading eyes staring at her, as they had at the moment of his death.

Judy shuddered.

She hoped he would leave her soon, but now she sat transfixed, unable to see today, consumed by the image of yesterday. Diana Krall's version of *I've Got You Under My Skin* was playing.

"Here you go," said Dorothy, placing Judy's regular order on the table. "Here's the paper in case you want to look—page twelve."

Judy tore herself away from yesterday and glanced up. "Oh, thanks Dot. Yes, I certainly do."

The paper was already open at page twelve, the *City Roundup* section. A collection of short pieces highlighting insignificant events that happened in the city the previous day.

Long time since I've held an actual newspaper. She inhaled. Having started her career at a newspaper, she still loved the smell of ink. *Wonder how long they'll keep printing them; everyone gets their news online now.* That Dorothy still had the newspaper delivered every morning didn't surprise her. Newspapers were as yesterday as Dorothy and her café.

Judy scanned the City Roundup section and found the item she sought.

Man Dies Outside Kansas Café

> Frank Farrington 48 died from a heart attack outside Kansas Café late yesterday morning. Mr. Farrington, who was divorced and had no children, was the owner of Phoenix Imports. He is survived by a younger brother and two younger sisters.

His parents had little imagination.

She looked out the window, hoping to see today, but it was still yesterday. The man—Frank—was still laying on his side, staring at her.

Frank Farrington is actually a powerful name, easy to remember. Three short sentences, not much of a legacy after forty-eight years.

Judy sighed. "That's just sad," she said to herself.

Judy often talked to herself, as people who spend most of their time alone do. She was curious. *What made him so angry? Perhaps his ex-wife?*

José, one of her former lovers, told her; "Nothing can make a man as angry as an ex-wife."

That makes sense. Frank had certainly been angry.

Judy had never married, not because she had any issues with the concept. It simply hadn't happened. Nor did she have any desire to be married. She liked her independence too much; her routine suited her perfectly, and she enjoyed the freedom to do what she wanted when she wanted. She supposed she'd never marry, but then again, she never thought about it.

Judy assumed being married to someone, you'd get to know a person's buttons, and being divorced would have no reason not to push them. *Could be something in that.* She reread the item. *Kansas Café. Wonder why Dorothy chose that name? Must ask her.*

"Three sentences. That's just sad, Frank," she said, looking at him.

Three short sentences were standard for a report of someone's death. S*till…*

"Must have been more to you than three short sentences."

Judy dragged her attention back to today. A feature—not quite finished—was due on Friday. She'd intended to finish it yesterday afternoon.

"Thanks Frank."

Must get it finished today. Fucking deadlines are the bane of my life.

Her former editor, Jeff Bowen, provided Judy with a solution: "I'm going to have to let you go, Judy. Too many missed deadlines. I like your work, so I'll make you freelance, and assign commissions, but miss a deadline and I'll stop using you.

"I'll give your name to anyone who's looking for a talented freelance writer, but if you want my advice; develop your own features and sell them when they're done, no deadlines. If they're interesting, they'll sell."

Judy still accepted commissions—her bread and butter—and she still hated deadlines. *Too much pressure.* She preferred her own features; no deadlines and she can sell the same feature in different markets. Significantly more income for the same amount of work.

Judy sipped her cappuccino and ate a little cheesecake. *Dorothy sure makes good cheesecake, best in the city.*

She studied Frank. "Why did you let yourself go? What made you so angry? Why didn't you buy new clothes? Did something go wrong in your life? And what do you want from me?"

God... I'm talking to a dead man now!

Judy sighed. *Could be an interesting feature... why do people let themselves go, and something about ex-wives pushing their former husband's buttons—why do they do that?* This was why she came to Kansas Café nearly every day. It's where she gets her ideas.

She retrieved her iPad. She always makes a note of her ideas for features. Almost one hundred now, each on a new page in her notebook app. As her ideas grow, she adds to them. When she has enough to work with, usually about a page of notes, she does research to complete her feature. Some ideas develop slowly, up to two years, others come to life in days.

Recalling the spiral notebook she bought the previous afternoon, Judy put her iPad aside, took out the notebook and fountain pen, inserted an ink cartridge, and was ready to start. *One idea per page. I'll pull the page out when I'm ready to write.*

She smoothed the page twice. Without thinking, she started writing.

Judy stared at what she'd written. Surprised by the words on the page, she examined the pen in her hand and the words on paper. It *was* her handwriting.

In Search of Frank Farrington.

"I *didn't* write that," she said, confused.

She retrieved her iPad, entered her new ideas in her customary manner, and added a third, *Why do friends lose contact?*

***

Judy hit the service bell on the counter.

Dorothy was out the back making a fresh cheesecake. Attending the counter, she said, "Oh, hello Judy, time to go?"

"Yes, things to do." Handing over her credit card, she said, "Put yesterday's on there too."

Judy turned to leave, and then remembered. "Oh, Dot, why did you choose the name Kansas for your café?"

"Well, my name is Dorothy and when I was a child, I loved *Wizard of Oz*, you know, because of the Dorothy connection. Must have watched that movie a hundred times. Anyway, that's where Kansas came from."

Never would've got that reference. "That's cool," Judy said.

"Was going to spell Café with a K, but it didn't feel right."

Moving Mountains

On the day he was to die, Frank Farrington ate his usual breakfast of cheap knock-off cereal. *Loopy Loops today.* He didn't enjoy them, he never did. *Taste like cardboard.* He placed his empty bowl in the sink along with his plate and frying pan from last night's dinner. *I'll wash the dishes later.*

Frank stood on the steel landing outside his dingy little apartment—converted mezzanine office space—inside the warehouse. He leased five interconnected warehouses, currently full of stock.

He surveyed his empire. *Mountains of stock.* By the end of the week, it would be empty, and then would fill up again.

"You know Frank," he said. "When I announced I would move mountains to make things right, I had meant it figuratively, not literally."

He stood, silently taking in the mountains before him.

He shook his head. "Better get to it if you want to visit Billy today."

The iron stairs clanged and groaned as he walked down.

Frank climbed into his forklift, intending to get the shipments ready to be dispatched early tomorrow. It was supposedly his rest day, the transition day between his receiving and dispatching weeks, but he always seemed to have stuff to do.

He stacked an empty pallet with mixed boxes of products. He seldom broke up pallets, but occasionally needed to.

"You'd think with all this lifting of boxes you do; you'd be in better shape," *and climbing in and out of the forklift all day.*

The boxes themselves—although full—were seldom heavy.

He farted. *God, I stink. Must stop eating this crap. Sure it's gonna kill me.* He recalled last night's dinner. A can of *Sham*, fried with canned potatoes, and finished with a can of baked beans, also fried. He ate it because it was free, left-over product.

"Meat and two veg," he told himself.

After creating a few *hills,* stacks of pallets loaded with boxes ready for early dispatch, Frank changed into his brown suit and left the warehouse, hoping Billy would be awake when he arrived.

***

Judy's first stop was Alice's Bakery, where she selected a small sourdough loaf, *best bread in the city.* The sweet, yeasty aroma of freshly made bread and cookies blended together reminded her of her grandmother.

Next, Lexington Deli, another of her daily rituals. She chose leg ham carved off the bone and extra tasty cheddar cheese, just two slices of each, sliced to order, then crafted herself a salad from the salad bar.

She arrived home, left her purchases in the kitchen, took her shoulder bag to her office, turned on her laptop.

Stepping into her office was like entering another world.

The centerpiece, a 1930s leather inlaid mahogany desk, had once belonged to her grandfather, and then her father. The only furniture she kept from her parent's home. When she furnished the office, she matched the style of the desk, giving the room hard masculine lines, in contrast to the soft, gentle, feminine lines of the rest of her apartment.

She returned to the kitchen to prepare lunch. A ham and cheese sandwich with handmade wholegrain mustard from Exquisite Jams, another high-end artisan food outlet. The salad she transferred from the plastic container to a plate. Judy didn't like to eat from plastic containers.

She cleaned up after herself and placed the rest of her sour dough loaf in her bread box for breakfast the next day. The day-old bread left from that morning's breakfast she discarded. *Mom would say it was wasteful, but I prefer to eat fresh.*

Judy ate lunch at her desk while finishing her feature.

She took her first bite of her sandwich and stopped working to savor the experience.

The ham was full of natural flavor from being cured on the bone, moist, a little salty, but with a hint of natural sweetness. Contrasted by the sharp bite of the aged extra tasty cheddar cheese, and a subtle heat provided by Dijon mustard. Seeds popped with each bite. The thick sliced sourdough added another dimension of texture.

Now, this is *a ham and cheese sandwich. Far removed from the so-called ham and cheese sandwich I used to eat,* from the shop in the newspaper building where she often ate when first out of college. Processed white bread, a scrape of margarine, a thin slice of processed ham, and another of processed cheese. *No taste at all.*

Judy returned her plates to the kitchen, and immediately washed, dried, and put them away, as she always did. She brewed some coffee, sighed, and returned to her work.

She finished her feature and saved it for the next day to have one last look before she sent it off, another of her habits. Judy's life was full of routines, rituals, and habits, but she didn't realize it.

She sighed and opened her spiral notebook, which contained just one sentence.

In Search of Frank Farrington.

"Okay, Frank, let's have a look at you."

Frank's eyes continued to stare at her.

She opened the city government's website and selected the birth records tab… "Let's see when you were born, Frank. My guess is around 1970." She entered a range of 1965-1975 and typed in what she knew.

Family Name: Farrington.

Given Name: Frank.

Other Names: she left blank.

She clicked search and waited for the result. There was one item.

Birth: Farrington, Frank. July 15, 1970.

Father: Farrington, John Charles.

Probably known as "JC" to his friends. Wonder why the father's name would be first. I should think the mother's name is more important.

Mother: Farrington (née Orman) Marion Marie.

Place of Birth: St Margaret's Maternity Hospital.

Judy added Frank's birth record and the little information she had to the notebook.

Divorced.

No children.

Brother.

Two sisters.

Phoenix Imports.

"Well Frank, I guess it's a start."

She did a quick search of social media, Facebook, Twitter, LinkedIn, and Instagram. Nothing. Many *Frank Farrington's*, but not the one she was looking for. *Unusual. Why no social media presence?*

She glanced at her notes: Phoenix Imports, underlined!

She stared at the page. *I didn't underline it.* "Strange."

Time to go to the Farmer's Market. A contradiction of routine and spontaneity, she went to the Farmer's Market every day, where she wandered around and selected whatever took her fancy for dinner that night. She preferred to eat fresh.

She didn't understand why people routinely ate the same food… *Monday we have this, Tuesday that, Friday fish… week after week.*

Another reason she couldn't see herself getting married. She hated the idea of a routine life. Judy sighed, packed up her desk, and left for the Farmer's Market.

***

The next morning, Judy headed to Kansas Café as usual. She sat on *her* sofa and looked out the window. Frank was still lying on the sidewalk, staring at her.

"You still here, Frank?"

She looked at him for a long time, not thinking or feeling anything. Staring back at him, trying to communicate, to understand what he wanted.

She didn't know how long she stared at Frank. The Flamingos' *I Only Have Eyes for You* was playing when she could refocus.

"Guess I should check your company out before it disappears, if that's what you want."

She searched for Phoenix Imports. It was in the low rent part of town.

"Can't say that surprises me."

She wrote the address in her notebook and added the observation; *Frank didn't like to spend money.*

She paid her bill, sighed, and left the Café. As she did, she said, "Well Frank, we're not in Kansas anymore."

She smiled to herself, amused by her own humor, as people often are when they spend a lot of time in their own company. She flagged a taxi and began the long journey across town.

Coffin

Billy sat on the edge of his bed, naked. The cleaning staff knew to do Billy's room in the afternoon. *Wish I accepted Frank's lunch invitation.*

Frank gave me money. Could've held some back for a drink after lunch, not that he actually paid his rent. *Didn't need to work.*

Don't know when I'll see Frank again, two or three months.

He glimpsed his reflection in the mirror….

***

Better get dressed.

Being released from solitary soon. Don't want to be. Maybe I can take a swing at the guard. It'll mean a beating. Not sure I'm up to it.

Been in ten weeks now. Billy thought about his life in prison. *Raped four times and shanked with a filed down comb, didn't know a comb could be a shank. Five years to go, don't know how I'm gonna survive.*

Three weeks in solitary for protection. He didn't want to be shanked again; the pain had been excruciating. *Wish I died.* He hadn't enjoyed being raped, either.

Billy's not gay and doesn't consider himself bisexual. Although there were parties, booze, drugs, whatever one wanted. Billy woke up in bed with a man occasionally, but not intentionally.

Wish I had enough money for a carton of smokes. Could pay someone to kill me. He was wallowing in self-pity. Billy didn't want to die, he only told himself he did. If he crossed the wrong guy, they'd off him for free.

***

Coffin sat at the computer in the prison library, pissed off. *Why can't I get the fucking thing to work?*

He wanted to smash it, but last time, he ended up in solitary for a month. He could ask for help. Anyone he asked would help, not that they'd want to. Everyone knows it's best to give Coffin a wide berth.

Coffin knew he wasn't smart. His father told him often enough.

"Boy, you ain't the sharpest tool in the box."

He hated being looked at like he was stupid. No one would say it to his face, but he knew they all thought it. He could see *that look* in their eyes. Making Coffin feel stupid had cost people their lives, and Coffin his freedom.

Everyone in the library knew Coffin needed help, but none would offer. You didn't approach Coffin unless summonsed. Everyone knew that, except the new guy, Billy, something.

"Look like you could use some help."

"Can't get the fucking thing to work."

"Let me try."

Billy pushed a few buttons. Coffin didn't know what he did, but it worked.

"Thanks," he growled.

"Anytime."

Coffin studied Billy. *Doesn't have that look in his eye. Not bad looking, but not young. He'll do.*

***

Billy saw Coffin talking to the guard Rodriguez. Coffin gestured towards Billy; Rodriguez gestured towards an inmate he had a run in with a few days earlier. Coffin nodded.

An hour later, Rodriguez transferred Billy to Coffin's cell.

"You'll be fine here," Coffin said. "No one'll touch you under my protection."

The next day, they found the inmate Rodriguez had pointed out, dead. His neck broken. They never found who did it, but Billy saw Rodriguez slip a carton of squares to Coffin. "Nice job."

Billy remained under Coffin's protection for almost four years. Coffin isn't gay, but he's in for life without parole. He has needs and the price of Billy's *protection* was to service those needs, as often as Coffin wanted them serviced. He never returned Billy's favors.

Coffin didn't speak much. People always looked at him like he's stupid when he spoke. Neither kind nor cruel, he had needs, and Billy didn't piss him off. Coffin liked Billy, but everybody likes Billy.

Billy's an addict. Frank put him in rehab twice. Addicted, at one time to just about everything. Booze, cocaine, heroin, parties, sex, *the life*, and gambling, the worst, at least in terms of the damage.

At first, Coffin's *needs* were more frequent than Billy liked. In time, Coffin's needs—which didn't change—weren't frequent enough for Billy.

***

Billy didn't miss Coffin; he could get his fix easily on the outside. When he first got out, he blew random guys in the park whenever he had cravings, then he worked out he could get paid for it.

O'Rourke Park was named after an influential and reputedly ruthless businessman, who controlled the docks with an iron fist more than a century earlier. One wonders how he'd react if he knew his park was now a renowned gay pick up spot.

Better get dressed, need to go to the office soon. Billy's office is a cubicle in the men's restroom of O'Rourke Park. His customers are mostly business guys looking for a quick blow job during their lunch break. The attendant keeps the cubicle locked for him, so it's available every day.

Billy sits in his office a couple of hours a day, sometimes longer. When business dries up, he takes his earnings–ten dollars a time, or twenty-five if they want to fuck him, no condoms–and crosses the road to The Shipyard. He drinks until the money runs out.

Wonder when I'll see Frank again, two or three months.

***

Billy wasn't the only one thinking of Frank.

Mike Eagleton was feeling guilty. When he read about Frank's death, his concern was for himself.

The only busy warehouses are Frank's. Trucks coming and going all day. Gave him something to do. *Now all I can do is turn the trucks away.* Not that *this* was Mike's concern. With Frank gone and many warehouses empty, the owners may close the complex. He'd be out of work.

Mike recently celebrated his sixtieth birthday. *How the hell am I going to find another job at my age?* Ten years earlier, when the factory closed, it took Mike nearly a year to find this job, and he'd only been fifty then.

Frank was a good guy. Mike liked him. *Worked hard, long hours.* Frank had a system. *Week in, week out,* Mike called it.

Poor bastard worked himself to death. Something Mike would never do. He'll miss Frank.

***

It took an hour to reach Phoenix Imports. Judy exited the taxi, looked around, and sighed.

A rundown, aging warehouse complex. Two strips of five warehouses with a driveway in between, and a security office—added some time later—in the center, controlling the comings and goings. The buildings were tall, constructed using corrugated metal sheeting, once painted cream, now fading, oxidizing, and peeling. *Seen better days, like Frank.*

Judy approached the security guy. *Talk about a stereotype.* She studied the man, and the name on his neatly pressed dark gray shirt. *Mike. Probably early sixties,* full head of gray hair, combed, and slicked straight back, *fashionable when he was young,* overweight, and looking bored as he sat on a high stool watching a small television. She sighed. *Why do people let themselves go?*

Many of these security guys are ex-police, but not Mike. *Can always tell by the way they carry themselves.*

She put on her sweetest smile. "Hi Mike."

***

Mike glanced up disinterestedly, but his demeanor changed when he saw Judy. *Seldom see women like this around here. Wonder what she wants.*

"Oh, good morning, ma'am," he said as he stood, subconsciously sucking his stomach in as best he could. "What can I do for you?"

"Looking for Phoenix Imports."

"Frank's place.... Well, it was. Frank passed away a couple of days ago."

"Yes, err... saw it in the newspaper. I'm writing a feature about Frank. Here's my card."

Mike examined Judy's business card, *Judy Vernon—Freelance Journalist* and her phone number and email address. Being a *journalist* impressed people more than *feature writer.*

"Frank passed away."

"Yes, I'm hoping to talk to some of his staff. Are they still here?"

"Frank's got no staff, it's just Frank."

"Which warehouse is Frank's?"

"Those five on the left."

"*All* five?"

"Yes ma'am, that's right."

"Really, five warehouses and no staff. Not very busy then?"

"Oh, he's busy, always working. Those on the right aren't busy, but Frank always has stuff going on."

"Did it all himself?"

"Yes, ma'am, has a system. One week trucks come in loaded with stuff, and he fills the warehouse. The next week, more trucks arrive and he empties it again. Since the day he started. Kept expanding and taking over more warehouses."

***

Explains the lack of social media presence.

"Sounds like a workable system with no staff. How's the warehouse now? Full or empty?"

"It's full ma'am. Trucks have been coming to pick stuff up, but I can only turn them away, you know, with Frank being dead and all."

"Mike, could I have a brief look inside the warehouse?"

"Don't know, ma'am."

Judy sighed, reached into her shoulder bag, unzipped the inside pocket, and took out a folded fifty-dollar note. Judy always carried a few for such an occasion. Her *fifty-dollar skeleton key*. It was surprising how many doors she'd unlocked with that key.

"Come on Mike. What harm could it do? And who's gonna know?"

She placed the new, crisp, folded bill on the counter. Mike squinted at the money for a moment, picked it up and put it in his top pocket.

"I guess it'll be okay, as you said, what harm can you do?" Mike handed her an old key with a yellow plastic tag with the number one written on it. "Here, first door on the left. Be careful in there."

"Thanks, Mike." She flashed him another smile. *Never fails.*

***

Mike watched her as she walked away, long flowing skirt swishing from side to side as she walked. *Damn fine ass.*

Phoenix

Judy approached a plain, once cream metal door, paint peeling in places like the rest of the building. The number one painted in faded black, with PHOENIX IMPORTS below the number, also in black but not faded. *Why do people let buildings go?*

She pulled the heavy door towards her; and stepped into Frank's empire. *Dark.* Light switch on her right. She flicked on the lights. A humming sound, then the first unit of the warehouse lit up.

Wow! Pallets upon pallets, stacked high on shelves nearly reaching the roof, and each filled with cartons; of what she didn't know.

"Frank, you surprise me."

Beyond the lit area, the pallets extended into darkness. Judy walked towards the second warehouse. S*potless. Dividing walls removed.*

She switched on the lights, more humming. The rows of pallets continued into the third warehouse. "My God, Frank, there is so much here. What've you got in these cartons?"

As she progressed to the fifth warehouse, turning on the lights as she went, surprise gave way to awe. Four warehouses filled with pallets of cartons. *A mountain of cartons.* Between each row, a space, to accommodate a forklift. *A whole mountain range of cartons, with a valley between each mountain.*

"Wow Frank." *He turns this over every two weeks.... by himself.* "You amaze me."

Each pallet contained the same type of carton. Covered with shrink wrap plastic, to protect them from the weather, and stop them from falling off. The cartons had information stenciled on them.

- ITEM CA1587/1
- QUANTITY 34
- ORIGIN PAKISTAN

Every carton on a single pallet contains the same item. A number. Still don't know what's in them.

The quantity in the cartons ranged from ten to one hundred. Countries of origin included Pakistan, India, Bangladesh, Sri Lanka, Vietnam, and China. Maybe others. *All low-cost manufacturing countries.*

The last warehouse was different. A series of small stacks of pallets. *The mountain range has ended, and the hill country begun.*

She inspected the first *hill.* Seven pallets, mostly undisturbed, and each pallet containing a single item. *He buys and sells items by the pallet without having to break up and re-stack them. Makes sense, easy for a one-man operation.*

"Smart, Frank."

Judy examined the packing slip attached to the stack.

CUSTOMER: DISCOUNT BAZAAR

DELIVER TO: The address.

ITEMS: a list of six items, a column for quantity and another for cost

TOTALS: QUANTITY 7 and COST $11,586.54

Simple and effective. "Well, Frank, you certainly had an efficient system."

Judy took photos of the mountain range, the hills and closeups of the carton stenciling and the packing slip/invoice.

She inspected another hill made from eight pallets: going to Dave's Discounts. A dozen such hills, waiting to be loaded onto outbound trucks.

The hill country becomes the plain. This is where Frank stores his equipment, a forklift, a pallet mover, and a sweeper. *Explains why the warehouse is clean.* All battery powered, and all plugged into a socket charging.

"Efficient, Frank."

In the corner, a washing machine.

Judy headed to the other side of the warehouse. Along all the walls, stretching the entire length of the five warehouses and two, sometimes three cartons wide, were open cartons. *Finally.*

Junk. Plastic toys, board games, jigsaw puzzles, low-quality clothing, cosmetics but brands nobody's heard of, shampoos and related bath care items, toothpaste, kitchen utensils, and low-quality processed foods such as knock off cereals like *Loopy Loops*, canned meals like ravioli and beef sauce, macaroni and cheese, bags of potato chips and similar empty calorie snacks, instant soups and instant noodles, coffee, teas.

Cheap crap one finds in those Two Dollar Shops. Not that Judy had actually been inside one. She continued looking. Tools, gaudy ornaments, even some flatpack furniture.

"God Frank, you sell crap."

Following the open boxes led Judy back to warehouse one. Black metal stairs hugged the wall, leading up to what she guessed was an office. She sighed and climbed up.

Not locked. She pulled the door towards her; it opened easily. Judy stepped in and flicked on the light.

All right, Frank, let's see what we can learn about you. An old wooden desk in the center of the room. Behind it, an office chair well passed its use by date. Along the back wall; a row of gray filing cabinets, old, scratched, and chipped. *Not surprised.*

On the desk, *neat and clean*, two filing trays marked *incoming* and *outgoing,* apparently for shipments, and an open laptop. She turned it on. *Please don't need a password... shit!*

Judy tried his name and birthdate without success. *Not a clue.*

07917051 appeared in her mind. *Frank's date of birth reversed. Makes sense.* She typed it in.

"Thank you, Frank."

No personal information, but a lot of files. Two interested her. *Accounting* and *Stock Control.* She took a thumb drive from her shoulder bag. Inserted it and copied them.

How many laws have I broken today? "But you don't mind, do you Frank?"

As she reached to retrieve her drive, the names of two more files appeared in her mind, as Frank's password had. *Billy* and *BC*. She copied them too, extracted her drive, and returned it to her bag.

It would surprise people what I keep in this bag. Experience taught Judy what *tools* came in useful. *Might make an interesting feature; what women keep in their handbags.*

Judy entered the room behind the office, a kitchen. She opened the fridge, *clean,* margarine, long life milk, a sealed container and two cans of beer, *not much in here.* She began opening cupboards; stocked full of cheap, low quality processed foods from Frank's stock. Cans of ravioli, corn beef hash, baked beans, beef stew, *Sham*, and various packets of instant *meals*… just add water. *More instant than canned ravioli?* Packets of chips and other empty calorie snacks, boxes of knock-off cereals, and instant coffee.

"No wonder you got fat, Frank, if you lived on this shit!"

The kitchen opened into a bedroom/living room. Old bed, threadbare sofa, a cheap TV, an old wardrobe along one wall, and a fraying rug over bare floorboards. Walls painted white, and a curtainless window overlooking the inside of the warehouse. The furniture, shabby and mismatched, *looks like it came from a thrift store*. It had.

"Did you spend money on anything, Frank?"

An ensuite bathroom in the bedroom's corner; toilet, sink, and a small shower. *Clean.*

The wardrobe contained Frank's clothes; outdated, and a size or two too small, like the brown suit he wore when he died.

Looking around the room, Judy sighed. *Clean, man clean. mmm could be a feature in that.*

"So, this was your life, huh, Frank? Not much of a life, your entire world in an old run-down warehouse in the cheap part of town. Wonder how you got here?"

Something's missing. It took her a minute to realize what it was. *A mirror*. Frank didn't have a mirror, other than a small one in the ensuite for shaving.

"Probably just as well, Frank."

Judy took photos of Frank's living area, switched off the lights, sighed, and left. She stood on the landing, looking over the landscape of Frank's empire, as he'd done the day he died.

She retraced her steps, shaking her head as she passed Frank's stock, made her way down the other side of the warehouses, switching off the lights as she did, stepped out of the warehouse and back into the daylight, locking the door behind her.

Judy glanced at her watch. She'd been in the warehouse for over two hours.

She approached the security office, Mike, watching TV, and looking bored as he was when she arrived.

"Hi Mike," she flashed a smile, as she offered him the key. "Thank you so much."

"Oh, hello ma'am, find what you were looking for?" Mike asked as he retrieved the key and returned it to its hook.

"Wasn't looking for anything in particular, just trying to understand how Frank's business worked, I guess. So, Frank lived in the Warehouse too?"

"Yes ma'am, he worked day and night."

"Sure is a lot of stock in there."

"Yes, ma'am, and it would be gone by the end of the week, if you know...."

"Have you looked inside since Frank passed?"

"No, ma'am."

"Perhaps you should before the warehouse gets locked down or cleared out. Lots of open cartons against the back wall. You know..."

"I think I will, always wondered what's in those cartons."

"You do that. Where can I get a taxi?"

"I'll call one for you ma'am, where are you going?"

Judy gave him the address of Alice's Bakery.

"Won't be long," Mike said.

The taxi arrived in minutes.

"Bye, Mike, thanks again. Don't forget those open cartons in the back."

"No ma'am, see you later."

***

He watched her walk towards the taxi. *Damn fine ass on her. I should check out those open cartons.*

***

In the back of the taxi, Judy retrieved her iPad and added her new ideas to her notes for features *Inside a Woman's Handbag* and *Man Clean.* She calls them ideas, but they're random thoughts. A collection of her features would be *Judy's Random Thoughts.*

She grabbed her phone and called Myron Myerson. *Now he's a guy who was a stereotype at birth.*

He answered immediately, "Judy Vernon. This *is* a pleasant surprise. What's up?"

"Hello Myron, are you free for dinner tonight?"

"Sure, I'd love to have dinner with you."

"Let's say seven at Franco's?"

"Beautiful woman, and a great restaurant. Looking forward to it."

"Me too, see you tonight, Myron."

Replacing her phone and retrieving her iPad, she added another random thought. *Are Stereotypes Real? Lots of ideas these days.* She settled back for the long taxi ride across town.

The Stereotypical Accountant

Judy prepared a lunch of sourdough bread from Alice's Bakery and broccoli and blue cheese soup from The Soup Master, who make the *best soup in the city,* fresh every day.

She reviewed her current feature, made a few minor changes, and sent it off. While the app was open, she checked her emails. *Two new commissions, nice!*

Might as well make a start, at least a plan, and work out what I need to research. Judy has a methodical way of working. It helps to get her head around what she needs to do. *One done.* She glanced at her watch. *Got time for the other, too.*

Judy sighed. "Now Frank, let's see what we've learned about you."

She added a few notes to her spiral notebook.

Apparently thriving business.

Efficient and hardworking.

No life beyond work.

Ate inferior quality food.

"Well, Frank, you were obviously smart. Not everyone could set up such an operation to be run by one person." She sighed. "You know, if you'd have eaten better and looked after yourself, you might still be alive today."

I wonder why people let themselves go. "Why did you let yourself go, Frank?"

A third feature? Why not? Why Do People Let Themselves Go? This was typical of her speculative feature selection process. If a random thought constantly recurred, it drove her to write. She was undaunted by the prospect of simultaneously writing three features.

"You've inspired me, Frank. Let's see what we can learn about your family."

She opened the city government's website and searched for the descendants of Farrington, John Charles. Five listed.

Frank

Susan Marie

John Charles

Peter James

Jenifer Anne

Five? The newspaper only mentioned three besides Frank. A little more digging. Peter had died when he was six.

"I'm sorry Frank, that's sad."

Why did the second son get the father's name? She changed her search from descendants to ancestors. Frank's grandfather, also Frank, passed away a few months before Frank was born. *That explains it.*

Judy sighed, switched to an app she used to trace people's phone numbers, and entered Farrington, John Charles. *Nothing, four entries for John and a stack of entries for J. Hope he's at least a John.*

She found Frank's brother on her third attempt.

"Hello?" A male voice answered.

"Hello, is this John Charles Farrington?"

"Yes, who's calling?"

"My name is Judy Vernon. I'm a journalist. Are you related to Frank Farrington?"

"He was my brother. Why?"

"I'm writing a feature on Frank. Could I talk to you about him?"

"A feature on Frank? *Why?*"

"Umm… I read the piece in the newspaper about Frank's passing, and I thought there must be more to a man's life than three short sentences."

"Yeah, I thought something similar. There *was* more to Frank than that."

"Would it be possible to meet tomorrow? Just to talk about Frank and his life… you know."

"I *don't* know. I don't understand…"

"I won't write anything you're not happy with. Didn't you say there was more to Frank? Don't you want people to know…"

"I guess… okay. I'm free at ten."

"Great, what's your address?"

John provided his details. "Thank you, John. I'll see you tomorrow."

Judy sighed. *Initial contact always feels stiff. Guess that's why it's cold calling.*

Opening her notebook, she added to the information she learned about Frank, details of his family, a brother who died as a child, and Frank named after his grandfather.

Coffee. She noticed the time. *Then I'd better get myself ready for dinner.*

"I wonder what Myron's going to find out about you, Frank."

What to wear? She selected a long, silky, low-cut crimson dress. Judy had written a feature; *How to Look Sexy Without Trying* a few years earlier. Matching lingerie from her *Fine Lines category*. Her *Aphrodisiac* lingerie was too much for the form fitting dress. She laid her clothes on the bed.

A quick shower to freshen up. She dressed. *A little makeup*.

She appraised herself in the mirror, *Glad I've never let myself go*. Her panty line was clearly visible. Walter, the one man she might have married—if he'd asked—told her men liked to see the outline of women's underwear. "It's sexy."

Judy wanted a big favor from Myron. *Is analyzing illegally obtained data against the law?*

***

Myron Myerson sat at the bar of Franco's—an upmarket Italian Restaurant—nursing his usual whiskey sour while he waited for Judy. Although, several years younger than Judy, he was, if he cared to admit it, more than a little smitten by her. Not to mention somewhat intimidated.

Before leaving his office that afternoon, Myron stood in front of the full-length mirror in his ensuite, inspecting himself. Since the first time they met, he always did so when he was going to meet Judy. Not that he needed to, Myron was always immaculate.

He fiddled with his tie to ensure it sat in exactly the right position; it always did. Like everything he does, Myron tied it precisely. He checked to ensure the cuffs of his shirt protruded from the sleeves of his suit—cut from finest quality super 150s wool—by precisely half an inch. Also, unnecessary because his family connections tailored both suit and shirt to his exacting requirements.

He inspected his handmade leather shoes, courtesy of a shoemaker uncle, another redundant act because his daily routine included the shoeshine stand at the Biltmore Hotel.

Judy had a way of looking at him, as if she's scrutinizing every detail, and he aspired to be perfect. He hoped she wouldn't find him wanting. He always felt like a schoolboy, trying to live up to his teacher's high standards when he met Judy. *If I had a teacher who looked like her, never would have left school.*

Now, sitting at the bar, he removed his glasses and, taking the cloth from his top pocket, cleaned them for the third time. If there was one minor smudge, he was sure Judy would notice.

Having half an eye on the door, he stood when Judy entered the restaurant. *My God, she's stunning.*

She smiled and made her way to him, with smooth, confident movements, ensuring her form fitting dress moved with her slender body, creating an image of graceful elegance. The looks the other diners gave her told him they shared his opinion.

He was self-conscious, as if she would know the effect her appearance had on his body, but he beamed.

"Hello beautiful."

***

Judy saw the look of admiration on Myron's face. *He'll do it.*

She returned his smile, kissed his cheek, and hugged him a little longer than necessary, feeling his desire as her body pressed against his. Judy knows how to ensure men want to please her.

"Hi Myron."

She cast an appraising eye over him. Tall and slim but fit, not skinny, with well-groomed short black hair, a slightly olive complexion, and a long nose. *Always immaculate, hasn't let himself go.*

"Shall we go to our table?" he asked.

"No, let's stay here and have a drink first," Judy suggested, and turning to the barman, said "Can I have a glass of house red please?"

Franco's 'house red' wasn't the usual low end house red. It was Antinori Tignanello, from Tuscany, a blended red wine with herbal, fruity and floral qualities, coupled with notes of mint, cocoa, vanilla, and licorice.

Judy first met Myron when writing a feature; *Men Who Hide Money and Assets from Their Wives*. Like Myron, her work enabled her to establish many useful connections.

Typical of those she considers friends, Judy knew little about Myron. His name and appearance, complete with round glasses, told people his occupation as soon as they met him, a Forensic Accountant. Highly intelligent, with an instinct for numbers and financial management, he has a lot of well-placed connections who owe him favors.

Myron differs from people's expectations. He has a compulsion for routine and order, but he's not serious by nature. He loves life and smiles easily. Myron's an acquaintance who, like many others, Judy calls upon when she needs a favor.

Judy swallowed the last of her wine, studied Myron through her empty glass before placing it on the bar, then tilted her head a little to one side in what she intended as an alluring gesture.

"Shall we go to our table?" she asked, mimicking his earlier suggestion.

Judy sighed. *Always takes me by surprise; such a warm smile, great sense of humor, impeccable timing when he tells a joke or an anecdote. Forgotten how much I enjoy his company.*

They went through the pretense of glancing at the familiar menu; both chose what they would eat hours earlier. The same starters and the same mains. It wasn't the first time Judy noted their similar tastes.

"So, Judy, how can I help you?" Myron asked, getting to the point now the small talk was over.

"Have you heard of a guy called Frank Farrington?"

"Frank Farrington? Let me think. Before my time, but if memory serves me… there was a Frank Farrington who was an investment broker, quite a good one I understand, but there was an embezzlement scandal. Lost his license permanently. Pretty sure there was a bankruptcy too, but I think he avoided prison. I can do some digging. Why do you ask?"

So Frank, you were a naughty boy.

"Frank passed away this week. Thinking of writing a feature on him. Anything you can find out would be helpful, thank you."

Judy reached into her bag and retrieved a thumb drive with a copy of the information she downloaded from Frank's computer. Her original thumb drive, appropriately labeled, was in what she calls *The Evidence Locker,* a cupboard in her office, where she keeps all such evidence.

She passed the drive to Myron. "Could you analyze these accounts for me, please? I'm interested in what Frank's been up to recently."

"Sure."

***

The nature of Myron's work taught him not to ask awkward questions about sources of data. Better for him, he didn't know.

Having concluded their business, they enjoyed their meal and each other's company, as they exchanged stories about what they'd been doing since they last met.

Peter

The next morning, Judy completed her exercise routine. Three days a week she did a series of floor exercises, sit-ups, pushups, squats, burpees, planks, glute bridge, which she learned from a feature she wrote, *Exercise to Keep Your Body's Tone.* Three days a yoga routine, another feature, *Yoga for Health.*

Now, Judy sat in her office drinking coffee and enjoying her sourdough toast. The same breakfast every day, unaware it was the same food routine she claimed not to understand in others. Judy always ate breakfast in her office. It catches the morning sun. The curtains, strategically open a few inches, invite a sunbeam to deposit itself on her grandfather's mahogany desk. She delights in watching the minute, otherwise unseen, airborne particles dancing in the beam.

Thinking about her dinner with Myron, Judy sighed. She knew a little more about Frank. A financier, an embezzler, and a bankrupt. The latter two may well explain why he was so angry. He became fat because of his poor diet, all that processed food.

Judy wrote a feature a few years earlier; *The Dangers of Processed Food.* Her research led to her commitment to always eat fresh. She was closer to understanding why Frank became a fat, angry man.

"You are becoming more interesting, Frank, and you've given me some insight into why people let themselves go. I wonder what motivated you to become such a naughty boy. Greed? Hopefully, your brother will shed some light on why."

She opened her notebook and added what she learned about Frank the previous day. Next, she opened her *Why Do People let Themselves Go* feature and added the insights inspired by Frank.

While she drank her coffee, Judy thought about Myron and sighed. *Enjoy his company, and his natural manner. Interesting and charming without trying to be. Should spend more time with him. Not only call him when I want something.* Myron attracted Judy, but she couldn't put her finger on exactly why.

His dress sense? *I do like a man in a good suit.* The energy of his understated fitness, his effortless charm, or that he's a cross between Harry Potter and a young Noah Wylie... *perhaps the complete package.*

Whatever the reason, Judy was more than a little aroused when she arrived home last night, possibly because she felt his desire when she hugged him.

Tired, she undressed, ready for bed. As usual, she slept in a short, silk nightdress, no underwear. She considered releasing the sexual energy built up courtesy of Myron, but it had been a busy, tiring day. She allowed herself to drift off to sleep, wondering why she wasn't fondling herself… *Getting old. When I was younger, never would have let myself sleep horny.*

When younger, releasing her sexual energy to help her sleep was a routine of hers whenever she didn't have company to do it for her. In the last few years, she let the routine go, and she didn't have company as often as she once had. *Definitely getting old.*

The last time she had company was almost a year earlier. Joanne, a cute African American girl she met in a bar.

Finishing her coffee, brought her back to the present. *Time to get ready for my meeting with John Farrington.*

She chose grey slacks and a white blouse, casual but professional. Judy understood the importance of *Dressing Appropriately for the Occasion*. Another feature. Much of what she learned about how one should live their lives came from researching features.

Retrieving her shoulder bag from her office, she sighed and set off to meet John Farrington. "What will John tell me about you, Frank?"

***

Exiting the taxi, Judy sighed and appraised John's home. A pleasant suburban home in a middle-class neighborhood. Three bedrooms, she guessed, brick construction, Autumn Lane colored, Hunter Green roof shingles, Swiss Coffee trim, with a neatly trimmed lawn, and well-kept gardens. *Respectable home.* She rang the doorbell. The door opened almost immediately. *Waiting for me.* She glanced at her watch. *A little early.*

"You must be John," she said, smiling. "I'm Judy Vernon."

She handed him her business card.

Obviously, Frank's brother. His frame, larger than Frank's and his hair darker, but no mistaking the resemblance. *Comfortably fit*, not overweight like his brother, but not the six-pack fit guys get when they work out a lot.

Clean shaven, with neat collar length hair, white shirt, beige slacks, and well maintained and polished gray leather shoes, not worn and scuffed as Frank's had been. He looks like exactly what he is, a middle class, middle management, white-collar worker.

John Farrington inspected her card. "Good morning, Judy." He returned her smile and offered his hand. "Please, come in."

Judy surveyed the living room, neat and clean, tastefully decorated with pastel shades and quality furniture. *Comfortable home, a step up or three from Frank's place.*

"Can I get you a coffee?"

"Yes, please." Judy said, hoping his coffee would be of better quality than the cheap and nasty stuff in Frank's kitchen.

While waiting, Judy studied the room again. *Welcoming.* That's the word she wanted. Noticing some photos on a display cabinet against the wall, she walked over to them. *You can learn a lot about people from photos.* Family photos, mostly of what she presumed were John's children. Some family photos of John with his wife and children. *Mmm, John's wife is an attractive woman.*

Two large group photos of extended families, one of which apparently John's wife's family, the other John's. The picture seemed about ten years old and included a younger, slimmer Frank. He wore a dark blue suit, becoming tight.

"Well Frank, not bad looking at all before you let yourself go."

"Excuse me?" John said as he returned with a tray containing two coffees, milk, sugar, and some cookies.

"Oh, sorry, I was talking to... myself." Judy joined him on the sofa. "Your wife is quite beautiful."

John nodded. "Alison... Ali." He smiled. "Yes, she's very attractive."

Judy lifted her coffee and inhaled the aroma before taking a sip. *Damn, that's wonderful.*

"What's this about? Are you trying to hurt Frank? Tarnish his memory?"

"Not at all. I'm not that type of journalist, I'm a feature writer. Besides, there's no reason to sensationalize. Frank isn't in the public eye."

"He used to be."

"Really? I didn't know that." Judy retrieved a digital recorder from her shoulder bag. "Would you mind if I record our talk for the record… I can send you a copy of the recording if you'd like."

John thought for a moment, then nodded.

"Thank you, John. I'm trying to build a picture of Frank, to understand his life and to get an… appreciation, I guess, of Frank's legacy. You know, what Frank achieved in his life and the impact he had on other people's lives."

"Why? Why are you writing about Frank?"

"Honestly, I don't know. I was sitting in a café and… umm… read the item in the newspaper about Frank's passing, and thought maybe I should find out about his life."

John nodded.

Judy smiled. "Let's start at the beginning. What was Frank like as a boy?"

"We weren't close as children, age difference… Frank was close to Susie, our sister Susan, still is… well, was. I was closer to Peter, only a couple of years younger than me."

"Can I ask what happened to Peter? If you don't want to talk about it…"

John was silent for a moment. "It's okay. I was with him. Peter, when he died. We were out riding our bikes. A car hit him. Not the driver's fault. Pete rode right out in front of him…" John became silent again as he relived the events. "I ran to help him… but I was a kid. Didn't know what to do. Kept thinking I should've protected him. Blamed myself… still do."

John inhaled deeply, closed his eyes, and bit his lip as he struggled to control his emotions.

Seems vulnerable. Think he needs to talk. Best be gentle.

"I saw him die, saw the life fade from his eyes.... still can." John went silent again. "Have you ever seen someone die? Have you ever seen the life fade from their eyes? It stays with you... forever."

Judy hesitated, unsure of what to say. "Yes John, I have."

"So, you understand."

Judy wanted to tell him how Frank's eyes haunted her, and she could still see Frank lying dead, staring at her, but she didn't want to lose the moment. Instead, she empathized.

"Yes John, I do."

"Devastation and grief enveloped our family. No one asked about me. I was only a kid, and had just seen my brother die, and no one asked me how I was, or what I was feeling. Not that they blamed me, or at least if they did, they never showed it. Blamed myself, of course...

"Frank asked me. Frank came to my room and asked how I was, how I felt. Just Frank. The only one. Even as a child, and even in his grief, he thought to ask how I was feeling. That's what I remember most about Frank, his ability to think about other people."

***

Frank stood in his room, staring out of the window.

One fucking vote. One lousy fucking vote and I would've been president. Vice president will look okay, I suppose. Wanted to be president. One fucking vote...

Susie burst in. He turned to admonish her for not knocking, but the look on her face stopped him short.

"Peter's dead, Frank," she blurted out.

"What?"

"Peter's dead!"

The strength drained from Frank's body. His legs became jelly. He reached for the back of his chair to steady himself. His mind went blank as he struggled to process what Susie was saying.

"What? How? Why?"

"A car hit him on his bike. He's dead. Peter's dead."

Every nerve in his body began screaming at him. *Fuck!* A hole appeared where his stomach had been.

"Peter's *dead*?"

"Yes, Frank."

He hugged his sister, and she, now crying and shaking, held him tight. Frank, numb, and unable to process what Susie was telling him.

"Where are Mom and Dad?"

"In the kitchen."

He gently disengaged her and headed to the kitchen. Jenny, the youngest, lay on the stairs crying. He sat beside her and lightly rested his hand on her back.

"Come and take care of Jen, Suse."

"I—I… I don't know what to say to her."

"Neither do I, just sit with her."

Entering the kitchen, his pulse racing, he took in the scene. His mother seated at the table, head in her hands, crying. His father standing behind her, hand resting on her shoulder, staring into the distance. He knew it was true. Peter was dead.

"What happened, Dad?"

"Peter's dead, Frank. Nothing the driver could do. Pete rode right out in front of him. That's what the police said. Nobody's fault, an accident."

"Wasn't Junior with him? Is Junior okay?"

"Yes, *Junior* is fine." He almost sounded bitter. "It's just Pete."

"Junior's a kid too, Dad."

"Don't you think I *know that,* Frank?"

Frank didn't know what to say. Emotion welled up inside of him as he processed the tragedy of his brother's death. His mother sobbed loudly, and his father squeezed her shoulder.

His father shuddered, his shoulders shook, his voice now softer, breaking. "I know it's not Junior's fault, Frank. The police said it happened too fast, nothing anyone could do. I can't see Junior now. I don't want him to think I blame him. I don't, but if I see him now…"

Frank's emotion was running down his cheeks. He stood beside his father and embraced them both.

He stepped back, wiping his face with his sleeve. "I'll go, Dad."

He walked back up the stairs. Susie, still crying, now sitting beside Jenny with her arm across her shoulders. He squeezed Susie's shoulder on the way past.

Reaching for the handle, he took a deep breath to calm himself, and entered the room Junior and Peter shared.

Junior was sitting on his bed, staring across at his brother's bed, as if willing Peter to be there. Not crying now, but his eyes were red, dry tear tracks visible on his face. Frank sat beside him and put his arm around his brother's shoulders.

"Are you okay, Junior?"

John

After taking a few minutes to compose himself, John moved beyond Peter's death, explaining, "After that, I paid more attention to Frank. Admired him. Wanted to be like him. Excelled at everything. Smart. Always did well at school, good at sports, and popular. Made the high school's first lacrosse team at fifteen, and in his senior year, captain of the team, and vice-president of the school.

"We thought he'd be offered a lacrosse scholarship from a top university. Scouts came to watch him play, close but no scholarship. This defined his life, I suppose, but Frank didn't like cigars, anyway."

"Where did Frank go to college?"

"City College on a partial scholarship. Our parents had little money, and Frank didn't want a student loan debt. He said, 'If I have an enormous debt to repay before I can start earning money, I'm starting behind everyone else'. Majored in Finance.

"I admired Frank, idolized him. I used to keep a scrapbook. Would you like to see?"

"Yes, *please*."

John went into a back room to retrieve the scrapbook. Judy sighed and finished her coffee. She reached for a cookie. *mmm... nice cookies.*

"Well, Frank, your brother is painting a different picture of you. Not at all like I imagined. What happened?"

John returned with an old, slightly yellowed scrapbook, which he handed to Judy. "In a box in the garage for years. Dug it out after Frank passed..." Noticing Judy's empty cup, he asked, "Say, would you like another coffee?"

"Please, John."

Exceptional coffee, smooth and aromatic, strong but without a hint of bitterness. Must ask him about it.

"May I take some photos of the scrapbook?" Judy called out.

"Sure."

The early pages were from the high school newspaper, a snippet about fifteen-year-old Frank making the lacrosse team, and reports from various matches. Frank was an outstanding player. Judy glanced at the cuttings, but didn't read them. She could do that later from her photos.

Cuttings from the school yearbook confirmed Frank was captain of the lacrosse team, and vice-president of the school, pieces from the City College's Alumni Newsletter, and then the newspaper clippings began.

Judy stared at them. She wanted to slap herself. Hard. *What kind of journalist am I? Searching newspaper archives when doing a background investigation is Journalism 101.*

"How could I have been so fucking stupid, Frank? Never occurred to me to check the newspapers. Sorry, I underestimated you."

John returned with the coffee. "There you go."

"Thanks."

Judy reached for another cookie as she perused the newspaper clippings. A small piece about Frank opening his own investment brokerage, with a partner, William Johnson.

"Frank had a partner?"

"Yes, that bastard Billy. Destroyed Frank's life. They were roommates in college…"

***

Frank headed to his dormitory to drop his books off before going to the cafeteria for lunch. *Wonder if my roommate has arrived. He's already two days late.*

He stepped into the dormitory and closed the door behind him before he glanced up and froze.

"Jesus, man, put some fucking clothes on."

"You must be my roommate. Billy Johnson," the guy said as he outstretched his hand.

Frank, raised to be polite, awkwardly reached out to shake Billy's hand.

"Frank Farrington."

"Good to meet you, Frank."

"Come on er.... Billy, put some clothes on and I'll buy you a welcome lunch at the cafeteria."

"Sounds great," Billy said as he bent down to retrieve his clothes, which lay strewn on the floor.

***

"Frank loved Billy. When he became successful, he took Billy with him. Wherever Frank went, Billy tagged along. Frank always looked out for people, especially Billy. But the truth is... Frank wasn't the best judge of character. I mean, Billy isn't a bad guy, likeable, but he's a fuckup and Frank carried him."

Judy had questions, but John was talking freely. Experience told her when people are talking, best let them talk. Usually, they answered her questions without her having to ask, and if not, she could fill in the gaps later. She limited her questions to the scrapbook.

Frank's company won the *Best Newcomer Award* and two years later, and for the next three years, *Best Investment Broker* in the state.

"So, Frank's business was successful?"

"Yes, very. Everyone liked and respected Frank. Smart, but not at judging people. That fuckup Billy is one, and that bitch he married. Never liked her, and Susie hated her. But... Frank loved her, was crazy about her and couldn't see her for the gold-digging bitch she was."

Judy turned the page, taking pictures as she did. A clipping from the society pages, Frank's wedding. She studied the faded photo, Frank, his wife, and another man. *Oh, Frank was quite handsome.*

"His wife is beautiful."

"Myriam. Can't think of one redeeming quality to be honest. That's Billy with them. Billy didn't like her, either. Think she used to nag Frank to drop Billy. Guess he should've. Billy's a fuckup, but he's not a bad guy. Myriam's a bitch.

"Susie's not as smart as Frank. None of us are, but she's an excellent judge of character. She warned Frank that Billy's a fuckup and told him outright that Myriam's no good. Frank didn't listen. He should've. Sure he wished he did... not that he said anything to me."

When Judy turned the page, she was astounded. Furious with herself and her lack of professionalism. *Can't believe I didn't do an archive search for Frank.* Frank ran for mayor. At least he announced he was running, but she never heard of him.

"Frank ran for *mayor*?"

"Everybody was sure he'd be mayor. A successful financier and popular with businesspeople, had a lot of backers. Everything going for him. I was proud of him then. Never happened, of course..."

"Why not? What happened?"

"Billy happened... the bastard!"

Judy sipped her coffee and waited for John to continue.

"Billy's a gambler, a drunk, and always in trouble with women. Got in deep with the mob or something. He owed some bad people a lot of money, so he began embezzling their investors' money to pay his gambling debts and save his own miserable ass.

"I think he believed he just needed one big score and he could pay the money back, but he always lost and got in deeper. Only a matter of time before they caught him. Frank's company destroyed and Frank with it. Look at the next page."

The cutting was loose. The headline said it all. *Leading Investment Broker in Embezzlement Scandal.*

"Frank did nothing wrong. All that bastard Billy. Didn't matter. Took Frank down with him. Frank's political career over before it started. Lost his Investment Broker's license, a lifetime ban... something about not meeting his Fiduciary Duty of Care. As senior partner, he was legally responsible even though he did nothing wrong. His assets seized and sold off to repay the company's debts... not enough, not nearly enough. Bankrupted Frank.

"At the trial, they exonerated Frank. Billy went to jail. Got five years, I think. Serves the bastard right. Destroyed Frank's life, and that bitch left him. Only positive to come out of it.

"Pulled back from Frank after that. Overnight. I'd gone from being proud of having a brother who was going to be Mayor, to being ashamed of having a brother who was an embezzler. He wasn't, but everybody thought he was. Ali kept telling me 'Frank did nothing wrong,'... but you know. I never even asked him how he was.

"After Peter died, Frank was the only one who asked how I was, but when Frank needed me... It's not Frank I should've been ashamed of. It's myself."

John became silent. Judy drank her coffee and turned the page, another loose clipping about Billy being jailed and Frank being found not guilty. The last clipping in the scrapbook. After taking a photo, Judy closed the scrapbook and carefully placed it on the coffee table.

"What happened to Frank after the trial?"

"Frank lost everything. Couldn't find work; no longer had an Investment Broker's License and besides, who'd hire an embezzler? Couldn't start a new business until he served his bankruptcy ban... five years or seven years or something.

"Susie was there for him. *I* wasn't! She took him in. Can't imagine what she'd have done if that bitch hadn't left him. Frank lived in Susie's basement for years, and she took care of him.

"Don't know too much about that time. The day after his ban from owning a company ran out, Frank registered a new company... Imports, I think. After that, none of us saw much of him, not even Susie. Working all the time. You should talk to Susie."

"Do you think she'll agree to talk with me?"

"If she likes you, she will."

"Could you let me have her phone number?"

"Sure, but best to ask her in person, I can introduce you at Frank's funeral."

"Oh... umm. When's Frank's funeral?"

"In two days, at St Michaels."

John retrieved a card from the display cabinet and handed it to Judy. A notice of *The Funeral of Frank Farrington* at St Michaels from 2.00pm. Judy took a picture of the card and offered it to John.

"I'll be there."

"No, you keep it."

"Thank you," Judy said, sliding the card into her shoulder bag. "Thank you again John, I won't take up anymore of your time. I'll call a taxi and get out of your hair."

Judy didn't turn her recorder off. Experience taught her to keep recording until she left. You never know what someone might say after the *interview.*

"No, thank *you*! Talking about Frank is exactly what I needed. Did me a lot of good."

Judy called a taxi. "Won't be long. Oh John, I meant to ask about your exceptional coffee."

"My one indulgence. Ali complains it's too expensive, but I think it's worth it. My personal blend, from Coffee Roasters downtown."

Judy knew the store. In The Gourmet District, where all the high-end artisan food outlets are.

"Took me a long time to perfect it… trial and error, but eventually I got it."

"Would you mind telling me the blend?"

"No need. Ask for the John Farrington Blend. It's kinda expensive and there's a one kilogram minimum on personal blends. About two pounds. Don't know why coffee's sold in kilograms."

"You have your own blend?"

"Many customers do. They keep a record of people's blends, and you can ask for it. Spin the beans so it's blended, otherwise you get different beans in patches, and every cup tastes different. They blend it for consistent taste and grind it."

"And I can order someone's blend?"

"You can order any blend, either a house blend, and they have a few, or someone else's blend, or create your own."

"You don't mind if I order your blend?"

"Of course not. If people order my blend, I earn points and can use them for discounts or gifts. Some people's blends are popular. Tell your friends about it too. The more people who order it, the better for me."

"Will do. Thank you again, John." Judy said as the taxi arrived. "I'll see you at Frank's funeral."

"Yes, and I'll introduce you to Susie. I'm sure she'll like you."

Judy climbed into the back of the taxi, sighed, and gave the driver the address of Alice's Bakery, unaware of how rigidly she followed her routine.

She turned the digital recorder off and returned it to her shoulder bag. She sighed again and settled back. *A lot to think about.*

Journalism 101

Judy left her shoulder bag in her office, sighed, and went to the kitchen to prepare lunch. Writing the feature about eating fresh and avoiding processed foods changed her eating habits.

"This is how we should eat, Frank. If you didn't eat all that processed crap, you might still be alive, and fresh tastes much better."

Returning to her office, Judy uploaded the digital recording to her computer. She kept her recordings in an *interview recordings* folder, each meticulously labeled and easy to find. Another lesson learned from experience. She listened to the interview with John Farrington, taking notes in her spiral notepad, which she now referred to as *Frank's book.*

She paused the recording and opened a new file in her *features in progress* folder, where she outlined another feature; *The Dangers of Stereotyping People*, something she's guilty of herself. She intended to use Frank and Myron as case studies. Writing four features simultaneously isn't unusual.

Listening to the end of the recording made Judy want a coffee. Opening the flat-bottomed bag she'd bought from Coffee Roasters, *The John Farrington Blend.* She inhaled deeply, relishing the aroma of freshly ground coffee.

She didn't realize she added a new routine to her repertoire. Most of her routines began this way. She discovered something by accident, like the first time she wandered into Kansas Café, or somebody made a recommendation such as John's coffee. If she enjoyed the experience, she repeated it.

She sipped her coffee, savoring the taste. *Excellent.*

"You've certainly impacted my life, Frank. Two features and great coffee."

She opened the newspaper archives, still frustrated with herself for not having done so as her first step. *It didn't occur to me Frank would've been in the newspaper.*

Judy hadn't treated her research on Frank as a feature she was writing, so she didn't plan as she usually would. She hadn't intended to write a feature about Frank, he somehow pushed her into it. *That explains it,* she justified to herself.

Most of the search results Judy had from John, but there were some more articles detailing the investigation of the embezzlement scandal. Being exonerated kept Frank out of jail. Beyond this, it hadn't helped him much. Judy entered *William Johnson* into the search field.

Her phone rang. *Caller ID is so convenient.*

"Hello, Myron."

"Hi, beautiful. Owe you an apology. Haven't had time to get into your Frank stuff yet."

"No hurry."

"Should've told you I have a court case going on. A dodgy entrepreneur sleazebag's been dipping into his employees' pension fund. I'm the star witness."

"You *are* a star."

"The money's *hidden* in one of those offshore accounts the government can't touch. Have a flag on it. If he moves the money, I'll know. Got himself an aggressive lawyer, John Snitter, who's throwing a lot of curve balls. Been able to dodge them so far. Adjourned now, a point of law. The judge is deciding if he can continue a line of questioning about how I tracked the money. The District Attorney's arguing I'm not obliged to reveal confidential sources. Going to be difficult to answer without…"

"Incriminating yourself, because your methods aren't entirely legal."

"As they say… *to catch a thief.*"

"So they say."

"Need to go over all my umm… *research* to anticipate what curve balls might come and work out how I'm going to answer them."

"You'll be fine, Myron. You're smarter than any lawyer."

"Can tell you it wasn't Frank. It was his partner."

"Heard that today, and it was in the papers." *Apparently.*

They said their goodbyes and rang off.

Men in particular enjoyed hearing Judy use their name often, and she knew it. Another technique experience taught her.

Judy returned to her search. Not much on Billy she didn't have, a small piece; they gave him parole after three years, nine months. Judy updated Frank's book.

"The more I learn about you, Frank, the more I like you. We might've become friends if we met under different circumstances. Well, if we met at all." *And if I didn't judge you based on your appearance.*

She sighed. *Time to go to the Farmer's Market.*

***

Despite having worked late into the night researching the four features, Judy arrived at Kansas Café at her regular time the next morning. Taking her usual seat, Judy looked out the window, expecting to see Frank lying wide eyed, dead in the street, but he wasn't there. She sighed, a little disappointed.

Judy retrieved her iPad from her shoulder bag, dutifully sitting beside her on the sofa. She glanced up and froze as she stared incredulously at Frank, sitting opposite her on the other sofa, his shirt stretched tightly across his chest and his bulging stomach. The buttons strained as if they'd fly off at any moment. That wide eyed in death stare gone from his eyes, replaced with the peaceful look he had moments before he died. The pleading remained.

Let's Fall in Love was playing, but Judy didn't recognize the artist. Dorothy was suddenly at the table, delivering Judy's usual order.

"Thanks, Dot," Judy said absently.

"You're welcome, hon."

"Oh, Dot… who's this singer?"

"Um…" Dorothy listened for a moment. "Caterina Valente. This version's relatively new."

Dorothy returned to whatever she was doing.

Judy needed to think. *Dot obviously didn't see Frank, so he can't be real despite appearances.*

"Just don't start talking to me, Frank. People will think I'm crazy if I'm talking to a dead man."

She stared at him for a long time, contemplating this development.

"I sort of understood why I could still see you in the street. Watching you die was a powerful experience, and somehow burned itself into my memory, or something. Can't explain it very well. Sure there's a psychological explanation for *that,* but why have you changed, Frank? Why are you sitting opposite me now?"

Judy sighed.

"For God's sake, don't answer me. Talking to a dead man would be too much! Why have you changed?"

Judy continued to reflect, looking for a satisfactory explanation. *Maybe I'm losing my mind.*

"Why have you changed Frank?" she asked again, praying he wouldn't answer.

"It's not you, is it Frank? It's me! The way I see you has changed. *That's it!* I saw you as a fat angry man who died in the street and nothing else… Now I see you as you were, a smart, kind, and capable man dealt a bad hand by fate. You've become a person to me. Someone who could've been a friend. The way I perceive you has changed. Makes sense, doesn't it, Frank?"

Judy sighed, drank her coffee, and ate her cheesecake.

"Would you like some Frank?" she asked, smiling at her own humor.

"Need to get going, Frank. A lot to do today."

Judy intended to spend the morning reflecting on the previous night's research, but Frank put a stop to that. She needed to write four features that day.

Judy paid Dorothy and left on her way to Alice's Bakery. She sighed. *Overcast and a little cool.*

"Soup again today, I think Frank."

A Man of Character and Integrity

The day of Frank's funeral arrived. Judy had worked late into the previous night, completing first drafts of her features. Writing features, even multiple features, was easy for her, as any job is easy for a seasoned professional.

She chose a dark blue suit and a white blouse from her solemn occasion collection. Not that Judy was aware she categorized her clothes into collections. In her perception, she spontaneously chooses what to wear each day, making sure she dresses appropriately for the occasion.

When Judy arrived at Kansas Café, Dorothy looked up from her newspaper.

"Oh. Hi Judy. So formal today."

"Frank's funeral is today."

"Frank?"

"The man who passed away outside last week."

"Oh… and you're going to his funeral?"

"Thought it would be fitting, as I saw him…."

"Good of you. Want your usual?"

"Please."

Judy sat on her sofa and looked across the table at Frank, who smiled.

"Good morning, Frank. Your funeral's today. You'll be able to go soon."

She was making mental notes for enhancements to her drafted features and thinking about Frank's funeral. *Don't know what to expect.*

Dorothy arrived with her order without acknowledging Frank's presence. *A good thing, otherwise we might have a ghost on our hands.*

"On the house today, on account of you representing us at, umm…"

"Frank."

"Yes, Frank's funeral. Had some extra business from his passing, mostly curiosity seekers, usually in the afternoons. A couple of them have been back, so he's been good for business."

"Oh... Thank you, Dot," Judy said as Dorothy returned to her counter.

"Even in death, you're helping people, Frank."

Judy continued to reflect on her features, occasionally discussing her thoughts with Frank, as she would have done with herself prior to *meeting* him. Mario Lanza's *I'm Falling in Love with Someone* was playing.

Her phone rang. Judy smiled when she glanced at the caller ID.

***

"Hello Myron."

"Hello beautiful. How're you placed for lunch tomorrow?"

"That would be wonderful, Myron."

He liked the way she said *Myron.*

"How does twelve thirty at Franco's sound?"

Franco's are a client of one of Myron's side businesses, Business Accounting Services, so they seldom charge him. Like Judy, he lives his life based on routine and habit, but unlike Judy, he knows he does so. Myron had introduced Judy to Franco's.

"Perfect! Are you busy tomorrow afternoon?"

"Nothing I can't reschedule."

"Great, let's make a day of it."

"Looking *forward* to it," Myron said with genuine enthusiasm, despite not knowing what Judy had planned. He enjoyed her company, and would enjoy the afternoon doing whatever Judy had in mind. "Oh, have a dinner tomorrow night."

"Understand, but we'll have the afternoon."

They said their goodbyes and rang off.

***

"Think you and Myron would've liked each other, Frank. Off to your funeral now… Guess I won't be seeing you anymore. Goodbye Frank."

Judy called a taxi.

"Time to go Dot, see you tomorrow," she said as she left the café.

Judy entered the church. *Nearly full, more than a hundred people. Wow Frank, this is quite a turnout.* Judy found an empty seat near the back of the church. An older man, sitting in the aisle seat, slid over to the next space on the pew, allowing Judy to take his seat. *A gentleman.*

"Thank you very much."

"Don't mention it. I'm Gerry, by the way."

Early seventies, I guess. Receding gray hair with a significant widow's peak, combed straight back, and slicked down. He wore a short-sleeved, open-necked blue shirt and gray slacks. A slightly bulbous nose and biggish ears, *typical in a man of his age.* Clean shaven with noticeable age spots on his lined face. Pale blue eyes, a little sunken and watery, but alive and bright. *Self-employed blue-collar worker.*

"Judy Vernon," she said, shaking his outstretched hand. "Big turnout."

"Yes, Frank was one helluva guy."

"Indeed."

A wonderful service. Half a dozen eulogies. His sister Susan and several others spoke about Frank in glowing terms. References to fate not being kind to him, and a common theme. *Character and integrity.*

This was what Judy took away from Frank's funeral; *a man of character and integrity*, a far cry from the fat, angry man she first encountered.

At the conclusion of the service, Gerry said, "Come on Judy Vernon, let's head over to the Church Hall for the reception before the line's out the door for some eats."

Judy learned about the reception from the Funeral Notice. It wouldn't be her type of food, but it was important to be sociable in her line of work. Like Gerry, she didn't fancy standing in a slow-moving food line.

"Good idea, Gerry."

A lot of food, not surprising with so many people. The food line had already started to form. *Mostly finger food.*

It impressed Gerry. "Looks like we got some good eats." He handed Judy a plate.

"Certainly, a lot of food," Judy said noncommittally. She selected a few fresh items.

Gerry wasn't so fussy. He unashamedly loaded up his plate. "Better load up now. Doubt there'll be seconds."

Judy smiled.

Gerry glanced at her plate. "Is that all you're having, Judy Vernon?"

"You know Gerry, at my age, a girl needs to watch her figure."

Gerry nodded. Judy half expected a quip about liking to watch her figure, but Gerry was a gentleman.

A large hall and mostly open space, with chairs lining the walls for those lucky enough to find a seat.

"Let's grab that quiet spot in the corner," Gerry suggested.

They found their seats and made themselves comfortable with their plates balanced on their laps.

"Did you know Frank well, Gerry?"

"Used to, before the trouble. Invested all my money with him."

"Oh, must've been a tough time for you."

"Nearly lost the house, but we got through it. Others weren't so lucky." He gestured towards the mourners.

"But so many people came today."

"Yes, and so they should. When Frank's partner stole our money, like most people, I blamed Frank. Couldn't believe I trusted the guy. Not him, of course, but few of us made that distinction. Pissed off because we lost our money. My lawyer told me there was nothing I could do until they settled everything. What they call an *unsecured creditor* or something."

He ate a little food, then continued.

"In the end, got about twenty-one cents in the dollar, not much, but enough to keep me out of trouble. Not happy with it, far from it. Wanted to sue Frank or somebody. My lawyer explained, 'No one to sue. Frank is bankrupt, he's already given everything and there's nothing left. As a bankrupt, his liability is over. They sent his partner to jail, so nothing to do there either.'

"A couple of months later, got a letter from Frank. Apologized for what happened and promised to pay the money back. Said it would take some time because he'd have limited opportunities to earn money for some years… forget how many. Took it to my lawyer, *proof that Frank's liable….* He said, 'Nothing you can do. Legally, Frank has no more liability. Obviously feels remorse, but not much he can do as a bankrupt. You need to accept you won't see your money again.'"

Gerry ate a little more.

"Years later, six or seven, I received another letter from Frank. This time, he attached a small check. Not much. He wrote, 'I stand by my commitment to pay you back, even if it takes the rest of my life.' Guess it did." Gerry said sadly.

"Took the letter to my lawyer again. Still bitter about losing my money and still wanting to sue somebody. He stared at it with an amazed expression on his face. I'll never forget his expression. He said, 'Can't believe it. Never heard of this happening before. Frank has no liability. Accept whatever he gives you and be grateful. Doubt you'll get much, but something is better than nothing.' Anyway, every month, I received another letter and a check from Frank. It always stated the amount paid and the amount owed. Over time, the checks got bigger."

"Frank *paid you back*?"

"Paid everyone back," Gerry said, again indicating the crowd of mourners. "That's why there are so many people here."

"He *repaid* all the money people lost?"

"He certainly did. Well almost, about ninety-five percent. Would've had us all paid back by the end of the year if he hadn't passed. I'm in the same house, but some people moved several times and Frank kept track of them. Investors who died got their money back too… Frank tracked their families down."

"Amazing," said Judy, trying to process what she'd learned that day. "Don't know what to say… *character and integrity*, I guess."

"Indeed."

They ate in silence, plates balanced on knees, occasionally looking around, both lost in thoughts of Frank. When he finished eating, Gerry resumed talking.

"I supported Frank when he ran for mayor. Had a printing business at the time and printed his campaign material. Would've made a great mayor. Can't think of the city ever having a mayor with the character and integrity of Frank Farrington."

From what she learned about Frank that day, Judy agreed. "No, neither can I."

"Character and integrity. I admit, Frank disappointed me when it happened. To be honest, I was more disappointed in myself for being such a poor judge of character. That's why I was so angry. Sure, losing the money hurt us, but I *believed* in Frank."

One of the catering staff collected their empty plates.

"Knowing I was right about Frank all along meant more to me than getting the money back. My wife understood what was making me angry, of course. Knew me better than I know myself. Always defended Frank, but I guess she was really defending me. Can see that now, couldn't then. She's gone now, passed a couple of years ago…"

"Sorry to hear that." Judy reached over and squeezed his hand lightly.

Gerry smiled. "Thank you. Not a day goes by when I don't miss her. Never underestimate the value of a good wife." Looking at Judy, he added, "or a good husband, I suppose."

Could be something in that.

"Met Frank's wife twice. Can't say I liked her much…."

"Hello Judy."

Judy looked up. John Farrington was standing in front of her. She introduced John to Gerry, who offered condolences.

"Judy been getting you to bare your soul?"

Gerry thought for a moment. "As a matter of fact, she has."

John smiled. "I'm sorry. I need to steal her away from you now. Judy, would you like to come and meet Susie?"

"I've enjoyed talking with you Gerry."

"Very much enjoyed talking to you, too, Judy Vernon. Glad to meet you, John."

As they made their way through the mourners towards the back of the hall, John said, "Susie's waiting in the anteroom."

On the way, mourners offering their condolences repeatedly stopped him.

"How are you holding up today, John?"

John smiled. He didn't answer immediately. "I'm actually doing okay, probably because of our chat the other day. Talking about Frank helped me come to terms with his passing."

In the anteroom, Susie was standing alone, lost in thought. She looked forlorn.

John said, "Susie, this is Judy Vernon."

Judy offered her hand. "Hello Susan, sorry for your loss."

"Thank you, and it's Susie. Everybody calls me Susie."

Judy handed Susie her business card. "Susie it is then."

"Junior tells me you're writing about Frank. Can I ask why?"

John rolled his eyes when Susie referred to him as Junior. *Of course, family would call him Junior, John Charles Farrington Jnr.*

She thought about her answer. *Best be open and honest.*

"Sorry I didn't tell you this before, John. I saw Frank die, called the ambulance. When I read those few sentences in the paper about his passing, I didn't plan to find out about Frank or write about him. After reading that piece in the newspaper, I opened a new notebook. Intended to make some notes about a feature I'm writing. Didn't know I was doing it, but I wrote 'In search of Frank Farrington'. It just happened…"

John asked, "Was it Frank? Was Frank the one whose life you saw leave their eyes?"

"Yes John, it was."

"I'm sorry Judy." He squeezed her shoulder. "It *never* goes away."

Susie gave John a puzzled look.

"Peter."

Susie nodded, then smiled at Judy.

"I'd very much like to talk with you about Frank."

"Have an engagement tomorrow, but how about the day after?"

"*Perfect.* The kids will be in school, so it'll just be the two of us. Why don't you come for lunch?"

"I'd like that."

Judy long ago learned the value of talking to people in a social setting. They're more open, and less guarded because they forget they're being interviewed. Judy has a way of making an interview feel like a conversation.

"Shall we say twelve thirty?" Susie asked, handing Judy a slip of paper with her address.

"Looking forward to it."

The door was open, but a man knocked, hesitated, and then nervously entered, appearing unsure if he should interrupt.

"Some mourners are ready to go, Susie. They're asking for you."

"Be there in a minute."

"Don't be long."

"My ex," Susie explained, which Judy had guessed from the contrast of familiarity and lack of warmth in their tone.

"Duty calls."

"Need to head off myself."

Judy was hesitant. The conversation had been a little formal, making it difficult to pick up cues. She trusted her instinct and hugged Susie, whispering, "Sorry for your loss."

"Thank you," she whispered back, returning the warmth of Judy's hug.

John said, "I'll walk Judy out and catch up with you, Susie."

"Okay Junior," again, John rolled his eyes.

Judy smiled. "You don't like being called Junior?"

"Makes me feel like a boy. I'm nearly forty years old."

"I'll call a taxi and get out of your hair. Won't be long, so better head out."

"I'll walk you."

They made their way back through the mourners, which took some time as John frequently paused to receive condolences.

When they left the hall and stepped into the sunlight, John explained, "Susie's husband left her a few years ago, such a cliché… took up with his secretary or assistant or something. Years younger, of course."

They passed alongside the church as they headed toward the road.

"Oh, I bought your exceptional coffee, by the way."

"Can't take credit. It was luck, not my knowledge of coffee that created it." John smiled. "Susie likes you, rarely invites people for a meal."

"I liked her, too."

The taxi was waiting when they reached the front of the church.

"Thank you for walking me, John. Hope we'll see each other again soon."

"Hope so too. Goodbye, Judy Vernon."

Men like to use Judy's full name, and when they did, Judy knew they'd remember her.

"Goodbye, John," she said as she climbed into the taxi and sighed.

She gave the driver the address of the Farmers' Market. Settling into the taxi, Judy retrieved her iPad and added a new idea to her list of potential features; *The Value of Having a Good Wife.* She sighed again. *Refine it later.*

***

Judy placed her produce in the kitchen and her shoulder bag in her office. *Coffee.* Running the coffee through the Italian percolator enhanced the aromatic qualities which filled her apartment and preempted Judy's coffee experience.

Seated at her desk and enjoying her coffee, Judy sighed and retrieved Frank's book from her shoulder bag.

"Well, Frank, quite a sendoff. You were an amazing man. Met no one like you, but wish I had."

Opening Frank's book at the first page, she struck a line through her first entry…

~~In Search of Frank Farrington.~~

She replaced it with a new title.

Frank Farrington: A man of rare character and integrity.

Turning to the current page, Judy added her notes from all she learned about Frank at his funeral, focusing on the eulogies and her conversation with Gerry.

"You know, Frank, Gerry is a proper gentleman, and I like Susie. And you… character and integrity indeed. You would've been an exceptional mayor."

Judy closed Frank's book and glanced at her watch. *Time to prepare dinner.*

Myron

Aphrodisiac lingerie today. Soft pink with a touch of lace, a silky pale pink dress from her sensual collection. *Short enough to be enticing, not so short, it looks slutty.* A little light makeup, and finished with pale pink shoes, just high enough to accentuate the shape of her legs. Judy inspected her reflection in the mirror and nodded appreciatively, *pretty in pink.*

"What do you think, Frank? Not bad, eh?"

Judy sighed, collected her shoulder bag from the office, and, curious to see if Frank was there, set out for her morning visit to Kansas Café. As usual, her shoulder bag didn't match her ensemble, but she never left home without her *toolbox.*

***

When she entered the café, Dorothy glanced up from her newspaper. "Oh, good morning, Judy. My, aren't you pretty today?"

"Thank you, Dot." Judy smiled, appreciating the compliment.

She sat on the sofa and glanced across the table. She sighed.

"Still here Frank? You had a wonderful service yesterday, so many mourners, with positive things to say about you. Can't believe you nearly repaid everybody."

She shook her head. *Difficult to conceive.*

"You *were* a man of rare character and integrity."

Judy had completed the second draft of her features the previous evening. She added the idea of John Farrington being referred to as Junior to her stereotyping article and his perception of being a boy. Mostly, it focused on Frank and Myron as examples without using their names. She touched on Mike, the security guard, in both this feature, and the one about *Why People Let Themselves Go.* She drew on Frank heavily for that, too.

Her style was to base her writing on actual people with authentic examples rather than focus on abstract concepts. The reason her work is popular and sells well, she believes. Judy turned what experience taught her into a routine, productive way of working. She believes she spontaneously draws on examples from real life when writing, rather than routinely incorporating them.

Ella Fitzgerald's interpretation of *Makin' Whoopie* played in the background. Judy reflected on her features and discussed them with Frank, as she had the previous day. Her usual practice was to complete three drafts before the final edit, and then one last review before sending them to publishers. It was important to draw a line on the drafting process. One could spend forever redrafting and never finish.

Judy sighed. *Time to meet Myron.*

She needed to call into Alice's Bakery on the way. *Didn't buy fresh bread yesterday.*

"Got to go, Frank, but I guess I'll see you tomorrow."

She paid Dot on her way out, feeling a little aroused at the prospect of an afternoon with Myron.

***

Myron was sitting at the bar with his usual whisky sour when Judy arrived at Franco's.

As she walked to him, Myron stared at her in admiration, as did most of the other diners who were predominantly business executives.

He stood. "Hello beautiful, you look amazing."

"Hi Myron, you look pretty good yourself."

Myron, immaculately dressed as usual, wore a steel gray tailored suit with a white shirt, a matching steel gray tie, and handmade black shoes.

She hugged him lightly and kissed his cheek. Myron held back from the hug a little, not wanting Judy to feel his arousal.

"Drink before lunch?"

"Sure. A glass of house red please, Tony."

After enjoying their drink and small talk, they moved to their table. Most eyes in the restaurant focused on Judy. Myron and Judy chose the same menu item: a smoked salmon salad.

"I analyzed Frank's books. You won't believe what I discovered."

Judy smiled. "Frank was repaying his investors."

"How do you know that?"

"I'm a journalist."

She wasn't Myron's perception of a journalist.

***

Not looking like what people perceived to be a journalist, helped Judy in her work. People forgot she was a journalist, so were less guarded, and more relaxed than they otherwise might be.

"Keep forgetting. You don't look like a journalist."

"Occupational stereotyping," Judy said, making a mental note to add it to her feature. "Why don't you start at the beginning?"

"I think Frank and I could've been friends."

Judy nodded.

"Frank put together the best business model I've seen; it's brilliant. Planning to use it for a client whose business is in trouble. Adopting Frank's model may save it. Do you think he'd mind?"

"He'll be happy to know his model is helping someone."

"Frank made millions from his import business. Four point three four million, to be exact. Took expense control to a new level. My family excels at controlling expenses, but Frank puts them to shame."

"Frank didn't like to spend money." Judy noted Myron's veiled reference, applying a stereotype to his family. *Must include that.* Typical of Judy, who's always working, but doesn't realize it.

"Frank wanted to maximize profits, not for himself, to repay the investors. He still has an excellent reputation in finance circles. Considered smart, a star of sorts. Some people think he should've paid more attention to his partner. Billy was average, hanging on to Frank's coat tails.

"Most consider Frank to be a victim as much as, perhaps more than, his investors. Many investment firms wanted to get Frank on board and made a concerted effort for his license to be reinstated, but the regulatory authorities wouldn't budge. They wanted to set an example that all partners have a fiduciary duty to their investors. Repaying his investors is astonishing. He did nothing wrong. Frank's a rare man."

"Gerry said he repaid about ninety-five percent of their money," explained Judy.

"96.76% to be exact."

Judy smiled. *Of course, Myron would know the precise amount.*

"Had he lived, Frank would have paid the debt in full, and nearly been a millionaire within a year or two."

They'd finished their lunch by this time, having continued talking about Frank while they ate. Myron opened his briefcase and withdrew a large buff envelope which he passed to Judy. "Here, prepared a full report and analysis for you."

O*f course you did.* "Thank you, Myron."

"I analyzed his business model, his finances and the repayment to his investors."

"Very thorough, thank you. I'll read it later." Judy slipped the envelope into her shoulder bag. "You really are quite brilliant. I could kiss you."

***

Myron—a little intimidated by Judy as men often are when they perceive a woman is out of their league—felt momentarily daring.

"Well, no one is stopping you."

He flushed at being forward. His words had slipped out.

Judy stood, leaned across the table, and kissed Myron directly on his lips. Not a light brush, as one might with a close friend. Judy applied pressure and held her kiss long enough for him to feel her intention.

She took him by surprise. His pulse quickened, providing an excess of blood to his face. His mind raced, chasing vocabulary away.

"Sh-sh-shall we have coffee?"

"Let's, but perhaps not here. I know a place with *the best coffee in the city*."

"Really? Let's go."

Myron removed his jacket from the back of the chair. He noticed Judy admiring his form as he reached his arms into it.

They gathered their belongings and as they were leaving, Judy said, "I should get the check. You've done so much for me."

"Already taken care of."

Outside, they flagged a taxi. Judy sighed and gave the driver her address.

Myron's temperature rose as she gently leaned against him in the taxi. He wanted to say something, but his mouth suddenly became dry.

When they entered Judy's apartment, Myron immediately removed his shoes, which pleased Judy. *Brought up right.*

Myron glanced around the living room, *spotlessly clean and everything in its place*, which pleased him. *Stylish, functional, and comfortable.*

"Make yourself at home. I'll freshen up and then prepare our coffee."

Judy dropped her shoulder bag in her office, sighed, and went to the bathroom. Then she retrieved her purchases from Alice's Bakery, taking them to the kitchen.

Myron called out, "I better, err… freshen up, too. Where's your bathroom?"

"Down the hall, second on the left."

Judy's bathroom, meticulous, not that he expected anything less, *not full of creams and lotions many women have all over their bathroom.* Finishing up, he ensured he left the bathroom exactly as he found it. As he returned to the living room, he could smell the aroma of the percolating coffee.

"That smells wonderful," he said.

Judy entered the living room carrying a tray with coffee and cookies. She noted with approval that Myron, now sitting on the sofa, had neatly folded his suit jacket and tie over the back of a chair. His briefcase stood beside the chair.

Outwardly, he gave the appearance of being his usual calm, confident self. Inwardly nervous, in the way people are when something long desired is within reach and they're worried they're going to fuck it up at the last moment.

Judy placed the tray on the coffee table in front of Myron and sat beside him.

Taking a sip of his coffee, he announced, "Excellent."

"The John Farrington Blend, from Coffee Roasters."

Myron looked a little puzzled.

"John Farrington, Frank's brother, introduced it to me. Has his own blend at Coffee Roasters."

"I have a blend there too, not a patch on this. I'll switch."

"Try a cookie."

He did.

"They're delicious too."

"White chocolate, macadamia, and mandarin. Hand made from fresh ingredients by Alice's Bakery, best cookies in the city."

Finishing his coffee, Myron said, "You're right, best coffee in the city."

He remained hesitant, trying to come up with the perfect move. Hard with desire, he wanted to take her right there on the sofa. But he didn't want to rush in like a schoolboy, even though that's exactly how he felt.

Judy's desire matched Myron's. Wet, almost dripping. She couldn't understand why he didn't make his move.

Judy sighed and said lamely. "Are you going to sit there, or are you going to kiss me?"

"Been thinking about it." *Pathetic*, but with his brain in turmoil as nervousness battled desire, it was the best he could come up with.

"Thinking is not doing Myron." *Lame again.*

She wanted to get her hands on the cause of the bulge in his trousers.

He leaned towards her; they kissed. Being aroused, almost to the point of ejaculation, created an additional concern. He didn't want it over as soon as it began. *Why does she make me feel like a schoolboy?*

"Mmm, coffee-flavored kisses… sure that's a line from a song." She laughed. *Why am I acting like a nervous schoolgirl?* "Please, sir, can I have some more?"

They kissed again, and Judy's hand drifted to Myron's chest. She felt the tautness of his body as she began unbuttoning his shirt…

She Did Not Sigh

The alarm on Myron's phone woke them. Time to meet his client for dinner. He kissed Judy lightly on the lips and gently caressed her silky-smooth skin. *Divine.*

Judy returned Myron's kiss and contentedly moaned, purring at his gentle touch, dancing lightly across her body, igniting her senses.

Myron said, "I'm sorry, I wish I could stay, but…"

Judy smiled warmly. "Nothing to be sorry for. Attend to your business."

As Myron dressed, he said "I hate to, you know…"

"Eat and run?" Judy suggested as she slipped on her short silk nightdress and headed to the bathroom.

Myron flushed. She *still* made him feel like a schoolboy, but he didn't know why.

When Judy returned, Myron, having regained his composure, said, "When something tastes so good, it's hard to stop eating…"

It was Judy's turn to flush, Myron noted with a little satisfaction. Normally, Judy took everything in her stride. Nothing seemed to faze her.

***

Judy was in the living room when he finished in the bathroom.

"Hungry?"

"Famished, but lazy to go out now. Someone has taken all my energy." She winked. "Can rustle up something here, or maybe order something in."

"Fancy a steak or something from Franco's? I can order one in for you."

"Oh, I would, but I didn't think they delivered."

"They do for me." Myron was almost apologetic. His shy smile conveyed humility.

Of course they do. Judy smiled. "Yes, I'd very much like a steak from Franco's."

Myron called the restaurant, speaking to the head chef.

"Rare with blue cheese sauce?" he asked Judy.

"Yes. How…?"

"Mario."

Judy nodded. Impressed, Mario knew what she liked.

Between kisses, Myron said, "I'll call you."

"Please do."

Judy watched him leave.

She retrieved the tray from the coffee table, washed the dishes, and brewed some fresh coffee before retrieving her matching robe, which was more modest. *Don't want the delivery guy getting distracted.* She prepared a tip and placed it on the small stand beside the door.

Judy settled in her office with freshly percolated coffee and the last of the cookies from Alice's. She took Myron's report and Frank's notebook from her bag, and began reading and making notes, but thoughts of that afternoon's activities distracted her.

Knows how to touch a woman, gently caressing her body as his fingers waltzed across her skin, subtly teasing her to saturation in the process… *Knows how to use his tongue too,* but if his fingers waltzed, his tongue tangoed…. Judy smiled contentedly at the memory.

Being a regular squash player ensured Myron was fit. *Certainly has stamina.* He satisfied her several times.

Pleasant as they were, Judy forced herself to push aside her reflections of the afternoon. *Work to do.* Myron's report was thorough, detailing how Frank started with a little borrowed money and built a successful business from nothing. Every penny he gleaned from the business, used to repay investors, meticulously recorded in the spreadsheet.

Frank hired a private investigator to keep track of the investors. *Keeping his promise literally consumed his life.* Judy felt a mixture of admiration and sadness, strangely tinged with the satisfaction she still felt from her afternoon with Myron. She carefully labeled the report and placed it in her evidence locker.

The doorbell rang.

Instead of taking her meal out of the hot box pouch, the delivery guy handed her the pouch. "Be careful. Heavy and hot."

She expected to transfer the meal from a plastic takeout container to her own dishware. However, it was served on Franco's distinctive earthenware, under a cloche that clipped on the plate. Separately packed was a sealed small ceramic sauce jug and complete cutlery. *Impressive. Anything for a friend of Myron's,* her thoughts romantically imitating a line from *Casablanca*.

Franco's was in danger of going out of business several years earlier. At the request of his father, Myron put together a creative finance and management package. Helped by 'investors' who pre-purchased a 'platinum membership' including free delivery anywhere in the city. Franco's survived and became one of the leading businessperson's restaurants in the city.

Judy intended to eat in her office, but the Franco's delivery was too sumptuous. A bottle of Antinori Tignanello had accompanied her dinner. She poured a glass and toasted Myron. *My man of stamina and class.*

Perfect end to an exceptional day, courtesy of Myron.

After dinner, Judy completed the final draft of her features, incorporating the additional insights inspired by Myron during lunch into her *Stereotyping* feature. She even included some inspiration from Myron's performance that afternoon in her *Why People let Themselves Go* feature.

Feeling well satisfied with her efforts that night, and very well satisfied with Myron's efforts that afternoon, Judy was preparing herself for bed when he called.

"Hello Myron."

"Hello Beautiful, I want to apologize again...."

"Nothing to apologize for. Besides, you bought me dinner."

***

Myron, buoyed by the events that day, and by having one more whisky sour than he should've at dinner, said, "I hope we can continue to see each other… socially, I mean."

"I'd like that Myron, very much."

"Oh, that's glorious news. My taxi is arriving." *And I'm so pathetic I can't stand it.* "So I must go. Good night, beautiful."

As she slid into bed, Judy didn't realize she hadn't sighed all night.

***

Judy arrived at Kansas Café in a buoyant mood after her afternoon with Myron. Dorothy commented she "seemed bubbly today."

She sat on her usual sofa, looking at Frank opposite, and listening to James Taylor's version of *You've Got a Friend.* She raised her cup and took a sip; closing her eyes to savor both the coffee and the music.

"Having lunch with your sister today, Frank. Wonder what else I'll learn about you? You've impressed Myron. Going to use your model to help save someone's business. Told him you'd be happy you're still helping people."

She was looking forward to her meeting with Susan Farrington. She instinctively liked her, although she wasn't sure why. Perhaps an air of strength, giving the impression she'd be fiercely loyal, but wouldn't tolerate nonsense.

Judy placed her belongings in her shoulder bag and was ready to leave. Usually, she might have sighed a dozen times while seated in the café, but that morning she hadn't sighed once.

Alice's first to buy some of her favorite cookies as an after-lunch treat, and she grabbed a bottle of oaked Chardonnay from Lexington Wines. Settling into the back seat of the taxi, she gave the driver Susan Farrington's address. She did not sigh.

Susan and Billy

Susie's home had a lived-in feel. As one would expect from a single working mother with two children.

"Come into the kitchen," Susie said. "Need to keep half an eye on lunch while we talk."

Judy nodded and followed her.

She studied Susie; she hadn't looked at her properly in the anteroom where they met. *Family resemblance is unmistakable.* Deep lines at the side of her eyes confirmed Judy's impression: easy to smile, easier to frown. Fine lines around her mouth suggested she was once a smoker. Grey roots in her otherwise brown hair. Susie cared about her appearance… when she had time.

Attractive, especially when she smiles, softens her, making her younger than her years. Frowning ages her, perhaps a decade. If I were Susie's partner, I'd be keeping her happy.

The rest, more impression than observation. Susie seldom became angry, didn't need to. A look would be enough for people to defer to her wishes.

A tiredness about her told Judy Susie needed something to release the constant pressure. She didn't know what that might be, but charged herself to make it happen, without knowing why. Judy shook her head to chase Frank's eyes from her mind.

She retrieved the chardonnay from her shoulder bag. "Maybe put this in the fridge to keep the chill on it."

Susie took the bottle from Judy and inspected the label. "Oh, nice. I'll prepare some coffee. John likes you, stopped in yesterday with some of his special coffee. Excellent coffee, but too costly for me… Ali thinks it's too expensive, but he doesn't drink or smoke, so she accepts it. Think she's happy to have a counter argument if John complains something she bought is too pricey. Marriage needs a careful balance, don't you think?"

Something about these Farringtons… Marriage Needs Balance, would make an interesting feature. Ties in with Gerry's idea about the Importance of a Good Wife.

"Suppose it does," Judy conceded, "but I never married. Do you mind if I use my digital recorder? Saves me having to take notes. Can give you a copy."

"John said you'll want to record our talk."

Judy frowned.

"A sibling thing. Only call him Junior to his face, because it annoys him."

Judy smiled; she could imagine Susie feeling a sense of pleasure when John rolled his eyes or grimaced at the mention of Junior.

"The aroma of John's coffee is so intense, it's like I'm already drinking it…"

"Exceptional coffee, probably worth the cost, but with two kids to raise, I can't justify the expense. Oh, lunch is in the oven, won't be long… mac and cheese."

"Sounds wonderful."

Judy didn't like mac and cheese, at least the common packet variety of low-quality pasta and a cheese sauce made from chemical laced powder. However, she knew not to be judgmental in any way when pursuing a story. Makes people defensive, sometimes aggressive, or worse, can shut them down. She'd happily eat and *enjoy* the mac and cheese.

Bringing their coffee to the table, Susie explained, "John's given us more than enough for another cup after lunch… well, after we've finished that chardonnay."

Judy sipped her coffee. "Heavenly."

"Certainly is, like a cigarette after sex, back when I smoked."

"Never smoked, but I bought some of John's coffee. Life's too short, as they say."

Susie gave a little laugh. "Funny… said that to Frank a couple of weeks ago."

Judy took another sip of her coffee and waited for Susie to continue; silence is often the best follow-up question.

Susie became distant, giving the impression of having momentarily drifted into the past.

"Finally convinced Frank to come for dinner. Seen little of him these last few years, since he started that import business. Must've been more than a year since he last came to dinner… Glad he came, at least I got to spend a little time with him before…" She swallowed and closed her eyes as she maintained her composure before continuing. "Frank really let himself go… put on a lot of weight. Spent the entire evening lecturing him about needing to take care of himself…." The timer on the oven interrupted her.

Susie removed the Pyrex dish from the oven and placed it on the kitchen island. "Needs to rest."

Judy could hear the molten cheese sizzling. She inhaled deeply as the wafting aroma reached her. "*Damn,* that smells *divine*!"

Susie grinned. "Frank said he was 'too busy to worry about anything but work,' but I told him life's too short, and he needed to look after himself before it's too late…. already too late for poor Frank…" Susie drifted silently into herself, then continued. "Don't think Frank lost interest in himself. He cared about repaying everybody more. Frank said, 'Don't worry. I'll finish repaying everyone soon and then I'll claim my life back.' He would've too… repaid everyone if he lived. An exceptional man… didn't deserve what happened to him."

Judy contemplated Susie's words before responding quietly. "No Susie, he certainly didn't."

"Time to eat." Susie stood to organize lunch.

She retrieved the wine from the fridge and handed it to Judy with a corkscrew and two glasses. "Pour the wine, and I'll fetch the food."

While Judy opened and poured the wine, Susie brought plates, cutlery, and a wine cooler to the table. She placed the mac and cheese between them.

"It'll change your idea of mac and cheese. Everyone loves it. People always ask me to make it, as if it's my signature dish or something."

Looks and smells amazing for a humble mac and cheese. Judy took a forkful. "Wow! That *is* amazing! Can't believe mac and cheese can taste *this good!*"

Judy took her time with her second forkful. A powerful kick of flavor from a generous amount of parmesan cheese with salty sweetness from a blend of oregano, marjoram, and basil. Creamy, the mozzarella cheese added gooeyness, and the macaroni had the slight bite of pasta cooked al dente. The noticeable contrast of textures surprised her.

"Secret's in the dairy, lots of cheese, cream and butter and quality pasta. This is *real* mac and cheese, nothing like that packet shit. Not healthy, I guess, too many calories, but tastes amazing…"

Susie became quiet and withdrawn.

When she spoke, she echoed what she said to her brother, the last time she'd ever see him. "Life's too short not to indulge occasionally."

Judy's turn to be thoughtful.

"Wrote a feature about the way we eat. The most important thing is to eat fresh, use fresh ingredients, create, and eat real food-based meals. Much healthier than processed foods, most of which are empty calories and of little or no nutritional value… someone described them as *products resembling food.* Fresh food is healthy, tastes much better and *isn't* indulgent. As you say, life's short and processed food only shortens it."

Isn't that right, Frank?

Judy asked, "Could I, umm… get your recipe for this?"

Judy had been a little concerned that the gooey creaminess would leave her mouth coated, but the wine acted as a palate cleanser.

"This wine is going down well with the mac and cheese. Excellent choice, Judy. Not my recipe. Found it online. British Chef, Marco Pierre White. Heard of him?"

"Can't say I have."

"Sure, I'll send you the recipe. This Marco is one of the leading chefs in the world, trained some of the world's best chefs I understand, including Gordon Ramsay."

Judy smiled. "Gordon Ramsay, I know. Now that man can cook… hot, too. Wouldn't kick him out of bed even if he couldn't cook."

Susie gave Judy a sheepish grin. "Well, maybe to cook breakfast."

"Why do I have the impression that's a fantasy you've enjoyed more than once?" Judy gave a knowing wink, which Susie ignored.

"*Anyway*, reading about Gordon Ramsay. This Marco guy made him cry. Intrigued me… looked it up. Liked what he said about the incident. 'I didn't make Gordon cry; Gordon chose to cry…' Wanted to find out about him and found this recipe…"

Susie cleared the table. Judy offered to help, but Susie waved her away.

"Perhaps take our wine into the living room? I'm fine here, but thanks for offering."

Settled in the living room, Susie was quiet, hesitant. Judy could see she wanted to say something, and was about to ask what was on her mind when Susie quietly asked, "Could you tell me how Frank died?"

Judy thought about the best way to describe the experience of watching Frank die. *Best trust my instinct instead of planning a response.*

"Often go to a café, Kansas Café. Downtown, near The Gourmet Food District, where John gets his coffee. An old café, getting pretty tired now, with threadbare sofas and faded decorations. A lot of character, and excellent music played at the right volume…

"The owner, Dot… Dorothy, makes the best cheesecake in the city. Fresh every day. I like fresh handmade food. Usually sit on an old comfortable sofa by the window, like to observe the people passing by… sometimes a passerby is interesting, and inspires an idea…"

Susie interrupted, "Been reading your features for years. Like the way you write… always looking for the positive aspects and not focusing on the negatives to sell a story. Can trust you with Frank…"

Judy smiled weakly, knowing she was waffling, stalling. She looked Susie in the eye, reached across and took her hand. They sat in silence—lost in the moment—until Judy took a deep breath and continued.

"Enjoying my coffee and cheesecake when I saw Frank walking past. He received a phone call and stopped walking… Couldn't hear what he was saying, and don't know who he was talking to, but the call made him angry… furious."

Susie became angry. "That'd be that *cunt* ex-wife of his! Never liked her from the minute I met the bitch, and the way she treated Frank after his trouble with Billy… I hate her, and I *never* hate people… she was a cunt to him, and I hate that fucking word and I hate her more for making me use it! But… there's no other word to describe her, horrible person… Never understood why Frank loved her, but he did."

Judy nodded. She squeezed Susie's hand before continuing.

"He was shouting into the phone, facing me… well the window and then everything seemed to be in slow motion… he dropped the phone and sank to the ground clutching his chest… before he passed the anger left him and he seemed at peace, like the weight of the world lifted from his shoulders. Somebody screamed at me to call an ambulance, which I did, but knew it was too late… I saw him go."

They remained silent for a while until Susie said, "Thank you for sharing. Relieved, he found peace in the end. Frank was a rare man who didn't deserve the hand life dealt him. Warned him about that cunt, and warned him about Billy, too."

"Poor Billy has no impulse control. Billy's not a bad person, sweet really, but he needs someone to keep him in check—can't control himself—does stuff which he regrets, but never learns. He deserved prison. Hurt many people. Frank, more than anybody, but he didn't handle prison well. Broke him."

Susie retreated into her mind again, but only for a moment. She picked up her glass and proposed a toast. "Billy," she whispered.

"Billy," Judy echoed.

"Dated Billy for a while. I was strong enough to keep him on an even footing… His grades improved when we were together because I made sure he stayed focused. Frank said I was good for him.

"Broke up with him because I felt like his mother. Didn't want to be anybody's mother. Wanted a guy who'd look out for me, not someone I needed to look out for. Can you understand that?"

***

"*Jesus Billy!* What fucking time do you call this? Been waiting fucking hours."

"Sorry Suse, I forgot."

"You didn't forget to go fucking drinking."

"I'm sorry…"

"Sorry doesn't cut it, Billy. You're always fucking sorry. Now get your ass to that desk and do your assignment. It's due tomorrow."

"What if I do it in the morning?"

"You won't, you'll do it now."

Easily defeated, Billy did as he was told. Susie spent the next few hours watching him do his assignment and suggesting improvements. After she made sure he sent it off, they went to bed.

Billy slept.

Susie didn't sleep. She lay beside him, thinking. *Can't do this anymore.*

When Billy woke, Susie was sitting beside the door, bag packed.

"I'm sorry Billy, I love you, but I can't do this. I'm not your fucking mother, and don't want to be. I'm done."

Billy slid out of bed, kneeling naked in front of her. "Don't go Suse, I'm begging on my knees. I can't cope without you."

"Sorry Billy. I'm leaving. Can't do this anymore."

"Please Suse…" he begged, tears rolling down his cheeks.

Susie's heart was breaking. She desperately wanted to go to him, hold him, tell him everything was going to be all right. Instead, she steeled herself.

"You're pathetic. Get some fucking clothes on and get your worthless ass to school."

She opened the door and stormed out—slamming it behind her—while she still had the strength to do so.

There was a finality to the slamming of the door and Billy knew it. Not that Billy knew much. There were only two things Billy was sure of.

He'd fuck everything up. He always did, and he loved Susie. He always would. Adopting a fetal position, he lay on the floor.

***

"I honestly believe if I stayed with Billy, it would never have happened. I could keep him under control. Billy can't control himself, but I could control him… so maybe? Not saying it wouldn't have happened, but *maybe* it wouldn't. In time, he may have resented being controlled and rebelled and it would have happened, anyway.

"Billy's a sweet guy, but there's something missing in him… an ability to know when he's doing the wrong thing and stop himself… take himself in hand. Poor Billy."

"What happened to Billy following his release from prison?"

"Frank would've known. Wherever Billy is, Frank would've been looking out for him. Frank blames… blamed himself for what happened to Billy. He never said so outright, but he alluded to it a few times.

"Felt he neglected Billy. Used to watch over him and rein him in when Billy went too far. In the end… between his political career and his cunt wife, he never had time for Billy. Left Billy to his own devices, which was always going to be disastrous."

Susan and Frank

"Frank lived in my basement when he lost everything. The creditors got it all and that cunt got nothing."

The smug look on her face told Judy this gave Susie more than a little satisfaction. *Why does she hate Frank's wife?*

"Frank spent all his time on the internet. 'Researching,' he said, 'Need to find a new business.' Chose import/export. Thought he'd relax then, start doing something other than being chained to his laptop, but he didn't. He kept at it twelve hours a day.

"He explained, 'Having decided what I'm going to do, I need to learn how to do it.' When his bankruptcy period ended, he was ready. The next day he registered a company, borrowed a little money from my husband. We were still together then—before my ex ran off with his secretary half his age—stupid bastard. Married now. Don't know if he's happy. Don't care. Not bitter. Guilted him into signing this house over and it's fully paid. Frank rented a warehouse across town with cheap rent. Seldom saw him after that. Want another coffee, hon?"

"Please." Judy reached into her shoulder bag. "Cookies… best in the city."

"Perfect, go nicely with the coffee."

Susie made her way to the kitchen and returned ten minutes later, with coffee and the cookies, now on a plate.

Trying one, she exclaimed. "My God! These *are* delicious."

"Macadamia, mandarin and white chocolate."

Judy sipped her coffee and slowly ate a crumbly, slightly buttery cookie. A soft crunch from the macadamia nuts, creamy sweetness from the white chocolate, and mild tartness of citrus followed by a burst of natural sweetness from the mandarin. Textures and flavors dancing in her mouth, each bite producing a different version of the dance.

She steered the conversation back to Frank. "Did you ever visit Frank's warehouse?"

"Thought about it a few times, but never got there in the end."

Judy was trying to decide whether to mention she'd visited Frank's warehouse. Luckily, Susie changed the subject.

"You said you never married. Seeing anyone?"

Judy flushed a little. "Sort of… I think so… just started… early days… well, a day."

"You obviously like the guy." Susie winked. "You're flustered like a schoolgirl."

"He's younger than me, but mature beyond his years…"

Susie smiled mischievously. "In my experience, younger guys have a lot of stamina."

The pink in Judy's face turned red. "He certainly does. Very fit. What about you Susie? Seeing anyone?"

"Nothing serious, seeing a couple of guys casually."

"Together?" Judy winked.

"Oh, God no! Not those two…" Susie became thoughtful for a moment. "Not that I haven't…. err… been the filling in a two-guy sandwich. I enjoyed being the err… center of attention." She laughed; almost a giggle. "I'd do it again if the opportunity arises… but they were a little competitive. Would've been better if they were into enjoying each other a little more and competing a little less. How about you… ever enjoyed dueling swords?"

Judy hesitated, not because she's uncomfortable with her sexuality, which she'd carefully crafted during her lifetime. She fashioned herself as a cute lesbian in college before transitioning to a happy bi-girl. Since then, she'd fine-tuned herself into what she now described as *gender irrelevant*. Judy enjoys sex with whoever attracts her. She hesitated because the conversation was being recorded.

"Not exactly. Been between a married couple."

"Interesting. How was that?" Susie asked.

"Much the same, I guess… competitive, but differently. She thought she needed to compete with me for her husband's attention, but she didn't. More interested in her than him, to be honest."

"Not surprised."

"Into girls at college and for a while after college; I um… matured I suppose, came to find guys could be more interesting… well, more attentive. Nothing as attentive as a guy who's trying to get inside of you. I became… adaptable."

"Gives you more options, I guess. My threesome would've been more enjoyable, if those two guys had been a bit more into each other." Susie laughed.

It's like we've known each other all our lives. Heard of this happening, but never experienced it. Read somewhere it's because of a past life connection, not sure about that.

Judy didn't want to pursue the subject on tape. People being interviewed often forget they're being recorded, but Judy never did. She changed the subject.

"If you don't want to… I understand, but I'm curious about Frank's relationship with his wife."

"Not sure if they ever had a threesome. Mind you, it wouldn't surprise me what she's into. Disliked her the moment I met her, but Frank loved her. Never understood why. Attractive, I guess, but not that deep beauty that lasts a lifetime. The pretty that doesn't age well. Not seen her in years. Thank God.

"Didn't care about Frank." Susie took a sip of coffee. "She cared about status and having whatever equaled success in her mind. Didn't like Billy hanging around, kept telling Frank they shouldn't be associating with people like Billy. He'd drag them down. Wasn't perceptive. Thought they should only associate with people of a certain status. Frank neglected Billy to keep Myriam happy. Without a stabilizing hand, Billy…."

Judy's journalistic instinct told her she needed to speak with Myriam and complete the story. *Damn Frank, would you get your eyes out of my head?* Judy shook her head to remove the image.

"What is it?" asked Susie.

"Oh… umm… Nothing. Please continue."

"Billy was a disaster, making one terrible choice after another… making bad choices to avoid the consequences of prior bad choices. Started gambling for the buzz. When he got in too deep, he continued gambling to get himself out of the hole… only made the hole deeper. It swallowed everybody. Frank should've paid attention to Billy. Wasting his time trying to keep that... Myriam happy. Complained all the time and constantly criticized. Do you know what constant criticism does to a man? It destroys his confidence."

What constant criticism does to a man. Must include that with Gerry's idea.

"Frank's confidence, already low because of that, err... woman, shattered when Billy's embezzlement came to light. She wanted Frank to hide assets in her name, which proved how little she knew him. He wouldn't do anything dodgy. If he had, would've ended up in jail with Billy.

"She left him. Surprised nobody but destroyed Frank. Wasted no time in divorcing him. Stupid bitch went for big alimony too. The judge awarded no alimony because Frank had nothing to give. Should've waited until after the bankruptcy period ended. Might've got something then. Glad she didn't... the cunt deserves nothing!

"Myriam, leaving is the one good thing to happen. Still tied to her, he never could've repaid people. The only important thing to him in the end. Think nearly paying everyone back brought him the peace at his passing.

"After that bankruptcy restriction, umm... ran out. Myriam tried for alimony again, but she outsmarted herself and I think the original judge didn't like her. No surprise there. She originally applied for some sort of binding alimony award which would bind Frank to pay regardless of his circumstances. The judge didn't deny her claim. He awarded her claim but awarded zero amount. Something like that... Don't really understand. The result was they bound Frank to pay nothing.

"Most people dislike Myriam instantly. Except Frank—possibly why he loved her, because everyone else hated her—Frank's like that, spent his life looking after Billy, well, trying to. Perhaps Myriam is another Billy in her own way, with none of Billy's redeeming qualities."

"Do you know where she is now?" Judy asked.

"No, and I don't care. A relief when she didn't come to Frank's funeral. Saved me a lot of aggravation."

"In the interests of painting a complete picture, I'd better talk to Myriam. I won't publish anything bad about Frank."

"You won't like her."

"Sounds like it. Do you have a number for her? Perhaps know what name she's using now?"

"An old mobile number… can't guarantee it's still connected."

Susie retrieved the number, wrote it on a piece of paper, and passed it to Judy, who thanked her and slid it into the inner pocket of her shoulder bag.

Susie cleared away their coffee cups. Judy glanced at her watch. *Getting late.*

"My God, is that the time? Sorry I've taken your complete day!"

"Don't be silly. A splendid afternoon. Must do this again soon. Don't be a stranger."

"Agree totally. We'll organize something soon. Been a long time since I had a girlfriend to confide in. Didn't realize how much I missed it."

Susie winked. "Oh, you're looking for a girlfriend?"

"God no, complicate my life too much," Judy smiled. "Looking for a *girl* friend." *Frank, get your eyes out of my head.*

"Anytime you want to chat."

"Same. I'll call a taxi."

They said their goodbyes when the taxi driver hit the horn to signal his arrival.

As Judy climbed into the vehicle, she switched her digital recorder off, and gave the driver the address of the Farmers' Market.

She took her iPad from her shoulder bag as she slipped her digital recorder into it. She added notes for more features; *The Effect Constant Criticism has on Men,* and *Marriage Requires Balance… A three-part feature?* Judy relaxed, reflecting on an enjoyable afternoon.

Myriam

After arriving home, Judy listened to the digital recording from her interview with Susie, discussed events of the afternoon with Frank and asked him questions which happily remained unanswered. She updated her notes in Frank's book.

Myron called. She invited him to dinner the next day. Judy often cooks at home, but hadn't cooked for anyone for several years. *Don't know what I'll make.*

***

Judy listened to Ray Charles singing, *You Don't Know Me,* as she enjoyed her morning cappuccino and casually discussed things with Frank. Judy no longer talked to herself constantly. Prior to meeting Frank, she'd fallen into the habit of being alone, not that she was lonely. Happy to spend her time in her own company, or in the company of her habits and routines, of which she had many.

If Judy were aware of drifting into the habit of her own company, she may think it might make an interesting feature.

Judy studied the recipe for mac and cheese Susie had emailed that morning. *Could prepare it for Myron.*

She retrieved the note Susie had given her with Myriam's phone number.

"Well Frank, hopefully I'll have the pleasure of talking with your ex-wife today. Can't say I'm looking forward to it. At least the result won't be as bad as the last time you spoke with her."

The phone answered after two rings... A woman, presumably Myriam, said, "Speak!"

"Hello, is this Myriam?"

"Of course it is. Didn't *you* ring me?"

"Hello Myriam, my name is Judy Vernon. I'm a journalist, writing a feature about Frank Farrington... I'd like to come and talk with you about him."

"Why are you writing about Frank? How much will you pay me?"

"Well Myriam, it's only a feature, so it won't make a lot of money. How does fifty sound?"

"Doesn't sound good. How about a hundred?"

"Okay, fifty when we start, and another fifty at the end of the interview. Okay?"

"Yeah, I guess."

"What time is convenient for you?"

"Anytime. Nothing better to do."

"In about an hour, then?"

"Fine. Bring the money."

"What's your address?"

Judy made a note of Myriam's address.

"Thank you, Myriam. I'll see you soon."

Myriam hung up without a goodbye.

"Off to meet your ex-wife, Frank."

***

Judy arrived at the address Myriam had given her. After getting out of the taxi, she put her digital recorder in the outside pocket of her shoulder bag. As she was paying for the interview; she didn't need to be open about recording it. The payment made it her property. Besides, people who seek payment for an interview usually demand additional payment to allow the interview to be recorded.

A small house, narrow, one story with a usable attic, she assumed because of the attic window. Cashmere woodgrain aluminum siding in need of a clean, with an unkept garden in a low-income part of the city, close to Frank's warehouse. An unpleasant odor coming from somewhere, but Judy couldn't identify it. She needed to knock twice before Myriam answered the door.

Myriam had that permanently tired look some people acquire from years of frustration and disappointment. Compared to the photograph in John's scrapbook, Susie's guess had been correct. Myriam—as unkept as her garden—hadn't aged well, as if she gave up on herself at some point.

Judy remembered something a Chinese woman told her, "No such thing as an ugly woman, only a lazy one." *Hmm, could be something in that?*

Myriam wore a very short, dark blue dress with white trim. A little tight. Judy couldn't decide if, like Frank, Myriam wore something she'd almost outgrown, or whether she bought it recently despite the style being too young for her, the way some women do.

Judy recalled an old expression. *Mutton dressed as lamb. Do people still use that expression? Could be a feature in that... maybe two.*

"You that journalist? Got my money?"

Not even a pretense of politeness. "Yes. May I come in?"

"Okay." Myriam turned and walked into her living room.

Judy followed her. *This could be hard work.* Myriam's living room displayed the same unkept qualities as Myriam and her front garden. The furniture—a standard sofa, two armchairs and a coffee table—seemed reasonably new, but appeared shabby.

A man sat in an armchair reading the paper. He looked up as they came in.

Judy smiled at him. "Good morning."

The man glanced at his watch. "Morning."

Warm and fuzzy house, this one.

"Don't mind my loser husband. Married three times and all fucking losers. Can you believe that? Married three fucking losers. How could one person be so fucking unlucky?"

The man looked at Myriam with disdain, sighed heavily, and stood, noisily folding his paper, before tucking it under his arm. He glared at his wife, but didn't even glance at Judy, as he almost stomped out of the room.

"Three fucking losers." Myriam shook her head. "Can you believe that? You got my money?"

"Yes, here you are, the other fifty when we're done, as agreed."

"Sure, whatever."

Myriam pointed to a sofa without inviting Judy to sit. The furniture sagged when Judy sat on it. Myriam sat in a chair opposite. Judy glanced at her. *Definitely too short.* In sitting, her dress became no longer than an extended T-shirt. The way Myriam revealed her panties left Judy unsure if it was by accident or design.

When Myriam crossed her legs, her short dress revealed more. White lacy panties, with small tuffs of pubic hair protruding from the lace. *Jesus, her vagina's as unkept as the rest of her.* Judy forced herself to drag her attention away from Myriam's untrimmed bush. On the cluttered coffee table between them were two cups of coffee.

"Made you a coffee," Myriam indicated the cup on the table.

Judy thanked her, picked it up, and took a sip. She nearly gagged, but hid it well behind the cup. *Cheap three-in-one instant coffee, like in Frank's warehouse.*

"Let's start at the beginning. How did you and Frank meet?"

"Don't remember. Think someone introduced us at a function. Thought he'd give me a good life, but turned out to be another fucking loser. Always dated losers. Thought Frank was different, so I married him, but I was wrong. Probably the biggest fucking loser of 'em all.

"Told him to dump fucking Billy. Another fucking loser, glad he ended up in jail. Bastard took everything from me… My only chance of a decent life. Wish he died in jail. Fucking loser and Frank, a bigger loser for not throwing him out of the business like I told him.

"Frank never listened to me. Every fucking day, I told him what he needed to do, but he never fucking listened. None of them do… these fucking losers I marry. Try to advise them, teach them, tell them what they're doing wrong and they never fucking listen. Losers. Don't know why I always marry losers.

"Fucking Frank is still giving money to fucking Billy. My friend saw Billy last week. Lives around the docks…. Fucking loser. Told her Frank gave him some money… Fucking Billy took everything from me, and Frank's still giving him money. Money he should give me. If that fucking Judge hadn't screwed me. Thanks to my fucking loser lawyer. Should've fucked the judge instead of him. Might've been okay then.

"Can't believe Frank's still giving money to fucking Billy. Both fucking losers, if you ask me. Deserve each other. Rang Frank when I heard... told him he's a fucking loser, to give me money instead of fucking Billy. Furious with me... don't know why. Only giving him advice, like I always did. Never listened. If he did, he would've dumped fucking Billy before he destroyed my life.

"Didn't always live like this." Myriam gestured widely, indicating her living room, but probably referring to her life. "Happens when you keep marrying fucking losers... Never fucking listen to me."

Myriam raised her voice, presumably so her husband—wherever he was—could hear her. "Now I've married *another* fucking loser. Always giving him advice, telling him how to do things better, but he never fucking listens. Fucking loser! Stops listening when I'm talking. Gets up and walks away without a fucking word. Don't even fucking pretend to listen. Fucking loser! Frank did that too the other day. One minute he's shouting at me... then he stopped talking. Fucking loser."

Myriam doesn't know Frank died. Have to tell her, not sure how she'll react.

"Myriam," Judy said, attempting to be gentle. "Do you know Frank passed away last week?"

Myriam became distant. Her face quivered, as if about to cry. She didn't. She swallowed hard, sat back in her chair, and straightened her body, almost becoming rigid as she steeled herself against the news. Myriam swallowed again and stared at nothing.

Having composed herself, Myriam resumed talking. "Really? No, I didn't. Nobody bothered to tell me. You'd think that fucking bitch sister of Frank's would've said something... How'd he die?"

"A heart attack." Judy was interested in Myriam's reaction. "While talking on the phone."

"Dead, huh? Heart attack... talking on..."

Myriam stopped talking. She stared sightlessly, but her face wasn't blank this time. She frowned, as though deep in thought. When she spoke, she was different, softer.

"That would explain it. Hanging up on me isn't something Frank does. He's strong. Walking away and ignoring me is something a weak man does." She nodded towards the door her husband used to leave the room. "No, Frank would've finished the call, even if it pissed him off. He must've died when talking to me. Can't believe the last thing I said to him was that he's a loser. I have to live with that now."

Myriam became quiet again. *Silently contemplating her realization.* Myriam shook her head. The abrasive persona returned.

"Guess that makes me a widow?"

"I'm not sure," Judy said, but Myriam seemed taken with the idea.

"As Frank's widow, it must entitle me to his estate. Wonder if he has much money. I'll need a lawyer. Can use that loser, Jeff. Not much of a lawyer, but cheap, and I can pay him with pussy."

"Pay him with pussy?"

"Yeah, he's a loser. Another fucking loser. I seem to be..." Myriam raised her voice, for her husband's benefit, "surrounded by fucking losers." She kept her voice raised. "Already used him for the alimony claim and two divorces. Instead of paying him, I suck his cock until he's hard, and then bend over his desk and let him fuck me until he shoots his load. Doesn't take long! He's cheap, but what a loser."

Paying with pussy... could be a feature in that.

Judy supposed this had always been Myriam's way, but as life had been less kind to her, her standards dropped. As fascinating, although somewhat distasteful, as Myriam was, Judy felt she should leave. Myriam needed time to process Frank's death. She obviously wouldn't allow herself to do so in Judy's presence.

Judy had half an idea Myriam herself could be the subject of a feature at some point, and definitely wanted to keep that door open.

Judy's gaze unwillingly returned to Myriam's lace covered vagina, from which she'd struggled to keep her eyes averted for the entire interview. In other circumstances and with another woman Judy would've found a flash of lace panties attractive, but if this was Myriam's interpretation of flashing her pussy, she needed to learn the difference between a flash and a spotlight. Judy didn't find Myriam's offering attractive, but it was hypnotic.

"Myriam," Judy refocused herself. "You mentioned your friend saw Billy?"

"Yeah, down by the docks. Fucking loser lives there now. Used to wish he got shanked in jail. Fucking loser bastard cost me everything. The only way I hear anything about Frank is from my friends who know people who know Frank. Can't believe none of 'em told me poor Frank died. You'd think someone would've told me. After all, I'm his widow!"

"Do you know Billy's address? Where he's living?"

"Billy doesn't have an address… lives down by the docks. Fucking loser's homeless now. Serves him right. Lost me my home. Had an elegant home once…" Myriam continued, raising her voice and looking at the open door. "Yes, had a grand home once, not like this fucking shithole. Would you look at the shithole that fucking loser gives me to live in?"

Judy clarified. "Billy is homeless, and stays around the docks?"

"Yeah, there's an early opening bar there. The Ship… something. One of those places where those disgusting homeless drunks hang out when they got a few pennies to buy something cheap and nasty to drink. Easy to find. Just follow the smell of those bums. Fucking losers, all of 'em like that fucking loser bastard Billy, and not all men. Some women bums there too… whores and dykes, I guess."

Myriam raised her voice again. "Not only men who are fucking losers. Some women are fucking losers, too. Knowing my luck, if I was a fucking dyke, probably end up with a fucking whore loser bitch, too. Story of my life. Attract fucking losers. Don't know why."

"Well, this has been enlightening, Myriam, thank you," she said, as she stood to leave.

Myriam stood too and stepped towards her as Judy passed her chair. Judy handed Myriam the second fifty, taking her hand as she did so. Judy, sure she wanted to talk to Myriam again, felt it was important to keep her on side and establish a going rate for any future encounters. On impulse, Judy hugged her.

"I'll call a taxi and get out of your hair."

As she left the house, Judy said, "Frank, would you get those eyes out of my head?"

In the taxi, and on her way to Alice's Bakery before she switched off the digital recorder. She expected to hate Myriam, but she didn't.

She took her iPad from her shoulder bag and made notes for features… *No Ugly Women—Only Lazy Women, Paying with Pussy, Mutton Dressed as Lamb—Why do Old Sayings Die Out, Myriam's Story?*

Idea wise, it had been a productive morning. She relaxed and thought about what to make Myron for dinner.

Dinner with Myron

Judy skipped lunch. *Need a decent coffee after that shit at Myriam's.* She opened the bag and inhaled deeply. *Love that smell.* She placed two scoops in her Italian percolator, put it on the stove, and turned on the gas, which clicked as it self-ignited. The nutty, burnt caramel aroma of the percolating coffee was enough to banish Myriam's three-in-one from her memory.

Judy sat in her comfortable office chair, legs curled up under her, lazily sipping her coffee. She didn't feel like working. She booted up her computer. *One last review before submitting them.*

She received two emails from publishers accepting features she previously submitted. This was not unusual. Publishers would either pick freelance pieces up immediately, or whenever they needed them. She opened the spreadsheet where she managed her publishers and updated her records. Judy kept track of the genre each publisher was interested in.

When she first met Myron, he offered to review her business plan and accounting management. Judy didn't take him up on his offer. Now, looking for reasons to spend time with him, she decided to do so.

As it was, she found herself decidedly moist at the prospect of Myron staying the night. Fidgeting in her chair, she shook her head; she needed to focus.

She planned a new commission and two freelance pieces, which could sell standalone or as a two-part feature. Versatility is important for sales. *The Importance of Being Married to the Right Partner,* and *The Importance of Balance in Marriage.*

Must ask Myron to explain cryptocurrencies… a feature comparing the newest and oldest currencies might be an interesting take. So many features inspired by Frank or connections to him.

"Well, Frank, you've certainly influenced my life."

She listened to her interview with Myriam.

***

Judy showered and changed. She wore a pale lemon blouse with mustard slacks.

Susie's mac and cheese recipe was in Judy's bag when she went to the Farmer's Market. She found all the ingredients needed. In the kitchen, while preparing dinner, she couldn't shake the feeling something wasn't quite right.

Returning to the bedroom, she studied her reflection in the full-length mirror a third time. *What is it? Oh. Our second date, and I'm wearing slacks!* She selected a white skirt.

After removing her slacks, she glimpsed herself in the mirror. Her lemon blouse, not long enough to cover her lacy lemon panties. *Ooh... now that looks... wow! Perhaps another day, if I open the door like this, Myron wouldn't give me a chance to eat dinner.* She pulled on her white skirt and returned to the kitchen.

***

Myron smiled and handed Judy a bunch of roses when she opened the door. The strong, familiar fragrance was almost intoxicating. She kissed him.

"Put your bag in the bedroom. Hang something in my wardrobe if you need to."

"I'll do that and freshen up."

"When you're done, come into the kitchen."

When Myron entered the kitchen, Judy handed him a whiskey sour. She bought the ingredients that afternoon. The roses, now in a Baccarat Spirale Crystal vase.

"Something smells wonderful."

"Apparently, I taste good too," she teased.

Myron flushed, which made Judy smile. "You do, but I was talking about dinner."

"Mac and cheese."

"Mac and cheese?"

"You'll see."

Judy took the roses into the dining room, placing them at the unoccupied end of the table. She needed the space between their settings for dinner.

As she walked past Myron, she stopped and kissed him. "Thank you."

Returning from the dining room, she kissed him again.

"You don't know what real mac and cheese is."

"I trust you. How was Frank's wife?"

"Ex-wife. On her third husband now, but not for much longer."

"Was she as bad as people said?"

"Yes. Fascinating person. Witnessed a car wreck once. Protruding bones and lots of blood. It was horrible, but I couldn't avert my eyes. Myriam reminded me of that."

"Find her interesting?"

"Yes, feel a little sorry for her. If you removed *fucking loser* from her vocabulary, there'd be little left. Might base a feature on her. Pays her lawyer with her pussy, apparently. A valid form of currency, she believes."

"Not ethical, but the oldest form of currency, they say."

"Had an idea this afternoon about writing a feature comparing the oldest currency with the newest currency. Know anything about Bitcoin?"

"I do."

"Thought you might," Judy smiled. "You can give me a lesson at some point. What about Frank? Did he become involved in them? Understand there's a lot of money to be made."

"He didn't. Had concerns about what might happen if trading in cryptocurrencies was a breach of his investment ban. Don't think it would've been. Frank wasn't taking any chances. Not that he didn't think about it. Developed a model for investing in Bitcoin. The BC file you gave me is a set of spreadsheets for a hypothetical Bitcoin investment. Would've made a great deal of money had he actually invested using his model."

"Can't say I'm surprised."

Judy took dinner from the oven to rest. The molten cheese sizzled and popped.

"Damn, smells delicious."

"So, Myron, how's Frank's model working out for you?"

Myron smiled. "Pretty well, actually. Wanted to test the model with a small investment. Frank was a smart man. Have a lot of respect for him. Personally, doubt their long-term viability. Speculative investment isn't my thing. Prefer direct control, but one could, if they gained the rights, sell Frank's Bitcoin model, and make a decent amount of money from doing so."

"Would you like another whisky sour, or would you like to switch to wine? I've an excellent chardonnay that goes well with the mac and cheese."

"Don't usually, but I might switch. Should try new things."

Myron put on the oven mitts and carried dinner into the dining room. Judy followed him with the wine and glasses.

"Help yourself," Judy said as she took the mitts from him and headed to the kitchen to retrieve the sourdough rolls she'd placed in the oven to warm.

She returned to the dining room. Myron had served her, and was now serving himself. *Thoughtful. Good upbringing.*

Judy offered a toast. "Beginnings."

"Beginnings." Myron echoed and sipped the wine tentatively. "Excellent, almost like tropical fruit with a hint of vanilla, but not sweet."

"Australian, somewhere called Margaret River."

Myron took some mac and cheese, breaking off the gooey, cheesy tail. Judy smiled, pleased she achieved the same creamy gooeyness as Susie. He blew on his fork, apparently eager to try Judy's cooking.

"My God. This *is* amazing!"

"Isn't it? Got the recipe from Susie."

"Susie?"

"Frank's sister, Susan."

"Frank's family has certainly had an influence on your life."

"Yes. Difficult to believe. Two weeks ago, I hadn't heard of Frank. When I first saw him, I wrote him off. Sent off two features inspired by him today. John's coffee, Susie's mac and cheese, and another two features I started today inspired by Susie and Gerry. There'll be at least one feature inspired by Myriam, and perhaps even a feature on Myriam herself."

"Maybe you should pay Frank a commission?"

"I was going to ask you about that."

"Paying Frank a commission?"

"No, no, no," Judy laughed. "Can you review my business and tell me if I can do something better?"

"Love to. We'll download some key files and I'll play with them in the office."

They each took a forkful of dinner, eating with intent to enjoy their meal, laying their forks down after each mouthful, followed by a palate cleansing sip of wine, and more conversation.

"Okay, and cryptocurrencies?"

"Cryptocurrency is virtual money that doesn't exist in physical form like paper money or gold. When you use a credit card to buy something, the money actually exists."

"Can people buy things with this pretend money?"

"They can now. The market is limited but growing."

"How do people make money from Bitcoin?"

"Same as buying regular currency or shares. People buy Bitcoin at say one hundred dollars and later sell them for one hundred and fifty."

They ate slowly, talking between mouthfuls, unusual for both, as each preferred to eat in silence. Myron was doing most of the talking, but Judy didn't eat while he spoke.

"Why doesn't everyone buy Bitcoins? Where does their value come from?"

"The value of anything, if we're putting a monetary value on it, is whatever somebody will pay for it. If nobody will buy Bitcoins, then all that's left is a line of code on a computer. Some people are risk averse and never invest in anything with a risk attached. Others prefer real or tangible assets rather than virtual assets, and some people know nothing about them."

"Guess Frank was risk averse."

"He was being overly cautious."

***

Myron was enjoying his dinner; in conversation, he was his usual confident self. The schoolboy was absent. It was only when attempting to express his feelings to Judy that his mind turned to mush.

"Why are you only getting involved now, testing Frank's system?"

"Several reasons. My upbringing for a start. My family are believers in tangible assets. Papa always tells me 'If you can't touch it, it's not real.' Our family's in property. Owning, not speculation, we're landlords."

They ate in silence, a sip of wine, rested forks.

"Papa says, 'People will always need somewhere to live, and we'll always have an income.' Not that we're stereotypical slumlords… far from it. Another of Papa's sayings is, 'Look after your assets and your assets will look after you.'

"Papa has lots of these sayings… *Myerson Lore,* he calls it. He's smart. He learns. Zayde's first building became worthless because the neighborhood died…"

Judy gave Myron a quizzical look.

"Zayde, Yiddish for grandfather. Bubbe is grandmother."

Judy nodded.

"Since then, we buy buildings in the same neighborhood, and maintain the buildings and the neighborhood. My family is tight with money in most respects, but for our properties, we're the opposite. Papa says, 'What we spend now, we recoup ten times in the future, we're not spending, we're investing.' We prefer clean, lower cost neighborhoods. Easy to rent properties, and always in demand."

***

Why didn't I take the time to get to know him previously? Has a lot of respect for his father, feels important. Perhaps because I wasn't close to mine?

"Pay attention because one day my family's business will be mine, but my business is business. I invest in people. Papa says, 'Invest in people, but keep control of the money'. Not sure why I'm telling you this. You're extremely easy to talk to... Can see why you're so good at your job; people want to talk to you."

"They do. People usually open up with very little prompting from me. Don't know why."

Myron frowned. "You really don't know?"

Judy shrugged. "Haven't thought about it."

"It's the way you use people's names."

"People seem to like me using their name."

"When you say people's names, your tone conveys intimacy, as if you're close friends, which creates instant rapport."

"I didn't realize..."

"Noticed it the first time we met. Walked away feeling I'd known you half my life, not that we'd just met."

Judy smiled. "I was thinking about Myriam—listening to you—her mind would whirl and ding like one of those old-style cash registers. Please continue. I'm too curious for you not to."

Myron said. "I can tell where people's interests lie by the questions they ask. You don't ask questions, which seems unusual for a journalist."

"Silence is the most effective question. If people don't answer my questions when they've finished talking, I can still ask them. Being patient and letting people talk is valuable. They answer questions I never thought to ask."

"Smart, and you sure can cook."

Myron stopped talking to savor a little more of his meal. A sip of wine, and he continued.

"Forensic Accounting is my passion, but I have several other businesses. One develops business apps, which is why Frank's Bitcoin model interests me. Not that I know much about apps, have people who do that. A client mismanaged his company; I found a buyer who wanted four of his five apps. I bought the one they didn't want back from them for five thousand. Ten apps and a dozen staff now.

"Most of my companies started accidentally when an unexpected opportunity presented itself. Usually, I help someone out of a difficulty and establish a business with them. The only one I started intentionally was my property management business, because I'll have to take over from Papa one day.

"Ten companies now. Quite varied, mostly giving people a second or third chance. Not interested in building up a business and then selling it at a profit. Not about money, it's about people, and creating value. How much money do people need?"

"I agree, more to life than money. People become obsessed with money. Those who have it want more, as if there's never enough, and others who don't like Myriam are equally obsessed with it."

***

Judy gave Myron access to her computer and left him to copy the files he needed while she returned to the kitchen to prepare some hot chocolate. Having decided that hot chocolate was an inadequate description when she first perfected it, she named it *heavenly chocolate.*

Judy knew Myron as an excellent forensic accountant with useful contacts. Always immaculately dressed and entertaining company. She knew nothing more about him. Frank, she wrote off as a fat, angry man of no interest. As she learned about both as people, she perhaps learned more about herself. She shook her head. *Frank, would you get your eyes out of my mind?*

She made her heavenly chocolate; heated full cream milk, with real chocolate shavings from The Knight Chocolatier, stirred in and melted into the milk. Judy used a blend of dark, milk, and white chocolate experimenting until she got the balance right, bitter, sweet, and creamy. Adding a shot of cognac and a little cinnamon, she let it rest while the flavors infused.

She didn't think it was healthy, but she didn't have it every night.

They settled in the living room, sitting together on the sofa. Myron sipped his.

"Damn, that's decadent!"

"I'd like some decadent kisses if you could oblige."

"Happy to oblige, ma'am."

He leaned in, his face close. She could smell the heavenly chocolate, before his lips brushed hers with a blend of intense chocolate and intense passion.

After they'd kissed, and returned to their chocolate, Myron asked, "What about you Judy? Always want to be a journalist?"

"No, but I needed to choose a major. If I wanted to be a journalist, I'd be more ambitious. They assign new journalists features because they're safe. Can't screw them up too much.

"Most want to get off them as soon as they can and become a proper journalist, maybe an investigative reporter who writes a Pulitzer Prize-winning story. Not me, happy writing features, don't want the pressures of deadlines.

"Becoming freelance made a difference. Can sell the same features to publications in different markets, which increases my earnings. Who doesn't want more money for the same amount of work? Lately, I've taken on ghosting work, and I don't mean Frank Farrington." Judy joked, "I should take more advantage of it, but I'm not sure how."

Myron had a quizzical expression.

"Writing or perhaps rewriting pieces others have written and will publish under their name, blogs mostly. Easy to do. Can do a standard rewrite in less than an hour on a rainy afternoon. Doesn't pay well, but sometimes feeds me ideas which I develop into features of my own.

"My parents passed over ten years ago, my mother from cancer, my father a few months later from a broken heart, I believe. Sold their big house, paid off my apartment, and found some safe investments for the rest.

"Don't want to work any harder than I do, because I like my life the way it is—perhaps a new interest. Talking of which, how about some more of those heavenly kisses?"

Finding Billy

Judy opened one eye as Myron was dressing. She watched him for a moment, lost in the memory of the previous evening. Her orgasms had been more intense than their first time together. She smiled.

"I think I'm still purring from last night."

"Oh, good morning, beautiful. Going for a run. Got to maintain our fitness routines. Too easy to let them drop and become lazy from what I've seen. Didn't want to wake you."

"You're right. It's easy for people to let themselves go. Wrote a feature about it."

"Sorry for waking you so early."

"As you have… you better come here and kiss me."

"Yes, ma'am." Myron crossed the room, leaned down and kissed her.

As Myron straightened, Judy slipped her hand down the front of his shorts and eased his hardening penis out. She slid her body down a little and opened her mouth, ready to take him.

"Let's see if we can convince you to workout at home."

"You already have." He said as her warm moist mouth encompassed him.

***

Judy got up long after Myron had left for work and was still—hours later—smiling contentedly.

When she turned on her computer, an email from Myron with a standard client agreement attached was waiting. She signed and returned it immediately. *The internet makes doing business easy.*

She used what remained of the morning, planning three features, and received a new commission. Another four features this week, a comfortable workload for her, which left her time to pursue whatever else interested her. Currently, Frank. *Lunch out before heading to the docks.*

She finished showering when Myron called.

"Just out of the shower, trying to decide what to wear."

"Naked?"

"I usually shower naked, easier to wash things."

"I like you naked."

"You don't like my clothes?"

"No… Yes… That's not what I meant. I mean…"

"I know what you mean," she giggled.

"Really? What do I mean?"

"I look great naked."

"You do."

"Did you call to tell me I look great naked?"

"Yes…. No… I have some preliminary recommendations for you. About your finances and business."

"Already?"

"Made it a priority."

"I *do* appreciate you."

"Dinner at Franco's tonight?"

"I'd like that."

"Maybe you can bring an overnight bag? Time you spent the night at my place."

"I'd like that too, very much."

They said their goodbyes.

There were many great things about a new relationship. One of which—arguably the best—having sex at every available opportunity. *Understand why some people move from relationship to relationship.* Perpetually in a new relationship. *Now that is true perpetual motion.* She took out her iPad and made a note for a feature: *Perpetual Relationships*.

She wore blue jeans and a white T-shirt and her *who cares* underwear for her visit to the docks. A light black jacket matched her slip-ons and would keep out any chill from the sea breeze if necessary.

***

Judy sat in Pie Eyed, an upmarket pie shop in the Gourmet District, waiting for the beef and burgundy pot pie she'd ordered for lunch. Handmade pies using high quality, fresh ingredients were Pie Eyed's specialty. *Best pie in the city.*

She massaged her jaw-hinge, which was a little sore. *Many years since I gave my mouth such a workout, not that I'm complaining.* She found the experience strangely soothing. *Like a pacifier, only very much bigger*. She smiled.

Her pie arrived. *Damn, looks delicious... mmm smells scrumptious too*. Judy appreciated the golden color of the pastry, not too light and not too dark. *Perfectly cooked.* The flake they got on the pastry lid always amazed her. The lamination created fine, crispy layers stacked upon each other. *Thousand-layer pastry.*

Judy lifted the layered pastry crust and put it aside to allow her pie to cool. The beef, so tender, it melted in her mouth. The burgundy sauce had depth and layers of flavor. Thick and rich, much time and care taken in its preparation.

Judy slowly enjoyed her pie, taking time to savor every mouthful. A small pie, even for one person, but packed full of ingredients. It felt like a large pie when eating it and certainly filled her up.

After lunch, Judy flagged a taxi and headed down to the docks in search of Billy.

***

The scent of the sea always makes the air fresh. Judy liked the docks district of the city. *Should spend more time here.* It has character, and not only the docks themselves, which are full of history and urban legend. Each of the piers has its own unique personality created by an often-checkered history. Judy had written a feature; *Urban Legends from the Docks.*

Pier four, known as *The Death Pier* because of a string of accidental deaths that occurred there in the late nineteenth and early twentieth centuries.

Pier nine, or *The Sex Pier* because of its proximity to the old Red-Light District, and the low-rent street walkers who used to sell their services to sailors in the shadows. Now crack-whores provide the same quick fix beneath the pier.

A new container terminal saw many piers repurposed, to house design studios, bars, and restaurants. The most famous being *Pier Two*, an upmarket restaurant.

Some piers are still working piers such as pier twelve, or *Fisherman's Pier*. Quiet now, but at four in the morning, it would bustle with activity. Pier twelve contained a famous eatery that would be closed soon. Their day ended early.

Bait & Switch opened for breakfast at four, servicing the fishmongers, traders, customers, and tourists who flocked to the early morning fish markets. They remained open for lunch.

Renowned as the premier seafood café in the city, lunch attracted a combination of business-people who would usually sit in the upstairs restaurant, while tourists and locals frequented the ground floor café.

Judy had eaten there many times. It didn't occur to her to have lunch there that day, perhaps it should have, but she was in the mood for a pie.

The taxi dropped Judy near *The Sex Pier,* the most likely place to find Billy's bar.

The Shipyard was located across from O'Rourke Park. She turned on the digital recorder in the pocket of her shoulder bag and entered.

A typical low-end bar, which has seen better days. A wooden bar counter, once varnished, now chipped and scratched. The bar itself, clean. Beer taps at the front, and shelves of cheap spirits on display behind. Under the bar, the usual fridges and a dishwasher for glasses, with rows of clean glasses on the counter waiting to be filled. Only a few drinkers in the bar.

Guess they'll renovate at some point, and it'll become trendy. Hope the barman knows Billy and his habits.

***

Dancer glanced at Judy with a little surprise. *Rarely get this class of woman in here, especially alone.* Sometimes a small group of tourists wondered in, but they seldom stayed long, usually one and done.

"What can I get you, ma'am?"

"Do you sell wine by the glass?"

"We do. Wouldn't recommend it. We have a couple of half decent bottles, Oaked Chardonnay, not expensive here, probably less than the cost of a couple of glasses up town."

"That sounds fine. Sorry, what's your name?"

"People call me Dancer," he said, noting Judy didn't ask the price, not rare in The Shipyard, for other reasons.

***

"Dancer?" Judy asked with a hint of skepticism.

Dancer was a big man, tall—the tall that somehow seems out of place—as if someone is too tall for their body so they are crouching down a little from a lifetime of trying to fit into their body or the world around them. Balding, and lines crossed his face, giving a casual observer the impression he's older than his years. *Not as old as he looks, in his fifties, I guess. Eyes narrow, but sharp. Doesn't miss much.* His mouth, one of those loose, easy to smile sort of mouths, and his teeth too straight and neat. *False.* Dancer's nose told his story. Bent in several directions, obviously broken more than once. Long arms and huge hands completed the picture.

"From your boxing days?"

Dancer smiled. "I wish. If I could dance in the ring, I wouldn't have my hooter broken so often. When I finished boxing, went to work for a loan shark as a debt collector. Became known as Dancer as in *dancing on people's heads*. Not that I ever did."

Judy smiled. *I like him. A good man to have in your corner if you were in trouble. Boxer, Muscle for hire, Bar Owner. Could be a feature in Dancer.*

"I'm Judy Vernon," she said, offering her hand.

"Pleased to meet you, Judy Vernon."

He poured Judy a glass of chardonnay and re-corked the bottle.

"I'll keep this in the fridge for you."

"Thank you." Judy sipped her wine. "Excellent choice, Dancer."

"Keep a couple in for tourists. The locals are more interested in quantity than quality."

"Dancer, I'm looking for Billy Johnson."

"Billy Blow?"

He glanced at his watch. "A little early for Billy, twenty or thirty minutes and he should be here… unless he works overtime."

"Billy's *working?* I thought he was homeless?"

"He's earning money so he can drink. Drunks and addicts have, err… creative ways to earn money. Don't think he's homeless now. His friend helped him a couple of weeks ago, paid for his room in a doss house round the corner. Old seamen's accommodation back in the day. Now cheap rooms for people at rock bottom."

"Do you think Billy is at rock bottom?"

"Billy passed rock bottom years ago. Half the time he's too drunk to find his way home and sleeps on a bench for a while, but he'll usually go home in the morning. How do you know Billy?"

"A mutual friend."

"Frank?"

"Yes…. How?"

"Billy only has one friend, talks about him all the time."

"Really?"

"Yeah, the more drunk he gets, the more he goes on about Frank, but he basically says the same thing. He destroyed Frank's life."

A customer came in. *Seventies or sixties having lived a hard life.* He stood in the doorway, his bulk blocking it completely. Stooped the way tall men often are. Slicked back gray hair, which almost matched the color of his watery eyes. He wore an old suit of indeterminate color, gray, pale blue. Time had leached the color out of it. A white shirt fraying around the collar. His gaze moved around the bar, as if surveying his environment. His protruding stomach had accompanied him for years, Judy guessed, because his clothes weren't tight. He had an air of authority. *Ex-cop; probably bent.*

Apparently satisfied with his inspection, he stepped up to place some money on the bar. About fifty dollars, from what Judy could tell. Dancer counted the money and put it in the till before pouring the man a beer and a shot of cheap whisky.

"Here you go, Georgie Girl. You seen Billy Blow?"

The man, Georgie Girl, downed his whiskey immediately.

"Still working, I think."

Dancer said, "You know better than that, George."

George muttered, "Sorry Dancer."

He took his beer to an unoccupied table.

"They're not allowed to drink at the bar," Dancer explained. "For their own good."

"Why Georgie Girl?" Judy was curious. The man didn't appear to have a feminine bone in his body.

"George found himself a coat one winter a few years back. A woman's coat, not that it matters. A coat is a coat in the winter. Proud of his new coat, he didn't realize it was a lady's coat, probably because it was big enough to fit him. Someone, I don't recall who, called him 'Georgie Girl', and it stuck the way these things sometimes do… nothing feminine about old George. At first, it pissed him off, so people kept using it to wind him up. Probably why it stuck. If he'd ignored it, it would have quickly died."

How people get nicknames. Could be a feature in that.

"What about Dancer? Who gave you that name?"

"From the loan shark I worked for, but not intentionally. He used to tell people if they didn't pay on time, he'd send me around to *dance on their head* and I became known as Dancer."

Another man came in.

"Here's Billy now."

"Whatever he wants on my tab, please Dancer."

Billy

"Lady to see you Billy," Dancer said.

"A lady?"

"This lady, Judy Vernon, friend of Frank." Dancer nodded towards Judy, who smiled and extended her hand.

"Hello Billy."

Billy took Judy's hand. "Hello. You're a friend of Frank?"

"Yes. Perhaps we can talk about Frank for a while?"

Dancer said, "The lady's buying, Billy," as he refused Billy's offered hand full of money.

"Why?"

Judy gave him her card. "I'm writing a feature about Frank. Nothing bad."

Billy appeared a little dubious, but kept one eye on the beer and whisky on the bar.

Common package at The Shipyard.

"I spoke with Susie earlier this week."

It was enough to clinch the deal.

"If Susie talked to you, you must be okay."

He picked up his drinks and headed towards a table in the corner. Judy glanced at her wineglass. *Nearly empty.*

"Can you fill me up please, Dancer?"

"Love to…" Dancer offered with a suggestive grin.

Judy flushed.

"Whisky gives them a fix, and the beer spreads it out." He explained without Judy needing to ask. "Otherwise, they quickly down shots until their money runs out and are back on the street looking for money for another fix in an hour."

Judy sensed Dancer watching her take her glass to the table. Not quite out of earshot, she heard him mutter, "Damn fine ass." She smiled.

As she sat down, Billy downed his whisky, shook his head, and sighed.

"That's better."

"My name is Judy Vernon. I'm writing a feature about Frank, so I'm talking to people from Frank's life to paint a complete picture of him. You knew Frank for a long time."

Billy nodded.

Despite being worn around the edges, Billy was handsome. Brown but graying hair, surprising clear brown eyes and a natural smile. He was likeable, but Judy couldn't put her finger on why. Life had dealt him a nice hand, she supposed, with Frank being his wildcard. Billy had fucked up the hand life had given him.

"I'd like to make a recording of our talk, Billy. Is that okay?"

"I guess…" Billy looked doubtful. "What about Susie? Did you record Susie?"

"Yes, I did."

"Then it'll be okay. If Susie trusts you, I can trust you."

Judy took the digital recorder from the pocket of her shoulder bag and placed it on the table.

"When did you meet Frank?"

Billy picked up his beer and studied Judy over his glass while he drank some before answering. "College. We were roommates. Frank's a smart man, smarter than me. Helped me get through college. Without him, doubt I could've graduated. Most of the time I scraped through, can't focus on anything… easily distracted. Sure there's a name for that—a formal name or something—I'm a fuckup. Always have been, always will be."

Billy shrugged his shoulders and drained what remained of his beer. He wiped the back of his hand across his mouth.

"Won't be a minute." He went to the bar to return the empty glasses and retrieve full ones.

Billy returned, sat down, and immediately downed the shot. *Why bother bringing it over from the bar? Dancer's rule. 'For their own good.'*

"While you're buying, I'm drinking. Got me at my best. Always at my best when I start drinking. First few shots calm me and make me feel normal and connected to myself. Used to be enough, not anymore."

Billy's shoulders slumped. "Before I leave here, I'll have trouble stringing two words together. Know what I am. If I could control myself, would've years ago, and my life would've been very different, and so would Frank's, but I can't. Anyway, where was I?"

"College."

"I'm not stupid. Can understand things, but I can't focus on anything for long, can't control myself. Susie was the love of my life, still is... Always Susie. We dated for a while in college, and I did well. Susie can control me, keep me focused. She's the part of me that's missing, the self-control. If she stayed with me, everything would've been different.

"Not that I blame her for my life. That's down to me. Susie's the missing part of me. Whatever is missing from me, Susie can give me. Make me a complete person. Too big a job for her, I guess. If I can't control myself, how can I expect anyone to do it for me?"

He stopped to drink some beer and examined Judy as if seeing her for the first time.

"Said she didn't want to be my mother. Can't blame her. My mother didn't want to be my mother. A whore, my mother. Don't have a father. I mean, I must have, but I never met him. Assume he was a customer. Don't know what she thought of me. Always sitting around half naked, didn't care. When we had dinner, I often dropped my fork to look at her pussy when I picked it up."

Billy went quiet. He absentmindedly raised his glass to his mouth, and became distant, remembering.

"When I was fourteen or fifteen, she needed to come to the school, some trouble I was in. She wasn't happy. Costing her money. After we arrived home, she showered and put on this short robe thing she used to wear, barely covered her ass, tied closed. Never bothered with underwear. She made me a sandwich and herself a coffee. I sat at the table to eat. She sat opposite.

"She had one foot on the ground, the other on the chair, which caused her gown to open. Her right tit hung out, her pussy exposed. Eating my sandwich, looking at her pussy and wondering how much she'd charge me to fuck her. She took a sip of coffee and looked at me. 'You know, Billy,' she said. 'I was minutes away from having an abortion. Sitting in the waiting room, they told me there'd be a fifteen-minute delay. Took it as a sign, never got the abortion… Wish I did.'"

He finished his beer, again wiped his mouth with the back of his hand, took the empty glasses to the bar and returned with full ones. He downed his shot before he sat down and resumed speaking immediately.

"No one's fault but my own, but for years, I blamed everyone else. Blamed Susie for not staying with me and keeping me under control. Blamed Frank for not helping me when I needed it. Truth is, Frank always helped me, still does."

Billy paused, stared at Judy, reached for his glass, and drank some beer. Judy watched him drink. He was pausing for a drink more frequently. He'd drunk a lot in a short time. It didn't appear to affect him. *Will the alcohol slowly take effect or hit him suddenly?*

"Don't have difficulty doing the right thing. Have no self-control. Probably a clinical name for it. Some sort of condition, but that's not relevant, is it? I'm a broken person—born with something missing.

"If I was missing a limb or an eye, people would make allowances, feel sorry for me. That people can't see the part of me that's missing doesn't mean it's not missing. Susie can give me what I'm missing. Love of my life. Didn't deserve her. Too young to take responsibility for me. Perhaps if she was older? Incapable of taking responsibility for myself."

Another pause, another drink, another mouth wipe with the back of his hand. He'd soon need another refill.

"Followed Frank into investment broking. Not good at it. Frank was. My skill was getting new clients. I brought the clients in. Frank looked after them.

"When Frank went out on his own, took me with him as a full partner. Biggest mistake he made in his life… gave me access to everything. Frank shouldn't have trusted me, not because I'm dishonest, despite what I did—I'm not dishonest. They scared me."

A pause to finish his beer. Judy surveyed the room. More patrons filled The Shipyard now. Some sat alone, drinking quietly. Others sat together, talking. *Myriam's right, not only men.* Billy didn't go for a refill immediately, nor did he wipe his mouth. He resumed talking.

"Stole millions. Saying I'm honest, because I never stole the money. I borrowed it to keep myself alive. They would've killed me…"

He stopped talking again, leaving his words hanging for Judy to reflect upon. *Who are they?* Judy expected him to take his glasses to the bar for a refill. He didn't. He stared at nothing, or perhaps his own thoughts.

"Would've been better for everyone if I let them. Maybe I would've if I had any self-control, but if I did, I wouldn't have been in that situation. Don't know what I'm saying. Later tonight I'll understand completely, but I won't be able to string two words together."

Billy picked up his empty glasses and headed to the bar for another round. Cheap whiskey and a beer. Judy sipped her wine and glanced around. The patrons—apparently a mix of functional and nonfunctional alcoholics—some looked like they held jobs, others appeared homeless. *So many stories in this room.*

Billy came back with his drinks, but after placing them on the table, he went off somewhere, without drinking his shot. He returned, smoking.

"You know," he began, and then took his shot, almost slamming the glass on the table. "I'm a born addict. Addicted to everything. Computer games at high school, not that they were much then. Sex more than once in my life. Booze, of course, and gambling. People, not generally, but to specific people… Did you know we can become addicted to people?"

"Never thought about it, but I can see it happening." *May explain people staying in abusive relationships. Might be a feature in there somewhere. Addicted to people.*

"Drugs, hard and soft. Sometimes, used one addiction to kick another. Put into rehab before I went to jail. Found other addictions inside. You name it, and I'll become addicted to it. Except for these things," he said, waving his cigarette. "Go figure. Most addictive things on earth, or so they say…"

"So they say." Judy agreed.

"… the one thing I never became addicted to."

"Frank shouldn't have trusted me, and he shouldn't have married that slut. Told him not to marry her. Best advice I ever gave him. Never listened. I introduced them."

"Really? Myriam couldn't remember how they met."

"Told you that? Lying cunt. She worked at one of the gambling clubs I went to; called them hostesses, but they were whores. The club paid 'em to keep guests company and encourage them to drink and gamble. Not about selling more booze. Getting the patrons drunk and making stupid gambling choices.

"Mostly female escorts because most gamblers at the clubs are white men, but they had a few gigolos. Being essentially whores, they were flexible enough to cater for fags and dykes, too. Could sleep with the guests if they wanted to. For love or money."

Billy stubbed his cigarette out in the ashtray, almost. He drank some beer. Judy reached across and finished stubbing it out. Judy could hear the alcohol taking effect, but as his words slurred a little, he used some higher-level vocabulary.

"Myriam decided I might be a good meal ticket. Always wanted something, and used her pussy, mouth, ass whatever she needed to pay for it. Explained it to me once. Treats her body like currency with different holes having different values. She's a slut. Not judging her. Stating a fact. I'm no different. Treat my body as currency. Useful lesson for me. In fairness to Myriam, if you've only got one form of currency, that's what you use."

Billy paused again and drank some more beer. Judy cast an eye around the bar, wondering about the other patrons and their stories. Billy wiped his mouth and heavily returned his glass to the table.

"So yeah, Myriam's a slut. She's also a lying cunt. Latched on to me for a while, which was fine. I had no illusions. I was a meal ticket, and she was an easy fuck… not a quality fuck mind. Like one of those twenty-four-hour buffets, they used to have near China Town… not great food, but always open. That's Myriam."

Billy's tone, his language, his focus, and his clarity were showing the effects of alcohol in different ways. He drained his glass for the umpteenth time. Judy had lost count. He said he needed to piss and headed to the restroom.

Judy took her glass to Dancer for a refill. He poured Billy another set, too.

"You still buying?" he asked.

"Yes."

"As long as you're buying, he's drinking, and then he'll go on to his own money."

"Will you cut him off?"

"Nope, not until he runs out of money. Not about the money. Don't know how much they give me or how much they drink. Always fair with 'em, but never let 'em drink on credit. If I cut 'em off, they'll go somewhere else and drink as many shots as their money will buy and then be back on the street getting into trouble. Better they stay here and pace themselves with beer."

"I think Billy better eat something. Do you have food?"

"Billy won't eat. They never do. Impedes drinking. They pick at any meal but don't really eat. Don't do food here, but have an arrangement with a cheap restaurant a few doors down. Maybe he'll pick at a snack platter?"

"Sounds good Dancer. Can you organize it, please?"

"No problem."

Another regular came in. He wore dirty blue track pants, and a red and blue checked flannel shirt, a size too big, with missing buttons. His long, thin nose displayed a road map of broken veins. Eyes almost closed, so Judy couldn't see the color. What teeth remained were yellow. Knotted white hair hadn't seen a comb since last cut. He was scratching at the itching stubble on his cheek, and had the scent of someone desperately in need of a bath. He handed Dancer a stack of money, mostly ones.

"Perhaps a second snack platter for the bar here? Your customers might pick at it while they're waiting for their drinks."

Dancer smiled. “Maybe they will. Never thought of it.”

Billy and Frank

Judy took their drinks back to the table. Billy joined her a few moments later. He threw back his shot, again almost slamming his glass on the table, and resumed talking.

"Where was I? Oh yeah… Fucking Myriam. I introduced her to Frank. She figured he was a better meal ticket than me. Got that right. Frank was naïve about women. Didn't recognize Myriam for the slut she is, or maybe he did, and loved her, so it didn't matter."

Although drinking at a rapid pace, Billy didn't seem to be deteriorating beyond the effect she'd noticed earlier. *Wonder when it'll catch up with him. After pausing to drink, he can resume speaking without forgetting where he left off.*

"Never loved anyone like that. Love Frank, and he must love me to still help me. Susie, love of my life, Susie. Never any love after Susie, someone for fucking and usually a slut like Myriam because I didn't have to work at it."

Does he know Frank's dead?

Billy paused, glanced around the bar, stared down at his beer, looked up at Judy, offered her a lop-sided smile, and continued.

"Myriam knew I was a degenerate gambler. Warned Frank about me. He didn't listen. Shouldn't have loved either of us. Loving the wrong people destroyed Frank's life. He was going to be mayor until I fucked his life up…"

A short, tubby man heading back to his table after having visited the restroom distracted Judy. A chair hit the tiled floor with a loud thud, as if thrown over. "You fucking bastard. You drank my fucking beer, you useless fucking prick!" the man shouted at his companion.

"I never drank nothing. Ya fucking drunk it before ya went for a piss, ya stupid bastard."

"Who you calling stupid? You fucking moron. I know what I drank."

The companion stood—a head taller and slimmer than his friend—he stepped towards him.

"Don't call me a fucking moron, ya fucking moron. Ya don't know what ya fucking drank. I never drank nothing."

Billy explained to Judy, "Abbot and Costello are always arguing about something. They're both fucking morons."

"Call me a moron again and I'll knock your fucking head off, you fucking moron. You drank my fucking beer."

"Ya couldn't knock the fucking head off a fucking beer. I never drank nothing, and yer a fucking moron, ya moron."

Dancer stepped up beside them, towering over them both. One look at Dancer, and they quietened down.

"You," Dancer said to the short man, "go sit over there." He pointed to a table.

"And you," to the taller man, "sit down."

The first man did as instructed, but whined, "He drank my beer, Dancer."

"I don't care who drank what," Dancer said. "Any more of this nonsense and I'll knock both your fucking heads off. Now sit quietly, and I'll bring you both a beer, on the house."

"And I ain't no fucking moron," the short man said, glaring at his former companion.

Billy paid little attention to the commotion. He used the opportunity to almost finish his beer, while Judy watched the argument.

Wiping his mouth with the back of his hand, Billy continued. "When he first started the business, I found investors and Frank managed their money with good returns. The investors introduced us up the line, giving us more money to invest, which meant Frank achieved better returns. They introduced us further up the chain and before long, we were sitting at the top, dealing with the city leaders.

"I loved it, loved being part of it. Not having any self-control, I got lost in the life. These people lived in a different world. My life was parties, coke, gambling and sluts.

"Sluts are someone to party with, no pressure, no commitment, just drinking, doing lines and fucking. You don't fucking marry them. If they become serious and controlling like a wife, you dump 'em and move on. Always another slut waiting to latch on. Poor Frank didn't understand, not his world. So, he married Myriam."

Billy picked up his glass. He didn't drink. He stared blankly into the distance.

"Two parts to that world. My part, indulgence and Frank's part, which controlled the city."

Occasionally Judy glanced around the bar, or took a sip of wine, but mostly, she listened to and observed Billy. *An air about him, a sense of likeability, a boyish charm, and in contrast to the life he's lived, a childlike innocence.*

"Only thought it was my world. A tourist who confused himself with the locals. Money, drugs, gambling, and sluts attract criminals like shit attracts flies. Investors too, but they invested in people's weaknesses."

He shook his head, downed his beer, wiped his mouth, and went for another round. Judy studied 'Costello', fresh beer in front of him, courtesy of Dancer, still muttering about not being a moron.

Billy consumed his shot on the way back to the table. He didn't sit down. Talking about the events leading up to the destruction of his and Frank's lives seemed to sober him up. Standing, he continued where he left off.

"Certainly invested in my weaknesses. Gave me credit and extended it as I continued to use… or lose it gambling. Didn't always lose. Sometimes won, but never enough."

He drank some beer, placed his glass on the table, and stared straight ahead, hands holding the back of his chair, once more looking at a distant memory.

"One day, as I left my office building, two men stepped out of the shadows, one on either side of me. Came from nowhere. Happened fast. Grabbed me and forced me into the back of a windowless black van. Neither of the men nor the driver said a word. You'd think I would've asked what's going on or where they're taking me. Didn't. Too scared to speak. Shitting myself, not literally, but almost."

He shivered at the memory. His grip on the chair tightened.

"The two men sat on a rear-facing bench seat. I was lying on a bare metal floor. The interior walls, painted black, the material covering the roof charcoal gray. If they designed the van to intimidate, they succeeded."

His body stiffened, and his arms shook a little as he applied more force to his grip on the chair.

"Drove me out of the city, into the woods. Stopped at the side of the road on a hill. Don't know where exactly. Couldn't see from the back of the van. They dragged me out. I could see down into a clearing where a black sedan had parked.

"A man took a phone from his pocket and made a call. He said 'Now.' One word. The only word any of them spoke. Could see what was happening, but wasn't close enough to see any detail. Two men dragged a guy from the car. Never knew who he was. Had a hood over his head, but even if he didn't, I was too far away to make out any faces. They forced him to his knees and put a bullet in his head."

Billy's gaze became more distant, more intense as he relived the events in his mind.

"Couldn't see the gun, but I saw a flash and a moment later heard the shot. Maybe I didn't. Perhaps I imagined the flash. No idea why they killed him. Never told me. Too far away to identify the guys who pulled the trigger, so I couldn't tell the cops. What was there to tell?

"They said nothing. I asked nothing. Still too scared to speak. Threw me into the van, drove back to the city, and dropped me at my office without a word. No threat, nothing."

Billy released his grip on the back of the chair and straightened up. He studied the imprints of the chair on his palms. Apparently surprised, he'd gripped the chair so tightly. He flexed his hands, leaned over to retrieve his glass, drank some beer and, still staring into his past, sat down absently.

Okay, so 'they' were the mob.

"Didn't go back to the club until they summoned me. Stayed in my office playing with the computer and thinking about how to raise some money. Didn't want to end up like that poor bastard."

He sat silently, eyes closed, not drinking. Not wanting to stare at Billy or interrupt his thoughts, Judy glanced around. People talking and drinking quietly. A normal day at The Shipyard. Dancer, standing behind the bar, watching her and Billy.

Billy interrupted the silence as if he hadn't stopped speaking.

"Set up an investment account and started channeling client's money into it. We did that, funneled several small investments into a single account to invest a sizeable amount which could net better returns. Stole people's investments, parts of them initially, and channeled the proceeds into the new fund I set up.

"Nobody noticed, so I kept doing it. Paid my debt, but didn't stop. Kept gambling, believing I'd get one big win to pay everyone back. No one would ever know. Never got the big win."

Judy said, "Gamblers never do." *Like all paths to hell, Billy paved his with...*

Billy stood. He picked up his glass and finished the remains of his beer. He fixed his gaze on Judy. "Drink, so I don't remember. Not working today. You're making me remember," he said bitterly. "Talking to you because I owe Frank that much."

Billy headed off to have his drinks refilled. Judy felt guilty, making Billy remember. *Frank's story needs to be told, don't know why.* She shook her head to shake Frank's eyes out of her mind.

Returning with his drinks, Billy sat down, swallowed his shot, and carefully placed the glass on the table.

"Investors started asking why they were getting low returns. Frank investigated and found the fake fund I syphoned money into. An honest man, he reported me to the authorities.

"Busy with his mayoral campaign—he'd have been a great mayor—otherwise would've noticed earlier. Myriam, pushing him hard. Wanted to be the mayor's wife. When Frank discovered my crime, he wasn't angry, perhaps disappointed. He didn't hate me. Almost like he pitied me. I hated that."

Billy fixed his eyes, full of pain and regret, on Judy.

My fault, but it's what Frank wants. Why else did he lead me to Billy?

Billy picked up his glass, and slowly drank a little beer, before carefully placing his glass on the table.

"Still helps me sometimes. Frank asked why I didn't come to him after they gave me that warning. He said, 'I could've spoken to the criminals, and I might've been able to do a deal. Criminals always have money they need laundered. I could've come up with a scheme that would not only clean their money but increase it through legitimate investments.' Frank could've done it too. He's smart."

Billy drank his beer, almost finishing it.

He doesn't know Frank's dead. Need to tell him!

Billy and Coffin

Dancer brought the snacks over to the table. Billy took a handful, not paying attention to what he chose. Dancer smiled at Judy and nodded acknowledgment, then returned to the bar. Billy followed him. Judy assessed the snacks, *mostly fried, processed foods*. They didn't tempt her.

Billy returned, downed the whisky, placed his shot glass on the table, and immediately began speaking.

"Should've gone to Frank. Perhaps I would've if Myriam hadn't been in the way. Gone through stages of blaming everybody else. No one to blame but me. Frank's the best person I know. Doesn't deserve a friend like me and didn't deserve a wife like fucking Myriam.

"I was going to jail. Worried poor Frank would too. He stayed out of jail but lost everything. Had to live in Susie's basement. Love of my life Susie is… If she stayed with me, it wouldn't have happened. She can control me. Something wrong with me, no self-control."

Repetition was creeping into Billy's retelling of events.

"Jail was hard at first. Got shanked—never learned why—thought I was going to die."

He paused and looked at Judy, sipped some beer, and became distant again, staring at something. He became morose, slumped further in his seat, his gaze dropped, his eyes appeared heavy. If he cried, she wouldn't be surprised. A mixture of alcohol and unwanted memories, she supposed. *Don't want to be the one who tells him Frank's dead.*

Billy sipped more beer. He had several ways of drinking. Sometimes he drank some, sometimes he gulped it down, and other times, like now, he sipped it. He continued, still staring at his glass, now tearing small pieces from a paper coaster.

"Those people will shank someone for looking at them wrong, or not showing respect, or to earn respect. Sometimes they'll shank someone for money. A carton of cigarettes is the going rate. What kind of person would kill someone for a carton of smokes?

"Coffin looked after me. Didn't want to know why they called him Coffin. No interest in running the prison, and didn't have a crew, but everyone left him alone. Nobody fucked with Coffin, no cons and no guards. People left him alone, and he left people alone.

"Coffin took a liking to me. People always like me. I'm likeable, I'm told. No idea why I'm so fucking likeable."

Certainly is likeable. Maybe it's that childlike innocence that remains despite everything, or maybe because he doesn't appear to have a mean bone in his body? As if adding emphasis to the point, a woman stopped on her way to the restroom and stared at Billy. She wore a yellow, green and blue floral dress, with an unbuttoned black and white check flannel shirt over it. She was absently scratching her unsupported left breast.

Billy yelled towards the bar. "Hey Dancer, Pissy Mary's at it again."

Judy was about to glance at the woman's face, but Billy was looking down at Mary's feet. Judy's eyes followed Billy's gaze.

"Oh, she's peeing on the floor!"

"Always pissing herself."

Dancer appeared beside her. He took Mary by the arm and walked her to the restroom.

"Jesus, Mary, can't you wait until you get to the fucking restroom?"

After the interruption, Billy resumed with more than a touch of bitterness.

"Likeable Billy, the degenerate fucking drunk, gambler and slut. Not everybody likes me. Myriam hates me…"

Billy gulped his beer. *He's not slowing down.* The alcohol was affecting him again. His mood had moved from morose to bitter, to affable in minutes. His method of drinking reflected his demeanor. He made his way to the restroom. *Gonna have to tell him soon.* Dancer arrived with a mop and bucket to clean up Mary's spillage.

"Had the carpet lifted and replaced with tiles," he explained.

Billy returned, draining his glass without sitting down.

"Hates me because I destroyed her and Frank's life. I hate me for that, too."

He grabbed some popcorn chicken as he headed to the bar for another round. *At least he's eating something. Not looking forward to telling him about Frank.* She felt guilty, letting him talk, not knowing Frank was dead.

Billy sat down. "Broken people."

He downed his shot and sipped his beer. "Broken people. Frank loves broken people; I'm broken. Myriam's broken. Frank loved us both. Perhaps he thought he could fix us. Maybe he was making up for his brother dying. Did you know one of Frank's brothers died when he was a kid?"

"Yes Billy, I did."

"Frank loves the wrong people. Still loves me. Not sure if he still loves Myriam. Coffin never loved me. Arranged with a guard to transfer me to his cell. Didn't want to know the details.

"Plenty of fit young guys, and plenty of fags inside, but Coffin took me for his bitch. Happy enough to accept him. Better than being raped and scared all the time. Let him do what he wanted—which means I let him stick his cock in my mouth or my ass—whenever he wanted. Paying for protection, peace, and a feeling of safety with my body. No different to Myriam, I suppose.

"Became a bitch in prison to survive. If I didn't, I would've been dead before I got out. Everyone knew I was Coffin's bitch. No one dared fuck with me. At first, I didn't enjoy it. Necessary for survival."

Billy's revelation did not surprise Judy. She had the impression he'd do whatever he needed to survive.

"God!" Billy took a long drink of beer and slammed the glass back on the table. "The damage I've done because I didn't want to be killed. If I let those gangsters kill me, I wouldn't have fucked up Frank's life. Would've been better if my mother got an abortion.

"Grew to love being fucked by Coffin. Sucked his cock whenever he let me. I'm an addict, and became addicted to sucking cock. Can you believe that? Knew people can become addicted to sex, but becoming addicted to sucking cock? I am. Not a bad thing. Funds my drinking. One addiction to pay for another… Sure there's a term for that. Not uncommon."

The concept of being addicted to performing fellatio was not new to Judy. Years earlier, a small adult classifieds newspaper was available in some newsstands and adult shops. Judy had read it occasionally out of curiosity. A man ran a regular ad, seeking guys who wanted their cock sucked. Judy had interviewed him—still had the recording—but hadn't used the material. She remembered Francine, who'd "Rather be fucked in the mouth than the pussy." *Might be a feature in that, after all; Addicted to Fellatio.*

Drinking seemed to help Billy focus, or perhaps gave him time to think. Judy sipped her wine. She was drinking more than usual, trying to summon the courage to deliver the news she didn't want to deliver. *For fuck's sake, woman, just tell him.*

Judy felt pity for Billy, for what his life has become, and for what she needed to tell him. Billy saw it in her eyes.

"Don't pity me. I don't hate my life. Have a job I love, which pays for my needs."

He finished his beer as if to make a point.

"Usually, have a room, but sometimes live rough. Frank pays for the room when he can. Guess he's doing it tough now. Never ask him. When it runs out, they kick me out."

Billy took a handful of fries and went to the bar. *He's still coherent, but he'll soon cross his line. Better tell him before he does.*

After placing his order, Billy headed to the restroom again. Judy glanced at her glass. *Almost empty.* She took it to the bar.

Judy smelled the man with the checked shirt before he arrived at the counter for refills. He grabbed a handful of snacks while he was waiting. *They're eating the snacks.*

"Good idea, those snacks," Dancer said. "Can't believe I didn't think of it."

"Glad to see they're eating them. Better than nothing."

Dancer nodded at the retreating checked shirt on his way back to his table.

"Called the homeless shelter. They'll swing by later and pick him up. Give him a decent meal, a bath, cut his hair and find him some clean clothes. A bed for the night if he'll take it. Either way, he'll be back tomorrow."

"Decent of you, Dancer. You mentioned Billy is staying around the corner at an old seamen's accommodation?"

"If it hasn't run out. Frank comes to see Billy occasionally, gives him a little money and pays for his room for a month or two. They always try to put him in the same room. When the money runs out, Billy leaves a bag in their storage room and lives rough until Frank comes again. Good man, Frank. Does what he can to help Billy. A better man than me. If it was me, I'd break Billy's nose every time I saw him."

"What's the name of the place?"

"Old Seaman's Lodge," Dancer said as he poured her wine. "Easy to find."

"Dancer, if I pay you for your time, can you make sure Billy gets home tonight?" She glanced over her shoulder. Billy was talking to one of his fellow drunks. "Need to give him some bad news, and I want to make sure he gets home."

"You don't *need to pay me*," Dancer said indignantly. "I'll keep him here to closing and take him home when I go, even if I have to carry him."

"Sorry if I offended you, didn't want to presume..."

"Don't worry about it," Dancer said with a smile.

Judy returned his smile and took her wine and Billy's drinks back to the table.

***

Dancer watched her walk to the table and sit down.

Damn fine ass. Just once in my life, I'd like to nail a fine woman like that, instead of the skanks around here.

Don't envy her task. He shook his head. He studied Billy, making his way back to his table. *Looking unsteady. Reach his limit soon. Can't believe he's lasted this long.*

If the bad news is what I think it is, poor Billy's gonna be a mess. Need to keep an eye on him for the next few weeks. No idea how he'll survive without Frank. George interrupted Dancer's thoughts by arriving for refills.

"Another round Georgie Girl?"

George stared at him like he was from another planet.

"Yeah, I know Georgie. Stupid fucking question."

Frank's Dead

Judy watched Billy return. Unsteady, meandering from chair to chair as he sought support. He bumped into another patron, but didn't apologize.

Reaching his own chair, Billy slowly and deliberately sat down, needing to concentrate hard on the simple task. For the first time, he didn't glance at his drinks. Instead, he looked at Judy, trying to focus.

"Are you aware Frank repaid the investors?" She was curious about his reaction, but felt guilty for stalling.

Billy studied Judy, glanced at his beer, looked back at Judy. "What?" he shouted.

The bar fell silent as everyone tried to hear what Billy was shouting about. Judy, startled, not by Billy raising his voice, but by the sudden silence. *A noisy place, suddenly silent, always feels eerie.*

He lowered his voice. He appeared in shock. "Frank repaid the investors? How? It was millions."

"Started an import business and spent every waking minute working to repay the investors."

"Can't believe that! I *can believe* Frank would do it. Told me I shouldn't worry, he'd repay everyone. He meant it, but I didn't think he'd be able to."

Billy became quiet. He downed his shot, placing the glass back on the table with exaggerated care, and then drank a little beer. His eyes were distant. "Frank would've been an exceptional mayor. Did you know Frank was going to run for mayor? Would've been the best mayor the city ever had. Robbed Frank of that opportunity and robbed the city of a great mayor.

"Could only think of saving my own miserable skin. Years inside gave me time to reflect. In saving myself, I hurt many people. A sobering thought. That's why I drink. The best thing about getting out is I can drink myself into a stupor. Don't have to think."

He raised his glass and paused, perhaps making a silent toast to drinking. He took two gulps, wiped his mouth with the back of his hand, and continued.

"After the first year, didn't mind being inside. They made all my decisions for me. Couldn't fuck up. The prison decided when I got up, when I ate, what I ate, what work I did—Coffin decided everything else—All I had to do was think about the lives I fucked up…"

He retreated into silence. Judy's eyes wandered around the bar. The men who'd been arguing earlier, Abbot and Costello, were sitting together. Georgie Girl was making his way back from the restroom. Dancer was behind the bar, pretending to clean it, his gaze firmly fixed on Judy and Billy. His gaze seemed to tell her to get on with it. *He's right Judy.*

"Coffin treated me well. Never beat me or abused me, never talked much. Not his way. All I needed to do was open my mouth or my legs whenever he wanted. Miss Coffin, but he'll never be released and I'll never go back, not even for a visit."

He picked up his beer and consumed what remained, which was most of it. He glanced at Judy. "Does the slut know Frank repaid everyone?"

"Myriam knows."

"Fuck! That would just about kill her. She'll be climbing the walls and Frank'll be every kind of loser you can imagine, and some you can't. Fuck me! Knowing Myriam will be crazy is almost as good as knowing Frank repaid everyone."

Laughing, Billy grabbed a handful of onion rings and headed to the bar for refills. He seemed steadier on his feet now, as if phasing in out of sobriety. *Seen no one react to alcohol like this. Need to tell him now, but how? Directly will be best.*

He returned and sat down, immediately skolling the whiskey. *Why doesn't he do that at the bar? Oh yeah, one of Dancer's rules.*

"Billy, I'm afraid I have some bad news for you… Frank passed away."

His body straightened with a jerk. The color drained from his face; he stared at Judy wide-eyed and said nothing. Dancer appeared beside Billy, placed two shots in front of him, and grasped his shoulder.

"Whatever you need, Billy," he said.

Billy downed both shots without acknowledging Dancer, who returned to the bar.

"Frank's dead?"

"Yes, Billy," Judy whispered. "I'm afraid he is."

"How?"

"Heart attack; it was sudden."

"What about the funeral?"

"Last week. Frank didn't tell anyone where you were, so no one knew how to contact you. Do you remember seeing a friend of Myriam's? That's how I knew where to find you. Myriam told me, but that was only yesterday. I'm sorry."

Billy nodded, pain in his eyes, too deep for words and even too deep for tears. They would come later. Judy could almost feel them building in him. Dancer arrived with another shot.

"Leave the bottle Dancer," Billy said.

"Give me your money, Billy."

Billy did. Judy gave Dancer a quizzical look.

"For safekeeping, otherwise he'll drink it away as soon as he wakes in the morning."

Dancer went back to the bar, presumably to retrieve a bottle for Billy.

Forlorn, as if his life had lost all meaning. Billy slumped in his chair, head bowed, and began whispering to himself.

"Frank dead? How can Frank be dead when I'm still alive? Those gangsters should've killed me. Should've died from a drug overdose. Should've died when I got shanked in jail. How's Frank dead, when I'm alive?"

Billy raised his head and stared at the bar. Dancer was busy with another patron. He drank most of his beer. He looked towards the bar again and waved at Dancer.

"Be right there, Billy."

Head bowed again, he resumed talking to himself.

"Frank's a capable man. Could've been anything if he didn't take me with him. Wanted to lift me up. I pulled him down."

Judy's brow knotted, overwhelmed by a blend of compassion and concern. *What should I do? What should I say? A wordsmith, lost for words. Feel useless.* She reached out her hand and gently rested it on Billy's arm.

Billy drained his beer and glanced towards the bar. Dancer was heading over to their table with a bottle. Dancer refilled both shot glasses. He picked up Billy's glass.

"I'll pour you another beer, Billy."

He took the bottle of whisky with him, seemingly absent-mindedly. Billy downed both shots without blinking.

Dancer delivered a beer.

"Where's my bottle?"

"Sorry, left it sitting on the bar."

Dancer returned to the bar and immediately began attending to another customer, forgetting Billy's bottle. Billy glared at Dancer but drank some beer. He stared at the whisky bottle and moistened his lips, still wet from the beer. He lost all strength and his head again went down. Judy could barely hear him now.

"Can't believe Frank's gone. How can Frank be dead before me? What sort of God would allow that to happen? Frank's the best man I ever met. Smart. Has an excellent character. Frank wanted nothing from me. Never took from me. Gave to me all his life…"

Dancer arrived with another shot. Billy found the strength to raise his head. He glared at the whisky bottle still on the bar, glared at Dancer, downed his shot, looked at Judy as if he was about to accuse her of something. Before he could, his head slumped again.

"Coffin made me feel safe. If I did anything to displease him, he would've dropped me. If I hurt him or damaged his reputation, he would've killed me without a thought. Frank wanted nothing from me. After I destroyed his life, he never dropped me. If Frank had become mayor, everyone would know what a great man he is."

Billy's gaze moved from Judy to the bar, and then to his beer.

"Susie's a superb judge of character, but not Frank. Love of my life. Always dreamed I'd pay Frank back, and maybe get Susie back. Too late now. Fucked up my life, and fucked up Frank's life. I'm just a fucked fuck up… fucking useless."

Billy stopped talking. His eyes glazed over, became empty and lifeless, as if shutters in his mind were pulled down. Apparently, on autopilot, he picked up his beer and drank. What had happened was strangely fascinating, but Judy wasn't sure what to make of it.

Dancer came over with a fresh beer.

"Billy's gone now," he said.

He placed a chair beside Judy and sat down.

"All drunks are different. Their addiction hits them in different ways, some chemical reaction with individual body chemistry, I guess. Don't know, it's what I see. Nor do they react the same way every time. There are variations and patterns they follow. Can only base it on my drunks, but been running this place and observing for years."

Billy was staring with lifeless eyes and taking occasional automatic sips of his beer. Judy changed her focus from Billy to Dancer, but remained silent.

"Today Billy was a concentrated version of normal, far more lucid and focused. Usually, he's all over the place, and very repetitive. He'll talk about a lot of random things which don't appear connected, and then hit repeat and go through them all again. The pattern repeats with decreasing lucidity. Scratched record, I call it."

Dancer looked at Billy with what Judy read as compassion. His eyes briefly focused on the bar in case anyone was waiting for service, then returned to Judy.

"Continues for hours sometimes. Annoying, as are many of their patterns, which is why I don't let them sit at the bar. With Billy, his record goes slower and slower and eventually stops and he ends up like this."

"Will he stay like this now?" Judy asked.

"Yes. I'll watch him. When he becomes fidgety, I'll take him to the restroom. If I don't, he'll piss himself where he sits. At some point he'll wander off—won't let him today—not knowing where he is or where he's going. Usually, he'll find somewhere to sit; on a bench in the park, or in a doorway if it's raining.

"He'll sit there staring and pissing himself until morning when he finds his way home for sleep and a shower, before going to work in the park for a couple of hours and then coming here to spend his money when he's done. Billy's life now. They're all the same with variations."

Judy glanced at Billy, picked up her glass, and drank a little wine.

"Does he do this every day?"

"Today he was different. He didn't jump around too much. His tracks played through. The only other times he's like this is when he's with Frank, but that won't happen anymore."

The man Billy had referred to as Abbot was heading to the bar.

"Duty calls," Dancer said as he stood to attend to Abbot.

"You can forget about Billy today. He's done. You won't get another word out of him."

"Need the restroom. I must've drank a bottle myself."

"You're well into your second." Dancer walked away, taking the remains of the snack plate with him.

"Oh."

***

She slid her digital recorder into the outside pocket of her bag and retrieved her glass.

"Goodbye, Billy."

She made her way to the bar to settle up.

"You seem to actually care about these people, Dancer."

"I do, but part of it is managing them. Rather take Billy to the restroom than clean the floor because he's pissed himself. If I don't look out for these people, who will? Can't take responsibility for them; learned that the hard way. Do what I can, not much, still better than nothing. Your snacks were a good idea. They've been picking at them when they come up for their drinks… I'll do it every day. At least they'll eat something."

Judy glanced back at Billy. *Do what I can for him.* She passed Dancer her credit card to settle her tab, and her name card.

"If Billy needs anything, you call me."

Dancer nodded. "Don't be a stranger."

"I won't."

Judy left the bar, headed for The Old Seaman's Lodge. She wanted to make sure Billy had accommodation organized, for a while anyway. She didn't know why; she only just met him, but she liked him. Yes, as everybody, well everybody except Myriam, said Billy was likeable.

***

Dancer's eyes remained fixed on Judy's ass until she was out the door. *Damn fine ass that, just once in my life I'd like to….*

The Old Seaman's Lodge

Dancer was right, The Old Seaman's Lodge was easy to find.

Beside the lodge, a souvenir shop appeared to occupy most of the ground floor of the building, but it didn't. The shop was in another building and had entrances on two roads despite not being on the corner.

A display stand beside the door contained brochures offering simple, clean accommodation. Judy entered the narrow lobby. In front of her were stairs to the upper floors and the guest rooms, according to the sign, but no elevator.

Reception was a small room beside the entrance, with steel bars in front of the counter, *a necessary precaution for twenty-four-hour budget accommodation in a seedy part of town.* Two charcoal sofas side by side against the wall opposite reception; between the stairs and the sofas were two vending machines, one with drinks, and the other with snacks; chocolate bars, candies, potato chips. Next to the reception room, opposite the other two, stood a third vending machine advertising hot beverages, coffee, tea, and chocolate. *Budget room service. Better than nothing.*

A door beside the reception counter was marked Baggage Storage—Private. *Presumably how staff enter reception.* From the front of the reception counter, Judy could see an internal door leading to the baggage room. *Hides baggage from view and provides an extra level of security.*

Everything in the lobby appeared outdated and worn around the edges, but exceptionally clean, including the receptionist. *Early sixties, clothes aged but laundered, receding gray hair in place, face lined, fingernails clean.*

Sure he has a story—everyone does—his might be interesting. An air of having been important once. Probably laid off. Maybe half-a-dozen years ago—difficult for people over fifty to find meaningful work—ended up as the receptionist here. The man wore a name badge: *Irving Jones.* Judy smiled.

"Hello ma'am," he said. "How may I help you today?"

"Hello Irving Jones. My name is Judy Vernon. I'm a friend of Billy Johnson, understand he's staying here."

"Yes, ma'am, but he's not here now. Probably find him at The Shipyard, around the corner."

"Thank you, Irving, but I just left him. I'd like to pay some rent for Billy, if I may."

"Yes, Ma'am, you certainly may." Irving smiled. He seemed genuinely pleased.

"His rent's nearly run out. Usually, Frank calls in and pays it in advance. Here a couple of weeks ago, but I think he must've given the rent to Billy to pay…"

"Don't think Frank will make it in again this month, Irving," Judy said, not wanting to explain Frank had died to another person.

How have I gone from witnessing the tragedy of Frank's sudden death to being the bearer of his death notice?

"Good man, Frank, been looking after Billy for years. Without Frank and Dancer, doubt Billy would survive. How long would you like to pay the rent for?"

"Sure you do your bit to help our Billy, too."

How has a man I just met and hadn't even heard of two weeks ago become our Billy?

"Think I'll pay three months now." She passed Irving her credit card.

"Okay ma'am, and thank you."

"Irving, Dancer will bring Billy home tonight. When he does, can you tell him Billy's rent's covered? Dancer looks out for Billy more than he lets on, I think."

"Yes, ma'am."

Not sure why I'm paying Billy's rent. Feel I should. Frank'll be pleased, which was important to her. She wasn't aware of this, nor the implications of her desire to keep a dead man happy.

When he returned her credit card, Judy handed Irving her business card. "If Billy needs anything, please call me."

"I sure will, ma'am."

"Goodbye Irving and thank you," Judy said as she made her way out of the lobby.

"No, thank *you* ma'am."

On the street, Judy flagged a taxi. Home to change before meeting Myron. As she settled in the back of the taxi, she reached into the pocket of her bag and switched off her digital recorder.

She took out her iPad and entered; *How People get Nicknames, Addicted to People, Addicted to Fellatio* and *Dancer?* to her feature list.

***

Judy copied her digital recording to her computer, but didn't listen as she'd intended. *Getting late.*

She showered, applied her usual light makeup, and chose white lacy aphrodisiac lingerie for a night with Myron. White limited her choice of outfit because Judy always matched her lingerie color with what she was wearing. Usually, she chose her outfit first, but thoughts of Billy distracted her.

A versatile white dress from her *sexy without trying* selection. Sleeveless and buttoned down to the waist, before becoming a form fitting skirt that stopped above her knees.

She enjoyed the caress of the light material, which hugged her shape without clinging. It didn't sit rigidly against her body, as a heavier material may have. The way it moved with her, almost flowing with her body, gave her a sense of gracefulness. A belt turned the dress's appearance into a blouse and skirt, and a pair of white high heels completed her ensemble.

Judy looked at herself appreciatively in the mirror. *That should get Myron hard during dinner. Glad I've never let myself go.*

She threw her jeans and some clean lingerie into her overnight bag, together with a pair of flat shoes. Judy needed little because she could wear her jeans over her dress, tucking the skirt in like a top.

As she left her apartment, she wondered, not for the first time, what Myron's apartment would be like.

***

Myron sat at the bar, drinking a whisky sour, and watching the door when Judy arrived.

The maître d' who greeted Judy took her overnight bag. "Let me take care of that for you, Ms. Vernon."

"Thank you."

Myron watched Judy make her way to him and stood to greet her. They shared a lingering, warm hug. He wanted her to feel the effect she had on his body.

"You look… Wow!" Myron said, "Just Wow!"

All he could think of to say. Coherent language suddenly absent. He tried again.

"Every man stared at you as you walked through the restaurant."

"Really? I wasn't aware of that," Judy lied.

"Would you like a glass of white?"

"Perhaps not. Wined out after this afternoon. Surprise me with something different."

"I'll have another," Myron said to the waiting barman, "and a Pink Gin for *my* lady."

Judy smiled.

"How was this afternoon?"

"Interesting, from many perspectives. Guessing there'll be some things to investigate after I listen to the recording. Billy's an interesting character, very likeable. Seems Frank's been helping him since his release from prison."

Judy collected her thoughts.

"Well, he's been helping him all his life, but it's surprising he didn't stop after Billy destroyed his life. Says a lot about Frank's character. He's a much better person than I would've been in the circumstances. Frank's been paying his rent in a low-cost guesthouse of sorts. Old but spotless. I paid three months' rent in advance. Frank wanted me to."

Myron had questions, but held his tongue. Letting someone talk usually meant they answered questions you may not have thought to ask.

A skill he'd learned from Judy. *Smart, beautiful, and kind. I'm a lucky man… or will be if this sticks.*

"Ashamed of myself. When I first saw Frank, I wrote him off as a fat, angry man in a bad suit. If he hadn't died, that's all he would've been to me. He was a smart, kind man of rare character and integrity."

The barman placed their drinks in front of them, but neither reached for them.

"His appearance and dress resulted from putting others first and keeping his word. He was angry because an unreasonable woman was abusing him for his kindness. Nothing about Frank was what it seemed at first glance. A valuable—if somewhat humbling lesson—I hope I never forget."

Myron studied her as she sipped her Pink Gin.

"Sweetheart, you live your life based on what you learn researching features. No reason you'll forget anything you've learned from poor Frank's life. We all judge, categorize, and box people at first glance. Makes us feel safe and comfortable. Our way of transforming the unknown into the known."

Myron picked up his glass and took a drink.

Judy squeezed his thigh gently. "Let's go to our table."

***

They studied their menus.

"I'm rather hungry," Judy said. "Had an excellent lunch, but that bottle of wine and the emotion of Billy…."

"Trust me?"

"With everything," she replied absently, and then the realization hit her. *Actually, do trust him with everything.*

Myron signaled the waiter.

"Would you ask chef if we can have tomorrow's special tonight? Happy to wait for it."

Her day with Billy had left Judy emotionally drained. She nearly finished her drink.

"This will take a while. Would you like another Pink Gin?"

"I would, thank you."

The waiter returned.

"Chef agreed."

Myron smiled. "Could we have another round, please?"

The waiter nodded and headed to the bar.

Myron finished his drink to keep pace with Judy.

"You were sure he'd agree."

"Yes, here when they arrived, too late for tonight's menu, but chef was so excited he described the dish to me. Knew he was dying to prepare it, plus…"

"Your relationship with the restaurant."

"That too. What's the name of that guesthouse where Billy is staying?"

"The Old Seaman's Lodge. Sort of apt for Billy, given his err… occupation."

"My family owns that building. In fact, we own the lodge too. A long story."

"That's a coincidence…" *Frank's eyes appeared in her mind,* "or not."

A Night with Myron

"You said dinner will take a while, so there's time for a long story," Judy suggested.

"Zayde bought the building cheaply fifty or sixty years ago to help a friend in financial trouble, not unusual in my community. Help the friend by buying the building and be rewarded by getting it cheap. I'm oversimplifying an accepted cultural formula, but that's the gist.

"Anyway, Zayde refurbished the building cheap. Good luck and cultural norms. The previous owner contracted for the building to be refurbished but went broke. The contractor ordered materials but didn't get paid. Zayde *helped* by acquiring the materials at cost, which meant the contractor didn't lose money, and Zayde saved a lot on materials he needed. Did most of the work himself, which was how we maintained buildings back then."

The waiter arrived with their drinks.

Judy proposed a toast. "To old seamen."

Myron echoed her toast.

"Took him two years to refurbish it. Offered double what he paid for the building. Over the years, my family could've made millions in property speculation. Not what we do. We're about security and community, not money. My thinking is similar, but for me it's people, not property.

"For the next thirty years various people owned and operated The Old Seaman's Lodge… Most not good at it and let the place run down. When Papa became more active in the business, he suggested they hire a manager and run it themselves. Zayde was skeptical, 'we don't know the hotel business.' Papa convinced him to try."

Myron paused for a drink, smiling at Judy as he reached for his glass. Judy joined him, using Myron to pace herself.

"We hired some poor managers over the years. After I started college, I developed theories about backing people who needed to be given a chance or thrown a lifeline. Papa could see the logic in this. Sometimes all a building needs to reach its potential is the right owner. Papa brings everything back to what he knows. So, he hired Irving, who had no experience with hotels, but desperately needed a job. Best manager we ever had."

The way the Myerson family's approach to managing properties had evolved through the generations fascinated Judy. *Wonder if I might find a feature in there somewhere.*

"A few months ago, one of my property management customers had a similar problem. The leaseholder on two of his hotels got into trouble and stopped making payments. Now my management company manages them based on The Old Seaman's Lodge model."

Myron paused again and reached for his drink. Judy mimicked him.

She sensed there was more to the story and was content listening to Myron after her emotional day with Billy. "Please continue."

"Papa passed the management of The Old Seaman's Lodge to me. We're working on branding. A small three property chain, with potential to expand. Moved vending machines into the properties. Provide a service to the guests and generate profit.

"All have free guest laundries which are underutilized, so the vending machine business is moving into the laundromat business. We'll install coin or card operated machines, and make the laundries open to the public, adding vending machines so people can get coffee and a snack while they're waiting for their laundry."

He finished his whisky sour. Judy kept pace. He signaled the waiter for another round.

"Let me talk to Irving and we'll see what we can do for Billy."

"Thank you, Myron, but I'm not asking…."

"I know you're not, sweetheart. Figure I owe Frank. Helped me a lot with his business model and his Bitcoin formula. From all you've told me about your friend Frank, I'm sure it's what he'd want me to do."

"You're right about what Frank would want, but I can't say he's my friend. I never knew him."

Myron smiled. "You know him now. Perhaps, better than most people did, and you feel in your heart he's your friend. I can tell by the way you talk about him, so yes, he's your friend."

"Suppose he is, but can one become friends with a person after they've died?"

"I don't know. The evidence would say they can. Might make an interesting feature. *Befriending the dead.* Doubt you're the only one with such an experience. Why not see if you can track some others down and write it?"

"Excellent idea. As soon as I finish my current features, I'll do some research."

Been so lucky these past weeks. Gotten to know two extraordinary men. One living, one dead. Both are intelligent, interesting to the point of fascinating, and both have depths that few people see. Judy looked at Myron. *Am I falling in love with him?*

Their meals arrived.

Myron glanced up. "Look at this."

Mario, who carried his creations himself, proudly announced; "Lobster Tagliatelle. Served in the shell on a bed of hand made and cut pasta, with a creamy tomato and herb sauce. Enjoy!"

The waiter followed Mario. "I canceled your drink orders. We pair the dish with a Chablis Grand Cru to bring out the complex flavors in the lobster. The oaky nature of many chardonnays would enhance the burnt butter taste instead."

The herbs made the aroma of the meal almost sweet.

"My God," Judy said. "That looks and smells amazing."

"It certainly does," Myron agreed.

The meat, sweet and moist, was delicious to the point of decadence. Being poached in burnt butter, it melted in the mouth. The pasta and sauce—in a circle on the plate with the shell sitting in the middle—complimented the protein perfectly. The sauce had a depth of flavor which enhanced but didn't overpower the dish.

Judy lowered her fork, closed her eyes, and enjoyed a food orgasm as she savored each mouthful.

"This is perfect, Myron, thank you."

She noticed Myron, likewise, savoring his meal.

Judy had shared high quality meals in the past. During the meal, her companion, usually a man trying to get into her pants—not that Judy blamed them for that—would keep returning to or alluding to the price. The constant reference to cost, subtle or otherwise, diminished the experience.

At no point did Myron refer to the price, nor compare the cost to the value. He only commented on the quality, how much he was enjoying it, and apologized for not talking.

"Myron, this is perfect, and you really *are* wonderful."

He flushed and focused on his dinner.

Having enjoyed their meal in a contented and comfortable silence, they waited until the table was cleared before either spoke.

As they finished their wine, Myron outlined his suggestions to enhance Judy's business. "We'll load your freelance features into a *Feature Bank* and offer an account to your publishers and new publishers. Having an account lets them read all features and purchase them online, as needed. You may need to update some of your older pieces, which would generate an item in your monthly newsletter."

"My monthly newsletter?"

"A monthly email informing publishers of new features, upcoming features, older features either updated or rewritten, perhaps a selection of features that are compatible as a series. If a publisher loses a feature at the last minute, they can buy one of your features to replace it.

"Other than a short newsletter, no more work than you're doing now. You keep doing what you do, and the *Feature Bank* will handle promotion and distribution. We'll set up a second site for blogs. You can write your own instead of ghosting others. The same process, but a *Blog Bank,* separate. No reason your customers couldn't subscribe to both sites.

"I've prepared a detailed report, analysis and plan for you, which I'll give you later. Read it when you're ready and tell me what you want to do."

"Myron, that's *wonderful*, but I only asked you last night."

"Already thinking about what I could do to make your life easier. Always make my resources available to family. What life's about... or should be. Helping people, especially family."

Judy smiled. *So now I'm family*? She liked Myron bringing her closer. *He's wonderful: as a person, in business, and in bed.*

"Ready to go home?"

"Yes, please."

***

Myron's apartment was what she expected. A penthouse, but not in the upmarket part of the city.

"Family owns the building." Myron said.

Functional and comfortable furniture. *Excellent quality. Leather, darker than mine. The male version. Impeccably clean, no surprise there. Everything in its place. As meticulous as his appearance.*

Myron had taken Judy's bag to his room and was now in the kitchen preparing hot chocolate. Judy smiled at the role reversal. She asked for directions to the bathroom.

The bathroom was spotless, everything in its logical place. The towels hung at precisely the same length. *Meticulous, not surprised.*

Judy now sat on the sofa, legs curled under her.

Myron entered with the hot chocolate. "Look like you belong."

"Feel like I belong." *Surprised how comfortable I am.*

***

Sitting beside Judy, enjoying their chocolate, Myron was nervous. He fidgeted. In love with Judy, but not ready to speak the words. Several times he opened his mouth to speak but didn't. *Why does my brain turn to mush when I try to talk about anything personal with her?*

"What is it, Myron?"

"Tomorrow's Friday."

"Yes Myron, very perceptive."

Myron smiled nervously. "I'm stalling."

What he needed to tell Judy had cost him relationships in the past, and he didn't want to lose her.

"Please, say what you need to say. I'm not one of those unreasonable dragon women you can't talk to for fear of their fire."

"No, I know." *You're the sort of woman who'd quietly walk away rather than deal with a distasteful confrontation.*

"Monday, Wednesday, and Friday morning I play squash. Enjoy it and keeps me fit. The squash courts are in high demand, so we need to book six months in advance. Have different partners. Can't just not go whenever I get a better offer. Sunday, Tuesday, Thursday I jog, and can easily not go—prefer to stay in bed with you—that mouth of yours is sensational."

Judy flushed, and Myron smiled.

"Sabbath. I'm not religious, neither is my family. Basically, just the pork thing and the Sabbath. There are many rules, but people follow the ones that suit them. Sabbath begins at sunset on Friday and ends at sunset on Saturday. We always stay home on the Sabbath, family only, our tradition.

"Spend Friday evening until Sunday morning with my parents. Have all my life. Hated it when I was younger, especially as a teenager, when all my friends were doing cool stuff. Now I figure, when they're gone, I'll be glad I spent one day a week with them. Have all day Saturday to talk with Papa about the business. Some people wouldn't allow business talk on the Sabbath, but my family is practical about such things. Unless the Sabbath is on the twenty-fifth, which is when I visit Rebekah."

"Rebekah?"

"My niece… well, cousin. Got herself into some trouble and is incarcerated. Her family and the community disowned her. I visit her once a month. She has no one else. She never says much, but I think my visits are important to her. It's important she knows when I will visit, gives her something to look forward to."

Judy smiled. "The more I learn about you…"

"Needed to explain things to you, Judy. We're spending more time together, which is what I want, but…"

"My parents are both gone. You won't regret having spent time with your parents. Knew your culture before I allowed you to seduce me and knew you played squash three times a week. More than comfortable with everything. In fact, I've ended relationships in the past to get one day a week to myself."

"I've had relationships end because they *didn't* want one day a week to themselves. So, I wanted to… Besides, I recall it was you who seduced me."

"Are you complaining? Do two things for me. Take me to bed and decide where you'll take me for brunch on Sundays. The second one you can do tomorrow."

"Yes, ma'am."

Rebekah

Fourteen-year-old Rebekah hated everything. She hated her life, hated being Jewish, hated feeling like a kid when she was with her friends, and hated being part of a strict family. So many fucking rules. She hated the daily lectures from her father about every-fucking-thing.

"You need to make sure the pleats on your skirt are in the proper order, not caught up and flattened. After sitting, you must check all your pleats are sitting correctly, otherwise people will think you do not care about your appearance. You need to take pride in yourself…"

She only half listened. *Who fucking cares about pleats? You've been banging on about pleats for a fucking hour, you stupid old fool.*

Outwardly, her only response was, "Yes sir," as her mother had taught her.

She appeared to be her usual docile, compliant self, but inside, every nerve was screaming. Something snapped in her. *Enough!*

"Fuck this shit!"

The horrified look on her father's face—an expression like she'd slapped him—gave her a deep sense of satisfaction as she spun round and stormed away. Her chair, she left, pushed away from the table—an Italian Baroque carved dining table, with eight leather seated chairs that had been in the family since before her father was born—and not neatly in its place as they taught her.

Rebekah stomped into her room, slammed the door behind her, locked it and threw herself face down on her bed. Her tearless eyes remained open. Attempts by her parents to communicate met with, "Fuck off and leave me alone."

Eventually, she stood and studied her reflection in the mirror. Her dress, the regulation four inches below the knees, decreed by her father. *I'll show him I can focus! Just watch me focus on not being part of this fucked up outdated family!*

Rebekah removed her dress and emptied her wardrobe onto the bed. Her mother had insisted she learn to sew. "Throwing clothes away before they're worn out is a waste of money. You need to learn to sew. You can repair and alter clothes when needed."

She replaced four inches below the knee with a new standard. Four inches above the knee. She spent the night focused on refashioning her wardrobe. In the early hours of the morning, she sewed her last stitch.

Standing in front of the mirror, looking at herself in her underwear, ready to try on her refashioned clothes, Rebekah's nostrils flared, and her head jerked back. *Hate granny underwear.* Whenever she changed for gym class, her friends, who mostly wore lacy briefs or thongs, laughed at her.

"Always wear clean undergarments," her mother told her many times, "in case you're involved in an accident."

Fuck underwear! She removed her granny pants, gathered the underwear from her drawer and placed it in the plastic bag with the off cuts from her dresses and skirts. *Won't wear any, then I'll be the cool one.*

Naked, she examined herself in the mirror. After coming into her room unannounced one morning and catching her masturbating, her mother had forbidden her from masturbation. After that, she kept her door locked. *Fuck that too. It's my fucking body.*

She flopped onto her bed, lying on her back, opened her legs and—thinking about a cool seventeen-year-old guy she often saw hanging out on her way home from school—doing things her friends had told her their boyfriends did; she brought herself to orgasm, savoring the waves of ecstasy that washed over her.

Wanting to leave home before her parents woke, she applied make-up—hidden in her school bag. She usually waited until she was on her way to school, removing it on her way home. She dressed in her shortened uniform, threw her backpack on, and picked up the bag of offcuts and discarded underwear.

Rebekah left the house. *Stop for breakfast on the way to school.*

She disposed of the bag in a dumpster and headed to Al's Breakfast Bar. The morning air, cool against the nakedness under her uniform, was exhilarating. *I'm free.*

She sat at the counter facing the window. *Wonder if passersby can see I'm naked between my legs.* Rebekah didn't need a menu; she knew what she wanted and delighted knowing it would repulse her family.

"Bacon and eggs. Oh, and a coffee," she said in response to the waitress.

"How'd you like that, hon?" the waitress asked.

"Oh. Umm… not sure. What do you like?"

"Sunny side up, and crispy bacon."

"Perfect. I'll have that."

The coffee arrived first. Rebekah inhaled the aroma, raised the cup, and took a sip. *Hot.* She blew on it to cool the liquid. She needed it.

Rebekah examined her breakfast tentatively. She inhaled deeply. The scent of bacon wasn't new to her, but she'd never eaten it. She cut a small piece and placed it in her mouth. *Saltier than I expected. Crispy and crunchy.* She didn't know how to describe the taste. *Tastes exactly as it smells.*

Rebekah liked it very much and devoured her breakfast. She was hungry, having missed dinner the previous evening. A second coffee and she was ready for school.

***

It was late in the day. The break before the last period. *Bored.* She glanced at her friends seated around her. Rebekah was the youngest in her class, having skipped a grade as part of a gifted young program. Her friends were older, sixteen. All had older boyfriends, none were virgins. They were the cool girls. Rebekah felt lucky they accepted her in their clique, even though she knew it was her brain they wanted. She also felt like a kid, excluded, especially when they were talking about boyfriends and having sex. She didn't want to be a kid hanging onto their skirts anymore.

Rebekah stood, slung her backpack over her shoulder, and said, "Fuck this shit, I'm gonna get laid."

Her friends, already shocked by the change in her appearance, stared at her open-mouthed.

***

She saw the boy she liked, sitting on the stairs in front of a building, as usual.

"Hi, pretty girl," he said.

She usually stopped to say hello, but never approached him. That day, she stepped over to him.

"Hi yourself. Never told me your name."

"Tony. Do you have a name?"

"Everybody has a name."

"What's yours?"

She didn't answer.

"Don't know your own name?" Tony asked.

"Thinking about it."

She didn't want that name anymore; it was her parents' name, not hers. *Want my own name.*

"Becky," she said.

"Becky?"

"Yeah, you live here?"

"Yeah, Three B."

"Parents home?"

"Nah, working."

"C'mon then."

Becky walked past him, opened the door and began climbing the stairs. She figured with being a few steps ahead of Tony, her short skirt and lack of underwear should telegraph her intentions.

She waited at his door. He arrived and fumbled with the keys. Flustered, he opened the door. She stepped in first. She didn't look around.

"Where's your room?" she asked.

"This one," he said, leading her into his bedroom.

Becky followed him in, shutting the door behind her. She slung her backpack on the floor, sat on the side of his bed, removed her shoes and socks, lay down and raised her skirt, exposing her virgin bush to the sunlight streaming in the window.

Seventeen-year-old Tony didn't need to be asked twice. In fact, he didn't need to be asked once. Shoes and socks off, jeans and undershorts on the floor, still wearing his T-shirt. He was on her in seconds.

Not wearing underwear, the slightest breeze had teased her all day. Thinking about the sexual encounters her friends described had made her horny. She was ready.

He didn't bother undressing her. No need. As soon as he was on top, he guided himself inside of her. No finesse, no foreplay. Becky winced as he penetrated her. It hurt. She winced with each thrust, and three minutes, fifty-four seconds later, he was done.

That was it. Her virginity, gone in under four minutes. It wasn't hers, anyway; it was Rebekah's. She stared at the ceiling. *No going back now.*

She sat up, swung her legs off the bed, and replaced her socks and shoes. She could feel Tony's semen running out of her.

"Where's the bathroom?" she asked.

He told her. It was easy to find her way in the small apartment. She wiped away the semen and blood, *not much blood, expected more*. She peed, took a washcloth from the shower, rinsed it in hot water, washed herself, rinsed the cloth and returned it to the shower, grabbed someone's towel and wiped herself dry. *Took longer to clean myself.*

Becky recalled what her friends told her, "First time's not so good, after that it's wonderful."

She flushed and returned to the bedroom. Tony, sitting on the side of the bed, half naked, a stupid grin on his face. She slung her backpack over her shoulder.

"Be better tomorrow," she said.

She turned, left his room, left his apartment, and walked home.

Her appearance would piss off her parents. *Don't give a fuck.* Her thoughts, occupied with school the next day, and announcing to her friends she'd lost her cherry.

***

Ten months later, Becky lay on the bed beside Tony. She wore one of his T-shirts. He wore undershorts. Her head rested on his shoulder.

The room was dark; the curtains closed. Tony rented the studio apartment after he found work. A motel room converted into budget accommodation. Two rooms, a living/bed room and a bathroom.

Tony said, "My mother told me I need to be careful, says you're a bad influence."

"Old people always say I'm bad. My friends think I'm cool. I don't give a fuck what anybody thinks."

"Your parents still giving you a hard time?"

"Papa still lectures Rebekah, but that's not me, so I don't listen. The police visited the other day. Reckon I smashed a shop window."

"You did!"

"Nah, home with my parents when it happened. At least, that's what they told the police."

"So, they're still looking out for you?"

"Nah, proud people, concerned about what the community will think. That's why they haven't taken the councilor's advice and put me in the system. Might yet. Keep saying they don't know what else to do with me. Probably be happier if I died. Better have no daughter than one that brings shame to the family."

"Don't think that's right."

"You don't know them or the community. Gotta plan to get out for good."

"Get out? Where will you go?"

"Here."

"Here?"

"Yeah. Need to piss and get dressed. Wanna go home for Sabbath dinner. I'll be back."

***

Becky sat at the table with her parents and Bubbe.

She announced, "Done with being a Jew. Gonna convert to Catholicism."

Bubbe began muttering in Yiddish. Papa looked at Becky and Mama alternatively. He seemed about to speak, but said nothing. *Not the response I expected, never seen him lost for words.*

Becky moved to phase two. She extracted a ham and cheese sandwich from her bag. She didn't know if they could smell the ham, so opened and closed the sandwich.

Bubbe looked like she was going to have a heart attack. Mama gasped. Papa stood and started pacing, wringing his hands, but still had no words for her. No lecture.

Having finished her sandwich, she lit a cigarette, which apparently carried the weight of the final straw as far as her long-suffering Papa was concerned. He turned to face the wall.

"I have no daughter," he declared.

"No, Papa, you drove her away a long time ago," Becky said quietly, and with more than a hint of sadness.

She collected the bag beside her, went to her bedroom, had one last look, then picked up the suitcase she'd packed earlier.

Becky paused as she walked past the dining room, looked at her family one last time, and left her home.

Becky

Fifteen-year-old Becky looked around her room. It was indistinguishable from any other motel room.

A double bed, a TV mounted on the wall, a two-seater sofa where Tony—now totally compliant to Becky's wishes—sat under the window. A bench along the other wall, a mini-fridge beneath the bench, and a microwave on top of it. The bench, which was long enough for two chairs where they sat when eating, ended when it reached a small wardrobe, usually crammed with their clothes, which were now stuffed in two suitcases in the trunk of Tony's car. They planned to leave the city as soon as they finished the job.

She finished going over her plan for the last time before putting it into action. She studied Spider and Flea—recruited by Tony on her instruction—seated in the chairs beside the bench, turned to face the bed.

"Got it?"

"Yeah, we ain't dumb," said Flea.

Becky knew his motivation for accepting the job was to look up her skirt at every chance he got. Spider did whatever Flea did.

Becky glanced at her watch. "Time to go."

They left the room and climbed into Spider's old Chevrolet G20 van, dull gray, scratched and dented in places. Spider would drive with Becky up front to show him the way. Tony and Flea would travel in the back. Flea generously held the door open for Becky to climb in. She guessed he was hoping for a glimpse of her naked bush and made sure she didn't disappoint; she wanted to keep him motivated.

***

Becky had devised a plan to rob Avi Jewelry. The family would be together at home, their shop closed because that family would have no business dealings—even by proxy—on the Sabbath.

The gang of four broke into the house. Brandishing guns, they tied the family up in the living room. Flea and Spider remained with the terrified hostages, to ensure Bela, the father, cooperated.

Becky and Tony drove Bela to Avi Jewelry Store.

Bela hesitated when he raised his hand to key in the alarm code.

"Come on, old man, get on with it. You don't want to leave your family with those two any longer than necessary, and no tricks. If we're not back within an hour, I won't be responsible for what happens," Becky said.

Bela appeared uncertain. "How do I know they will be okay?"

"We just want the stuff. Turn off the alarm, and we'll go in nice and quiet. You'll open the safe, and we'll take those diamonds you've got in there. We'll clear out the display cases, and you'll be back with your family in no time. No one will get hurt if you co-operate. If not…"

Becky nodded at Tony, who lifted his shirt to reveal the gun tucked into his jeans.

Bela nodded. His hand shook as he entered the code to turn the alarm off. He took the keys from his pocket and unlocked the door. His hand still shaking, he pushed the door open. All three stepped inside.

"You see, old man, cooperate and it's easy. Now open the safe and don't try pushing a hidden alarm button or any nonsense like that," Becky said.

Bela led Becky to his office and got down on one knee to open the safe.

Tony pulled three garbage bags from his pockets and began emptying the items from the display cases into the bags.

Becky smiled. *Everything's going to plan.* Take everything they could, return the old man to his home and leave him tied up with the others. Meet a fence Spider had lined up, offload the stuff from the display cases, split the proceeds, and go their separate ways. Becky hadn't told Spider and Flea about the diamonds, which she'd once overheard Bela mention to Papa.

Becky figured they had a day or two to leave the city and head south before concerned staff investigated and discovered the family on Monday morning.

***

Harry White was an aging police officer. A beat cop all his life with no desire to do anything else. His job was to keep his community safe and to ensure it remained a good place for decent people to live. One of the few remaining foot patrol cops in the city. Radio cars had replaced most of them.

Harry's beat included the Diamond District. The business owners believed a visible police presence was important. The district business association had no shortage of funds, and donations to successive mayors' election campaigns ensured they kept a police presence.

Harry knew the people on his beat, knew what they did and when they did it. Harry used this expression a lot when training rookies. Borrowed it from NYPD Blue. *Best cop show ever made.* Harry knew their habits and peculiarities. He knew the neighborhood so well that if anything was out of place, he'd recognize it.

Harry smiled, remembering something he'd read that morning in Judy Vernon's latest feature. He'd been reading her features since being the subject of one several years earlier. *Saturday morning. Light's on. Someone in the Avi Jewelry Store. That's wrong.* Some of the other stores, jewelry or otherwise, employed non-Jewish people to conduct business on the sabbath, but not this family.

Harry crossed the road to investigate. They always pulled the blinds in the front windows down when closed. A gap between the blinds allowed Harry to peer inside without being seen. He glimpsed a young man emptying the display cabinets.

He stepped away from the store so he couldn't be overheard and radioed for backup.

"Quietly," he said. "Don't want to alert the perps."

The first radio car arrived in minutes. Two officers exited the vehicle, parked a hundred yards away so as not to alert those inside. They approached Harry.

"Robbery in progress. Only eyeballed one perp, probably more. Possibly armed. Position yourselves either side of the door, and we'll grab them when they come out. I'll move back to the window."

When Becky, Tony, and Bela were about to exit the store, Harry whispered, "Two perps, one male, one female. The old man's the owner. Take the perps and I'll look after the owner."

The officers nodded acknowledgement.

Harry used his fingers to provide a countdown. Three, two, one.

***

Becky was excited. *It worked. Pick up those morons, sell the stuff and we're home free. Enough to buy a quality ID. A new life.*

"You go out first, old man, and no tricks, or we'll leave your family at the mercy of those two."

Bela glared at her, but did as he was told.

As Becky and Tony exited the store, two officers with guns drawn met them.

One ordered, "Against the wall and assume the position."

Becky's heart rate quickened, her breathing shallow. *Fuck! Run. They won't shoot a white kid.* She took a step, but the officer grasped her arm and pushed her against the window. *Fuck!*

She glanced at Tony, hoping for a distraction, but he complied with the officer. *Of course he would.* The officer who'd issued the order holstered his gun and frisked Tony.

"Gun!" He removed the gun from Tony's jeans.

"Okay," he said, "Hands behind your back."

Tony complied and was handcuffed.

The other officer, one hand grasping Becky's arm, frisked her lightly, with Harry—who kept them covered—as a witness.

Upon having her arm released, Becky tensed, ready to run.

"Don't even think about it," the officer said.

The handcuffs felt tight on her wrists. Having her arms secured behind her back hurt her shoulders. *Fuck!* Tears built up behind her eyes. *Don't cry.*

A second radio car arrived.

"You guys take this one, and we'll take the girl," the arresting officer said.

One of them took Tony by the arm and led him to the police car, shoving him, not too gently, into the rear of the vehicle.

The arresting officer likewise escorted Becky to the first radio car, guiding her into the back seat. He stared, then smiled. She realized her skirt had ridden up. The glimpse of naked young pussy seemed to make his day.

"Let me go, and I'll give you a taste," she offered.

He ignored her, collected the bags of stolen items, and placed them securely in the trunk.

***

Harry took Bela aside.

Bela pleaded, "Please Harry, they have my family."

"You're safe now, Bela. Tell me what happened from the beginning."

Bela explained the situation.

"Okay, Bela, we'll take care of it. Let me talk to my sergeant. I've an idea."

Harry used his mobile for the call.

***

Anxious for his family, Bela was frustrated. He could only hear half of the conversation.

"Sarge, everything's under control here. Two perps in custody. However, we have a hostage situation at the owner's residence."

Bela listened to Harry's explanation.

"If we set up a wide perimeter, so we don't alert the perps, we can lure them out quietly. Avoid a siege situation which will be hard to control. I know the female perp, young girl, Rebekah. We send her in there with Bela, the owner. She ties him up as planned and leads the two perps still in the house out to the van, where we'll be waiting."

Bela tried to focus on what Harry was saying. Wringing his hands, his legs weak, his stomach nauseous, his mind in turmoil. He couldn't hold a coherent thought.

"It's a risk Sarge, she could alert them, but I can convince her it's in her interest to cooperate. If a hostage were to get killed in a siege situation, she's facing felony murder. Got an attitude, but smart enough to know what's in her best interest."

Bela's concern was to protect his family. *That evil girl can't be trusted.*

He trusted Harry. "Keep my family safe."

Harry nodded. "We'll do our best, Bela."

***

Harry assisted Becky from the back of the radio car. He noticed her lack of underwear, rolled his eyes, and sighed.

He explained, "Rebekah, you're going to jail, the only question is for how long?"

"It's Becky, and I know that. I'm not stupid."

"Okay Becky, understand this. If any of the hostages get killed when we arrest your accomplices, you'll be charged with felony murder. That's life. Do you want to go to jail for life?"

"Fine, when I left them. Nothing to do with me."

"Linked to the same crime. Your involvement in the crime is enough for you to be convicted."

"But I'm not there."

"Doesn't matter. Nothing's going to save you from doing time, but if you cooperate, I'll testify on your behalf. Should result in a reduced sentence."

"Cooperate how?"

"We'll take you and Bela back to the house in the van. You take Bela inside, tie him up as planned. Tell your accomplices the stuff's in the van. Lead them out and we'll arrest them when they're safely away from the hostages. Don't get any ideas about warning them or thinking you're going to get away. You won't. The place is surrounded. You'll get an increased sentence. Do you understand?"

"I'm not stupid. I want immunity. I'll testify."

"We don't need you to testify. We caught you in the act."

"Then I want a suspended sentence, or whatever it's called. Don't wanna do time."

"Not gonna happen. Armed robbery is a serious offence."

"Okay, a guarantee, a couple of years in juvey."

"I'm not allowed to give you any guarantees, and we don't have time to arrange one. We need to act quickly."

"Well, what can you give me?"

"My word that I'll testify."

"Your word?"

"Yes. Will you do it?"

"Don't have a choice."

***

Flea glanced at his watch for the fourth time in less than five minutes.

"They should be back by now," he said to Spider.

"Yeah. Give 'em another twenty minutes. If they're not back, we get outta here."

Flea ogled the young girl he'd been toying with for the last hour. "Okay, you keep a lookout."

Spider turned to the window and looked out, as he'd done since Becky and Tony left.

Flea returned to the young girl tied to the chair in the dining room. He resumed talking to her. Asking if she wanted to go upstairs, asking if she ever had her pussy touched, stroking her hair, and touching her thigh. He crouched in front of her, opened her legs, and touched the inside of her thigh. He slid his hand up and forced his fingers inside the white cotton panties.

Spider said, "They're back, reversing into the drive… Becky's getting out, flashing her pussy as usual. What's a fine piece of ass like that doing with a dropkick like Tony? Looks like Tony's staying in the van. She's dragging the old boy out of the van now. We should get ready to tie him up."

"Looks like I'm gonna have to leave this pretty girl for another day," Flea said, inhaling her scent on his fingers. "Don't worry sweetheart, I'll be back for your cherry. Hope they got enough stuff. Getting worried they were gonna do a runner."

***

When they arrived, Harry, who was driving, reversed into the driveway, which placed the van between anyone looking out the windows and himself.

"Remember, young lady, help us get those two out with no one getting hurt, and you may have a chance of a life when you get out. Anything goes wrong and I'll make sure they throw away the key."

"Relax, I know the score. I'm not fucking stupid."

Bela said "No, just evil, your poor Papa…"

"Shut up, old man. I don't have a Papa. You better not screw this up. Keep your fucking mouth shut, and let us tie you up, and your family will be fine."

"I am supposed to trust you?"

"You got no choice. Besides, you agreed."

"I trust Harry."

"When we get inside, do exactly what I tell you."

Harry said, "Enough. Bela, it's not perfect, but it's our best chance to keep your family safe."

"I know, Harry."

"All right, get going before they wonder what's taking you so long. Remember, we got the place surrounded."

Becky was about to say something to Harry, but thought better of it, instead she addressed Bela. "All right, old man, I'll get out first, open the back door and drag you out. When we get inside, I'll tell you to sit down and shut up. You'll do exactly that. Say nothing, keep your eyes down."

Becky got out of the van, opened the back door, and dragged Bela out. She led him to the back of the house and inside, told him to sit in a vacant chair and keep his mouth shut. Flea tied his hands behind the chair. Becky quickly grabbed the duct tape and, none too gently taped his mouth shut, still worried he might say something and screw everything up. She threw the tape to Spider, who taped his legs to the chair.

Flea asked. “Everything go okay?”

“Yeah, like I said it would. Tony’s waiting in the van with the haul. Let’s get the fuck out of here.”

She noticed the frightened look in the girl’s eyes.

“You didn’t do anything stupid, did you?”

“Relax sweetheart, I wouldn’t cheat on you.”

Becky rolled her eyes. “Come on then, play your cards right and I might give you more than a flash, just this once, to celebrate.” Becky shuddered at the thought.

They left the house and were surrounded by police and arrested.

Flea glared at Becky. “Fucking bitch, I’m gonna slit your fucking throat.”

Becky glared back. “They had the place surrounded. I was saving your worthless fucking lives.”

***

They gave Becky five years. Juvenile detention until she turns eighteen, then transferred to a women’s prison.

Spider got ten years, Flea received the ten and an additional three for sexual assault. Tony was sentenced to seventeen years, including seven years, for the statutory rape of Becky. It didn’t matter; he was dead, shanked within two years.

Slave

The corrections officer opened the dark blue metal cell door and shoved Becky inside. "Your new home, enjoy. Jack, you got company."

Jack's welcome was to let go a long, loud fart.

Jack's way of saying hello? The officer locked the door with an ominous clunk behind her. White walls in need of painting, dark gray vinyl tiles over concrete. Toilet and washbasin in the corner, a fixed light gray Formica bench table with a yellow plastic chair on either side, an almost empty shelf affixed to the wall above the table, and a bunk bed against the opposite wall.

Guess the bottom bunk's mine. She threw the few items they gave her—toilet paper, towel, soap, toothbrush and toothpaste—on her bed, and sat on the edge.

The bed creaked and grunted as Jack moved above her. Jack climbed down. One foot on the floor, the other still on the ladder at the end of the bunk, Jack farted again. She strode to the middle of the cell and leered at Becky, one side of her upper lip curled up.

Becky studied her cellmate. Thickset, short dark hair, cold brown eyes, arms covered in tattoos. *Don't look too friendly. Dyke.*

"I'm Becky."

"My cell, my rules."

"Sure."

"Stand up!"

Becky did as instructed. Jack walked around her, as if inspecting livestock. She stroked Becky's long, light-brown hair and slapped her ass. After two circuits, she stood in front of her and stared into Becky's pale-blue eyes. Becky, uncomfortable, intimidated, nervous, unsure what was happening.

"We're gonna get along fine, princess."

Without another word, Jack returned to her bunk.

Becky lay on hers and stared up at the bottom of Jack's bunk. *What the fuck was that about?*

***

An officer unlocked the cell door. Jack climbed down from her bunk, and Becky swung her legs off hers and stood.

"C'mon, Princess, dinner time. Usually go to the rec room between work and dinner, but a couple of stupid bitches got into a fight yesterday, so we're locked in our cells after work. Don't know how long this time."

Becky followed Jack to the mess hall.

Jack nodded towards a stack of trays on a stainless steel trolley. "Grab a tray and line up."

A tall girl, looking bored and disinterested, carelessly slopped lumpy mashed potato, peas, meatballs and something like runny shit on her tray. Becky sat beside Jack. Other girls joined them.

One girl nodded towards Becky, "Who's this?"

"New cell mate… Princess."

It was the only time they acknowledged her presence during dinner. The girls at the table deferred to Jack. They talked about other inmates and guards referring to them by nicknames. Becky didn't know who they were talking about and couldn't follow the conversation. After they ate, they returned to their cell.

***

Becky lay on her bunk, waiting for the lights to go out. *Nothing to do. Jack doesn't want to talk. Don't know what to make of her.* Other than their initial encounter, she seemed friendly enough, but the way Jack looked at her made Becky uncomfortable. *Like the way Flea looks at me, but worse.* Becky felt vulnerable.

The lights went out. The bed squeaked and groaned. Jack was on top of her.

"Okay Princess, let's get those panties off and see what your muff's made of."

"I'm not a dyke…"

"You will be by morning."

Becky didn't see the punch coming in the dark, but she felt it connect with the side of her face. Stunned, pain chased all thought from her mind. Becky had never been hit so hard. She'd never been hit.

Becky began to scream, but was silenced by a second blow, landing in the same place as its predecessor. Pain caused stars to flash before her eyes or in her mind. *Thought that only happened in cartoons.*

"Keep your fucking mouth shut, bitch. Attract the screw's attention and I'll break your fucking neck."

Not wanting to be hit again, Becky raised her pelvis, and Jack removed the panties the officer had insisted she wear. Jack wasn't gentle. Jack's fingers entered her body. Becky felt no pleasure. Eventually, Jack brought her to orgasm. *Oh... didn't expect that.*

Jack moved down the bed.

"Now we've got you juiced up. Let's see what you taste like."

Jack brought Becky to orgasm again. This time it was good. *Maybe this won't be so bad.* Jack raised her head and belched loudly.

"You taste good, Princess. Your turn."

She dragged Becky down the bed, reversed her position and lowered herself onto Becky's face.

"I don't..."

The tingling between Becky's legs was replaced with blinding pain as Jack's fist landed. Tears coming from her eyes, she tentatively extended her tongue and did as ordered.

"God bitch! Not like that. Put some fucking feeling into it."

Becky sensed Jack raise her fist again and began licking harder. *Never smelled a vagina up close before. Heard jokes about it smelling like fish. Doesn't smell like any fish I ate.* Nor was she sure how to describe the taste. *A little salty, a little sweet, and a little slimy.* It reminded her of something, but she couldn't think what. She didn't like it, but didn't hate it. *Better than being hit. Suppose I'll get used to it. No choice.*

Satisfied, Jack raised herself to climb off, paused and farted in Becky's face. Becky felt the wind from Jack's fart. *Cold. Thought it'd be hot. Smells like... shit.* Jack climbed off and returned to her own bunk.

Becky turned to the wall and stared at nothing. She thought she was strong, but rebelling against her conservative parents and controlling the easily gelded Tony hadn't prepared her for someone like Jack. A few hours inside revealed the truth.

***

Becky woke to the sound of Jack dropping a deuce. Her face and her vagina were sore. Jack didn't pull her punches. She reached her hand up to her face and tentatively touched it; swollen.

Jack said, "If anyone asks, you tripped and hit your face on the table."

Becky nodded.

"Been thinking, don't need a princess, need a slave. From now on, you follow me around and do what I say when I say it. You got that Slave?"

Becky nodded. *What does that mean? Something to do with my performance last night? Didn't I make her cum?*

***

They placed their breakfast trays on the table and sat. Scrambled eggs, baked beans, and half a tomato. Becky reached for her bread roll.

"I didn't say you could eat Slave," Jack said. "I'll tell you when you can eat."

Becky sat back and waited.

One girl asked, "Rough night Princess?"

Jack said, "Don't need a princess, that's Slave."

The girl repeated, "Rough night, Slave?"

"Tripped and hit my face on the table."

Jack ate her own breakfast and more than half of Becky's.

She belched loudly. "You can eat now, Slave."

Becky ate what Jack left. She couldn't quite process this world life thrust her into. She was powerless. All she could do was appease Jack to avoid being hit until she worked out how to regain control.

***

Becky—assigned to work in the laundry with Jack—was folding clothes, as Jack instructed. There were a dozen girls working there, supervised by one officer. It was a typical commercial laundry, two large washing machines, two gas powered dryers, a flat-iron for sheets and an ironing press for clothes. Concrete floor painted glossy gray. Hot despite two commercial fans. Jack worked the ironing press.

A girl, with dark hair cropped short on the front and sides, but long at the back, shouted, "Fuck this! These fucking sheets are burning my fucking hands."

She was alternatively shaking her hands, blowing on her fingers, and cursing the sheets coming off the roller of the flat-iron. Becky looked at her, small and wiry, nose ring, pierced tongue, seven earrings, a cross tattooed on her forehead. *Looks tough, could be a useful ally.*

The girl noticed Becky looking at her. "Hello pretty, looks like you had a rough night. If you need protection, we can work something out."

Jack said, "Back off, bitch, that's mine."

The girl nodded, looked Becky up and down and asked, "Is it for rent?"

"What you offering?"

The girl studied Becky again.

"Five."

"Done."

Jack turned to one of the other girls.

"Jo, you need to take a dump. The screw will escort you."

Jo nodded and made her way to the officer.

"Make it a long dump," Jack added.

After the officer left the laundry, the girl passed Jack five smokes, which Jack tucked inside her underwear. She approached Becky, who didn't understand what had transpired.

"Slave, go to the storeroom with her and do whatever she wants."

Becky began, "I don't want…"

A sharp pain radiated from her elbow when Becky landed on the hard concrete floor. She may not have seen it coming, but she knew exactly what hit her.

"Wasn't asking."

Becky used her sleeve to wipe the blood from her lip, split against her teeth, and rubbed her elbow. She dragged herself up and followed the girl, who was already lowering her pants as she entered the storeroom.

The girl, slacks and panties around one ankle, half lay on a stack of towels, and opened her legs. Becky had never seen a pierced clitoris before.

"Get to it, bitch. Don't have much time."

Becky glanced over her shoulder, thinking she might make a run for it. Maybe the guard would be back. Jack was standing at the doorway, watching. Not being able to think of anything else, and not wanting to be hit again, Becky meekly did as instructed. The girl grabbed her head and pushed it between her legs.

"Hard bitch."

Becky vaguely heard the laundry door being unlocked when Jo and the officer returned.

Jack shouted, "Time's up!"

The girl tensed, and suddenly her orgasm exploded into Becky's unsuspecting mouth. Gagging and coughing as the liquid forced itself down her throat, Becky collapsed to the floor.

The girl reached down to pull up her pants, saying, "What up bitch, never been with a squirter before?"

***

After work, an officer escorted them—in groups of four—to the showers and stood outside. Ten minutes later, the officer would stick her head around the door and yell, "Time's up." The ten minutes were flexible depending on the mood and character of the officer on duty.

Smoking is prohibited. Jack produced a cigarette and lighter from inside her folded towel. Lighting her cigarette, Jack said. “Wash me, Slave, but don’t wet my fucking smoke.”

Becky did as she was told. Despite her attempt to be careful, Jack’s smoke got wet.

Jack grabbed Becky’s hair and pulled her head back. She stuffed the wet cigarette into Becky’s mouth and forced her to eat it. Becky gagged and vomited a little. The water washed away both her vomit and her tears.

“Stupid bitch. Told you not to get it fucking wet.”

***

Two weeks later. Becky was sitting on the side of her bunk, wondering how she was going to survive five years of this hell. *At least things can’t get any worse.* She was wrong.

Jack, who was on the toilet having her morning dump, said, “Don’t know why I’m wiping my own ass when I got a fucking slave. Get over here and wipe my ass.”

“I’m not wiping your fucking ass.”

Jack stood, and with two steps, was beside Becky. She dragged Becky up by her hair and flung her across the room. Becky hit the wall, hard, and crumpled in a heap on the floor. Before she had time to react, Jack rolled her onto her back and rubbed her shitty ass in Becky’s face.

Jack stood to finish wiping herself with paper. Becky, gagging and retching, jumped up, ran to the sink, and vomited. She ran the water hard to wash the vomit away, picked up the soap and scrubbed her face with soap, water, and tears.

“Not fucking asking Slave. From tomorrow, you got a choice. Either wipe my ass with paper like a civilized fucking human being, or I’ll wipe it on your face.”

***

A month after her incarceration began, an officer told Becky she had a visitor. *A visitor, who? Didn’t expect to have visitors.*

As she left her cell to follow the officer to the visitor's area, Jack whispered, "One fucking word and I'll slit your fucking throat."

Becky tentatively entered the visitor's area. Uncle Myron was waiting for her. She was unsure how they were related; everyone in her community seemed to be related, fifth or sixth cousins or something. *What's he doing here? Haven't seen him in years.*

"Hello Rebekah."

"Hello Uncle Myron."

"Wanted to make sure you're okay."

"I'm fine."

"Do you need anything?"

"No."

The conversation continued in this vein for fifteen minutes. Myron reaching out, and Becky responding with a word. She wanted to talk to him. His visit made her feel less alone, but she worried she might say something to piss Jack off. She believed Jack could easily slit her throat, or worse.

Myron's visit gave Becky something she'd lost on her first night inside. A sliver of hope. She wanted to tell him how much his visit meant, but didn't.

Myron said, "Okay Rebekah, guess visiting time's over. I'll be back next month. If you need anything, let me know then. Deposited fifty dollars into your account in case you need anything. Will every month."

"Thank you, Uncle Myron," she said, hoping he could feel her appreciation. He reminded her there was a real world outside this hell.

A solitary tear caressed her cheek as the officer escorted him out.

Conversations with Frank

Myron had gone when Judy woke the next morning. He'd prepared coffee, John Farrington Blend ready to be percolated, and a loaf of fresh sourdough bread from Alice's Bakery ready to be sliced and toasted. Judy smiled. A note.

Enjoy your breakfast sweetheart, help yourself to anything, let yourself out when you're done. The door is self-locking. Sunday brunch at Bait & Switch. Talk later. M.

Along with the note, Myron left the promised *Report and Recommendations for Judy Vernon*. She glanced through it while she ate. *Straightforward, exactly as he explained.*

She showered, wishing Myron would return home and join her. *Certainly reawakened my flagging sex drive.*

Judy dressed and gathered her possessions. She felt comfortable at Myron's apartment, but wanted to talk to Frank about Billy. She called a taxi, collected her overnight bag, and headed downstairs.

Settling into the taxi, she gave the driver the address of Kansas Café, pulled out her iPad and added; *His and Hers Furniture* to her list of potential features… She remembered Myron's suggestion, which she also added, *Making Friends with the Dead.*

"Going somewhere, Judy?" Dorothy asked when Judy arrived at the café.

"Coming back."

"Usual?"

"Please, Dot." Judy made her way to her sofa, and the man who was always waiting for her.

"Good morning, Frank," she said, as if she expected him to answer, relieved when he didn't.

"Didn't get here yesterday, err… busy with Myron in the morning. You'd like him, have a lot in common. Says you and I have become friends. Do you think the living and the dead can become friends?"

Frank smiled at her, the pleading still in his eyes, but Judy was no closer to knowing what he wanted.

"I think we've become friends. Tell people we are, but are we? Think we would've been if I'd known you. Had we met, I wonder if I would've taken the time to know you, or continued to take you at face value as I did when I saw you?"

Dorothy delivered Judy's order.

"Thanks Dot."

B.B. King's version of *To Know You, Is to Love You* was playing. Dorothy returned to her counter. Judy resumed her one-sided conversation.

"You and Myron are similar. Both smart, and both much kinder than you need to be, perhaps than you realize. I admire Myron for creating opportunities and second chances for people, picking up those others have thrown away."

Judy took a sip of coffee, replaced her cup, took a small forkful of cheesecake, conveyed it to her mouth, but didn't chew. She let her taste buds absorb the flavor. She closed her eyes and allowed the music to wash over her. After swallowing, she opened her eyes, looked at Frank, and smiled contentedly.

"Seeing you reminds me how important it is to take time to enjoy the simple pleasures of life while we still can."

Another sip of coffee.

"Doubt you ever had Myron's stamina. Maybe you did, before you let yourself go. Perhaps I should ask Myriam about your stamina, Frank?" Judy laughed at her own joke.

"Met Billy yesterday. Easy to like. Has an interesting life now. Can't believe after everything, you still helped him. Says a lot about you, perhaps more than what you did to repay the investors. You truly are a man of rare character and integrity. I keep saying that, because it's true. Proud to be your friend."

"Billy doesn't want to remember he destroyed your life. Drinks until he forgets. Then he can find peace of sorts, not knowing where he is or what he's doing. Not an ideal solution, nor is the way he earns his drinking money."

Another sip of coffee, another bite of cheesecake, another moment savored.

"If one doesn't kill him, the other will. Been thinking about our Billy this morning. Don't believe there's anything to be done to help him. His lifestyle is more than a series of addictions feeding each other. It's Billy's choice. Guessing in time, forgetting will become his way of being. Poor likeable, weak Billy."

The sound of her phone interrupted her. She glanced at caller ID before she answered. Susie, who invited her to a family barbeque the following day. Judy happily accepted. Jenifer, the youngest of Frank's siblings, wanted to meet her.

"Well, Frank, seems I'm being adopted by your family."

Judy retrieved Myron's report from her shoulder bag. She read it carefully, paying attention to every detail. Bottom line was more income for little to no extra work.

Judy studied Frank, still staring at her, eyes pleading for she didn't know what. The Mel Tormé version of *Autumn in New York* was playing in the background. She felt at home and dreaded the day when Dorothy closed Kansas Café. *What'll happen to Frank?*

Judy worked because she enjoyed what she did, not because she needed the money to survive. Their similar outlooks, as well as their similar lifestyles and tastes, attracted her to Myron. *Has fingers in a lot of pies and likes what he does. Not motivated by profit.*

"Myron's an interesting man. Enjoys creating new ways of doing things and taking dead space and turning it into something productive. Uses disused retail space for pop-up adult vending machine outlets. Reaches out to fallen people and gives them the opportunity to get back on their feet. Think you and Myron would've been friends," she said, almost as if seeking Frank's approval.

She took a sip of coffee, picked up her phone and called Myron.

"Hello, sweetheart. Still at home?"

"No, but thank you for preparing exactly what I like for breakfast. At my café now, but will go home soon and do some work."

"Talking with Frank?"

Judy flushed.

Before she could respond, he continued. “You can tell Frank I took care of another three months’ rent for Billy.”

“That’s wonderful, but I wasn’t asking…”

“I owe Frank.”

“Why I was calling, other than to thank you for breakfast, was to accept your offer to establish those feature banks.”

“You’re welcome. Doubt it was as, err… vigorous, as yesterday’s breakfast.”

Judy wondered if Myron felt her flush through the phone.

“A woman called Sin… Linda Sinclair will be your account manager; she’ll call you later today.”

“Thank you. Oh… going to a barbecue at Susie’s tomorrow.”

“Enjoy yourself. Interesting how you’ve become integrated into Frank’s life.”

“Honestly, don’t know how it happened.”

“Sorry sweetheart, have a meeting in a couple of minutes.”

“Don’t be sorry. Attend to your business.”

Judy had the impression he was going to say something else, but he didn’t.

***

It took will power for Myron not to add three words when he said goodbye to Judy.

Judy’s unintended reference to Kansas Café as *her* café sowed a seed in Myron’s mind, which he planted to see if it would grow.

***

Judy shifted her attention to Frank.

“Myron took care of Billy for another three months. Safe for six months now. Myron makes a valid point. How did I become integrated into your life? Time to go. A lot to do this afternoon. See you tomorrow, my friend."

Judy gathered her belongings, paid Dorothy, and headed to Alice's Bakery, and then Lexington Deli, where she chose a fresh Caesar salad for lunch.

She reviewed the recording of her interview with Billy and updated Frank's book before writing her features. Sin called her during the afternoon to set up the feature and blog banks. When she finished her work, Judy went to the Farmer's Market.

***

"Morning, Frank," Judy said as she sat down on her usual sofa the next day. She was in a cheerful mood. Yesterday had been productive. Not wanting the pressure of work left undone when she attended the Farrington barbeque, she not only wrote, but later reviewed, her latest features.

"Pork chops for dinner last night, Frank. Can enjoy them while Myron is home with his family. His cultural obligations won't have a negative impact on my life. I'm certainly enjoying the orgasms he gives me, but Miss Kitty needs a rest. Damn, that man has some stamina."

Dorothy arrived with Judy's cappuccino and New York style cheesecake. Judy's habits would adjust and adapt to include Myron, but she would remain a creature of habit, and remain unaware of it.

Judy retrieved her iPad and opened the file containing her random thoughts, or, as she interpreted them, ideas for features.

"Need to write a few blogs next week, Frank. Thought I should go through my potential features and decide if any would be more suitable as a blog. Don't like the word blog. I'll think of them as *mini features*."

Harry Connick Jnr crooned his version of *It Had to Be You.*

She reviewed the list and began moving items more suitable as mini features.

"What do you think is trending, Frank?"

That's what I should do. Write mini features about whatever is trending. They'll sell better and establish me as a freelance blogger.

"Brilliant idea, Frank."

Judy opened *Google Trends* and began exploring. Most of the trending stories related to celebrities, politics, and sports, none of which appealed to her. She found what she wanted in the *Realtime Searches* section and decided on four mini features she believed she could easily write.

She glanced at her watch. "Goodbye Frank, off to spend the day with your family. *You* should've spent more time with them."

Farrington Family

Despite having stopped at Lexington Wines to collect two bottles of chardonnay, Judy arrived at Susie's earlier than expected. She pressed the doorbell. Susie opened the door immediately. *Must've heard the taxi.*

"Hello Judy, thanks for coming."

"Hi Susie. Thank *you* for inviting me. Am I first to arrive?"

"Wanted you here before the others so we could talk."

The women embraced. They'd moved beyond the light, pretend hug of acquaintances. Judy followed Susie into the kitchen.

"I'll put these in the fridge."

"You brought wine? Thank you. Fancy a cup of John's coffee?"

"Please, love that coffee. Myron's buying it now."

"Things going well with Myron?"

"Very."

"Could've brought him, still can."

"Sabbath," Judy explained. "Spends Sabbath with his family."

"Oh… is that a problem?"

"Not at all. I have free time each week to make plans around. Besides, the old girl needs a rest."

Did I tell Susie that? Told Frank, but that's different.

"A problem I'd be more than happy to have," Susie said as she brought their coffees—in mugs—to the table. "Speaking of which, did you see that cunt?"

Judy smiled. She guessed why Susie wanted her to arrive early.

"Yes, I talked with Myriam."

"What did you think?"

"Well…" Judy hedged. "She certainly is different."

"Can't trust her. She lies."

“She does. Just so you know, said she’ll contest Frank’s will.”

“She won’t. Frank didn’t have a will. According to the lawyers, if there’s anything, it’ll go to me, John, and Jenny. The cunt’s got no claim, but I figure she’ll try.”

Glancing at her watch, Susie went to turn on the oven.

“Time to cook the mac and cheese.”

“I was hoping you’d make it. First meal I cooked for Myron.”

“Seriously, are things going well with Myron?”

“Early days. The man has style and class. I’ve always enjoyed his company. That helps. We have similar tastes, which makes everything easy. No need for compromise.”

“Not to mention his stamina.”

Judy flushed. “That too.”

Susie returned to the table. “Are you complaining?”

“No, just need to give the old girl a rest now and then. Saw Billy too.”

“Really? How is he? How’d you track him down?”

“How is he?” Judy repeated. “Not a straightforward question. He’s a drunk. Drinks to forget. Once a choice. Doubt it is now. Beyond choice and beyond addiction, if there’s such a thing. More a lifestyle than an addiction. His only thought is the drink. No concern about what he’ll eat, if he’ll eat, or where he’ll sleep.”

Judy sipped her coffee and looked at Susie, who had become silent, a distant expression on her face. *What’s that look? Love? Guilt?*

Judy continued. “Getting money to buy booze is where it starts and ends. If not for Frank, paying rent on a room in a cheap boarding house, he’d be homeless.”

“Frank was *still* taking care of Billy? That surprises me. No, it doesn’t. That was Frank. People underestimate what a good person he was. Typical of him. Continue to take care of Billy and not tell anyone. My brother was a man of rare character.”

“He was.”

"What about poor Billy now? Do you think I should help him, pay his rent or something? Maybe I should see him?"

"He'll be okay for a while. I covered his rent for three months, and Myron's taken care of another three. Dancer, the barman at The Shipyard where Billy spends his time, will call me if he needs anything. If you visit him, go early in the afternoon, and only stay about an hour. That'll be when you catch him at his best, before…"

"Why would you pay Billy's rent?" Susie interrupted. "You don't know him."

"Billy won't pay it and that would put him on the street. Everyone says he's likeable. He is." Judy shrugged. "It's what Frank wanted."

"Everything you say is right, but why would *you* do it? You *don't* know Billy and you *didn't* know Frank."

Is she put out because I'm helping Billy? Guilt?

"You're right. I didn't know Billy, but I instinctively liked him. He still loves you, by the way. Walked away feeling he was a friend, same as I did when *we* met."

"Oh, I am, sweetheart. Felt the same, and you helping our Billy confirms that. I'm curious, and surprised."

"After one meeting, I referred to him as *our Billy.* Frank's inspired several features, so I figure I owe him a commission. From all I learned about Frank, I'm sure he'd want me to help Billy.

"Myron asked me if people can become friends with somebody after they've died. I feel Frank and I've become friends, but…"

"You certainly act like Frank's friend. One more question, sweetheart. Why would Myron pay Billy's rent?"

"Myron's taken to calling me sweetheart, too." Judy smiled. "Perhaps that's one reason, but I don't think he actually paid it, just took care of it. Myron's family owns The Old Seaman's Lodge where Billy lives."

"Oh… so if you two stay together, Billy should be okay for a place to live."

Definitely guilt.

"Think so, even if we don't stay together, but I believe we will."

"I hope you do. I like to see you happy, not that I've seen you any other way… Somebody's arrived." Susie noted as a car pulled into the drive. "Listen Judy, I have an ulterior motive for organizing the barbeque, Jenny. You spoke with me and John, and Jenny feels left out…."

"Sure, I was planning to speak with her."

"Hello Junior." Susie called out as she opened the door. Judy could imagine John cringing. "Judy was just saying she hopes you brought coffee because we finished my supply." To John's children she said, "Hi guys, your cousins are in the back watching *Harry Potter*."

Susie returned to the kitchen with John's wife.

"This is John's wife Alison. Ali, my friend Judy."

Wow! Even more beautiful in person. Judy stood and reached out her hand.

"Hello Alison, pleased to meet you."

Alison's stunning green eyes mesmerized Judy, almost the color of polished emerald with tiny flecks of gold, perhaps canary. Alison caught her breath. They held the handshake for what seemed an eternity, frozen under mutual intensity. Susie cleared her throat, dislodging the hypnotic handcuffs. Their eyes unlocked and each took a breath.

"Call me Ali. Heard a lot about you from John."

She turned to her sister-in-law. "Is that your amazing mac and cheese I smell?"

"In the oven, and Judy's got some chardonnay chilling in the fridge."

John came in carrying a box of groceries. Susie winked at Judy.

"Put those on the bench, Junior."

John looked at Judy, grimaced, and rolled his eyes.

Judy smiled. A few seconds of interaction carried layers of meaning. *I'm accepted into the Farrington Family. People take these moments for granted. They underestimate their significance.*

Drawn to his work in college, she mentally recited a few lines of a Rod McKuen poem…

While traversing a lifetime,
we should not concern ourselves
with steps that lead us
day to decade
or even year to year.
Moment to moment is enough…

"… are you with us, Judy?"

"Oh… sorry. Hello John, how've you been?"

"Very well, thank you, Judy Vernon," John replied exuberantly.

"Been much better in himself since he talked with you," Ali said.

John flushed and gave his wife a pained look.

"What about you, Judy? Talked to anyone interesting?"

Susie jumped in, "Judy's been talking with our Billy, and that cunt, Myriam."

"Really?" John asked. "How'd you find Billy?"

"Myriam knew how I could get in touch with him."

"How's your feature on Frank coming along?" John asked.

"I'll make the salad later, Susie," Ali said. "Don't want to make it too early. Better fresh."

Making the salad fresh. My kind of woman. Responding to John, Judy said, "Progressing, Frank was an amazing man. Hoping to talk to Jenny today, and then a few loose ends to tie up."

Another car arrived. Susie said, "Sounds like Jenny and Dave. Junior, can you get the door?"

John rolled his eyes. "Yes Susan," he said as he left the kitchen.

Ali laughed. "He hates being called Junior."

"Yeah, I know."

"Keep telling him you only do it because it annoys him, and if he stopped reacting, you wouldn't do it." Ali explained.

"He's a man," Susie said. "Men never fucking listen. Only pretend to when they're trying to get into our pants."

"That's the problem with being married," Ali said. "They don't listen, and they lose interest in what's inside our pants."

Judy said, "Yeah, a line in an Alanis Morissette song sums it up for me; *you wined me, dined me and sixty-nined me, but you never listened to a fucking word I said*, something like that."

Susie asked, "What about Myron, Judy? Does he listen?"

"I believe he listens, but that's his character. Myron listens to everyone and pays attention to detail. Can't say if he'll follow my advice, not given him any."

"So, a new relationship, and he's in every chance he gets?" Ali asked.

Judy flushed. "I give him lots of chances."

"Enjoy it while you can hon, after you marry, they lose interest; stop taking the chances you give them."

Susie said, "… but they still look for opportunities to get into other women's pants. They're all bastards."

"Married or not, they lose interest. For most, the hunt arouses them and when they no longer need to chase, there's nothing to make them horny," Judy observed.

Susie said, "Yeah, the magic is in the hunt, and it doesn't matter what they're hunting."

"Not only men," Ali said.

"True," Judy agreed.

"Well, Miss Alison, that's a conversation we'll certainly be having later."

"What're we having later?" John asked as he entered the kitchen.

"Mac and cheese," Susie said. "Not quite ready yet."

"Smells good."

"Sure does!" Agreed Dave.

"Hi Dave," said Susie. "Put your stuff on the bench. We can organize it later. This is my friend Judy. This is Jenny's husband, Dave."

Judy and Dave shook hands lightly.

"Junior, perhaps you and Dave can light the barbeque. Beers in the fridge. Jen," she called out to her sister in the living room with her children. "The kids are in the back room. Check if they need any snacks or drinks."

John grabbed two beers. "Come on, Dave, let's get this barbeque warmed up."

"Wine ladies?" Judy asked, bending to retrieve a bottle from the fridge.

Dave studied her ass as she bent over. Susie and Ali exchanged glances with a smile.

"Men," Susie said.

Susie placed four glasses on the table and handed Judy a corkscrew as Jenny entered the kitchen, saying, "Kids are fine."

"Judy, my sister Jenny."

"Hello Judy, pleased to meet you. Hi Ali."

Judy poured the wine and passed the glasses around.

Susie proposed a toast. "Cheers ladies. Here's to men, for all their faults."

Susie took the mac and cheese from the oven to rest.

Judy retrieved her digital recorder from her shoulder bag, suggesting she and Jenny go talk in the living room before the barbeque began.

Jenny nodded.

As she and Jenny left the kitchen, Judy overheard Susie say, "Well, Ali, just us now… tell me everything."

***

Ali shrugged. "It was a long time ago. Ancient history."

"So it won't matter if you tell me," Susie suggested.

"It's a long story."

Susie nodded at the door to the living room. "They'll be ages."

She's not gonna let me off the hook. Buried images and forgotten memories had created a kaleidoscope in Ali's mind since she met Judy. *Suppose talking about it will help put it into perspective.*

The Bored Housewives Club

Ali understood John needed to work overtime to support them and enable her to give up work and care for little Frankie, named after his uncle and godfather, Frank.

She appreciated John's sacrifice, but hadn't expected him to be working late every night and on weekends. Being short-staffed, John's employer was happy to give him all the extra hours he wanted.

"Better take it while I can get it," John said. "When they hire more staff, it'll dry up."

She considered asking him to work less, but didn't want to be one of *those* wives who was unappreciative of her husband's efforts.

Ali was the first in her circle to have a baby. Her friends were busy with their lives, and their activities weren't usually conducive for a woman with a baby in tow. She was lonely.

Reading the local newspaper while she enjoyed her morning coffee had become a daily ritual. Uninterested in the news, but it was something to do. She picked up her cup with two hands and sipped her coffee. Glancing at the classified section, an announcement for a meeting of *The Bored Housewives Club* caught her eye.

Thinking she might meet some women in a similar situation to herself—someone to talk with, and perhaps some activities to become involved in—she rang the contact number.

A woman answered. "Hello."

"Oh… Hi. I'm interested in learning more about *The Bored Housewives Club.*"

"We're always happy to meet new ladies. There's a meeting tomorrow. Would you like the address?"

"I… Yes, I was…"

"Thirteen-twelve Nightingale…"

"I know Nightingale. I wond…."

"Ten thirty-eleven, we usually start."

"Okay, what…"

"Got something on the stove. Can't talk now. See you tomorrow. Don't need to bring anything, just turn up. Bye."

Ali stared at the silent phone. *Know nothing about the club or their activities.*

***

Ali parked a few doors down from the address given. *A suburban home.* She got out of the car and surveyed her surroundings. *Quiet street, indistinguishable from mine.* She removed the stroller from the trunk and set it up on the sidewalk, with easy practiced movements. Carefully lifting Frankie from his seat, she placed him in the stroller. He looked around with what appeared to be mild curiosity.

She was thankful life blessed her with a quiet, undemanding child. Prior to giving birth, she read horror stories about difficult babies who required constant attention. If Frankie had been one, she didn't know if she could cope.

Last, she clipped the diaper bag—which contained more than diapers—on the handles of the stroller. Without the counterbalance of Frankie, the weight of the bag would upend the stroller.

She pushed the stroller along the sidewalk, turned into the driveway of a split-level Ash Gray brick home, and eased it up the three small stairs to the porch, and a white double front door. Ali pressed her finger against the doorbell, which chimed inside, and waited.

A woman appeared beside her. The woman stood uncomfortably close. Ali couldn't get a clear look at her. Slim faced with shoulder length light brown hair, brown eyes—Ali could only see one, but assumed she had a matching one—she wore a white blouse or dress.

"Nancy," she introduced herself.

"Ali."

"First time?"

"Yes, thought I might come to see what this *Bored Housewives Club* is about."

"Great, guess that makes me your welcome partner."

Before Ali could respond, the door opened. A dark woman with a big welcoming smile and sparkling, almost black eyes greeted them. A little dark inside, and with only the light from the open door to illuminate her, the woman seemed all white teeth and sparkling eyes to Ali.

"Hello Shy," said Nancy. "This is my new friend Ali who's joining us today."

"Hey Nancy. Pleased to meet you, Ali," Shy said, holding out a hand.

Ali took Shy's hand and lightly shook it.

"You too, Shy, thank you for having us." Referring to herself and Frankie.

Nancy led Ali inside, who followed, pushing Frankie's stroller. Nancy was wearing a dress, but being behind her, Ali saw little else of her. She still hadn't confirmed Nancy had a matching eye.

Shy announced to what appeared to be eight women in the room, some with babies and some—like Nancy—without, "Nancy has arrived with her new friend Ali."

They sort of collectively said hello to Ali, but none introduced themselves individually. The way she introduced her, gave Ali the impression Shy thought she came with Nancy. Unsure whether to correct her, Ali said nothing.

She examined the darkened room, curtains closed and lights off. *Strange.* Sofa and two matching armchairs, glass coffee table, a tall lamp in the corner, television mounted on the wall. The lack of light made it difficult to take in the room's detail or see the attendees clearly. Two women sitting on the sofa, the others standing in pairs. After introducing them, Shy sat in an armchair.

Nancy steered Ali to the vacant, comfortable looking high-backed armchair with wide arms. Ali wasn't sure of the color, pale mustard, she supposed.

"Would you like a glass of wine, Ali?" Nancy asked.

"Please, but just the one. I'm driving."

"Me, too."

Nancy headed off to get the wine.

Ali left Frankie in his stroller, content examining the people in the room with his usual mildly curious gaze. A quiet baby, easy to forget he was there. She positioned him beside the armchair.

Almost as soon as Ali settled herself in the armchair—as comfortable as it looked—Nancy returned, handing Ali a glass of white wine.

Nancy perched herself on the arm of Ali's chair.

The dimly lit room, being busy with Frankie, and Nancy's tendency to keep herself very close, made it difficult for Ali to gain an overall impression of her appearance. About ten years older than Ali, with fine lines around her mouth and eyes. A small, slightly pointed nose, a few scattered freckles, only noticeable because she sat so close.

Nancy offered a toast. "New friends."

Ali clinked Nancy's proffered glass and echoed her toast.

The wine tasted a little unusual. *Citrus notes, a hint of lime perhaps,* not what Ali expected. "This is different."

"Chablis, French, from the Burgundy region, I think."

"Nice."

"Just got the one?" Nancy asked, nodding towards Frankie.

"Yes, Frankie. What about you?"

"Got a couple, but they're at school now, thankfully."

Thus, Ali spent her afternoon chatting with Nancy—who, sitting on the arm of the chair, leaned in towards Ali—about nothing in particular.

Nancy was attentive, and made Ali feel welcome, as she suggested she would. Offering and fetching juice, coffee, and snacks.

Unusual. Doesn't appear to be any activities. Women stood or sat together talking to each other, mostly in pairs. *Don't know what I expected, not this. Friendly enough, nonthreatening.*

Music played softly in the background, mostly eighties love songs. *Eternal Flame, I Want to Know What Love is, Crazy for You.*

She didn't talk to anyone other than Nancy.

Nancy was saying, "… so your husband neglects you?"

"I don't feel neglected, not in that way. I mean, it's not as if he'd rather be at work than home with me…" she glanced at Frankie, who remained fascinated with all the new people to look at. "… us. Doing what I asked him to do. Didn't expect him to be working as much, is all."

"And you're bored looking for something to do with your time.

"Having an easy baby is a godsend, but it adds to the boredom, and I'm a little lonely, to be honest."

"Perfect. I'm free tomorrow. I'll come for lunch and bring a movie."

Nancy invited herself, but made it sound as if Ali invited her.

"Usually have salad for lunch, so I have little lunch stuff in," Ali explained, weakly hoping to dissuade Nancy.

"Love salad."

They exchanged phone numbers.

Nancy left the same time as Ali. They said goodbye to Shy, and the other women whose names Ali never got.

Nancy walked Ali to her car. After helping put the stroller in the trunk while Ali settled Frankie into his car seat, Nancy embraced Ali and kissed her on the cheek.

"Looking forward to our date," Nancy said as she headed to her own car.

"Me too," responded Ali absently.

Ali drove home, unsure what this *Bored Housewives Club* was, but she had someone to talk to all afternoon, and made a friend. Maybe that's what the club is, an opportunity to make new friends.

Alison and Nancy

Arriving at the front door, Nancy pressed the button. A melodic chime sounded inside. Ali didn't respond immediately. Nancy waited. *Must be busy.*

When she opened the door, the sunlight caught Ali's green eyes and canary flecks turned gold, which made them sparkle, like emeralds under a spotlight. *Those eyes.*

"Hello Nancy, please come in."

Nancy stepped through the doorway before responding.

"Hi Ali."

She walked in far enough to enable Ali to close the door, but kept herself close. Nancy placed her bag on the floor and embraced Ali, kissing her lightly on the cheek. Ali returned both.

Nancy didn't release her embrace directly. She held it much longer than one normally would when embracing an acquaintance. Ali didn't pull away. She matched Nancy's embrace for duration and intensity. Nancy smiled with satisfaction, kissed Ali's cheek again, and released her.

"Come through to the kitchen," Ali said. "Feeding Frankie, and then I'll toss the salad."

"Lead the way…" *and I'll check out your cute ass while I follow.*

Nancy glanced around the open-plan kitchen and dining room. A wooden dining table, with matching cloth upholstered chairs, marble kitchen benches, over wooden cabinets, almost the same color as the dining table. Nancy didn't pay attention to the detail. It wasn't Ali's furniture and fittings that interested her.

"I brought a bottle of wine," Nancy said. "Not driving. Took a taxi, so we can both have a drink."

"Good thinking… on both counts." Ali sat beside Frankie, feeding him lunch. "There's some fresh coffee in the pot. Cups are on that tray," she said, pointing towards a tray on the kitchen bench. "Pour us a cup while I finish feeding Frankie."

Nancy poured their coffee and brought the tray to the table. Ali had placed a small jug of creamer and a bowl of sugar cubes on the tray. The milk jug and sugar bowl matched the crockery.

"Milk and sugar?" Nancy enquired.

"Milk, no sugar."

They chatted about their husbands and kids as they drank their coffee.

Having finished giving Frankie his lunch, Ali took the tray with their now empty cups back to the kitchen, rinsed and placed them in the dishwasher. As usual, Frankie was quiet other than an occasional belch. They may have forgotten he was there.

Nancy studied Ali as she prepared their salad. Almost black shoulder length hair, a smile that would open doors. Nose and ears the appropriate size for her face. Her eyes were her one distinguishing feature, and without the flecks of canary or gold depending on the light, they'd be nothing more than pale green eyes. *Ideally proportioned.* None of Ali's features, other than her eyes, were remarkable, and yet, as a complete package, she was stunning.

Nancy smiled as Ali handed her two glasses and a corkscrew, saying, "Would you mind?"

"Not at all." *I'll open anything you want me to.*

Ali prepared a chicken Caesar salad, which Nancy enjoyed without giving it any thought.

Frankie, still sitting in his highchair, watching them eat with a strangely curious look on his face. *Surprised, Ali didn't put him down for his nap immediately after his lunch.*

Ali appeared to have read her mind. "Don't like to put him down as soon as he's finished eating. Change his diaper shortly, and he'll go down easily. Always does. He's a good baby, never any trouble or fuss. Seems happy to observe everything around him."

"Noticed that. Going to be a deep thinker when he grows up."

Nancy watched Ali clear away their plates. She enjoyed watching Ali. Every movement, fluid, economic and graceful. No movement exaggerated, nothing stood out to grab attention, and yet the symphony of her movements demanded attention.

"Why don't you take our wine through to the living room while I attend to Frankie?"

"Sure, I'll top up our glasses. I brought a DVD. *Thelma and Louise*."

"Wonderful, love that movie."

Nancy took the DVD from her bag, collected their glasses, and did as Ali suggested. She set the wineglasses on coasters and the DVD on a wooden coffee table and sat on a soft white sofa. The living room gave the impression of being clean and comfortable, but Nancy ignored the detail of the room.

Ali came in, turned on the television, and opened the DVD player with the remote. She picked up the DVD, removed the disk from its cover, and bent to insert it into the player. Nancy drank in every fluid movement and savored the experience, not taking her eyes from Ali and not blinking. Nancy waited until Ali sat on the sofa, leaving a standard comfortable distance between them, and then excused herself to go to the bathroom.

On her return, she sat beside Ali, leaving no distance between them, feeling Ali's body against hers. She smiled when Ali didn't adjust her position.

As they enjoyed the movie, chatting about what was happening on screen, occasionally sipping wine, Nancy slowly made herself more comfortable. Before long, her head was resting on Ali's shoulder, who didn't seem to mind.

The car sailed over the cliff. The closing credits began, and Nancy raised her head from Ali's shoulder as Ali turned to say something. Ali's words never left her throat. Nancy was very close, and Ali froze.

Nancy raised her hand to Ali's chin and guided their lips together. Ali hesitated for a moment and then relaxed into their first kiss.

They exchanged no words. Their eyes said whatever they needed to say. With one hand, they gently caressed the other's cheek, seeming to mirror each other. Their other hands lightly entwined. They kissed gently, exploring each other's mouths softly.

Frankie's cries broke the spell. Ali disengaged herself and silently left the room to attend to her son. When she returned with Frankie, she placed him in his playpen. She hadn't spoken since their first kiss.

Nancy said, "Better get going. Mine'll be home from school soon."

She retrieved her bag from the kitchen, took out her cell, and called a taxi.

Returning to the living room, she said, "Won't be long."

Ali ejected the DVD and replaced it in its cover. She wordlessly handed it to Nancy, who slid it in her bag, which she then placed by the door. Nancy turned and looked at Ali, who followed her to the door. Ali said nothing, her gaze fixed on Nancy's eyes.

Nancy stepped forward, stopping as her body touched Ali's. They embraced, lips still tingling from their earlier encounter, silently found each other. Nancy's hand slid down Ali's back and rested on her ass, which Nancy gently fondled, before using it to pull Ali into her. Ali didn't resist, her breathing quickened.

Frankie watched silently from his playpen, with that same curious look on his face.

The sound of the taxi's horn ended their embrace.

Nancy whispered, "I'll bring lunch tomorrow."

Ali said nothing.

Nancy collected her bag, opened the door and stepped outside, momentarily startled by the daylight.

***

Ali inspected herself in the mirror. A light raw cotton ice-mist blouse, neither loose nor tight. She undid one more button, revealing enough of her cleavage to show the lace of her sea-foam bra. Ali liked the color sea-foam because it was the closest color to her eyes. A short powder blue skirt, not too short, but short enough so any touch on her thigh would be against skin. Opened toed white shoes, with enough height to accentuate the shape of her legs.

She smiled, satisfied she'd be attractive to Nancy, assuming she was reading the situation correctly. She knew her ensemble would be attractive to a man. *Don't know if it will be equally attractive to a woman.*

She'd never kissed a woman before yesterday, not even as an adolescent. Kissing Nancy excited her. At least that's what she called it. In truth, it aroused her, but that, too, felt like an understatement. Unsure how to interpret the experience, she hadn't known what to say, so she said nothing.

Ali wanted more of those long, soft kisses. *Never been kissed like that. Should have told her. Should have said something.* She didn't know if it was how women kissed, or how Nancy kissed her.

Wonder what she'll bring for lunch. Ali was almost finished feeding Frankie when the doorbell sounded. She practically jumped up and ran to the door. When she opened it, Nancy stared at her. She heard Nancy catch her breath. Ali smiled, trying to appear in control. "Are you going to stand there staring, or are you going to come in?"

Nancy stepped in without taking her eyes from Ali, who closed the door and turned to face Nancy.

They stepped towards each other, embraced, their mouths connected, saying everything they needed to say without words. Nancy's hand glided down Ali's back, but didn't stop, instead it continued down to the edge of Ali's skirt before gliding back up to fondle her ass inside her skirt.

Ali—chest rapidly rising and falling with her heightened breathing—could have easily gotten carried away, but she pulled away, saying, "Need to finish feeding Frankie."

She led Nancy into the kitchen, and returned to feeding her son, as Nancy poured their coffee and brought it to the table, after placing their lunch—burgers—in the oven to keep warm.

An hour later, with Frankie in bed, and lunch consumed, they adjourned to the white sofa, settling down to enjoy the DVD Nancy brought, *Remains of the Day*. They needn't have bothered starting the movie. Neither watched it.

As the opening credits began, so did Nancy. Ali felt Nancy's hand against her cheek as she gently turned Ali's head and directed their lips together. Nancy's hand rested lightly on Ali's inner thigh.

The movie and Nancy progressed. Ali's pulse quickened as Nancy's hand slowly edged its way up her thigh. She opened her legs to allow Nancy's skilled fingers to ease the crotch of her panties aside and find the promised land. *My God, she knows her way around a woman.*

Nancy brought Ali to orgasm as the movie reached its climax. She did so in a measured, practiced way. Ali was ready almost as soon as Nancy touched her directly. Nancy somehow held Ali's orgasm at bay, bringing her to the edge of release, and then causing her to hold back. Ali didn't know how she managed it; she wouldn't have believed it possible.

Prior to marrying John six years earlier, Ali had experienced several boyfriends. She certainly enjoyed sex with them, never needing to fake an orgasm. This was something different. The constant building and relaxing, Ali didn't know how else to describe it, created an intensity she hadn't imagined possible.

Frankie woke.

Nancy glanced at her watch. "Time to go, I guess."

Ali sat up and buried her head in Nancy's shoulder, close to tears.

"Thank you," was all she managed to say.

Her mind, her whole body, spinning.

Nancy's hand was under her chin as she lifted Ali's head to her own and kissed her in that soft manner of hers. Nancy stood, lifting Ali with her. They embraced, kissing goodbye.

"Tomorrow?" Ali whispered.

"Tomorrow."

Ali's eyes followed Nancy as she walked into the kitchen to retrieve her bag and call a taxi. She studied her when she returned to the living room and deposited her bag by the door before making her way back to Ali, who hadn't moved. She liked the way Nancy guided their lips together. They kissed long and soft until the taxi's horn ended it.

Ali watched Nancy leave, and then turned to attend to Frankie, who was becoming impatient.

***

Ali returned to the living room after putting Frankie to bed. *I don't know what to do. What if I'm not good at it?* Nancy exited the bathroom and crossed the room to her lover. She took Ali's hand and kissed her gently on the lips.

"Tell me," Nancy whispered.

"I've never touched a woman, I don't..."

Nancy placed her finger against Ali's mouth.

"Take me to bed and I'll teach you."

Ali nodded, but didn't move.

"Take me now," Nancy said.

Ali led her into the bedroom.

"Undress me," Nancy instructed.

Ali began fumbling at the buttons on Nancy's blouse.

"No. Slowly. Follow my lead."

Nancy released a button on Ali's blouse, and gently caressed the newly revealed skin, nibbled on her ear, and moved to the next button. Ali matched Nancy, release, caress, kiss, until they stood together naked.

"Hold me, feel my skin against yours."

Ali stared at her lover's naked body, observing or perhaps absorbing every detail, pale skin, with an occasional dark freckle. Nancy's breasts sat neatly on her chest. They didn't dance, but moved slowly up and down in time with her breathing. Pink nipples did nothing, but beckon Ali's mouth. A neatly trimmed, light brown triangle hid the delights below. Ali stepped forward until their bodies touched. Nancy's soft skin against her own made her tingle as if her pores were dancing. *What's this? What's she doing to me?*

"Let your instinct take over. Touch how and where you want to."

Ali closed her eyes, using her fingertips to see, to sense, to drink in Nancy's features. Sparks of light and images took form in Ali's mind and her consciousness. *Is this because it's Nancy, or because she's a woman?*

Keeping her eyes closed, Ali eased Nancy onto the bed. She used her senses to maximize her experience, reveling in the sound of Nancy's breath, sometimes quickening, and sometimes deepening. Groans, moans, whimpers, squeaks, and breaths combining to create a symphony of pleasure.

The scent, or scents of a woman, of this woman beneath her, a blended and fluid aroma bathing Ali in a bouquet of delight.

Ali savored the tang of Nancy's skin, and dipped lower to taste the beads forming between Nancy's breasts, and around her hardening nipples. When Nancy writhed beneath her, Ali moved lower, her tongue parting swollen moist lips for the first time and being rewarded with layers of intense flavor bursting along her tongue.

Is this what making love to a woman is like? It's as if I'm exploring a celestial temple.

Nancy began whispering instructions to guide Ali's actions. Directing Ali's fingers to stimulate the perfect places on her clitoris and within her vagina. Nancy not only directed the placement, but also the pressure and intensity of Ali's touch.

Nancy tensed under Ali's touch, released something between a scream and squeal and her body began to jerk and shake as an orgasm—building for days—exploded in waves of ecstasy.

Ali lay contentedly beside Nancy. She could feel Nancy's body buzzing in the afterglow, or imagined she could. A self-satisfied expression graced her face.

Nancy said, "I think you got as much pleasure from giving me an orgasm as I got from having one."

"It's the first time I've given a woman an orgasm."

"Believe me, girl, it won't be the last."

Alison and Sara

Their relationship lasted three months before Nancy's visits became less frequent. As their encounters all but ceased, Ali wondered what she did wrong.

The day of a *Bored Housewives Club* meeting. Ali had attended several meetings—always with Nancy—and understood the purpose of the club.

When Shy opened the door, they embraced warmly and kissed on the lips. *Wonder what it would be like to be with an African American woman.*

She entered the living room to find Nancy sitting on a sofa, with her arm around another woman. Ali froze. Frankie's stroller in front of her. She stared at Nancy, not knowing whether to cry or scream.

Sara, who came in shortly after Ali, spoke before Ali gathered her wits. "No point looking at her with those puppy dog eyes. For Nancy, it's about the conquest. Once she's conquered, she loses interest. Preys on fresh meat. You're not the first and won't be the last."

Ali looked at Sara, whom she met two or three times. "You too?"

"A long time ago."

Ali glanced around the room. All eyes seemed to be on her. *Everyone knew what was happening, except me. I'm so stupid. What was I thinking?*

Pulse racing. Face heated. Breathing shallow. Scream building. She felt Sara's hand on her arm. *Calm down.* Her eyes returned to Sara. *Gotta get outta here.*

"Wanna go somewhere? I have my car."

Sara smiled. "Sure, let's do lunch. There's a decent café nearby."

***

She directed Ali to a small suburban café.

Sara entered first and held the door open for Ali to push Frankie's stroller through.

Wood-grained Formica tables, and black metal framed chairs with orange vinyl upholstery. Metal napkin dispensers, and a round metal tray containing plastic squeeze bottles of ketchup, yellow mustard, a bottle of McIlhenny's Tabasco sauce, and salt and pepper shakers. *Tacky, but spotless.*

Ali settled herself, stroller beside her. Sara retrieved a chrome highchair from against the far wall. She lifted Frankie from his stroller and settled him into the highchair.

Ali took a container of pureed food from her diaper bag and placed it on the table, intending to feed him while they ate. For now, Frankie was happy inspecting a new environment.

"Such a quiet boy," Sara said, nodding in Frankie's direction.

"Yes, always looking at things, as if he's taking everything in. Often wonder what he's thinking."

"My daughter's a little older. In preschool every day. Well, six days a week. I'm in retail, so I work Saturdays. Sundays and one day during the week off, which suits me. Every other Sunday, she's with her father."

"You're not together?"

"Divorced. Knew I was a lesbian when I got married. A mistake. Getting married, I mean, not being a lesbian. You?"

Ali was about to say no, but hesitated while she gathered her thoughts. *Oh... she's asking if I'm married, not if I'm a lesbian.*

"Yes," she said. "John."

Sara, looking at the menu, asked, "What do you fancy?"

Am I a lesbian?

"What?"

"What do you want?"

I want to know if I'm a lesbian.

"I don't know. I'm happy with my life as it is, I suppose…"

Ali noticed the amused expression on Sara's face, and the menu in her friend's hand. As she pieced the question together, her cheeks warmed.

"Oh… sorry. I um… not sure." Regaining her composure, Ali asked, "Anything you recommend?"

"Their chicken and avocado sandwich is delicious."

That'll do.

"Sounds great, and a coffee, I think."

"Me too, I'll go order."

While Sara ordered, Ali contemplated the question. It had never occurred to her she was a lesbian. Her automatic answer was no. *Maybe I am a lesbian. Thought it was just Nancy.* She shook her head. *Does having a three-month relationship with one woman make me a lesbian?*

Ali studied Sara as she returned. She'd paid little attention to her when they met previously.

Thick shoulder length dark brown hair, big brown eyes—what people described as cow eyes—Ali supposed. Matched by an almost bovine nose, which didn't look out-of-place, perhaps because of a mouth which reminded Ali of the entrance to an amusement park she once visited. She had deep laugh lines on either side of her mouth, with a hint of dimples. Sara was chubby, which her tight jeans did nothing to disguise. Her large breasts strained against her tight white T-shirt.

Cuddly, not chubby. Ali smiled at Sara. *Amiable. I like her.*

"What?" Sara asked.

"Nothing. Thinking how much I like you."

Ali's words earned her an enormous smile.

"Might see if I can have Frankie's lunch warmed up a little."

Ali returned almost immediately. "They're going to bring me a bowl of hot water to sit it in."

"Most of the girls at the club are married," Sara said. "That's why I joined. Not looking for a relationship, just some company sometimes."

"Took the name of the club at face value. Met Nancy on the doorstep the first time I went."

"Oh, so you weren't looking for…."

"No. Didn't know I could until Nancy."

"No experimenting when you were younger?"

"Never."

Sara opened her mouth to speak, but the café owner arrived with a bowl of hot water and their coffees on a tray. Ali placed Frankie's lunch in the water to warm. He was content sitting in the highchair, looking around him.

"Wouldn't be surprised if he becomes a writer," said Sara. "He seems to take everything in."

"Yes, he's always curious."

Their sandwiches arrived.

They finished eating, consumed their coffee and all but exhausted the small talk.

"Better take him home for his nap, and he needs changing, but I live nearby so that can wait 'til we're home. Do you, umm… have any plans this afternoon?"

Sara smiled. "I do now."

"I'll get the check, and we'll head out."

"Already taken care of."

"Thank you. Let's go."

***

Having attended to Frankie, Ali came into the living room where Sara sat on the white sofa, enjoying a glass of wine. Ali extended her hand, inviting Sara to stand. She pulled her close. Lips connected for the first time.

Ali smiled at her body's reaction; her motivation for inviting Sara home had been her own curiosity about her sexuality rather than a specific attraction to Sara. *Not only Nancy, who makes me wet.*

She led Sara to the bedroom, where each slowly and deliberately removed the other's clothes, studying unfamiliar bodies as if reading braille. *She's a little shy, but has no reason to be.* Ali guided Sara to the bed. She enjoyed being the one to take the lead.

After they made love, Ali cuddled into Sara contentedly. *Cuddly.*

"Sara," Ali began gently caressing her lover's soft stomach, "would you like to make this a regular, err… liaison?"

"I would."

Ali kissed Sara's left nipple.

***

Ali and Sara had been dating—perhaps an exaggeration—for around six months. They met for sex, usually at Ali's place. It never occurred to Ali that John might come home from work unexpectedly. Occasionally, on a Sunday, they took in a movie and went back to Sara's for a matinee.

Ali now accepted that despite a lifetime of heterosexual relationships, she was a lesbian. She reflected on her close friendships with various women she worked with or girls she attended school with. In hindsight, what she put down to strong bonds of friendship had been something more, something she might have learned earlier in her life, if any of them had made a move on her.

She was contemplating divorce. She loved John, *a good husband.* They still had sex once a week. She didn't hate it. Never had. *Sex with men isn't bad, but not even close to what I experience with a woman. Two women. I've had sex with two women.*

She supposed she could remain married to John and take her pleasure with the ladies of *The Bored Housewives Club. Feel guilty cheating on him.* At first, she told herself, *being with a woman isn't cheating. Horseshit.*

This was how she spent her time now—when not entertaining Sara—speculating on what she should do with her life.

Alison and Frank

"Fuck! Fuck!"

Ali stared at the stick in her hand.

"Fuck!"

It told her exactly what the two discarded sticks in the trash told her. *How the fuck can I be pregnant? How do you think, you dumb bitch? You shouldn't have let this happen.*

"Fuck!"

What the fuck am I going to do? Have an abortion? Keep it? Won't tell John. Suppose I'll have to if I keep it. If I get an abortion, I won't tell John. Won't tell anyone. Don't I want a divorce?

Ali stood, loosened her robe and allowed it to drop to the floor, stepped into the shower, and turned the water on. The hot water stung as it cascaded over her shoulders. She didn't flinch. She wished the water would wash everything away. *Don't want to give up Sara.*

After her shower, she dressed, made herself a coffee, and sat at the dining table. *Glad Frankie hasn't woken up.*

"Fuck me!"

Isn't that how we got into this mess? Need to talk to someone. Sara? No, she can't help. Wants me to divorce John. Move in with her. So much for not wanting a relationship. John? Fuck, what would I tell him? Susie? No, she'll probably tell me I'm a stupid bitch. Already know that. Frank? Guess I can talk to Frank...

She picked up her cell, chose Frank from her contacts and selected call. The phone rang once, then he answered.

"What do you need, Ali?"

"Need to talk to someone. Can you call in for lunch? Little Frankie misses you." She added, trying not to sound desperate.

"Supposed to have lunch with Billy... not important. Twelve-thirty, okay?"

"Perfect. Thank you."

"You wouldn't ask unless it was important."

They said their goodbyes and Ali went to wake Frankie.

***

Ali heard the melodic tone of the doorbell and glanced at her watch. *Twelve thirty-six. Frank.* She opened the door. When he stepped inside, she hugged him as though she didn't want to let go.

"I appreciate you coming, Frank. I know you're busy, but…"

"Nonsense Ali, nothing's more important than family."

"Come through to the kitchen. I'll finish feeding Frankie and then make lunch. Schnitzel, okay?"

"Perfect. Would you mind if I fed Frankie?"

Ali smiled. Frank was his usual calm, patient self. A little of the tension left her.

"Please, he'll like that. I'll make some coffee and prepare lunch."

"Hello little man," Frank smiled warmly at his godson, who laughed and waggled his legs at the sound of the familiar voice.

Ali brought their coffees on a tray. Her hands shaking a little as she set the tray on the table.

"Sit down Ali. Tell me what's on your mind, while we have a coffee. Lunch can wait a few minutes."

"Waiting on the potatoes, anyway."

Ali sipped her coffee, trying to keep her hand steady. She studied Frank.

"I, um… not sure where to start."

"Start wherever you're comfortable starting."

"I don't… I…"

Ali took another sip of coffee. Her mouth dry, her hand still shaking.

"Take your time. We've got all afternoon."

Her breathing, fast and shallow. She forced herself to take a deep breath.

"I-I-I'm a lesbian."

Her words hung in the air. Speaking the words, for the first time in her life, eased her mind, despite her apprehension of Frank's reaction.

"Okay." Frank shrugged his shoulders and continued feeding Frankie.

His calm acceptance gave her confidence to continue.

"My girlfriend…" as the words passed her lips, their truth warmed her, as she acknowledged the reality to herself.

"My girlfriend wants me to divorce John and move in with her."

Frank didn't answer immediately. He studied her.

Ali searched his eyes for judgement but saw none.

"It'll break his heart, but he'll recover. John's resilient."

Not the response Ali expected. "Thought you'd tell me I shouldn't."

"John's my brother and I love him, but I can't ask you to sacrifice who you are for him."

"I'm pregnant!"

Silence.

Ali wanted to scream. *Say something!* She tried to read his eyes. She could almost see his brain working in overdrive, but he said nothing. *Jesus Frank, would you speak to me?*

Finally, he said, "That complicates things."

That's it?

"Going to have an abortion, divorce John, and move in with Sara."

That'll get a reaction. It didn't. Ali picked up her cup and sipped her coffee to calm herself.

"Does John know you're pregnant?"

"John knows nothing. Doesn't know I want a divorce. Doesn't know I'm a lesbian and doesn't know I have a girlfriend."

"What do you want from me, Ali?"

"I want… I don't know what to do."

"Sounded like you know exactly what you want to do."

"I don't. What should I do Frank?"

Frank shrugged. "Make lunch and let me think about everything."

Make lunch? I throw a handful of grenades, and your response is make fucking lunch? At least, I would've got a reaction from Susie. Ali fought the urge to send her cup flying into the kitchen. *Make fucking lunch! Are you fucking kidding?* Ali wanted to scream. Not knowing what else to do, she returned to the kitchen to finish making lunch.

Frank said, "Frankie looks ready for his nap. I'll put him to bed."

Let's ignore the elephant and focus on the mundane.

"He'll need changing."

"I can change a diaper, easier these days than when I used to change Jenny's."

Ali was placing lunch on the table as Frank returned to the dining room.

"Smells wonderful," he said.

After he sat down, he ate some schnitzel and mashed potato together.

"This is excellent, Ali, much better than I'd be eating if I lunched with Billy."

Yes, Frank, I asked you here to assess my culinary skills.

"Maybe, but you wouldn't have the drama."

"It's Billy… I probably would."

After this, he ate in silence. *For fuck's sake, say something!* Ali barely picked at her lunch. The butterflies in her stomach weren't hungry. Her tension returned, her nerves screaming on her behalf.

When he finished eating, Frank said, "I can't tell you what to do, Ali."

What? All that thinking and nothing!

He continued, "Whatever you decide, I'll be here for you."

More than I would've got from Susie.

"Thank you, Frank."

"What I can do is offer you two questions and an observation."

Finally!

"Okay."

"How did you feel when you looked at Frankie for the first time?"

Not expecting that! Ali didn't answer immediately. She recalled the birth of her son, remembering her first reaction.

"He took my breath away. I stared at him in wonder."

Frank nodded. "Have you met a lady who took your breath away the moment you saw her?"

Nancy took my breath away the first time we had sex. "Not when I first saw her, no."

"You supposed I'd tell you to stay with John because I don't want him hurt, and yet I was the one you confided in."

Ali remained silent; her mind, which had been in turmoil, went blank.

"You don't need *me* to tell you what to do."

Her silence continued.

Finally, she said, "Thank you, Frank."

Ali cleared the table and made them another coffee. After coffee and small talk about the family, which seemed surreal to Ali, Frank stood to leave.

He embraced her. "Whatever you decide, Ali, I won't judge you. I'll be here for you. Count on it."

***

Sara was excited, as always, on Ali-day. *Love spending time with Ali. Love Ali.* She wanted to bed Ali the moment she saw her walk into the club meeting. Could barely contain herself the day they lunched in the café. When Ali invited her home, she was trying to work up the courage to suggest it herself. *Didn't think Ali would be interested in a fat girl like me.*

She expected it'd be a onetime deal, Ali looking for validation, having confirmed Nancy moved on. When Ali suggested they continue to see each other, she was ecstatic. Ali's the most beautiful woman she's been with. *Didn't count on falling in love.*

She didn't expect Ali to divorce John and move in with her, but she hoped. Sara thought about Ali constantly, and the more she thought about her, the more she loved her. When she's honest with herself, she suspects Ali's fond of her, but doesn't love her. She's not always honest with herself.

Sara appraised her image in the mirror. *Wish I wasn't so fat. Ali doesn't seem to mind. Cuddly, she says. Time to go.*

When Ali opened the door, Sara sensed something in Ali's manner. *Going to tell me she won't divorce John. Didn't expect her to. She's fucking beautiful.*

Sara stepped into Ali's living room, closing the door behind her. They embraced and kissed. Sara savored the moment, as she always did. *Something's different. Something's not right.*

She followed Ali to the dining room. *Frankie, already in bed. Lunch on the table. Gone to a lot of trouble.* Sara's stomach sank, her nerves were on edge, the elation she always felt on Ali-day deserted her. *Something's wrong.*

Sara sat at Ali's invitation. *Not her usual confident, graceful self.*

"What's up, Ali?"

She didn't want to know, but wanted to get it over with, whatever it was. She focused on Ali. *Flustered, nervous, hesitant. I don't like this.* She waited.

"I'm sorry, I can't divorce John." Ali began.

Is that all? Knew that.

"Didn't expect you to, but I hoped."

"Been seriously thinking about it. Told my brother-in-law I was thinking of divorcing John and moving in with my girlfriend."

Girlfriend! Brother-in-law?

"You told your brother-in-law? John's brother?"

"Needed someone to talk to."

You can talk to me.

"And he told you not to divorce John?"

"No, he didn't. Thought he would, but he didn't."

Something more. Bad news coming. "There's more, isn't there?" *Not looking at me.*

"I was thinking about leaving John, but everything has changed now."

"Why?"

"I'm pregnant."

"Pregnant? How?"

"The usual way. Thought about an abortion, but I can't do that, even for you, Sara."

"Don't want that. Would never ask you to…"

"I know Sara. Being pregnant changes everything."

"Doesn't have to… we can still."

"No, Sara, I can't keep living this double life. Was going to divorce John. Can't now with the baby."

Sara was trying to process what Ali was telling her. "What're you saying, Ali?"

"We can't see each other after today. This is our last time together."

"I-I-I…"

"No, Sara, I'm sorry, but I can't do this anymore. I want you to take me to bed, make love to me one last time."

Sara needed time to think. *No, no, NO! This can't be happening. Can't end. Not like this. Everything's been going so well. Pregnant. How'd she let herself get pregnant? Don't want this.* "We can raise our children together. Get married. I love you, Ali. Please don't do this. We can make it work…"

"Thought of that, Sara. Everything you say is right. I know it is. But… I can't do that. I can't take John's children away from him. He's a good man. He doesn't deserve that."

"What? I'm not a good woman?"

"Oh darling, you are. You're an amazing woman. I love being with you. It's just…"

You don't love me.

"They're John's children."

Can't do this… Gotta get outta here. Sara's pulse was racing, her stomach in knots. Her heart held together by a thread. She wanted to scream, wanted to run. "Please Ali, I'll do whatever you want."

Ali sat at the table; head bowed. Their lunch untouched. Sara took in the lunch on the table. *Ali went to a lot of trouble.* She stared at Ali. *Forlorn. Ali's hurting, too. This must be so hard for her.*

She stood. Unsure what to do or what to say. She was numb, suspended somewhere between acceptance and hope. Sara took Ali's hand and led her to the bedroom. She undressed the woman she loved, slowly and purposefully. She wanted to savor every moment.

Sara made love to Ali, knowing it was the last time. She could sense Ali had decided.

Spent, Sara lay staring at the ceiling. Ali was cuddling against her as usual, gently caressing what Sara considered her flabby stomach. She was self-conscious the first time Ali had done that after they made love. Since then had reveled in Ali's touch. Until today.

Today, her touch felt surreal. Sara sensed it was the last time she'd feel Ali's touch. She couldn't endure anymore; she was barely holding herself together. "Sorry, Ali, I need to go."

Sara got up and quickly dressed. Ali got up too, and put on her dressing gown, following Sara to the kitchen to retrieve her bag and then to the living room. Reaching the front door, Sara turned to embrace Ali as they wordlessly said their last goodbye.

Sara felt Ali shudder. Saw her eyes fill and overflow as tears streamed down Ali's face.

Unable to hold herself together for even another minute, Sara turned, opened the door, and stepped into the daylight. She almost ran to her car, fumbling with the keys, desperate to get away.

In her car, Sara wanted to speed away. She couldn't. No longer able to hold her emotion at bay, she sobbed uncontrollably as her heart shattered.

***

Ali stared at the front door. When Sara closed it, she knew it was the last time she'd see her. She cried silently, tears rolling down her face, like raindrops quietly rolling down a window.

Only now, at the end, did Ali realize she was in love with Sara.

Numb, she turned and slowly made her way, one deliberate step at a time, to the bathroom. She allowed her robe to slide off her body and lay crumpled on the floor. She turned the shower on and stepped in, willing the water to wash away her tears and her love.

***

The next morning, Ali sat at the dining table. She picked up her cup and sipped her coffee. *Have to tell John soon. Not ready yet. One more thing I need to do.* She grabbed her cellphone and called Susie.

"Hi Ali, what's up?"

"Hey Suse. I'm pregnant."

"Congratulations. How'd John take the news?"

"Haven't told him yet. Waiting for the right moment."

"Okay. No one will hear anything from me."

"Need a favor. Would you be able to take Frankie today? Something I need to do."

"Sure, he's no trouble. He'll just sit and watch me all day."

"All he ever does. Drop him around in an hour."

"Fine."

"Thanks again, Suse."

"It's nothing."

Ali ended the call. She had one more call to make.

***

Ali pressed her finger on the button and heard the familiar chime from inside. Shy opened the door and Ali stepped in.

They embraced and kissed, but not as usual; Ali held the kiss much longer.

"What's up?" Shy asked.

"I wanted to tell you in person. I won't be able to attend club meetings anymore."

"Women stop coming all the time, usually they just disappear. You didn't need to come tell me in person."

"It's just that…"

"Don't need to tell me why."

Ali looked at her.

"Wanted to say goodbye."

Shy nodded.

Ali took a step closer and kissed her again. Slowly and intentionally. Her hand drifted down to Shy's blouse, and she began undoing the buttons. Shy slid her hand down Ali's back and began fondling her ass.

They undressed each other, letting their clothes fall to the floor. Naked, Shy took Ali to the bedroom and lay her on the bed.

After they delighted in each other, Ali dressed, kissed Shy goodbye, left, and walked thoughtfully to her car.

***

Shy stood at the door, watching Ali walk away. She smiled. She'd wanted Ali since the first time she saw her standing at the door with Nancy. Shy had no illusions; she knew what it was about. *Not the first time I got lucky because some cute slice of vanilla wanted a taste of chocolate.*

It was why divorced Shy, and married Nancy, had established *The Bored Housewives Club.*

***

Ali sat in her car. She retrieved her cell from her bag, called Frank, and told him of her decision.

One thing about Ali that few, if anyone understood, was her ability to single mindedly pursue a goal, at the exclusion of all else. At that moment, sitting in her car, still feeling the glow of making love with Shy, she resolved to focus her energy on being the best wife and mother she could.

Her desires, her nature, she buried deep within herself and from that day, she would not permit herself to even look at another woman.

***

A dozen years passed. Ali never allowed herself to think about *The Bored Housewives Club.* Never allowed herself to think about Nancy. Never allowed herself to think about Sara. If a memory tried to resurrect itself, she buried it deeper.

She buried that time of her life so deep she almost forgot it happened. Feelings and experiences erased from her existence.

In a single moment, when she took Judy's hand and their eyes connected, everything changed. It all came flooding back.

Jenifer and Billy

Judy sat on Susie's sofa observing Jenny, who glanced around the familiar room, then sat beside Judy instead of in the chair opposite.

We're going to be friends. "Do you mind if I record this?" Judy asked. "It saves taking notes."

Jenny studied Judy, as if assessing her, then nodded. "A long time ago… I was a different person then. Where do you want me to begin?"

Intriguing "Start wherever you want, and we'll see where it leads, but first…" Judy picked up her glass. "Frank."

"Frank," Jenny echoed. She savored the wine or her brother's memory before swallowing, then set her glass on the coffee table.

Judy said, "From what I learned, your brother was a rare man."

Jenny began. "People think they knew Frank, but they didn't. They assume I didn't know him well because there's a big age gap between us, but Frank had an enormous influence on me. There was a depth to our conversations, which made us close and revealed a part of Frank few noticed."

Jenny paused, leaned forward to reach her glass, sipped her wine, and returned it to the table. Judy mimicked her.

"Some say Frank was naïve, which is why Billy and Myriam destroyed his life. He wasn't. He knew who they were and accepted them because of who he was.

"Frank said, 'If we try to change someone, to help them be our idea of a better person—we don't really love them—we love our image of them. Many relationship problems exist because we confuse who people are with who we want them to be. Love is acceptance without qualification, or condition.' Frank never wanted to change Billy or Myriam. He wasn't naïve about them either."

Jenny stood. She picked up her wine and took a sip. Still holding her glass, she began pacing.

Judy used the opportunity to observe her. Light brown hair that finished halfway down her back, almost the same shade as her curious eyes. *A woman who pays attention to what's happening around her.* Her features, unmistakably Farrington, but softer than her siblings. Jenny wore a pale pink—more of a blush than a color—T-shirt with tight blue jeans and lace-up runners. *Nice figure.*

Jenny stopped pacing but didn't sit. No longer looking at Judy, she began talking.

"If I'm going to talk about how we became close, I need to put it in context. So, I'll tell you everything."

Judy said, "I won't publish anything you don't want me to."

"When we reach puberty and discover masturbation, it's wonderful. Normal, but I was insatiable. At it all the time. Many nights I didn't sleep. I didn't know what was wrong with me. Now I understand… addicted to the chemicals produced within my body by the orgasms." A thoughtful expression, another sip of wine and more pacing. Judy remained silent, watching her, waiting for Jenny to continue, and admiring the way Jenny's body moved in concert with her fitted jeans.

"Never looked into it, nor did I have treatment or go to meetings. They have them, you know, groups for sex addicts like Alcoholics Anonymous. Mine just went away, thankfully. I assume it was hormonal changes. Something like the way a hormonal imbalance causes bad acne in some people. Progressed from masturbation to having sex with older boys—many. Problem was, they never lasted long. Sometimes they came before we barely started. Developed a reputation as the school slut. Didn't care. Only cared about my need."

Jenny drank some wine, paced some more, and then stopped. She smiled at Judy and rejoined her on the sofa. She began talking again, quietly confiding in a friend.

"One day, when my parents had gone away for a few days—don't remember where—I bunked off school, dressed in a very short, pleated skirt, and button up blouse, put on some makeup. Planned to go to a bar and pick up an older man." She shrugged. "Tired of boys who couldn't satisfy me."

Judy nodded.

"Almost ready to leave when there was a knock on the door. Billy. Assumed he was looking for Susie and told him she wasn't home. He said, 'No not Susie. Sometimes drop in to scrounge a coffee and sandwich from

Marion.' My mother. Offered to make him a coffee, put the kettle on, but never made the coffee. Seduced him instead. Not that it took much to seduce our Billy. Sex with Billy was good. The only man I ever met whose sexual appetite matched mine."

With a wistful look in her eye, Jenny continued. "Crazy in love with Billy. All I wanted to do was fuck, and he obliged. Only a matter of time before someone caught us… Luckily, it was Frank."

***

"We should close the door, Billy."

"Yeah, in a minute Jen." Billy didn't close the door.

Sitting on the bed, naked, he pulled Jenny on top of him. She straddled him, wrapped her arms and legs around his back, buried her head into his shoulder, and began riding him. She liked to be in control of the rhythm.

Jenny sensed rather than heard someone at the door. She raised her head and opened her eyes. "Frank!"

She was on the point of orgasm when she leaped off Billy and dived under the sheets in a single motion.

***

Startled, Billy jumped out of bed and almost froze naked. The only part of him that voluntarily moved was his eyes. His gaze alternating between Frank and his clothes, strewn on the floor. His erection shriveled involuntarily. *Fuck! Should have learned from that time he nearly caught me with Marion.*

"Frank. I…"

"For fuck's sake Billy. Get some fucking clothes on. I'll be downstairs."

***

Frank sat at the kitchen table, drinking a coffee. When Billy stepped in, he pointed him to the chair opposite.

"She's underage Billy."

"I guess… I didn't mean to. I…"

"I'm not angry Billy. From what I saw, she was more than consenting. Doesn't change the fact she's underage. You could both be in a lot of trouble."

"Yes, I…"

"I won't ask if you considered the consequences. I know you didn't. You never do…" Frank said with a hint of bitterness.

"I didn't think…."

"No Billy. If someone catches you, you'll go to jail, having to register as a sex offender for the rest of your life."

"I didn't…"

"Do you want to go to prison, Billy?"

"No. Are you telling me not to see her anymore?"

Frank shook his head. "That's between you and her. I want you to promise me you'll tell no one about having sex with Jenny."

He studied Frank. *We're the same age, but he always seems so… Like my older brother.* Frank was frowning, his face a blend of concern and confusion. *He's as protective of me as he is of Jenny.*

Billy nodded. "Okay, Frank, I promise I won't tell anyone."

"Good enough. You should go now."

Billy opened his mouth to speak, but changed his mind. He stood, walked to the door, stopped, turned to look at Frank, opened his mouth again. Shook his head, turned and quietly left.

***

Jenny glanced at the clock. *Half an hour since Billy went downstairs. Guess he's not coming back.* Jenny's need gnawed in the pit of her stomach.

She rolled onto her back, opened her legs, and slid her hand between them. She didn't think of anything; didn't need to. Attending to her need didn't take long; she was almost there riding Billy.

She barely smiled. The experience was more mechanical than sexual. She allowed her orgasm to wash over her, giving the fix a chance to do its job.

The gnawing diminished, but remained. *Not surprised.* Doing it herself was like being with those inept schoolboys. Being with Billy was different. Her orgasms were intense and always satisfied her. She opened her legs and slid her hand back down for an encore performance.

She allowed her second orgasm to wash over her. The gnawing gone, she smiled. She felt normal.

***

Frank was on his third coffee when Jenny walked into the kitchen. *Surprised he's still here.* She sat opposite and stared at him defiantly.

"I love Billy. I *won't* give him up."

"I'm not asking you to, Jen, but you're only sixteen. If you get caught, Billy will be in a lot of trouble, probably go to jail."

"Are you telling me to stop fucking Billy?"

"I'm not telling you what to do. I need you to understand there could be consequences."

"Did you tell Billy to stop fucking me?"

Frank studied his sister over the rim of his coffee cup.

"Told him if anyone finds out about you two, he'll probably go to jail."

Her posture became less tense, her attitude softened.

"But you didn't tell him to stop?"

"No point. People think our Billy doesn't know right from wrong. He does. Billy thinks he can't control himself. He can. Billy's problem is he can't grasp the concept of consequences. He doesn't consider the consequences and ignore them. That step doesn't exist within Billy. He's almost like a child, surprised his actions have consequences."

"I love Billy. He's the only one who can satisfy me. I want to spend the rest of my life with him."

"He's an easy person to love, but he'll destroy your life at some point. He won't want to, and he won't mean to, but he will. You need to understand that."

"Is that why Susie dumped him?"

"No, Susie can control him and keep him out of trouble. She chose not to accept the responsibility."

"I can. I can accept the responsibility."

"No Jen. You're not Susie. You're soft and kind. Susie is strong willed."

"You mean she's hard and judgmental?"

"She might be, but she'd move heaven and earth to get you out of trouble if she needed to."

"Maybe I can become more like her, learn to control Billy?"

Frank smiled and drank more coffee, now cold.

"Susie is Susie. You're gentle and kind, just be you."

"I need Billy, Frank. I have a problem. Do you want me to go back to being a slut?"

"I want you to be yourself, whatever that is."

"Even if I'm a slut?"

"I'm your brother. I love you. No matter what you do, I'll always love you. If we love someone, we love them exactly as they are, even though they're flawed. We're all flawed. How can I love you and put conditions on my love?"

Frank looked into his sister's eyes and said, "I love you, Jenny."

Jenifer and Frank

"Talking about Billy that day was the moment me and Frank connected. We remained close until he passed."

Jenny's lip quivered. She closed her eyes. Despite her efforts, half a tear escaped from one. Her face tensed as she swallowed the tears back. Judy reached out and gently touched Jenny's hand.

Jenny took a deep breath and finished her thought. "I stopped fucking Billy, but didn't stop fucking. Billy had an enormous appetite for sex. Others couldn't match my appetite. Glad it went away. Thought I might need to become a porn actress to survive."

Jenny drained her glass and looked at Judy, who mimicked her.

"You want another wine?"

"Please, Jenny."

Jenny headed to the kitchen under the guise of needing to refill their glasses. Judy guessed Jenny wanted to compose herself and allowed her to do so privately.

Judy stood and stretched. Then, right arm across her chest, resting lightly on its counterpart just above the elbow, and left hand gently cupping her chin, she wandered aimlessly around Susie's living room. *Obviously prepared what she wants to say, but she's right, even people who loved and believed in Frank sold him short.*

Ali... not affected like that for a long time. Ever? Lost in thought, Judy didn't notice Jenny's return, who appeared beside her and handed Judy a glass.

"They're all out the back."

"Guess they'll be ready to eat soon."

They clinked glasses, each sipped their wine, and returned to the sofa. Judy pushed images of Ali out of her head. Jenny began talking almost as soon as she sat down.

"The second conversation I want to talk about happened years later, when Frank was running for mayor."

She sipped her wine again, then put the glass on the table.

"A function at Frank's home, family, friends, clients, and the guys supporting him. I slipped upstairs to use the bathroom where it was quiet, with no one waiting. Opened the door to discover Myriam with Frank's main backer.

"Couldn't stand the guy. He was fat and sleazy. The type of guy who makes you shudder and cringe in disgust by the way he looks at you. Didn't seem to bother Myriam… on her knees giving the fat, sleazy bastard a blow job."

Why do people use fat as an adjective to emphasize the negative traits of a person? Fat, sleazy bastard. The man being overweight isn't related to him being a sleazy bastard. Being a sleazy bastard is far worse than being fat, but adding the adjective fat seems to make sleazy bastard worse.

I saw Frank as a fat, angry man, not an angry man. Why did I do that? Possibly a feature in there somewhere. Being fat isn't a negative character trait, is it? God! Too much to think about. Judy shook her head to refocus herself.

"I waited until the event was over and took Frank into his office for a chat. Told him what I witnessed. Frank said, 'in Myriam's mind she's helping me.'

"He didn't get angry or appear hurt or upset. I was confused. He explained. 'There are three types of people in the world: people who are self-aware, people who aren't self-aware, and people who think they're self-aware, but they're not. Few people are the first type. People who are the second type can't know it. Myriam is like most people. She's the third type, but thinks she's the first type.'"

Jenny reached for her wine, apparently buying time to think. A look of concentration on her face gave the impression of trying to remember Frank's words accurately.

"I asked Frank to explain. He said, 'People create a persona which they present to the world. People will often be self-aware of their persona or image because they created it. They believe they're self-aware, but because their self-awareness doesn't extend beyond their persona, they're not really self-aware.' People underestimated Frank. He had a depth few recognized."

Judy believed she was self-aware. Like most people, Judy was Frank's third type; self-aware of the persona she spent a lifetime meticulously crafting with the aid of the features she researched.

Jenny offered her glass to Judy for a toast. Judy retrieved hers from the table and touched it against Jenny's.

"Frank," Jenny proposed.

"Frank," Judy echoed, looking not at Jenny, but at Frank's eyes firmly implanted in her mind.

Jenny continued. "Frank said, 'Myriam has gotten lost in life. She believes all she has of value is her sex. She's created a persona based on her belief that her self-worth doesn't extend beyond how she can use her body to get what she wants in life. There's much more to Myriam. She doesn't see it, but I do and I love her.'

"I asked if he wanted to break through her persona so she could develop into this better person he saw. He said, 'For many, their persona is all they have. If we take it away from them, they may have nothing. I see Myriam as she is, both the persona and the person beneath. I love her and accept her. Even if Myriam doesn't believe in herself, I believe in her.'"

Susie entered the living room.

"Lunch will be ready in around fifteen minutes."

"Okay Suse," Jenny responded.

Judy nodded.

Susie left without interrupting further.

Jenny continued, "I asked if Myriam going with other men broke his heart. He said, 'Not important. If Myriam stops loving me, it wouldn't break my heart. Love doesn't need to be reciprocated to be real, although life is better when it is. Love grows when it's reciprocated. Love feeds on love.' He thought about it for a long time, then said, the only way Myriam could break his heart is if she stopped believing in him."

Jenny stood, took her glass from the table, and began pacing again. She stopped and studied Judy. "Frank made me think about love and relationships, probably why I can accept Dave, despite… Changed my opinion of Myriam. Stopped hating her. She's a slut, but I'd been one too.

If my hormonal imbalance—or whatever—hadn't corrected itself, still would be.

"Myriam saw me leaving Frank's office and glared at me. I smiled the sweetest smile and suggested she use the strongest mouthwash she could find before she kissed my brother with that mouth."

A Taste

Noticing Jenny's glass was empty, Judy drained her own.

"My turn," she said, heading to the kitchen to refill their glasses.

Ali was preparing the salad when Judy entered.

"Oh. Hi Ali."

Judy tried to remain calm, despite being aware of Ali's presence. She placed the glasses on the island bench and retrieved the wine from the refrigerator. When she straightened and turned, she felt before she saw Ali beside her. She placed the wine beside the glasses and turned to face Ali, who stepped close to her.

"Here," she said, offering a spoon full of salad dressing. "Try this."

Ali raised the overfilled spoon to Judy's lips. Judy opened her mouth to taste Ali's offering. A little of the creamy, thick liquid escaped her mouth and trickled down her chin. Ali raised her other hand and gently wiped away the overflow.

She studied her outstretched finger and then fixed her gaze on Judy. Eyes locked on Judy's, she raised the finger to her mouth, extended her tongue and, using the tip, she licked her finger clean, with three long slow passes of her tongue.

Judy stared at Ali's tongue. Her pulse raced, and her breathing quickened. She fidgeted; unsure if she twitched or imagined it. Judy tried to swallow, but her mouth was dry. Extending her own tongue, she moistened first her top lip and then her bottom, with slow deliberate movements. She forced herself to look away.

"I, umm… better get this wine back to Jenny."

Ali said nothing and returned to the salad.

Judy refilled her and Jenny's glasses, and noticing Ali's glass, nearly empty, stepped over and filled it.

"Salad dressing, mustard, honey and macadamia. Found it in that shop with all the homemade jams and stuff near the Farmer's Market." Ali explained.

"Exquisite Jams. I know it."

"Anyway," Ali continued. "Over there the other day for John's coffee, and I had a walk around. Don't get to the gourmet district often. Browsing and noticed some tasting pots on the counter. Interested because it's kinda expensive. So, I try the dressing and wow! Had to buy some. Told John if he can buy his special coffee, he can buy my special salad dressing. He couldn't think about arguing."

Smooth, almost silky. Luscious yet a little zesty. Perfectly balanced. Must get some. "It tastes amazing."

Ali looked directly into Judy's eyes, but didn't respond immediately. Judy wanted to look away but couldn't.

Eventually Ali said, "Oh, I'm sure *it* does!"

Oh, God! Judy's still racing pulse carried an excess of blood to her face.

"I-I-I… Jenny's waiting."

She absent-mindedly placed the wine bottle on the bench, retrieved their glasses, and almost scurried to the safety of the living room.

Jenny, still pacing, stopped and looked at Judy.

"You seem flustered. Did something happen?"

"I-I-I… No. No, nothing. I'm concerned I'm keeping you from your family. They'll be ready to eat."

"Nonsense. They won't start without you. You're the guest of honor."

"Oh. I…"

Judy calmed herself, walked over to Jenny, and unsure which glass was whose, handed her a full glass. They clinked glasses in a silent toast and returned to the sofa.

Having regained her composure, Judy prompted. "You mentioned a third discussion."

Jenny resumed. "It happened after Frank lost everything. I expected he'd hate Billy, but he didn't. Still loved him. Frank wasn't concerned about Billy going to jail, said, 'Billy's adaptable. He'll survive and come out the other side.'"

True, but he didn't walk out unscathed.

"Myriam stopped believing in him, which broke his heart. Frank said, 'There's a solution to any problem, but people usually give up if the solution requires time. People don't like time, want immediate or at least foreseeable solutions.' Myriam didn't believe Frank could solve their problems. She left him. Everybody assumed her leaving broke his heart, made him bitter. Not bitter, disappointed."

Jenny offered her glass to Judy, in another silent toast to her brother.

"Frank said, 'I can't control the time it'll take to resolve my problem, because of the bankruptcy. On the bright side, it gives me time to learn new skills, and develop a workable plan. Need to repay everyone who lost money because they believed in me, before I can re-establish my life.'"

Oh Frank, so close.

"I suggested the bankruptcy meant he had no obligation to repay people. He said, 'Legally perhaps, but I can't take my life back unless I repay people. If I did, it wouldn't be *my* life.' People thought Frank was hiding in his room depressed because Billy and Myriam destroyed his life. Not true. He was learning new skills, developing ideas, building and testing business models until he perfected one. Frank never believed his life was destroyed. It had been dismantled, but he could rebuild."

Sorry you ran out of time, Frank.

"When you write about Frank, don't sell him short, or portray him as a victim of trusting the wrong people. He ran into a problem that required time to solve."

"I won't." Judy offered her glass. "Frank."

"Frank. Better go out to the barbeque now," Jenny suggested.

"Yes, sure they're waiting for us."

"Enjoyed talking with you. Remind me of Frank. You're not judgmental. I like that. Besides, in our family, Susie has enough judgement for us all. You're a listener like me. I like that too. I'm the only listener in the family. That's why Frank could talk to me."

"You've given me a lot to think about, and revealed a depth to Frank I hadn't discovered previously." Judy stepped to Jenny and hugged her.

As they made their way out of the living room, she passed Jenny her business card. "Would love to catch up any time. We can meet for coffee, dinner, or whatever you fancy and just listen to each other for a while."

"I've every intention of seeing you again. Susie and John seem to have adopted you, so you're almost part of the family now." Jenny said, as they entered the kitchen on their way outside.

***

After the barbeque, Judy helped Susie wash the dishes.

Susie said, "Bloody Dave couldn't take his eyes off your ass."

"Really? Didn't notice," Judy lied.

"Yeah, you did. Not exactly subtle."

Judy laughed it off, but admitted to herself she liked the attention.

"You were certainly the center of attention; Ali's eyes were glued to you all afternoon."

Susie seemed to be taking the credit, but Judy was unsure for what.

"Oh, I…"

"And you spent the afternoon avoiding looking at her."

Did she miss anything? "Oh, I…"

"Like you're avoiding looking at me now."

"Oh, I…"

"Our Ali made quite the confession."

"Really?"

"Yes, apparently she used to be a lesbian."

"*Used* to be?"

Frank, You've Changed

Judy was looking forward to her brunch with Myron. She sat on her sofa at Kansas Café, staring at Frank who'd lost weight.

His clothes now sat comfortably against his body; the buttons no longer strained against his bulk. *Do ghosts have a body?*

She frowned, attempting to process what she was seeing and understand why Frank had changed. She'd deduced previously it was her perception of him that changed, not Frank. This didn't prevent her from asking the question.

"Why have you changed, Frank?"

Frank Sinatra's *Beautiful Strangers* began playing, which distracted her thoughts away from Frank and towards Ali.

Recently, her appearance received more attention than it had for years. *Perhaps something to do with the energy I'm putting out since I became involved with Myron.*

She recalled the woman in the bookstore the day she met Frank and wondered if Myron was a result rather than the cause. Frank was possibly the catalyst for the sexual energy she now exuded. Maybe the experience of watching Frank die had somehow caused a change in her body chemistry.

Whatever the reason, she enjoyed the attention. She no longer felt she was getting old. *Better do some research to find the best exercise to ensure my ass remains damn fine for many years to come. Could be a feature in that.*

Dorothy arrived with her cappuccino but no cheesecake. Judy didn't want to spoil her brunch appetite.

"Here you are, hon."

"Thanks, Dot."

Judy reflected on her interview with Jenny the previous day. Irritated with herself. She hadn't intended to talk with Jenny. She assumed the age gap between Jenny and Frank meant they weren't close.

This was against everything she'd learned about not assuming what people did and didn't know, and to interview everybody with an open mind. One reason Judy had developed her interview technique of letting people talk. *The second time I didn't follow the principles of Journalism 101 since I began investigating Frank's life.*

She returned her attention to Frank.

"Why do I keep forgetting the basics with you? Why have I been making assumptions about you since we met? Why, like everyone else, do I continually sell you short?"

Frank shrugged. She studied him, as if waiting for him to answer her questions. "And why have you changed?"

Judy raised her cup, closing her eyes as she inhaled the faint aroma, muted by the milk. She allowed the warm, creamy liquid to rest in her mouth before swallowing. She replaced her cup and instinctively picked up the napkin to wipe the milk foam—always deposited by the first sip of cappuccino—from her upper lip.

"Did anyone other than Jenny understand your depth, Frank?"

Silence.

"Yes, I suspect you're right. Perhaps Myriam. I certainly need to talk with her again."

Another sip of cappuccino while she reflected on what she learned yesterday.

"I think you may be right, Frank. Every problem has a solution, but time is often the barrier, and must be removed from the equation."

Judy stared silently, allowing a solitary tear to slowly make its way down her face. Brushing the tear away, she continued. "You really were a remarkable man. Every time I think I understand you, I discover another layer. Learning about you, my friend, is like peeling an onion."

Frank gave her a silent half smile that seemed tinged with sadness.

"I'm not sure if I understand more or less since meeting you. I don't understand how there have been so many changes in my life. How did we become friends? I believe I know you better than anyone. How did we become such close friends that I've become part of your family?

"How have my pheromones cranked up to my teenage levels, so that my *damn fine ass* has become a magnet with people of both genders wanting a piece of it? Not that I'm complaining..."

Judy took another drink of her coffee, wondering if it would be preferable if Frank answered her questions or remained silent.

"If you are... well, were so wise and deep, how did you become so obsessed with paying everyone back and neglect yourself? Unless you knew you had a heart problem and wanted to repay everyone before you died? Is that it, Frank? If so, why doesn't anyone know?"

Why not just have treatment? Frank was not forthcoming with any answers.

That's it! "I see you at your best now. You're more handsome this way. Shouldn't have let yourself go, especially if you had a heart condition."

Frank smiled at her, but the pleading remained in his eyes.

"And I wish you'd tell me what you want. Why are you still here?"

Judy finished her coffee. Myron would collect her soon. Her attention switched from Frank to the other man in her life.

"Why has Myron fallen in love with me?"

Silence.

"Yes, Frank, I *do*. Can tell by the way he looks at me. Well, yes, I have... I guess *he* can feel it too. What about our age difference? I'm older than Myron, and then there's the religion thing. Also, children. Not interested in having children, too old and settled for that nonsense now.

"I like things exactly as they are, but I'm old enough to understand relationships need to evolve, but what can this grow into? I blame you, Frank, not sure how, but I know it's your fault. If we could stay as we are now, it would be perfect for me. I think for Myron too, actually. He's an only child, and I'm sure his parents will want him to carry on the family name or something. Speaking of children, why didn't you and Myriam have children?"

Her phone rang. She glanced at the caller ID. *Of course, it is.*

"Good morning, Myron."

"Hello sweetheart, I'll be there in around ten minutes."

"I'll be waiting outside. Missed you, by the way."

"Missed you too. Very much, in fact."

She organized her stuff into her bag, glad she put in several hours' work last night after the barbeque and had all features and mini features almost finished. She needed to review them again before she sent them off.

Judy settled with Dorothy, said her goodbyes, and went outside to wait for Myron.

Sunday Brunch

Judy leaned against Myron's shoulder. They quietly held hands during their ride to the docks.

The taxi stopped at The Old Seaman's Lodge.

"I have a bag in the trunk," Myron explained. "I'll leave it in the storage room rather than lug it around all day."

"Good thinking."

Judy expected to see Irving sitting behind the desk, but it was another man, *also past his prime*, who was on duty.

"Hello Jeffery," Myron said. "Need to leave my bag here."

"Hello Myron." Jeffery buzzed the door of the storage area open. "I'll let Irving know if you haven't collected it when he starts."

"Thanks," Myron said as he exited the storage area, allowing the door to close behind him.

They began walking to the restaurant, holding hands.

As if he read her thoughts, Myron explained. "Few people between twenty-five and fifty work in our companies. Usually, kids out of school or people over fifty, prematurely put out to pasture."

"No bright young men like you?"

"We want people no one else wants. Older people bring years of experience and a work ethic from another era. We value them, treat them with respect. They reward us with loyalty and dedication."

They crossed the road and stood in front of O'Rourke's Park.

"Time for a stroll through the park?"

Myron glanced at his watch. "Sure."

There were few people in the park, mostly men wandering around aimlessly. Judy guessed their purpose. On the way to the seawall, they passed the public facilities.

"Billy's office." Judy observed.

"Will he be working now?"

"A little early, appears to be a few potential customers hanging around."

They reached the seawall; Judy leaned against the wall and closed her eyes. Myron stood behind her, hands resting gently on her shoulders. The cool breeze from the water caressed her face, making her hair dance gracefully. Inhaling the salt air, eyes closed, she listened. Quiet except for the sound of the wire halyard lightly tapping morse code against the flagpole, and a few seagulls squealing like a squeaky gate in the wind. The sea barely whispering as it gently caressed the seawall.

She opened her eyes and took in the bay's vista before her. Silhouettes of fishing boats docked at the Fisherman's Pier, resting until dusk, when they'd head out to sea for their night's work. Perhaps a dozen small sailboats silently gliding across the water, weekend sailors getting the most out of the light breeze. The sun reflected on the water, bright stars of sunlight appearing and disappearing as the sun painted images on its choppy canvas.

Judy could've stayed in that moment all day, but it was time for brunch.

They walked past pier nine, The Sex Pier. Judy noticed a police car parked adjacent and glanced under the pier. Two officers talking to the working girls, who were hoping to earn enough for their morning fix. *Should pay them a visit one day. Might be an interesting feature.*

Late morning, and the dock area was quiet.

Judy resumed their conversation, interrupted by their stroll through the park. "So, you don't hire people in their prime?"

"People in their prime have one eye on their job and the other on their exit strategy to the next step, the next challenge, the bigger paycheck, and so they should. They're not loyal, nor are they dedicated to any employer. Hiring older, discarded people makes good business sense, and it's the right thing to do for the community."

At Bait & Switch, they sat upstairs in a window seat with a view of the harbor and the adjacent dock. The décor was unremarkable: woodgrain Formica tables, padded black vinyl covered chairs, both with a black metal frame. It was the fresh seafood, the location on Fisherman's Pier and its popularity, which created the atmosphere. Judy smiled and reached out to take Myron's hand.

"Thank you. I don't get down to this part of the city as much as I should."

Myron smiled, raised her hand, and kissed the back of it.

"I come here for business, but I should come here to enjoy the atmosphere sometimes."

"I wonder why different parts of the city have different atmospheres? Why do they feel so different? Is it their history?"

Myron shrugged, "Perhaps their usage?"

"When the atmosphere of a district changes, what's the catalyst for the change?"

"Maybe demographics?"

"I might write a feature. In fact, I'll write a series. Could do a feature on each of the city's districts and then round it off with a piece about what makes them different."

"Like to read that. I read all your pieces, have since we first met. Mama will read it too. Turns out she's a fan, been reading your features since you began in the newspaper!"

Why is he discussing me with his mother?

Judy opened her mouth to ask, but the waiter arrived to take their order. *Frank, I blame you.*

Myron looked at Judy. "Seafood platter for two and a bottle of Chardonnay?"

"Perfect."

As the waiter left with their order, Judy said, "You discussed me with your mother?"

"Yes, sweetheart. Told my parents about a smart, beautiful, warm, kind, amazing woman I'm seeing."

"Really?"

"Yes."

Judy looked away, and then, raising an eyebrow as she looked at him sideways, asked. "What did you tell them?"

Myron smiled and winked. "Told them you're sensational in bed, easily the best sexual partner I've had…"

"Enough Myron!"

The temperature rose in her face, despite a big, beaming, shy smile.

"… and that your ass is so sexy, every time I look at you, I get hard."

Attempting to regain control of the conversation, Judy said, "I feel the same, my best sexual partner and a tongue a thirsty lizard would be proud of."

The waiter arrived with their wine in an ice bucket. Judy avoided eye contact, as the thermometer that was her face skyrocketed. After filling their glasses, he retreated to the safety of his station.

Trying to compose herself, Judy took a sip.

Myron laughed, amused by Judy's loss of composure. He offered a toast. "Us!"

She repeated his toast. They maintained eye contact while they sipped their wine.

Judy said, "I do like the way we fit together; our thinking, our values, our taste, our outlook on life."

Myron smiled. "Not to mention how well we fit together physically. Being inside you is like sliding into a velvet pouch…"

"Myron please! You're going to have me cuming in my panties."

"*That* I would love to see," Myron said with a smile.

Wishing to change the subject, Judy said, "Myron, I understood shellfish wasn't kosher?"

"It's not. Pork and shellfish. Basically, comes down to the animal's diet. We can eat animals with a plant-based diet, but not those whose diet is meat-based or are scavengers."

"Do all Jewish people avoid pork?"

"I understand the percentage of people who identify as Jewish and don't eat pork is less than eighty percent, but don't know for sure. Some only eat a little pork, like bacon. The percentage of Jews who don't eat shellfish is even lower, and those who don't eat meat and dairy together are less again."

Myron picked up his glass, offered Judy a silent toast, sipped his wine and continued.

"I don't eat pork, but that's all I don't eat based on my religion, more culture than religion. I love shellfish. My parents' generation is stricter. They don't eat pork, nor shellfish. Meat and dairy in the same meal never happens."

"Meat and dairy?"

"Yes, I love a Rueben Sandwich but having corned beef and Swiss cheese together is prohibited. If I followed that rule, I'd never have tried a Rueben Sandwich."

"Interesting."

"When I'm with my parents, I follow their strict diet because I respect them. I don't want to make them uncomfortable."

Judy frowned and studied Myron's face. "You were talking to your mother about me?"

"Mama's been reading your work since your newspaper days. Has an alert set up on her search engine for your new features. Surprised she knows how to do that. Mama likes your positive outlook. She said, 'In a world where everyone seems negative, and every news item is critical, it's refreshing to have someone looking at everyday life positively and raising issues for people to think about. No negativity, and no judgement.' She said, 'What she has to say makes sense.'

"Made me proud of you," he added.

Waves of emotion washed over her. *Being with him is like having multiple emotional orgasms. Is there such a thing? Is our sex great because I'm having both physical and emotional orgasms? Emotional Orgasms, there's a feature in that.*

Myron continued. "When I told her I was dating you, she said, 'Well, that explains it.' Apparently, she read your latest feature about stereotypes, and it felt familiar to her. I read it too. An interesting and insightful piece."

"I didn't realize it was published. Did you mind me drawing on you for one of my examples?"

"Not at all, sweetheart. As Mama says, you're not a critical writer. Gave me some stuff to think about... positively. Mama asked if I had an issue with being given such a Jewish name. I don't! I like my name, it fits me. Sometimes people not seeing beyond the stereotype is useful. I asked Papa if he read your work. He said, 'I don't need to because Mama is always reading something she's written to me.'"

"Really?"

His parents apparently like me. Important. If they didn't, it would put pressure on our relationship. Judy decided her three concerns; age difference, culture, and babies, would wait for another day.

Myron excused himself.

Judy took her iPad from her shoulder bag and entered the details of her new feature ideas, *Psychology of the City Series, A Glimpse at The Life of a Crack Whore, Emotional Orgasms*.

The waiter brought their seafood platter, placing it in the middle of the table.

"For two?"

"Yes, ma'am."

"It's huge."

"Yes ma'am, enjoy."

Judy studied the platter. Mostly grilled or barbequed. She took inventory: lobster, crab, langoustine, mussels, scallops, oysters, tiger prawns, shrimp, fish, squid, and char-grilled octopus. It came with two sides: large cut chips and a salad.

Who needs sides? Glad Myron eats shellfish.

Myron returned.

"Wow! So much food, and it looks amazing."

"Yes. Far too much for us."

"Well, too much for one sitting. Rather than waste it or keep eating until we become uncomfortable, we should take what we don't eat home. Can use it as the base for our dinner later."

"You must've read my mind. Contemplating, picking up some Lobster Bisque from The Soup Master on the way home. Create a seafood soup with what we can't eat now."

"Wonderful idea. Doing anything with you is easy. No debate and no drama."

"Are you suggesting I'm easy?" Judy asked with a mischievous smile.

"I certainly hope so, because my…"

"Eat Myron!"

Judy sampled the platter.

Why do people over-eat to save wasting food and make themselves uncomfortably full just because they've paid for it? Changes the experience and diminishes a memorable culinary occasion. Could be a feature in there somewhere.

They ate slowly, taking time to enjoy brunch and each other's company. When they were comfortably full, they asked for what remained to be packed up.

Glad we agree on everything. Some couples can't agree on even the most insignificant and unimportant things.

Judy retrieved her iPad from her shoulder bag and added three notes to her list of ideas for features: *Uncomfortably Full*, *Waste or Waist* and *Constant Bickering.*

Everybody has random thoughts. Judy derives an income from hers.

The packing of the remains of their platter was impressive. Everything individually wrapped and placed in a Styrofoam box with containers for the salad, chips, dressing, and sauces. The box was in a netted carry bag. Very hygienic and convenient, but perhaps not environmentally friendly.

An amazing way to spend our Sundays. "Myron, can we make a permanent booking here for Sunday brunch?"

He smiled. "Already have."

They left Bait & Switch and headed for The Shipyard. Judy wanted to check on Billy and ask him some follow-up questions.

Myron and Dancer

Dancer, standing behind the bar as usual, glanced up from the liquor order he was completing when they entered and beamed.

"Judy Vernon. Didn't expect you back, and certainly not so soon. An unexpected pleasure. And young Myron didn't realize you knew each other."

Judy shot a look at Myron. He hadn't mentioned he knew Dancer. Not that Myron, knowing Dancer, was a surprise. *He seems to know everybody.*

"Hello Dancer," Judy said. "Good to see you again."

Myron smiled and winked at Judy. "Hello Dancer, been a while."

"Five years."

"You thought anymore about my offer to renovate?"

"What, and turn this place into a fag bar? More money in it, but who would look after this lot?"

"Yeah, but I could put the rent up."

Dancer had been busy since they entered the bar. He gave Myron a Whiskey Sour and opened a bottle of wine, the same Chardonnay as the previous occasion for Judy.

"Good people Myron's family," he said to Judy. "Haven't increased my rent for ten years."

Judy squeezed Myron's arm.

He helps a diverse range of people, and few—other than those he helps—know about it. Most—like I did—write him off as that Jewish Accountant.

"Dancer made me my first Whiskey Sour."

"Your family owns this building, too?" Judy asked.

"Same building as The Old Seaman's Lodge. A strange sort of backwards J shaped building. The builders tried to acquire the entire block but got into a dispute with some owners who refused to sell. In the end, they built around the existing buildings. Heritage protected, so all we can do is maintain it and refurbish the interior. Maintaining heritage buildings in this city has tax breaks. Not all bad."

"How's Billy?" Judy asked Dancer.

"Billy is Billy," Dancer said. "Back in the pattern of his life, but a little sadder and a little quieter. When we explained you paid his rent, he cried."

Georgie Girl came to the bar with his empty glasses. While waiting for the drinks, he nibbled some bar snacks.

Judy smiled.

Dancer said, "Smart girl, you got there young Myron."

"Yes, she is."

Judy, still smiling, became lost in thought. She searched her feelings, trying to understand why she was feeling overwhelmed.

Concern for Billy. Joy at the success of my bar snack idea. Shy self-consciousness at Dancer and Myron's praise of me. Admiration and respect for Dancer and the subtle way he manages and cares for his drunks. Curiosity about what happened in Georgie Girl's life. Love for Myron.

She marveled at people's ability to experience diverse feelings simultaneously. *I can identify my feelings. What if someone experienced all these simultaneous feelings, but couldn't separate them? What if they were just all mixed up together? Very confusing.*

She watched Georgie Girl return to his seat. *Perhaps a series of features about broken lives. Each one based on the life of one of Dancer's drunks. How many ideas for features have I had since I met you, Frank?*

"Let's move to a table and wait for Billy," she said to Myron.

Myron asked Dancer to put their takeaway box in the fridge and joined her. Judy apologized to Myron as she made notes on her iPad.

"No need to apologize. I love watching you do what you do. I can always see when you have ideas. If I had as many ideas as you, I'd need to write them down too."

Judy finished making her notes and smiled at Myron.

"Really? You can see when I have an idea. Interesting."

Could be something in that. Judy reopened her iPad and added a note: *Watching People Have Ideas*. Closing her iPad, she felt Myron smile. She looked up. He had an amused smile on his face. Myron laughed as she opened her iPad again. Judy typed, *Can We Feel Smiles?*

"I can't believe one person has as many ideas as you do," Myron said. "You amaze me."

Judy winked. "Forgot to mention my digital recorder's been on since we entered the bar. Have it on record you think I'm amazing."

"For the record, it's not what I think, it's what you are! A fact, not an opinion!"

Judy smiled. "Here's Billy now."

"I'll chat with Dancer while you talk to him."

"You didn't tell me you knew Dancer."

"Want to have a little mystery, so you don't get bored with me."

Can't imagine I would.

Myron grinned. He stood and gently squeezed Judy's shoulder before he headed to the bar.

Billy, beer in one hand, whisky in the other, made his way to Judy's table.

***

Myron sat at the bar and drained the last of his drink.

Dancer mixed him a fresh one without being asked. Myron didn't pay for his drinks at The Shipyard and now, neither would Judy.

"Fine woman, you got there," he said as he placed the drink in front of Myron.

"I know it."

"Art and Ruth keeping well?"

"Yeah, how about you?"

Dancer shrugged his shoulders. "Getting older."

Myron sipped his drink. “Better than the alternative.”

Dancer surveyed the room. Abbot and Costello would be at each other’s throats before long. Most of his customers drank alone, silently battling their demons with mind numbing alcohol. “Perhaps not for everyone.”

Myron followed Dancer’s gaze around the room. “Seriously, if you want to renovate…”

“As I said, what would happen to this lot? Need to be done at some point. The district’s changing. An office building in the next block’s being converted into condos. That’s the start of it.”

“Papa says the city plans to rejuvenate *The Docklands,* which is what they’re calling it now.”

“The proximity to the city means undersized, overpriced apartments. This lot’ll be forced out, won’t be able to afford to live here anymore. Every silver lining has a cloud.”

“Still two or three years away, I think.”

“Can imagine the type it’ll attract, familiar with the area from visiting the park at lunchtime. Plenty more business for Billy, I guess… if he lives long enough.”

Myron nodded, thoughtfully. He sipped his drink, trying to decide whether to ask Dancer what he meant. Dancer continued and Myron chose not to pursue it.

“What about you guys? Plan to refurbish your buildings?”

“Seaman’s will need to be refurbished at some point, but Papa wants to leave the apartment block as it is, affordable for working people.”

“Good to hear.”

Dancer had lived in one of their apartments since he took over The Shipyard. The rent, bundled into the lease of the bar.

Costello had gone to the restroom. Abbot came to the bar for another round, so he wasn’t tempted to finish his friend’s beer, Dancer guessed. He turned away from Myron and attended to Abbot.

Billy Revisited

"Hello Billy," Judy said as he joined her at the table.

"Hello Judy Vernon. Before I forget, thank you for taking care of my rent. I appreciate it."

Judy smiled. "It was what Frank wanted."

"Think so too, not that I deserve it."

"May I ask some more questions?"

He downed his whiskey and shrugged. "Sure."

"Why didn't you mention you had a relationship with Jenny, as well as Susie?"

Billy didn't answer immediately. "How?"

"Jenny."

He nodded. "Frank made me promise never to mention my relationship with Jenny. Said I'd go to jail. Never went with her after Frank found us. Guess he told her to stop seeing me. A pity. She was a great fuck."

"Frank never asked her to stop seeing you. It was her decision. She loved you and didn't want you in trouble. She was underage."

"Sweet of her. Great kid. Guess she's not a kid anymore. Didn't love her. Loved Susie. Always will. Love of my life, Susie. Jenny really enjoyed fucking. We fucked at every opportunity. Both addicted to sex. I'm addicted now, but that was different."

Billy picked up his beer, drank half, and glanced around the bar before continuing.

"After Jenny, I found a slut in a bar… can't remember her name. Together for a while, but moved on when she tried to complicate things. Life was simple then, working… wining and dining potential clients, and fucking. Guess my life's simple now too…. Working to pay for the booze, drinking until I forget, and sleeping. Nothing complicated in that."

No, it's the remembering that complicates things. "Did Frank criticize you for sleeping with Jenny?"

"No. Told me to tell no one. Thought it was Jenny's reputation, never occurred to me he was protecting me. Jenny too. Only a kid and protecting me. Frank was always protecting me. I'm broken and can't protect myself."

Raised voices at a nearby table distracted them. Abbot and Costello were arguing about something, but Judy couldn't work out what.

Billy muttered, "Fucking morons."

He drank half of what remained of his beer, and continued.

"Frank *never* judged me. Never said I disappointed him, except once. Not disappointed, I ripped everyone off. It was because I didn't tell him about the problem, so he could find a solution. Frank always said there's a solution to every problem."

He stood and drained the dregs from his glass.

"Except being dead. Guess Frank found a problem without a solution."

Billy took his empty glasses to the bar. Frank's pleading eyes appeared in Judy's mind. *Jesus Frank, I wish you'd tell me what you want.*

Judy eavesdropped on Abbot and Costello's conversation.

Abbot was saying, "What's the matter, ya miserable bastard? *That's* funny."

Costello replied, "Not true, old joke… and you tell it every fucking day, you fucking moron."

"Don't call me a fucking moron, ya fucking moron."

Billy returned with full glasses. He quickly downed his shot, and noticing Judy's glass almost empty, returned to the bar to have Judy's glass filled and convinced Dancer to give him another shot.

Billy downed his extra shot before sitting down. He continued, as if his recounting of events hadn't been interrupted.

"Frank said, 'Most problems need time, but people want an immediate fix. Problems develop over time, and we need time to fix them.' I argued the people I owed money to wouldn't give me time. He said, 'They will if it's in their interest.' I think Frank was right. Thought so at the time, but it was too late."

Billy sipped some beer, momentarily lost in thought.

Judy surveyed the room. Few patrons, Pissy Mary, sitting in the corner by herself.

"Frank said, 'All you've done is solve one problem by creating a bigger problem, also solvable, but it'll take longer.'" Billy's head dropped. When he looked up, his eyes were full of regret. "Right again. He solved it."

"He was a wise man," agreed Judy. "I wonder if he was naïve about Myriam, or if he accepted her the way she is and loved her?"

Billy thought while he drank his beer and then headed to the bar for a refill. When he returned, he sat down before throwing the whiskey down his throat.

"Frank loved four women in his life. I fucked them all. He knew about three of them and never held it against me. Don't think he knew about the fourth one... If he did, things might've been different."

He stared at his full glass for a long time.

Susie, Jenny, Myriam. The fourth?

Billy contemplated his beer or something else. Judy sipped her wine and waited for him to continue.

"One hundred and twenty-five dollars," Billy said bitterly, eyes still fixed on his drink. Then he stared at Judy. "That's what my own mother charged me. I was sixteen."

Oh, he.... oh.

Eyes still fixed on Judy, he picked up his glass, raised it to his mouth, but didn't drink.

"Frank accepted me exactly as I am. Accepted me and loved me even though he knew—better than anyone—I'm broken, and unfixable."

Billy finally drank and placed his glass on the table with excessive caution.

"Never tried to change me. Never lectured me about controlling myself. Thought it was because I'm unfixable, but you're right. In his mind, there was nothing to fix.

"As for Myriam, everyone knew she was a slut. One of those sluts who may as well have the word SLUT tattooed on her forehead. Some people are sluts, but you'd never know. Others, like Myriam, seem to shout slut from every pore."

He stared straight ahead, giving the impression he was looking at Myriam.

"The moment someone meets her, they know what she is. So yeah, Frank accepted her and loved her the same as he did me."

Billy was fast reaching the point where he'd talked enough. She recalled Dancer's words, 'Some days Billy crosses the line quickly.' Today was apparently one of those days.

Tempted to ask him about the fourth woman, perhaps another day.

Billy became lost in his thoughts and memories.

When sober, he can remember everything, including details. Understand why he drinks. Only in banishing his memories can he find peace. Best leave him in peace now.

"Thank you for talking with me, Billy. I'll be back from time to time to see how you're doing. If you need anything, Dancer can contact me."

Billy smiled and drank some beer. He held on to his glass.

"Anytime Judy Vernon, I enjoy talking to you, even if you make me think too much." He held his glass towards her in a mock toast. "As long as you're buying." Billy paused for a moment before completing the toast with a swig of his beer. "Why are you being kind to me? You don't know me."

"Two reasons; I like you; you're a good man. Second, it's what Frank wants."

"I can feel you like me," Billy said with a smile and a wink. "Besides, I'm likeable… apparently. Looking after me is what Frank would want. His life's work… poor bastard. But I'm not a good man. I'm a cheat, an embezzler, a destroyer of lives, a degenerate gambler, an addict, a drunk, and a whore." He drained his glass. "I know what I am."

"Perhaps, Billy, but you're not malicious, and that makes you a good man. We don't need to be perfect to be good."

"You're a kind person."

Billy stood when Judy did.

He hugged her goodbye and announced, "Need a piss."

***

Judy joined Dancer and Myron at the bar.

"Dancer, call me if Billy needs anything."

"Why are you being so kind to Billy?" he asked.

"Because I like him, and Frank wants me to."

"That's what Myron said."

Judy smiled. "I'll pay the tab. Cover Billy today, too."

"Already taken care of."

"Thank you, Myron," Judy said, smiling and gently stroking his arm.

"Don't thank me. Dancer took care of it."

"Part of the rent," Dancer explained.

Judy nodded. "We'd better be on our way, Dancer. Still have some things to do."

Dancer passed Myron both his overnight bag and their takeout lunch box. Judy gave Myron a questioning look.

"Had Irving send it round."

After saying their goodbyes to Dancer and leaving The Shipyard, they flagged a taxi.

Judy gave the driver the address of Alice's Bakery and took her digital recorder from the side pocket of her shoulder bag to turn it off. She dropped it back into her bag and snuggled against Myron contentedly for their ride downtown to the Gourmet district.

New and Old Habits

After Alice's, they stopped at The Soup Master for some bisque, and Exquisite Jams for some of Ali's honey, mustard, and macadamia dressing.

Judy picked up two bottles, and her mind filled with images of Ali. The way Ali's tongue had lingered, as it cleaned dressing off a finger, and where Judy had imagined Ali's tongue was positioned.

Stop it. You're NOT going there. Goose bumps prickled her skin. Frank's eyes appeared in her mind. She shivered.

Myron's hand was on her arm. "What is it?"

"Oh… nothing. Someone just walked on my grave."

***

They arrived home. Myron removed his shoes, took his bag to the bedroom, and used the bathroom.

Judy smiled. Myron was comfortable at her place. She prepared their coffee, and white chocolate, mandarin, and macadamia cookies for a light afternoon tea. Thoughts of Ali banished, replaced with those of domestic bliss with Myron.

When Judy took the tray through to the living room, Myron was on the sofa, waiting for her. *Perfect.*

"Interesting talk with Billy?"

"Yes, appeared to make him think about some things. Hope it'll be good for him. Maybe help him feel a little less guilty. Not saying making Billy feel better about himself was my intention. That ship has sailed.

"Frank wasn't the naïve poor judge of character people assumed. He accepted people as they are without wanting to change, fix, or improve them. Frank had a rare ability. Easy to accept someone like you, as you are, but being able to accept Billy and Myriam as they are… he was a better man than me."

Myron laughed, "Glad you're not a man. You're so amazing, I'd love you, anyway. As I'm not as err… versatile as your Billy, that would be difficult for me."

Judy, distracted by deciding whether to be open with Myron, missed what he was really telling her.

"If *you* were a woman, it wouldn't phase me at all, but I'm glad you're not."

Myron shrugged. "Not surprised."

Myron didn't probe, ask for details, question her, or become some sort of macho man because he felt threatened. Judy smiled and snuggled closer to Myron.

Coffee finished, Judy suggested, "Perhaps we should adjourn to the bedroom for, umm… a rest."

"I'm not tired."

"Perfect. I have a saturated vagina with your name on it."

"Is that a thing? People getting their lover's name tattooed on their genitalia."

"Ooh, I don't know. If it is, might make for an interesting feature. Know a couple of tattooists, I could ask."

Myron smiled. "Been looking forward to drinking from your velvet cup for days."

***

Myron left early the next morning for squash. Judy didn't go back to sleep. She worked, finishing the final review of her current features and blogs, and sending them off. The commissioned features to their publishers, and her freelance features and blogs, to Sin, who would use them to launch *The Judy Vernon Feature Bank.*

Judy drafted a launch email for Sin, accepted three new commissions and chose a feature and two blogs of her own to write. *Going to be a busy week.* The research for her Frank story was almost complete. She needed to decide what to do with it.

***

Judy sat on her favorite sofa at Kansas Café. She smiled across the table.

"Morning, Frank. You're looking well. Had a wonderful day yesterday. After brunch I talked with our Billy. Your ears must have been burning. Do you still feel stuff like that?

"Home for a matinee with Myron, then we prepared dinner together. Heating the bisque, we picked up at The Soup Master and shelling, shucking, cutting, and stirring our left-over seafood into it. Wonderful soup. Everything about yesterday was wonderful. After dinner, we cleaned up together, which I liked. Then an early night..." *A new relationship is good for the sex life.*

Dorothy brought Judy's usual cappuccino and New York style cheesecake. *Walk On By* played in the background. *Haven't heard this version before.*

"Dot, who's this singer?"

"Um... from memory, a guy from New Zealand, Marc Hunter, and spelled with a c, I think. Enjoy hon. Gotta get back to the kitchen, making fresh cheesecake."

Judy searched *Marc Hunter* on *Wikipedia*, an excellent source for preliminary quick research she found. Apparently, Hunter, who died from cancer, had been the lead singer of a rock band, *Dragon,* and other bands.

Curious. Many modern singers record albums of the old standards and reveal vocal talents surpassing—in my musically uneducated opinion—the talent they displayed while performing with their band. Could be a feature in there somewhere.

"Yes Frank, our Billy seems well, or as well as can be expected. Lucid and reflective, at least while I talked to him. Still trying to drink his guilt away and with it, his memories, and his mind. Only a matter of time before he succeeds, but I guess you know that.

"Must hurt you to watch Billy drinking himself to death. If you were alive, would you try to stop him, to save him from himself, or would you continue to accept him the way he is?"

Judy sipped her cappuccino and cut a small piece of cheesecake to accompany it.

"Suppose you're right. Depends on Billy and what he wants. Who's to judge if Billy is wrong in choosing his slow death, and who's to determine if saving, or trying to save him, is right? It would be arrogant for us to assume that we know what's best for Billy, more than he knows what is best for himself."

More coffee and cheesecake while she contemplated Frank and Billy.

"I agree. We can only judge Billy by our standards. What right do we have to apply our standards to anyone other than ourselves? He must live by his own standards and live with the consequences. Suppose one could argue if we live in society, we should live by society's standards, which create the consequences. Not that society's standards are always right.

"A few decades ago, a gay man would've been jailed for being gay. Now a gay man can live openly and even marry, so society's standards can change to align themselves with the individual's standards.

"God Frank, all this thinking you make me do, does my head in. Will homosexual men still be *gay,* now they can marry? There aren't too many happy marriages, are there Frank? Talking of which, hoping to see your Myriam today. Better ring her now."

Myriam answered, "Speak."

"Hello Myriam, Judy Vernon. Are you free this afternoon? I'd like to ask you a few more questions."

"Bring a hundred and I'll be free late this afternoon. Gotta see my loser lawyer first."

"Great. Four, okay?"

"If you got the money."

Myriam ended the call. Judy stared at her phone and shook her head.

She called Myron.

"Hello, sweetheart."

"I'm seeing Myriam late today. Dinner at Franco's and back to my place?"

"You read my mind."

"Say seven?"

"Perfect."

Hanging up from Myron, Judy's attention returned to her coffee, cheesecake, and Frank.

"Thinking about seeing Myron tonight is arousing me. Don't know what you've done to me, Frank, but I'm as horny as a teenager who's discovered sex for the first time, not that I'm complaining. Did I tell you Myron has stamina? Sore from yesterday, and it's only Monday. Guessing by Friday I'll be glad of the Sabbath to give the old girl a rest for a couple of days…."

Frank was smiling.

"And you can wipe that silly grin off your face. I'm sure it's your fault."

Judy shook her head and finished the remains of her coffee before looking back across the table.

"Those eyes! Wish you'd tell me what you want."

Leaving the café, she said, "We're not in Kansas anymore, Frank," laughing at her own repeated semi-joke.

She headed to Alice's Bakery for her sour dough bread and then to Pie Eyed for lunch, before her meeting with Myriam.

Myriam Revisited

Judy switched on her digital recorder before she exited the taxi. Myriam answered the door almost immediately. She wore a tight white blouse and a denim skirt, even shorter than the dress she'd worn at their previous meeting. *Guess I'm in for another show.*

A distinct change in Myriam's demeanor. *Friendlier and less surly.* Myriam settled Judy on the sofa, left the room and returned with what smelled like decent coffee in a French press, and some packaged oat and raisin cookies from the supermarket. A major improvement from the cheap instant coffee provided last time.

"He's gone," Myriam said. "Don't need to tolerate shit coffee and crap food anymore. Trying to drive him away. Happened suddenly, but planned for some time, apparently. Probably as long as I worked on driving him out. Married him, looking for security, but never liked him. Thought I'd learn to, but didn't. Hated the miserable, useless bastard."

Myriam's face had an expression of distaste, as if she smelled something vile.

"Needed him to leave because I wanted alimony or something this time. By the time he left, had it all arranged with his lawyer. I only needed to agree. Did better than I expected."

Myriam was wearing sheer, lacy red panties. The shortness of her skirt placed her vagina front and center. At least the center of Judy's attention, who again struggled to avert her eyes from Myriam's lace covered offering, partly because of Myriam's constant fidgeting.

"Are you alright Myriam? You seem a little uncomfortable."

"I'm okay, a little sore is all. Paid my lawyer's fee this morning."

"Oh," said Judy, not understanding Myriam's point.

"Frank didn't leave a will for me to contest, but I'm putting in a claim for his estate. Waste of time, my lawyer says. Told him if he's successful, I'll let him fuck me in the ass, which he's been on about for ages. He agreed.

"Jeff said if he can get me this house in the settlement, he wants to ass fuck me. I agreed because I want a house, but in hindsight he already knew the settlement offer. The bastard."

Myriam leaned forward to press their coffee, then poured two cups, passing one to Judy, who made a show of raising the cup to her nose and inhaling the aroma.

"Smells wonderful."

Myriam smiled. "Better than that other shit." She waved her hand towards the tray. "Milk and sugar."

Judy nodded and reached for the milk. Myriam opened the cookies.

"Help yourself."

Judy selected one. *Important to accept hospitality when interviewing someone.* She took a bite. "These are nice."

Myriam nodded.

"Anyway, my husband wanted a clean cut, no alimony, and no reason to see me again. The deal is I get the house, free and clear, with no mortgage or anything. Better than I hoped for."

Myriam sipped her coffee, and Judy mimicked her. Replacing her cup, Myriam sat up and made a show of slowly crossing her legs, causing her minimalist skirt to creep up further.

Oh, God! Judy forced herself to look away.

"Never owned anything before, never. Now I own this house. It may be a bit of a shithole in a shitty neighborhood, but it's *my* shithole. Mine. My security. Never had security before…."

Myriam paused, momentarily lost in thought.

"Signed the agreement today. His lawyer sent it over signed, a done deal. Needs to be rubberstamped by the court, a formality. After I signed, Jeff wanted his fee paid. Thought, why not get it over with? I'm sore and uncomfortable, but that'll pass… and I have a house. Not complaining."

Myriam drank a little coffee, ate a cookie, and changed the subject.

"Never went to college, didn't get my high school diploma. Nearly did, but learned a lesson about trusting people instead. No good at math. My talent lay elsewhere. My math teacher was a lonely middle-aged dyke. Asked her to tutor me, but seduced her instead. Made her think she was seducing me. First time with a woman. Liked it a lot.

"I had a friend back then, Julia. To be honest, I loved her. Only loved two people in my life. Seduced her too and did some stuff I'd learned from the math teacher. She's still a dyke, I'm told."

Myriam stopped talking. Judy recognized the distant look in her eyes as she relived the past, temporarily abandoning the present. After finishing her coffee, Judy waited for Myriam to return.

"Julia wanted to know why I knew how to make love to a woman. Knew about all the guys I fucked because I told her everything. Told her about the math teacher. No reason not to. I loved her and trusted her.

"The cunt reported me. Got kicked out of school. Broke my heart. Never saw or spoke to her again. If she hadn't reported me, my life would've been very different. Maybe we'd be a pair of happy dykes? Never knew why she did it. Never understood it, and never asked.

"Found work in a shop with the help of my mother—a bitch, by the way—earned shit. Wanted a car, too cold to go to work in the winter. Had an idea. If I seduced my stepfather, could blackmail him into buying me one. Almost worked, but my mother found out and threw me out."

Her face told Judy Myriam harbored much bitterness towards her mother.

"Her own daughter. She didn't throw him out for fucking her daughter… She threw me out. The bitch!" Myriam spat out those last words, as if she'd bitten into a sour lemon.

"Found a shitty room near my job and stayed there until I was old enough to work in bars. Good at it. Well, working in bars and fucking. Now the agreement's signed, I can work again. Lined a job up at a bar a few blocks away. Current manager is fucking useless, and the owner likes me because I worked for him before… Not to mention, I suck his cock. I'm going to make more coffee… You want some?"

"Yes, please Myriam."

Judy always accepted hospitality when offered because you never knew what would offend somebody. Judy wouldn't risk Myriam shutting down. She liked this open, honest, perhaps vulnerable Myriam.

When Myriam returned with the coffee, Judy asked, "What happened to your math teacher?"

"Lost her job. They charged her, but the charges didn't stick. I refused to testify. Held in custody for a while when she was first arrested. I denied it, said I made it up to impress my girlfriend, but the teacher felt guilty and admitted it.

"Thought she was a stupid bitch. Now I kinda admire her. May have worked out for her. Heard she ended up living with her dyke prison guard. Guess I did her a favor."

Myriam pressed and poured the coffee, and then made another show of crossing her legs, making sure Judy had an eyeful. *That's intentional.*

"My mother and my stepfather separated within a year. Tried to go home, but my mother wanted nothing to do with me, called me a 'Worthless slut' and told me I wasn't welcome. Fucking bitch!

"After I started working in clubs, I became half a whore. Liked the work, and the atmosphere, meeting people, becoming friendly with the regulars. Run right, a bar can have a family feel. Hated working in a shop, only seeing people for a few minutes and never getting to know them. That's why I like bars. Plus, my body is my only asset. Use what I have to get by."

Myriam sipped her coffee, looking through Judy into the past.

"When I met Frank, my life changed. I loved Frank. Only the second time in my life that I loved someone. Both ended badly. That'll teach me."

Judy looked at Myriam, silent and distant. *Yes Frank, I can understand why you loved her. Now get your fucking eyes out of my head.*

"People thought I was a gold digger, conning Frank for whatever I could get. Not true. I really loved him.

"All I ever wanted was something that was mine, just mine. Frank never gave me that. Everything was his or ours. That's why I got so angry.

If Frank had put the house in my name, it would've been mine and it would've been safe.

"Everything's changed now. I have something that's mine. A sense of security and belonging. Looking forward to starting my new job, too. Perhaps he'll give me a piece of the bar if I do a good job of running it? I'll treat it like it's mine, anyway. Make the customers feel at home.

"I'll never marry again, and never live with anyone, either. Don't wanna risk losing what's mine. When I want company, can bring someone home from the bar… for love or money.

"Frank told me, 'It'll take a long time, but I'll get our lives back.' Too angry to listen. Broke his heart when I didn't believe in him. Didn't care. Too pissed off to care about Frank. *Wanted* to break his heart. Wanted him to hurt. That's the truth. Frank was right, or would've been if he didn't die. Should've listened. Maybe he'd be alive if I did."

Judy studied Myriam as she reached for a cookie and washed it down with coffee. She no longer saw Myriam as a curiosity. She felt drawn to embrace her.

"Heard people talking. Saying poor Frank was naïve and stupid for taking up with a no-good slut like me. One thing for sure, Frank wasn't stupid. He had no illusions about me. Frank knew what I was. He never criticized me, never blamed me, never wanted to educate me, never wanted to teach me… to make me a better person. He accepted me. I loved him for that, and I know he loved me.

"People are funny. Write others off as being stupid when they don't understand them or can't agree with their choices. People treat me like I'm stupid… *A dumb slut.* I'm not the sharpest knife in the drawer, but I'm not fucking stupid. I may not be book smart; but I'm street smart, and I know how to read people."

Judy said, "I had an interesting chat with Billy after we last spoke."

Myriam smiled. "Always liked Billy; everyone likes Billy. We were together before I was with Frank. Suited us both. I was a slut and Billy was an addict and a gambler. Understood each other. Both loved *the life.* Partying every night, booze, drugs, and gangsters. Oh, and fucking, we were always fucking. A good life, but no future.

"Life with Frank had a future, or so I thought. Maybe it would've if I wasn't so angry. Loved Frank. Didn't love Billy."

Myriam looked thoughtful as she drank a little coffee.

"Billy, for fun. Frank, for life. Billy treated me like a slut. Frank never did. The only man who never treated me like a slut."

Judy began, "I was talking to Jenny…."

Myriam interrupted her. "That fat sleazy bastard…" she shuddered. "Couldn't stand that fat fuck, but he would've been important to Frank's political career, so I sucked his cock. The things we do for love, eh?

"He wasn't the only one. I was trying to help Frank. Only reason I did it. Wouldn't have sucked or fucked that guy for any amount of money. Couldn't stand to be in the same room as him. Wouldn't do it for money. I do have standards, but I did it for Frank."

Myriam fascinated Judy more than the first time they met.

Her manner, way of speaking and expressing herself, attitude, outlook, everything except perhaps for the constant flashing, was different. The change in Myriam intrigued Judy and left her wondering if the change was conscious or subconscious.

Has Myriam's demeanor changed because she now owns a house? Is Myriam taking the interview seriously this time and was she just playing for effect last time? Has Myriam subconsciously adapted to her situation? Perhaps it's simply because her husband—whom she had been trying to drive away—has now gone, and she doesn't need to maintain her obnoxious persona.

Myriam continued. "I was worried Jenny told Frank."

"She did."

"Really? Surprising. Frank never let on. I was sensitive to his attitude because I expected him to react. Assumed he didn't know."

"I believe he understood your thinking and motivation."

"He would. Smart, my Frank. Not naïve, like people assumed. He was accepting. He was an extraordinary man, but my anger got in the way. A combination of everything… not one thing—not even Billy's nonsense—destroyed my marriage. Billy, Frank's character, my anger and frustration… Nothing could have survived.

"A long time ago. If I'm honest, I miss Frank. Didn't realize it. Still angry with him. After your last visit, I spent a lot of time thinking about Frank. *That one* finally left, and I was alone with my thoughts. I thought of Frank… maybe your visit bringing up the past, or the end of another marriage, perhaps Frank passing or a combination. Most things in life are motivated by a combination of factors, I think.

"Funny you should bring up me blowing that fat, sleazy bastard. When Frank's political career died, I was angry with him because I blew that fat cunt for nothing. Nothing to do with Frank. He didn't ask me to, and he wouldn't want me to… My own warped thinking about how I could help him… Still, I was pissed off with Frank."

Myriam stopped talking. She fought back tears and struggled to maintain her composure.

Suddenly she said, "Enough talking now."

"Okay Myriam, I'm sorry if I upset you."

"Not your fault, except you're too easy to talk to. Do people open up to you without realizing it? I bet they do, *all* the time. There's something about you Judy Vernon."

"Thank you, Myriam. Perhaps we'll meet again. I hope so."

"Me too," Myriam said quietly.

Myriam stood, smoothed the front of her skirt down, and reverted to her persona of their first encounter to regain her composure.

"Which do you prefer, white lace pussy or red lace pussy? You think I didn't notice you can barely take your eyes off it? Offer you a taste, except I have my period. Always wear red panties when I have my period, my little joke."

Judy flushed and looked away. She focused on calling a taxi.

Myriam continued. "Could smell the dyke on you the minute I met you. Short skirt and lacy panties are very effective in getting the attention of men and dykes. Anytime you want a taste, you come back… I reckon you have one sweet pussy yourself."

Judy composed herself and smiled. “You leave little to the imagination Myriam, I won’t forget your offer.”

She was relieved when the taxi arrived quickly. Myriam walked her to the door, leaned in unexpectedly, and kissed Judy on the lips. The kiss startled Judy, but she didn’t mind. She returned Myriam’s kiss. *I blame you, Frank.*

She gave the driver the address of Franco’s.

She arrived early. Happy to wait for Myron. A drink-alone-at-the-bar sort of day.

Rebekah and Myron

Seventeen-year-old Slave sat on the edge of her bed, contemplating her choices. Her eighteenth birthday was in two weeks. She'd transfer to an adult prison, which may give her an opportunity to escape Jack, but she couldn't be sure. Jack was also due to be transferred, and it was possible they'd transfer together.

Don't know if I can endure another day of this hell. She'd acquired a shank, now hidden in her mattress. *If I cut Jack's throat, I'll be in for life. If I cut my own, I'll be free.*

Twenty-fifth of the month, the day Uncle Myron visits. Be here soon, always comes at precisely ten forty-five. Looking forward to seeing him. His visits keep me sane.

She didn't say much, but sitting with him for fifteen minutes each month made a difference. *Wish I could tell him how much his visits mean to me. Think he knows.*

The fifty dollars he deposited in her account every month had been a godsend. She used it to appease Jack. Important to keep her cell mate happy. If not, Jack would find new and more degrading tasks for her.

An officer appeared at the cell door. "Visitor, Slave."

Everybody referred to her as Slave. Her name now. Everybody except Uncle Myron, who called her Rebekah, her name once, two lifetimes ago.

Myron stood when she entered the visitors' area, as he always did. "Hello Rebekah."

"Hello Uncle Myron."

Slave looked at the room for what she believed would be the last time. A small windowless room, walls painted white, light gray tiles on the floor. The room always seemed sterile, with a scent of lavender disinfectant. A single orange plastic chair on one side of a table—intended to keep visitors and inmates separate—two identical blue plastic chairs on the other. Maximum of two visitors. She walked past him and sat down. Inmates must face the guard standing beside the door.

They didn't touch; not permitted. The conversation began as it did every visit.

"How are you, Rebekah?"

"Fine."

"You'll soon be transferred to an adult prison. How do you feel about that?"

Slave tried to speak, "I-I-I…" Her words stalled, but her tears flowed, taking her by surprise.

Myron jerked his head around and looked at the officer enquiringly, almost pleadingly. The officer—one of the kinder ones—nodded. Two steps and Myron crouched beside Rebekah, arms around her. She buried her head into his shoulder and cried.

Through her tears, Slave whispered an account of her life in hell. Her name is Slave; beatings whenever she displeased Jack, who sat on her face every night, even when Jack had her period, her daily ass wiping duties, having to wash Jack in the shower, and being pimped out for a few cigarettes.

She told him everything, including the shank hidden in her mattress. As she spoke, her body quivered, disguised from the guard by her sobs.

The officer cleared her throat.

***

Myron returned to his seat and studied Rebekah. *Knew she was struggling. Saw it in her eyes, despite her saying she's 'fine' every month. No idea it was so bad.*

He couldn't say much in front of the officer. Fortunate, because he didn't know what to say. *Can't imagine what it was like for her these past two years. Need to get her out.*

He was silent—trying to communicate with his eyes—his brain was moving in overdrive. Assessing and analyzing the situation, recalling people who owed him favors and may help, beginning to connect the dots and formulate a plan.

Myron glanced at the clock on the wall. *Visiting time will soon be over.*

"Stay strong Rebekah. I can't promise, but I know some people and I'll attempt to get you a parole hearing. Even if we can, there's no guarantee it'll be successful, but let's try."

Slave nodded.

"I'll put an extra fifty dollars in your account this month. Maybe you can use it to, err… keep everything calm."

"Thank you, Uncle Myron."

"Time!" The officer announced.

Myron stood and for the first time in nearly three years leaned across the table and kissed Rebekah on the cheek.

The officer cleared her throat again.

"Be strong," he whispered.

He turned and followed the officer out.

***

Slave watched him leave. She understood what he meant when he said, "Be strong." *Don't do anything stupid with that shank.*

Can't imagine how he'll be able to arrange a parole hearing. The possibility gave her hope. Almost. She dared not hope when chances were it would end in disappointment. *Please God.*

Talking to Myron, finally telling someone about the years of hell, helped. The extra fifty dollars would help too. She could keep Jack in a good mood by indulging her with her favorite cookies.

The officer returned. "Come on, Slave, back to your cell."

***

The clear blue sky and bright sun made Myron squint when he left the corrections facility, as it often did. Today it gave him hope, which even the foreboding heavy black gate with its thick bars topped with spikes didn't dampen.

He began making calls while waiting for a taxi in front of the gate. His first call was to John Snitter. “John, Myron Myerson. I’d like to retain your services.”

“Glad to hear it. You been a naughty boy?”

“No, on behalf of my niece. Is it possible to have an early parole hearing scheduled?”

“It’s been known. I have some contacts; send me the details and I’ll ask around. We’ll see what we can do. The best thing would be a recommendation from the sentencing judge. How old is she?”

“Just about to turn eighteen and be transferred to an adult prison.”

“Good timing gives them a reason. Parents?”

“Disowned her.”

“What’s she in for?”

“Armed robbery and unlawful detention.”

“Anyone hurt?”

“No, thanks to her cooperating with the police.”

“That helps. Not strictly necessary, but with the absence of parents, are you prepared to assume legal guardianship until she turns twenty-one? It’ll show the board she has a stabilizing influence.”

“Yes.”

“Call your friend the DA, ask him to make a recommendation to the judge, and see if we can look at their file. That’ll be useful.”

“I can ask.”

“He owes you.”

“My taxi’s arriving. I’ll send you the details. Let me know if you need anything else.”

“Sure, talk later.”

In the back of the taxi, Myron called the district attorney—whom he knew well—having frequently been an expert witness. He answered almost immediately.

"Hello Myron, what can I do for you?"

"I'm looking for a favor. Trying to organize a non-scheduled parole hearing for my, er... niece. Was hoping you might request the sentencing judge to make a recommendation."

"It's doable, providing there's nothing untoward in her file. On my way to a meeting. Send me the details and I'll pull the file when I return. No promises, but I'll look."

"That's all I'm asking."

"Have you retained a criminal lawyer?"

"John Snitter."

"Shitter is formidable, but you know that."

"He suggested it might be helpful to look at your file."

"Be disappointed if he didn't. It's possible. If there's nothing.... Sorry, need to go. Send the details and I'll get on it as soon as I can."

***

Myron sat at his desk in his office. High-backed leather chair, with a hint of red, to match his redwood desk. The only two items on which were his computer and a coffee. He always kept his desk clear except for what he was working on. He liked order. His suit jacket was hanging in his closet.

He reflected on Rebekah's situation. He learned it was not unusual for young offenders to have a parole hearing prior to being transferred to adult prison, but a hearing wasn't scheduled for Rebekah. The judge hadn't made a recommendation when sentencing.

Myron had work to do if he was going to secure Rebekah's release. He needed to have her sentencing judge make a recommendation and have the parole board schedule a hearing. John Snitter couldn't appear at the hearing, but he could advise and prepare Rebekah for it.

He called Burt Rogers, who managed Myron's property management company, and sometimes hired parolees as maintenance workers. He explained the situation.

"Burt, do you know a parole officer who can give us advice about a program we can get Rebekah into?"

"Frank Dunn, I'll call him."

"Thanks Burt. Incoming call, talk later."

It was John Snitter.

"Parole hearings at the detention center are on the tenth. When's her birthday?"

"Sixteenth."

"The DA will have contacts. Should be able to add her to the list. Spoke to a family court judge I went through law school with. No guarantees, but he'll move your guardianship application to the top of the list. His clerk is putting in a call to social services. An application is being couriered to you now."

"Thanks John."

"You're in a sound financial position and squeaky clean…"

"How…"

"Investigate everyone I cross-examine, never know what'll turn up. A couple of glowing personal references and it should be a formality."

Finishing his call with Snitter, Myron called the mayor. He was leaving nothing to chance.

"Myron. What can I do for you?"

"I'm applying for guardianship of my cousin. May I use you as a personal reference?"

"Of course, use my private mobile number. Fax me a copy of the application and I'll have a word to the director. Make sure it's not lost in the system."

Myron thanked him and rang off.

The courier arrived.

Myron was completing the paperwork when the DA called. "Examined her file. Won't be a problem. My people are copying the documents, get Shitter to send the paperwork, and we'll release it to him, legal. Put in calls to the sentencing judge and the parole board. Should be able to add her to the list for the tenth. Anything else you need?"

"Thank you, appreciate it. Filling out a guardianship application now. Can I put you down as a personal reference?"

"Sure."

Ending his call with the DA, Myron smiled. *Need to make sure she gets parole.*

***

Slave lay on her bunk. Despite herself, she hoped Uncle Myron could somehow get her a parole hearing and began imagining walking out of her cell, her hell and never looking back.

Jack was sitting at the table, eating the cookies Slave had bought her. She cocked her leg and farted loudly. "What's going on with you, Slave? You bin acting strange since your uncle came."

"I… err… nothing going on. Just thinking he won't visit here again. Don't know where they gonna send me. What if it's upstate and he can't visit? What'll I do for money?"

"Thinking 'bout that too. Only a few weeks behind you. Might ask the screws if I can transfer early… Can go together. Gonna miss that tongue of yours."

Slave shuddered at the thought, but Jack seemed too intent on her cookies to notice. *Please God no.*

It's Not What You Know…

Three days later, April Smith sat in the visitor's room of the Juvenile Detention Center. Appointed advocate for Rebekah *Something*, the previous evening. She shook her head. *Swamped, no time to examine the file.* The guardianship hearing was that afternoon; according to the yellow post-it note stuck on the front of the file. *Why is it being fast tracked?*

While she waited, she perused the file. The applicant's personal references caught her attention. *The guy has connections.*

***

Slave was working in the laundry when the officer approached her. "Slave, you got a visitor."

Jack glared at her. Slave shrugged.

As the officer escorted her to the visitors' area, Slave asked, "Who?"

"Social services."

"Why?"

"How would I know?"

Slave entered the visitor's room. A middle-aged woman with dark hair was reading a file. The woman looked up and removed her glasses when Slave sat.

"Hello Rebekah, my name is April Smith."

"Hello."

"How are you?"

"Fine." Slave was nervous. *Are they going to transfer me early?* "What's this about?"

"I'm your advocate. That means I'm here to represent your interests." She consulted the file. "Myron Myerson has applied to be appointed your legal guardian until you are twenty-one."

"Wh… Oh." Slave smiled. *Why?*

"The hearing's this afternoon. Do you have any objection to him being appointed your guardian?"

"No, of course not."

April made some notes. "Is there anything you want to say about him?"

"Uncle Myron is the only one who's visited me since I've been here. He comes every month."

After making more notes, April asked, "Do you agree to Myron Myerson being appointed your legal guardian?"

"Yes." *Why?*

April passed her a form. "Sign here please Rebekah."

Slave signed. *Must be something to do with getting me a parole hearing.*

The officer escorted her back to the laundry.

Jack was on her in an instant. "What the fuck was that about?"

Slave shrugged. "Social Services. A formality before I'm transferred to adult prison or something. I dunno."

"If I find out you're up to something, bitch, I'll slit your fucking throat."

Unless I slit yours first, you evil cunt. "I ain't up to nothing."

That afternoon, the court appointed Myron as Rebekah's legal guardian.

***

Two days later, the sentencing judge issued a formal recommendation for a parole hearing. The parole board officially added Rebekah—already penciled in following a call from the DA—to the list for the tenth. The recommendation from the judge ensured no awkward questions would be asked.

Securing the hearing was a start. Myron needed to give the parole board a justifiable reason to grant Rebekah parole.

Through Frank Dunn, Burt Rogers learned of a culinary training program for young offenders that saw them attend culinary classes twice a week, supported by a work placement. Myron had Rebekah accepted into the program and registered her for night classes two nights a week in a program which would lead to a *Certificate in Hospitality Management.*

Everything was falling into place, but Myron wasn't satisfied. Thorough by nature, every dot needed to be connected. He'd ensure the parole hearing became little more than a formality.

***

Judy sat on her sofa at Kansas Café, Myron sat beside her, and Frank—unseen by Myron—sat opposite. They were having coffee, cappuccino for Judy, black for Myron, nothing for Frank, and sharing a single slice of New York style cheesecake.

Myron said, "Spoke with Papa. Easy to find a suitable apartment in one of our buildings for Rebekah, but first I need to find her a work placement. Better she doesn't have a long commute."

Judy nodded, took a forkful of cheesecake, and fed it to Myron. He swallowed and smiled.

"The correct work placement is critical. One hears stories about parolees being mistreated, and taken advantage of by employers. She doesn't need that. The poor girl's done her time in hell. We need somewhere quiet, with no pressure to give her time to recover and adjust."

Frank was looking around the cafe. A change from him staring at her with those pleading eyes. He turned his attention back to Judy and smiled. *Great idea Frank.*

To Myron she said, "What about this place? If Dot agrees, would this be suitable for Rebekah?"

"It would be perfect. It meets the work placement criteria, and it's quiet, no pressure. Tell Dorothy I'll cover Rebekah's wages."

"Let me out, and I'll ask her."

Judy—pausing to kiss him on the way past—headed to the counter to talk with Dorothy. She glanced over her shoulder, and smiled at the two most important men in her life sitting together, waiting for her return.

"Dot, have you got a minute?"

"Sure."

Best get straight to the point. "Myron's niece, Rebekah, got herself into some trouble as a kid. She's nearly eighteen now, and we're hoping she'll be paroled. Myron has her accepted into a culinary program, and she'll be doing a hospitality course two evenings a week. We need to find her a work placement so she can get paroled. Would you consider taking her on? Myron will cover her wages so…"

"When we first opened, we were busy. Had a couple of girls working for me then. It was a wonderful time; we were like family. I miss those days. Yes, Judy, I'd be happy to take the girl…"

"Rebekah."

"… Rebekah on. Be nice working with someone again."

"Thank you, Dot. We really appreciate it. Myron will have some paperwork to sign, I think."

"That's fine."

"Now, we need to find her somewhere close by to live…"

"I've got a spare room in my apartment upstairs. She could take that. I'll be glad of the company, to be honest."

"Oh, Dot, that'd be wonderful, but you don't know her. Are you sure it won't put you out?"

"I've known you nearly ten years. You wouldn't ask if she wasn't suitable. Besides, it gets lonely living and working alone. She'll be doing me a favor."

"Thank you again, Dot, for…"

"Nonsense, it's nothing."

Judy returned to Myron and relayed Dorothy's response.

He retrieved two partially completed forms from his briefcase, one for housing and one for employment. "I'll have Dorothy finish completing these forms and sign them. Need to connect all the dots."

Judy smiled. *Of course you do.*

As Myron headed to the counter, she noticed her cup. *Almost empty.*

"Maybe order some more coffees, darling," Judy called after him.

Myron turned and nodded.

Judy drained her cup and glanced at Frank. He was smiling, but the pleading in his eyes remained after what had been many months.

"Thank you, Frank. An excellent idea solved two of our problems. Have to admit, you're quite useful to have around."

Judy sat chatting with Frank while she waited for Myron to finish the paperwork.

Myron returned and placed the documents in his bag, fussing through them to ensure he had everything.

"I don't know if they've told Rebekah it's happening yet. She wasn't on the original list, so I'm hoping not. John Snitter and I will visit her the day before her hearing. Don't want to tell her too far in advance in case it causes her problems."

Dorothy delivered their coffees.

Myron said "One more thing. The arresting officer testified on her behalf at the trial, which is why she got a reduced sentence. The DA says the sentence reduction is why the judge didn't set a non-parole period. I'm thinking it could help if he—Harry White—would testify again."

"Harry White, the beat cop?"

"Yes, from my community. I know him a little. I…"

Judy reached for her phone, scrolled her contact list, found Harry's name, tapped call, and put the phone on speaker. Harry answered after two rings.

"Judy Vernon. This is a surprise."

"Hello Harry, how've you been?"

"They're making me retire or sit on my ass in the station. Don't want to, no idea what I'll do without my beat. Can't avoid it. Too old to be a real cop, they tell me. If you want to do another feature, it had better be soon."

"Not why I'm calling, but that's a good idea, a follow-up feature on *The Retirement of a Beat Cop*. I'll put in a call to public relations and set it up."

"An interesting way to spend my last days… with you tagging along again."

"I was calling to ask if you remember an attempted robbery a few years back? A young girl and some others, you testified on her behalf…"

"Young Rebekah? Yeah, I remember. Other than a jealous husband who knifed his wife, the only excitement I've had on this beat in the last ten years. Not a bad girl, just acting out."

"She has a parole hearing in a couple of days, and we were wondering if you'd be willing to testify on her behalf again?"

"She must be due to be transferred to a women's penitentiary soon. Doesn't need that, just a mixed-up kid. Yeah, happy to testify. Need to clear it with my sergeant, but won't be a problem."

"I'm with Myron Myerson. He'll give you the details."

"Hello Harry," Myron said.

"Myron, I haven't seen you around for a while…"

***

Slave was working in the laundry, when an officer came in. "Visitor, Slave."

Jack glared at her.

She shrugged. "I don't know."

On the way, the officer—the one who'd allowed Myron to hug her—said, "Your uncle and another man."

Slave entered the visitor's area.

"Hello Uncle Myron."

"Hello Rebekah, this is your attorney, John Snitter."

"H-hello."

"Hello Rebekah, pleased to meet you," Snitter said.

He glanced at the officer. “Officer, I’d like to speak to my client in private.”

The officer looked at Myron.

“Her legal guardian,” Snitter said.

“I’ll be right outside the door if you need me,” the officer said as she left the room.

Slave looked questioningly at Myron. *What’s going on?*

Snitter explained. “You have a parole hearing tomorrow.”

“W-what? P-parole? Tomorrow? How? I don’t…”

“Your uncle pulled some strings. We don’t have a lot of time, so let me tell you what’s going to happen tomorrow and how you’re going to act…”

***

Slave waited for the officer to return after escorting her visitors out. *Don’t know how Uncle Myron did it. Can’t believe it. This time tomorrow I could be out of this hell. Please God, don’t let Jack fuck it up.*

The officer returned to collect her a few minutes later.

“Come on, Slave, let’s get you back to the laundry.”

“Please, ma’am, don’t say anything to…”

“Nobody’ll hear anything from me. I’m on duty again tomorrow. I’ll be discreet.”

As soon as Slave returned to the laundry, Jack asked, “What was that about?”

“My Uncle. In the neighborhood. Called in on the off-chance they’d let him visit. We still don’t know where I’m being transferred.” *Glad I didn’t mention the extra fifty.* “He paid in another fifty.”

The extra money was enough to appease Jack, apparently.

***

When the officer came to collect them for their work detail the next morning, she said, “Not you, Slave. You stay here, you’re on special duties today. I’ll come and collect you.”

Jack asked, "What special duties?"

"Mind your business, and get your ass to the laundry," the officer replied.

Slave surveyed her cell. *Nothing I'll miss. Nothing.*

She checked the shank was in place, hidden in her mattress. *If the hearing doesn't go well, Jack'll be in a rage because I didn't tell her.* She studied her surroundings again. *Nearly three years and not one good memory.*

It felt like an age before Slave heard the officer's footsteps as she was using the toilet for the third time since Jack left. She wiped herself and adjusted her attire.

"You ready?" the officer asked.

Slave nodded.

"Come on. Hope it goes well."

"Me too." *Please God.*

***

Parole hearings are held in a purpose-built room at the facility. A long table with the three board members seated behind it. A chair to the right, facing the board for Slave, with the corrections officer standing behind her. Another chair to the left for the witnesses, who entered one at a time, offered their testimony and left.

Slave studied the parole board. *Seem friendly enough. Smile and look me in the eye, none avoiding eye contact.* Their demeanor put her at ease a little. Despite this, her mouth was dry, her mind racing, worried she'd forget what Snitter coached her to say. *Don't say too much, just tell them what they want to hear.* She wiped her sweaty palms on her pants every few seconds and tried without success to silence her pounding heart.

As the witnesses provided their testimony, the board made some notes, nodding occasionally, but asked few questions.

Harry White explained how Rebekah had helped the police keep the hostages out of danger.

The Juvenile Offenders Warden testified Rebekah had a clean disciplinary record, and had completed her high school diploma.

Uncle Myron, her newly appointed guardian, outlined the employment, training and residential arrangements in place for Rebekah.

When asked to make a statement, Slave told them, "I made foolish decisions when I was young. Being estranged from my parents, some older boys influenced me. I've learned my lesson. I'm looking forward to building a life for myself." Exactly what John Snitter had told her to say.

The hearing didn't take long. Almost an anti-climax. *Feels like a formality rather than a hearing.*

They granted Rebekah parole for the remaining two years and four months of her sentence.

***

Slave never returned to her cell, never saw Jack again.

At the insistence of Snitter, they took her to the processing area. The escorting officer handed Slave a package. "Your uncle brought you some clothes. You can change in there," she said, nodding towards a small room.

Slave nodded, took the package, and changed into a grey tracksuit. *My own clothes.* She folded her prison uniform and placed it on the table. She still wore her prison issue underwear.

Dragonflies danced in Slave's stomach. She repeatedly wiped her hands on the legs of her track pants, and glanced over her shoulder while they processed her out, worried she was going to be told her parole was a mistake.

The processing officer brought a box to the counter. She removed the lid and extracted a T-shirt and a skirt; the clothes Slave was wearing when she arrived. The officer peered inside the box. "No underwear?"

"Never used to wear any."

The officer nodded, and extracted the last item, a watch. She opened a white plastic bag, slid the items inside, folded and sealed it with tape. She slid a form across the counter saying, "Sign for your belongings."

The officer glanced at the paperwork and, satisfied all was in order, slid the package across to Slave. "Good luck."

Everything happened quickly. Slave's mind was numb. She couldn't believe it was happening. *I'm really getting out.*

Slave stepped out of the detention center's main entrance. The sun was bright; much brighter than the small, enclosed exercise yard she was used to. She squinted as the natural light stung her eyes.

Uncle Myron was waiting beside a taxi.

She ran to him.

She never looked back.

Never would.

She threw her arms around him and buried her head in his shoulder. Tears flowed; her body shook with her sobs. She released years of degradation.

Slave died.

Rebekah said, "Thank you, Uncle Myron." *Thank you, God.*

After Winter

Mid-morning on a Saturday. Winter had come and gone since Frank passed.

Judy sat on her usual sofa at Kansas Café, talking with Frank, who, months after his death, continued to sit opposite. She visited the café and spoke with Frank nearly every day. The pleading in his eyes remained. The Julio Iglesias version of *As Time Goes By* was playing in the background.

"Wish you'd tell me what you want, Frank. Dorothy's been making noises about retiring. I may need to find another café. If this place closes down, what will happen to you?"

Her concern for the well-being of a ghost didn't feel strange to Judy.

"Yes, Frank. I guess you could follow me to a new café, but don't start following me around. People will think I'm crazy if I'm always talking to you."

Rebekah brought Judy's cappuccino and New York style cheesecake. She worked in the café by day and attended culinary school two evenings a week. Another two evenings at business school. Having stopped observing the Sabbath before her incarceration, Rebekah worked on Saturdays.

"Thank you, Becky," Judy said as Rebekah placed her order on the table. "You've settled in well. It feels like you belong here."

"I do. I love working here. Dorothy's always telling me stories about the café. My courses give me a future and I've made some friends. My parents still won't see me. Burned that bridge. Doesn't matter." Judy detected a hint of sadness. "Try the cheesecake, Aunt Judy. Made it myself."

Judy cut a piece of cheesecake and slowly raised it to her mouth, making a show of taking Rebekah's request seriously.

"Does it taste as good as Dorothy's?"

"Easily as good."

"Really?" Rebekah beamed.

"Yes."

"Thank you, Aunt Judy."

Rebekah almost skipped back to the kitchen.

"No Frank. Sitting at the back of the café, nobody notices. Well, yes, Myron and Ali know, but they love me, so they don't think I'm crazy."

Susie, Jenny and, most frequently, Ali, often joined Judy for coffee. Judy had them sit beside her, and opposite Frank. She enjoys their company, and it gives Frank the opportunity to spend time with his family, despite them being oblivious to his presence. Ali sits very close and often holds Judy's hand, which especially amuses Frank.

Regular family events were now part of Judy's routine, such as a girl's Friday night out every two weeks with *The Farrington Girls.*

A Farrington Girls' night out always follows the same routine. They meet for dinner at Ozzie's Burgers and then head off to Moonglow—a nightclub on the edge of the Gourmet District.

Judy smiled as she recalled Jenny's description of a night out for *The Farrington Girls*, "Susie on the prowl, me watching, and you and Ali dating."

"How did I become a *Farrington Girl?*"

Silence.

Judy retrieved a letter from her shoulder bag, still her constant companion on the sofa beside her.

"Look at this Frank, The Merchant's Association of the Gourmet District is giving me an award."

> *In recognition of the positive impact your blogs have had on the Gourmet District, we are pleased to inform you that a plaque commemorating your "Outstanding Contribution to the Gourmet District" will be unveiled on April 14. At the unveiling, we will present you with a replica of the plaque.*

"You know, Frank, I can trace all the positive things in my life directly back to the first time we met."

***

Ozzie's Burgers @ The Farmer's Market is owned by an Australian guy, everyone calls Ozzie. Judy doesn't know his real name, but knows she likes his burgers. Her favorite is the Sunny Burger.

The first time she'd enjoyed a Sunny Burger, she sat at the counter to watch it made.

Diced onion caramelized using a little oil directly on the hot plate. Sausage meat—already mixed with herbs and spices—formed into a ball. The onion gathered in a pile using a wide metal spatula, that appeared to be a paint scraper.

Balled meat placed on top of the onions and flattened with the spatula and the heel of Ozzie's hand, imbedding onion into the meat. The onion that escaped corralled into a second pile, and the process repeated when Ozzie flipped the patty.

The meat sizzled, aromas of beef scented with a blend of seasoning, and spices infused with the caramelized onion wafted over Judy, igniting her taste buds and causing her to salivate in anticipation.

A hamburger bun with sesame seeds on the top, baked—Judy discovered later—by Alice's Bakery, halved and toasted. Equally generous portions of barbeque and tomato sauce spread on either half, both sauces handmade by Exquisite Jams.

The cooked meat was placed on the bottom half and topped with a slice of tasty cheddar cheese. It may not melt into almost liquid as processed hamburger cheese does, but it has flavor.

A large lightly pickled slice of beetroot added color and contrast on top of the cheese. Judy found it strange to put beetroot on a hamburger and nearly told him not to, but decided to try the authentic burger. She later learned it's usual to include beetroot in a hamburger in Australia.

A lettuce cup, sliced tomato and sliced cucumber topped with a Caesar dressing, also from Exquisite Jams, comprised the next layer.

A slice of canned pineapple—lightly caramelized on the hotplate—was next, followed by two rashers of crispy bacon. Finally, a sunny side up egg, before the top half of the bun completed the burger. *A balanced meal.*

Ozzie cut the burger, allowing the egg yolk mixed with tomato sauce to run down through the hole in the pineapple ring which directed the yolk into the burger instead of down the side.

Looks appetizing—made fresh, and mostly unprocessed ingredients.

She struggled to pick up half the burger without the contents spilling. Mouth wide-open, she maneuvered it into her mouth and bit into her first Sunny Burger. A little egg yolk and sauce ran down her chin.

My God! Fucking delicious!

She reached for a napkin and dabbed the spillage, closing her eyes to savor the flavors and textures which complimented, rather than battled, each other.

The bacon's saltiness balanced the sweetness of the pineapple. The juices from the meat mixed with the sauces. A snap from the bacon, crunch from the salad, smoothness from the egg and cheese, and soft bread. Tangy from sauces and spices. A bite from the cheese and a sweet bite from the pickled beetroot and caramelized onion, finished with a gooeyness from the egg.

Wow! When she finished, she wanted to order another, not that she could eat it.

She described her Sunny Burger experience to Frank the next morning, who inspired her to write a mini feature about it; *Sunny Burger: A Party in Your Mouth.*

As usual, lifestyle sites picked it up but then, food and local sites also ran the mini feature. Print media published it as a filler. Ozzie's Burgers hung a framed copy on their wall. Their business doubled, with a flow on effect to the Farmer's Market, making Judy almost a local celebrity.

She never pays for a burger at Ozzie's now. They refuse to accept her money.

The success of her Sunny Burger mini feature, and requests from publishers for more inspired her. She wrote another, *Coffee Roasters' John*

Farrington Blend. Also popular, resulting in multiple sales for Judy, increasing Coffee Roasters' business and making the John Farrington Blend their best seller.

A framed copy of Judy's mini feature is on display in the shop, and there are many benefits for John Farrington, who, like Judy, no longer pays for his coffee purchases.

Judy's glad she doesn't need money, otherwise she might be tempted to solicit and charge businesses for promoting their products and services. She only writes about products she believes in and uses, the ones she considers *the best in the city.*

Her third food mini feature was *Alice's White Chocolate, Mandarin and Macadamia Cookies: Each Bite a Different Version of the Dance*, with similar results. Now, many of the businesses in the Gourmet District have a framed *Judy Vernon mini feature* on their walls.

Judy never accepts payment from business for writing about their products, but she seldom needs to pay for anything in the district.

***

Judy glanced at her watch. *Nearly time for Sabbath dinner.*

After meeting Myron's parents twice, they accepted Judy as part of the family, and invited her to join them for Sabbath meal.

Myron still goes to his parent's home after work on Friday and stays until Sunday morning when he collects Judy for their weekly brunch at Bait & Switch.

Judy joins the family for Sabbath meal on Saturday afternoon and leaves again that evening. An arrangement everyone's happy with.

"How's this happened, Frank?"

Frank didn't answer.

"When I met you, I didn't have a family. Now I have two. How am I integrated into these families, like I've always been part of them?"

Frank smiled and tilted his head slightly. There seemed to be a twinkle in his pleading eyes, as though he were taking the credit.

Judy shook her head. "See you tomorrow, Frank."

Art and Ruth

Judy arrived at Myron's parents' home.

From the first Sabbath meal she'd shared with the family, Judy took to referring to them—at Myron's suggestion—as Mama Ruth and Papa Art as a sign of respect. The significance of Myron's suggestion wasn't lost on her, but referring to them as Mama and Papa felt natural, and Judy never gave it a second thought, let alone dwelled on the implication.

Judy placed her finger on the button and pressed lightly.

***

At the sound of the familiar chime, Ruth glanced at the clock on the kitchen wall and smiled. *That'll be Judy.* She made no move towards the front door. Myron would be hovering near the door, waiting as he did every Sabbath.

Being the only girlfriend Myron had introduced to them confirmed he was serious. She liked them as a couple, and the idea of Judy as a daughter. *Much more suitable than Malka.*

***

Myron and Malka arrived home. She headed to the living room. They exchanged no words. Myron seldom spoke to her. *Little point. She never listens.*

Myron studied his fiancé. Waist length dark brown hair, slim body and long legs. Brown eyes, full of determination, but not a hint of kindness. *Glorious body. No denying she's attractive, but she doesn't do it for me. Sex is mechanical, functional, and lacks passion. Guess she doesn't like me much either. Wish Mama made a better match, someone who at least tried to understand me.*

With Malka—the daughter of one of the leading families in the community—conversation usually focused, as it had on their way home, on properties to be bought and sold for profit. She was trying to interest Myron in investing in a property which she speculated they could sell a few years later at a handsome profit.

Myron's response, always the same. "I'm sorry Malka, we don't sell properties."

"But Myron, we can make a lot more money selling properties than holding on to them. Nobody understands why you don't sell your properties."

"We don't need money."

"Everybody needs money."

"Enough for living a comfortable life, and for security against the unforeseen. We have enough."

"We could buy a big house and let everyone see we are successful."

"Being seen as successful doesn't mean someone *is* successful."

"What's the point of being successful if no one sees it?"

"Success, as they say, is like beauty in the eyes of the beholder."

Malka rolled her eyes. "More Myerson lore?"

"No, a cliché."

Malka switched to her sullen mode.

If she means to influence me, she doesn't know me at all. He went to his room and returned to his current repetition of analyzing the situation. No matter how he tried, he couldn't connect the dots to picture how everything would work. Nor could he work out how to extract himself from the situation without Mama losing face in the community.

***

Art looked up when Malka entered and sat on the sofa opposite him. Hearing her and Myron arrive, he noted she came straight to the living room without stopping to pay her respects to Ruth. *Not even a pretense of respect.*

"Hello Art," Malka said.

Art glanced at his watch. "Good morning, Malka."

Malka's eyes were fixed on the large beige envelope on the coffee table. "Is that Myron's medical report?"

"I believe so."

She reached for the envelope. "What's it say?"

"Don't know. It's addressed to Myron."

Malka withdrew her hand, but continued to stare at the envelope.

Medical report. This is more like a business transaction than a marriage. She's more interested in our properties than our son. Art turned away. He didn't want her to catch the look of disdain on his face.

***

Myron entered the living room after stopping in the kitchen to say hello to Mama. Before he had a chance to sit down or greet Papa, Malka grabbed the envelope and passed it to him.

"Your medical report."

He nodded, took the envelope, but didn't open it. He crossed the room and hugged Papa hello.

Malka frowned at him. Twice she opened her mouth to say something, but evidently thought better of it.

Still standing, Myron carefully opened the envelope. He glanced at Malka, on the edge of the sofa, looking anxious, like she wanted to rip the report out of his hands. He extracted the document and placed the envelope neatly on the table. *Am I moving slowly to annoy her?*

Myron read it thoroughly, then smiled. He studied Malka, waiting expectantly. When he re-read the report, his smile broadened. He winked at Art before passing the document to Malka.

***

Malka stretched forward and almost snatched the paper from Myron's hands. She studied the results quickly and intently.

"Says I'm in perfect health," Myron said, still beaming.

Malka's eyes widened. She stared at the paperwork and then glared at Myron. *Unlikely he will father children! No, no, no. Who will carry on the bloodline? No, this isn't possible.*

"Says you can't father children."

Art gasped, but she ignored him.

"No, but the important thing is, I'm in perfect health."

"*Perfect?* How can you say perfect when you can't father children?"

"That's not important."

"It *is* to me! How can our bloodline continue if I don't continue it? I'm an only child. Bad enough I'm female, and our name will only carry on added to yours."

"We can adopt."

"What? Someone else's bloodline?"

"Blood doesn't make family."

"*You people* have no idea what's important."

Malka glared at Myron and then at Art. *Defective! Myron and his damn Myerson lore. Both defective.*

"Says unlikely, not impossible." Myron argued.

She threw the document on the table. Art glanced at Myron, who nodded. Art picked it up and began reading.

"This whole family is impossible." Malka glowered at Art and Myron. "Marriage is impossible."

"I'm sorry, you feel…" Myron began.

"You're defective! I won't invest in anything defective. It's bad business."

Malka stood, looked at Myron with disdain, jerkily pulled the engagement ring from her finger and flung it on the table. She shook her head, and with an audible sigh, snatched her bag off the sofa, turned and stormed out without another word.

***

The slamming door startled Ruth. *What's going on?* She wiped her hands on the tea towel she was holding and went to the living room.

Myron standing, smiling. Art sitting in his usual chair, reading a document. Malka gone.

"Myron? Art, what's happened?"

"Myron's medical report. Seems unlikely Myron will be able to father children." Art explained.

"Oh, Myron!"

Myron smiled, and looking pointedly at the discarded engagement ring, said, "There are worse things than being unable to father children."

Ruth followed Myron's gaze, noticing the ring. "Malka?"

"Failed business merger," Art opined.

"She decided if I can't father children, she couldn't marry me."

Ruth—still trying to grasp the situation—looked at her son, smiling, beaming. *Given a choice of marrying that girl or not being able to father children, Myron prefers the latter.*

"I'm sorry. Word will get around, but I'm sure I'll still be able to find you a good wife."

Ruth looked at Art for support. He seemed about to say something, but Myron spoke first. "Mama *please*. I don't need help to find a woman. I always knew you'd find me a wife, and accepted it, but it didn't work out."

She glanced at Art, and back to Myron. Finally, her gaze settled on the engagement ring. "I admit, Malka wasn't the best match for you. But I've not known you to date anyone. You've never mentioned anyone…"

"Really Mama. Do you want me to discuss my sex life with you?"

Ruth flushed. "No, of course not."

"I don't date girls from the community. Most have a narrow outlook on life, and pressure from the community places too much stress on the relationship."

"Told you he's not gay," Art said. "He always looks at girls with short skirts, not guys with cute asses."

Ruth looked at her husband, but didn't respond.

She studied her son and slowly nodded. "Don't worry. I've learned my lesson. I won't interfere again."

"You weren't interfering, Mama; you were doing what you thought best. Arranged marriages are the way of things."

"Not anymore."

Art said, "Worked out for me, but I was lucky."

Ruth flashed Art a smile, then turned her attention back to Myron.

"How do you feel about being unable to father children?"

"Haven't had time to process it. All I can think is it's better than the alternative." He fixed his eyes on the engagement ring. "Being a father has very little to do with blood, and everything to do with heart. Perhaps I'll marry a single mother or adopt. No point in worrying about it now."

Ruth nodded. "Why didn't you introduce us to any girl you dated before Malka?"

Myron shrugged. "Never dated a girl I thought I'd like to spend the rest of my life with."

Ruth nodded. She never raised the subject again. She trusted her son, put his happiness first, and ignored the gossip and pressure from the community.

***

Learning Myron can't father children removed Judy's biggest concern about being able to maintain their relationship. She was open to the prospect of adopting, although they'd never discussed it. Myron would be more likely to adopt an older child no one else wanted and Judy was comfortable with that. She wasn't surprised when Myron accepted guardianship of Rebekah.

Ruth smiled when Judy entered the kitchen to ask if she needed help to prepare Sabbath meal.

Having been reading Judy's features since she started writing, Ruth felt she knew her and considered Judy a friend before they met. When Ruth saw how happy Judy made her son, she fell in love with her and accepted her as family.

Judy embraced Ruth and kissed her cheek. "Anything I can help with, Mama Ruth?"

"No, I'm waiting for dinner to finish cooking. The cold dishes are on the table."

"I'll say hello to Papa Art and come back to help take stuff to the table."

"Thank you. Perhaps take the wine on your way."

Sabbath meal is a late lunch, referred to as 'dinner'. Judy couldn't eat after such a big meal, so she supposed it was an early dinner. She quite enjoyed the wine served with the meal; Manischewitz Concord Grape Wine is sweet and fruity.

Art stood when Judy entered the living room.

He liked Judy the moment they met. His fondness for her grew when he saw how she and Myron were together. It was obvious she loved Myron and he could see Myron loved her.

"Hello, Papa Art." Judy embraced him and kissed his cheek.

"Hello Judy, everything under control in the kitchen?"

"Mama Ruth says dinner won't be long. I'll help her take everything to the table soon."

The effect Judy had on his wife and his son sealed the deal for Art. Judy was family. He considered her a daughter.

"Oh Judy, I have something for you." He reached down to the coffee table and picked up a key, which he passed to Judy.

"You shouldn't have to ring the doorbell like a visitor."

Judy took the key and smiled. Overwhelmed, lost for words. "Thank you, Papa Art," was all she managed.

Judy and Alison

The next Farrington Girls' night, Judy and Ali, were enjoying each other on the dance floor. Jenny sipped her vodka tonic as she watched the waitress place another two pink gins on the table.

She nodded towards the drinks, commenting to her sister, "Those two are hitting it pretty hard tonight."

"You counting?" Susie asked.

"Noticing."

"Notice that guy heading this way? I'm trying to decide whether to take him home or out the back. Dance with him again and see what happens."

"How do you decide?"

"Don't know. Just a feeling."

Jenny took another sip of her vodka tonic and smiled as her sister met the guy and headed back to the dance floor. This break from the reality of the life of a working single mother had done Susie a world of good. Judy was right. Susie needed to release her tension, and often found a guy, sometimes two, to go home with.

Jenny occasionally dances, but mostly sits in their booth, watching the *goings on* as she describes it. *I might do a psychology course.*

Not for the first time, Jenny wondered what it would be like to take a guy 'out the back,' into a laneway with dimly lit alcoves. Ideal for a quick fuck or blow job, and avoids the complication of taking someone home.

Jenny wasn't sure why she hesitated. She didn't believe in fidelity in marriage. She found infidelity useful. When Dave has someone on the side, she knows. She says nothing, but uses his guilt to get what she wants without argument. Last month, his guilt paid to have the living room wallpaper replaced.

Judy and Ali returned from the dance floor, downed their drinks, and signaled for another round before they sat. While they waited, they kissed, as they often did. Everyone at the club assumed they were a couple. *Look like they belong together.* Despite Susie's assurances, Jenny wouldn't be surprised if they slept together. They always took separate taxis home, which might be a ruse.

Ali slid her hand inside Judy's skirt. Jenny studied Judy's reaction. She opened her legs a little wider, kissed Ali passionately, and slid her own hand inside Ali's skirt.

Interesting. How far will they go now alcohol's diluted their inhibitions? Never been attracted to women, so why is watching them arousing me?

A waitress arrived with another round, interrupting the action on the other side of the booth. Judy and Ali downed their drinks and returned to the dance floor.

***

Ali stared sightlessly out the window of the taxi on her way home, imagining Judy's face reflected in the glass.

These past few months had left her infatuated with Judy. Nothing could come of it, given their present circumstances. *No idea why I feel this way about her or what to do about it. She's the love of my life, my soulmate, or perhaps it's the way our chemicals react?*

Her first glimpse of Judy always made her breathless, pulse racing and unable to sit still. *Why does it always feel like I'm seeing her for the first time?*

They spend the night holding hands, dancing and kissing. Less than Ali desired—less than she believed they'd have—if their circumstances were different. She longed for Judy's touch, for Judy's taste.

When she arrived home, Ali could barely contain herself long enough to shower—she told John she was washing the sweat off after dancing all night—her fantasy, always the same; Judy's fingers, not her own, bringing her to orgasm.

***

Myron heard Judy open the door and hurried to greet her when she arrived for Sabbath dinner. She was her usual warm self, but had a distant look in her eyes.

Something on her mind. Not avoiding eye contact. No coldness towards me. Probably thinking about her latest feature, or something to do with Frank.

Enough for Myron. *Talk about it when she's ready.*

***

Sunday morning, Judy sat at her desk, eating breakfast, staring into the sunbeam as usual.

I love Myron. Haven't told him. Sure he knows. Never been so compatible with someone. Considerate, predictable and a wonderful lover. No need to compromise on anything. Perfect for me. I don't want to lose him.

Ali sets my senses afire. How can fire make me wet? The prospect of an unfulfilled promise? Perhaps more alluring in restraint?

Judy lost herself in the dance of airborne particles alive in the sunbeam until they came together. No longer particles, instead transformed into Frank's eyes, staring back at her.

"Frank! This is your fault! I was perfectly fine with my life before you came along. No complications."

Silence.

"Two years? Surely not that long."

There was that one girl I met in the bar....

"No Frank, one drink doesn't break a drought."

I was tired of failed relationships.

"Point is Frank, if I was single, I'd be free to be with whom I wanted, when I wanted."

It wouldn't have been the first time Judy had simultaneously been involved with people of different genders. Similar, she supposed, to visiting the Farmers' Market and deciding what to eat for dinner.

"No, I'm not saying I want to repeat my slutty behavior. That was a decade ago."

Why does talking to Frank feel like I'm talking to my father?

"Your fault, Frank. If you didn't give me your accounts files, there'd be no reason to contact Myron, and if you didn't die, I wouldn't have met Ali."

That's harsh.

"Sorry Frank, I didn't mean that like it sounded."

Don't know what I want....

"Well yes, I suppose I do."

I want everything to stay exactly as it is.

"You're right Frank. Nothing needs to change."

She finished her coffee, smiled, picked up her phone, selected the contact at the top of her list, and pressed call.

"Meet me in an hour. People's Park, East Gate."

***

Ali was unsure if the command she'd received signified what she wanted or didn't want to hear. Her thoughts had been distracted since Friday night; well, distracted for months, since the moment their eyes connected at Susie's barbeque. Ali thought and fantasized about Judy constantly.

Did I over-step or take things to the next level?

Perhaps everything will be okay, Judy reciprocated. Her touch—even through my panties—nearly made me cum right there in the club, with Jenny watching. If that waitress didn't bring our drinks, I would've.

Now I've received a royal summons. The possibility of not answering the command hadn't occurred to her. Her nerves raw, her heart pounding, she changed. A white blouse, buttons undone enough to reveal her lacy bra and cleavage, and a short white skirt.

She appraised herself in the mirror and nodded approvingly. *Ready to meet my fate. Please God, don't let this be the end.*

"Keep an eye on the kids for a couple of hours John, need to meet Judy."

Ali was out the door before John responded.

***

Upon arriving in the park, Judy rang Myron. "Something to do. I'll meet you at Bait & Switch. I may be a little late."

The butterflies in her stomach were playing basketball, dashing from one end of the court to the other, as her thoughts debated whether Ali would agree. From her vantage point on a bench near the park entrance, Judy saw Ali as soon as she entered. She stood and waved.

When Ali reached her, Judy took her hand. "Let's find somewhere quiet."

Ali said nothing. Judy led her to a bench surrounded by trees, released her hand, and sat. Ali sat beside her, hands fidgeting in her lap.

Judy took Ali's hand again and began. "Time… had we met at another time in my life, I would've bedded you within an hour. Wouldn't have cared if you were married. Wouldn't have asked."

"You're very sure of yourself."

Judy fixed her gaze on Ali's green eyes, daring her to look away.

"*Please.* You ogle me like I'm Fine Belgian chocolate, and the only decision you're contemplating is whether to consume me immediately or slowly savor every morsel."

Ali smiled despite herself. "Definitely the second."

"No matter how much I might desire you, I *won't* risk losing Myron, and I *won't* be disloyal to John."

"You desire me?"

"You knew the moment our eyes connected."

"I admit, I felt something," Ali said.

Judy studied Ali. A single tear escaped Ali's control and was making its way down her cheek. Judy brushed Ali's face, capturing the tear. She examined her thumb as if inspecting the drop before extending her tongue and licking Ali's salty overflow.

"I don't want to lose you, but I need you to understand we can never go further than we did on Friday night. I must draw a line, because if I cross it, I doubt I'll be able to control myself. That's my condition. Never inside my underwear. That way, I can convince myself we're only flirting."

***

Relieved, Ali lost her iron control. Tears flowed, but not the bitter tears she'd expected and fought. She embraced Judy, burying her head in Judy's shoulder, and let her tears flow.

Ali composed herself. "Sorry darling, I made your blouse wet."

"Not only my blouse, but we're *not* going there."

Ali closed her eyes, allowing her imagination to play with the image Judy gave her.

"You can wipe that silly grin off your face. You look like a man who thinks he's gonna get laid. I'm serious. It's set in stone. I want your promise."

Made yourself clear; I won't get laid.

"I promise, I won't try to put my hands… or anything else inside your stone panties."

"That's not enough."

Ali opened her mouth to speak, but Judy continued before she could.

"If I get carried away and try to touch *you*, promise you'll be strong enough to stop me."

Oh, she feels the same about me. Ali reached out and placed her hand over what she estimated was Judy's heart. "I promise, I'll never let you touch me inside my panties, no matter how much you beg me to."

Not a promise Ali wanted to make, but one she resolved to keep. They sat quietly with Ali's hand resting on Judy's chest until Judy said, "I think you can remove your hand now."

***

Judy stood and reached down to take Ali's hand. "Let's walk for a while."

They strolled through the park holding hands, occasionally stopping to kiss, appearing to the world like a happy couple. They entered a circle of trees, which hid a rose garden.

Ali commented, “Oh, didn’t know this was here.”

“Don’t know why it’s encircled by trees. Suppose when the trees were first planted, they didn’t anticipate they’d grow so tall.”

They followed a cobblestone path around the outer circle of roses, stepped down a small linking path, then followed an identical path between the two outer rose beds. Color, in shades of pink, white, red, yellow, and peach surrounded them. The air, full of the fragrant, unmistakable scent of roses.

“So pretty,” Ali observed.

“Yes, you are.”

Ali squeezed Judy’s hand.

They strolled around the circular paths surrounding two more rows of roses.

“So many rose bushes.”

“Seventy-one, counted them once.”

Reaching the center, the world was silent. The only sound, a simultaneous intake of breath as the women caught sight of the central garden, which contained a single plant.

An ancient rose, its limbs gnarly and twisted like an arthritic nonagenarian, its leaves sparse. It offered a solitary bloom. A wine-red perfection of a rose that had recently fully opened. One glimpse of the bloom and it became clear why the rose has been exalted throughout history.

The central rose had a mystical quality, as if the much younger plants which surrounded it in four neat circles had come to pay silent homage to the ancient. The sun hadn’t reached its zenith, but a ray of sunshine found its way between the trees and illuminated the single rose like a spotlight.

“Almost as if we’re being blessed.”

"Yes," agreed Judy, as Frank's eyes appeared in her mind. "But by whom."

They sat on one of the four curved benches surrounding the central rose. Silently holding hands and leaning into each other, absorbing the moment of spirituality.

Eventually, Judy glanced at her watch. *Time to go.* More than a little disappointed and conflicted, she wanted to meet Myron, but she didn't want to leave Ali.

"I need to meet Myron for brunch."

"Better go myself. John'll be wondering what I'm up to."

They stood and made their way out of the park, hands and hearts entwined.

"Not sure what this is, and nothing can come of it, but I'd like us to spend more time together. Nothing in particular, just enjoying each other."

Ali winked. "Didn't you make me promise we wouldn't enjoy each other?"

"Not sexually. Sex is off the table. I love the way you make me feel when I'm with you."

Ali grinned.

"What?"

"Thinking about what I want to do to you, on the table."

"Behave yourself."

"My promise relates to my actions, not my thoughts. Those I can't control."

Judy's turn to grin. "Nor me."

"Of course I want to spend more time together. I'm infatuated with you. You're all I think about. Don't know what it is about you, but I felt it the moment I saw you."

Judy squeezed her hand. "I can sense it, darling."

Their eyes connected. It seemed to Judy they spent a lot of time communicating with their souls. An unfamiliar experience for her.

"The truth is, I love you, Judy."

"I can feel."

Judy hadn't expressed her love to anyone for more than a decade. Expressing love made her vulnerable. The last time she expressed her love, she'd been hurt deeply, and had sworn off women and began dating men. That she could admit loving Myron to Ali, but not to Myron, wasn't lost on her.

They embraced when they reached the park entrance, and kissed.

"You better go," Ali said.

Judy stepped out of the park and onto the sidewalk without another word. She flagged a taxi, gazed at Ali one more time, and climbed into the back.

Dickensian

Judy settled into the back of the taxi, gave the driver the address for Bait & Switch, and became lost in her thoughts.

Frank's fault. Before he came into my life, I was content. Just me, but I liked it that way. A tranquil life, no complications. Now I'm working twice as hard, and I've fallen in love with two people.

Not that this is unusual. Complicates lives and destroys relationships. Don't want my life complicated.

Best be honest. What's that saying? Everything in moderation, including the truth.

I'll be moderately honest.

Judy relaxed.

Frank's right. Nothing needs to change.

***

Myron appraised Judy as she made her way to their usual table. *She's beautiful.* He no longer felt like a schoolboy when he was with her, nor did he feel she was out of his league. *She's exactly my league.* He signaled the waiter, who was ready to take their order.

They embraced and kissed. Myron examined her eyes. *Seems to have resolved whatever was troubling her.*

"Sorry I'm late, needed to see Ali."

"Doesn't matter. Brunch won't be long." He nodded towards the waiter, heading their way. They sat silently as the wine was opened, poured, and the bottle placed in the ice bucket.

"I've something to tell you, Myron. Let me finish before you respond."

When do I not? "Sure."

Myron studied Judy. *Not fidgety or defensive. Nothing to worry about.*

"I'm attracted to Ali. We've become close. We're dating on Friday nights, and we'll be seeing more of each other."

He wanted to hear her out before he thought about his reply. He always listened to understand, not to respond like most people do. *Nothing I don't know from the way you look at each other.*

"We, umm… flirt on the dance floor, and kiss sometimes, as far as we go. I promise I'll never have sex with Ali as long as you and I are together. But I have strong feelings for her. Nothing I can do about that."

"You don't need to ask my permission to spend time with Alison."

"I'm not asking permission. At least, I don't think I am. I'll be seeing more of her, and I don't want to sneak around as if there's something to hide." Judy looked at him expectantly.

Myron nodded towards the waiter who was bringing their seafood platter. "Let's eat."

He studied Judy while he ate. *May not have spoken it, but she loves me. Can feel she does. People think love is intangible, but it's not. It can be felt, experienced, and lost. I've felt a woman's love dissipate and become extinct more than once. No reason to believe Judy's love for me has diminished since she met Alison. If it had, would've felt it. Judy made a promise, didn't need to. Wouldn't ask for or expect one. Trust her. If I didn't, we wouldn't be together.*

Quite like Alison. Judy can't control her feelings any more than I can. Feelings don't work like that. Didn't have feelings for Malka, no matter how hard I tried. Alison's not a threat. Love isn't a competition. Besides, those who win in a love triangle ultimately lose in the relationship.

All I can do is keep loving her and trust she'll keep loving me. If I pressure her or make her life difficult, I risk losing her. Don't want to lose her. The only threats are my insecurities and jealousy, and I feel neither. No problem here.

Situation analyzed; dots connected. He smiled.

***

Judy knew how his mind worked. He took a similar approach to every situation he encountered; analyze the issue from all angles, draw on his experience, see how everything fits together, and then connect the dots to ensure there were no gaps. A natural process for him.

Normally, she studied the process in fascination. Myron once commented; he could see her have ideas. His observation sparked an idea for a feature. Turning the tables and watching Myron think nurtured the idea. Judy spent several days riding buses, observing the passengers and watching them as they became lost in their thoughts. She wrote a feature: *Watching People Think.*

Today, she didn't want to watch him think. She wanted to hear him talk. The butterflies in her stomach were impatient for his answer.

Finally, he did. "Sweetheart, I feel where your heart lies, and as long as I feel your love, I've no reason to be concerned. If that ever changes, we'll need to talk."

"I can feel you too, all the time."

***

On the way home, Judy received an intriguing email alert on her phone.

When they arrived, Judy went to her office, while Myron went to the bathroom.

She sat at her desk and excitedly read the email. She re-read it to be sure she understood it correctly, opened the attachment, and selected print.

When she finished her research on Frank Farrington, Judy knew she had a book, not a feature. She only needed a final chapter. She considered seeking a publisher, but it was difficult to attain one. Months of sending out manuscripts might not result in a publishing deal, even if one had contacts like Judy. Not to mention there would be pressure for the final chapter.

In the end, Judy stuck with what she knew. She took a Dickensian approach to publishing her book, serializing it, publishing one chapter a month. *Sure a few magazine publishers will take it. Buy me time to find a final chapter.*

Judy made the right decision. She sold her serialization to more publishers than expected, reaching a global audience.

The email was from a company interested in publishing *Frank Farrington: A Man of Rare Character and Integrity*, in book form. They enclosed a contract and offered a sizeable advance.

"Look Myron!" she blurted out as he almost had one foot in her office, pointing to the printer.

Myron scanned the document, then stepped over to the desk and kissed her.

"Congratulations, sweetheart."

"Today may be the best day of my life."

Frank's eyes appeared in her mind.

Myron reached down, pulled her to her feet, and hugged her. She buried her face in his shoulder. Her happiness flowed as tears soaked into Myron's polo shirt. Regaining her composure, she extracted herself from his arms.

"I'll put the coffee on. Can you read through that and make sure everything's in order? Want to sign it before they change their mind."

Judy carried the tray with their usual Sunday afternoon coffee and cookies to the living room.

Myron finished reading the contract. Having an experienced eye, it didn't take long.

"Standard contract," he said. "Nothing untoward, except the deadline to produce the manuscript is only six weeks. They want to take advantage of the interest generated by the serialization."

"Finished other than the final chapter. Gives me six weeks to come up with a conclusion."

"Can you do it?"

"I'll have to."

Judy took the contract, returned to her office, signed, scanned, and sent it to the publishers. Deal done.

Returning to the living room, she said, "Take me to bed and make this day perfect."

***

Judy was still buoyant the next morning when she arrived at Kansas Café.

"Frank, we need a final chapter for your book. Any ideas?"

Frank smiled, but remained silent.

"I guess I could. Let me think about it."

Rebekah delivered Judy's regular order and returned to the kitchen.

"Actually, Frank, it's a good idea. Perfect ending. Can't promise, but I'll have Myron look into it."

She opened her iPad and began making a list of all the features and mini features inspired by Frank, about Frank, or related to Frank.

It took longer to compile the list than Judy anticipated. Ali and the weekend's distractions caused her to neglect her current features. She needed to get them written, edited and reviewed before the fast approaching deadline. *Fucking deadlines.*

She inflicted more pressure on herself by accepting an invitation from Ali for a midweek spa and sauna day at a retreat in the hills outside of the city.

***

Ali got the kids off to school. *One last look at myself.* Eggshell slacks and a sea-foam colored cotton blouse. Not that it mattered, they would spend most of the day wearing robes provided by the spa.

The layer under her clothes was more important. She wore her best lingerie, lacy satin in shades of red and white, named *Liquid Abstract.* Mostly they'd be naked—sauna, jacuzzi, full body scrub—but she wanted to wow Judy, even if nothing would come of it.

She called Judy. "On my way," then climbed into her Dark Garnet Red Pearl Chrysler 300 and headed off, excited at the prospect of spending the day with Judy.

Don't know why she makes me feel like a kid on Christmas Eve. Hope the feeling never goes away.

***

Judy inspected herself in the full-length mirror, trying to decide whether to leave two or three of the lower buttons open. A knee-length tiffany blue button-down dress, gathered at the waist. She knew what attracted Ali's attention, because her eyes were always rivetted on Judy's crossed legs when she wore short skirts. Underneath she wore her aphrodisiac lingerie, powder blue.

Ali called. "On my way." Judy's heart skipped a beat. She studied her reflection one last time. *Three buttons.*

Today was a test for Judy. *Can I spend the day naked with Ali and not cross the line, not break my promise?* The question consumed her. *If I can't, need to decide between Myron and Ali.* A decision she didn't want to make.

***

Neither pretended not to stare as they undressed beside each other, and carefully hung their clothes in their lockers. They assisted each other to unfasten their bras, which was unnecessary.

They stood naked beside the closed lockers, unashamedly staring, conscious of the other's nakedness but unconscious of their own. Frozen by the same hypnotic handcuffs that bound them the moment they met.

Both aroused, neither moved. They listened to the echo of heavy breathing, knowing if they moved, they would start something they couldn't stop. Everything would change. Although their bodies remained apart, their souls intertwined.

An attendant entered, creating a distraction which released them. She handed them towels, which they wrapped around themselves, then followed the woman to the pool room.

A quick shower and they stepped into the unoccupied sauna. They opened their towels and sat naked, allowing the heated air to open their pores. Despite their heated libido, neither opened their legs.

They held hands, perhaps to keep their hands occupied.

After the sauna, they showered together, washing the sweat off themselves and each other, being careful not to cross their agreed upon boundaries. Next the Jacuzzi, before heading for a body scrub, now their pores were open and relaxed.

And so, they spent the day together, naked and bonding as they adapted to their unusual relationship. Unconsummated lovers.

***

Ali dropped Judy at the Farmers' Market when they returned to the city. Judy selected the items needed for dinner. When she arrived home, she reviewed her current features, made some minor adjustments, and sent them off.

She climbed into bed that night, still aroused. She remembered her promise to Myron. *I promised not to have sex with Ali; I didn't promise not to fantasize about having sex with her.* She slid her hand between her legs. *That woman makes me so wet.* In her fantasy, Ali's hand touching her, as she'd wanted Ali to do all day.

After she satisfied herself, she smiled contentedly. *Guess I'm not getting old anymore.* She drifted off to sleep.

***

When Ali arrived home, her children sat at the kitchen table doing their homework. Empty plates and glasses told her they helped themselves to an after-school drink and snack. *Everything under control here.*

"Gonna take a quick shower, then I'll make dinner," she announced.

She stepped into the shower and allowed the hot water to cascade over her body. *So horny. Don't know how I didn't touch her.* As she did on Friday nights, she slid—what was in her mind—Judy's hand between her legs, and relieved herself of sexual tension.

This is gonna work out just fine. She turned the water off and grabbed her towel. *Must get dinner organized.*

***

The next day, Judy finished her list of Frank related features and mini features. *Hmmm... More than I imagined.* She emailed the list to Myron and called him with a request to calculate how much money she'd made from Frank.

The answer to her question would, she hoped, enable the seed to grow into an idea and, from the idea, a conclusion for her book.

Sabbath

Judy called into Kansas Café for a coffee and a chat with Frank.

"I'm hoping what Myron tells me today will give us the ending for your book."

Frank smiled, but remained silent.

"Instead of sitting there smiling, I wish you'd tell me what you want. You've had that pleading look since I met you, and I'm no closer to knowing what it means."

Rebekah arrived with Judy's coffee and a small piece of brownie.

"Everything good, Becky?"

"It's like I've woken from a nightmare. I love culinary school, learned I can cook. Dorothy always tells me stories about this place in it's prime, makes me feel I was there."

Her self-esteem has improved. "I'm happy for you."

"Aunt Judy, could you try my brownie and tell me what you think?"

"Love to."

Judy made a show of eating the brownie, slowly and deliberately. "Oh my, that's amazing. Is it kosher?"

"Not if they have meat in the meal because it contains dairy, but as a standalone snack, sure."

"I'll take two pieces with me. Art and Ruth can have them tomorrow."

Rebekah nodded and grinned. "Is it really good?"

"Yes, Becky."

Judy smiled as she watched Rebekah return to the kitchen. She and Myron had effectively adopted her. For Judy, it was a trial run for what she expected would be in their future.

She raised her cup and inhaled the aroma. *I have an unhealthy relationship with coffee.* She took a sip, savoring the flavor, before replacing the cup on its saucer, taking a napkin and absently wiping the foam from her mouth. She reapplied her lipstick.

Judy returned her attention to her companion. He was usually smiling at her, conveying his emotion through changes to his smile. His eyes never changed.

"Yes Frank, everything is well with Myron." She rolled her eyes. "And with Ali."

The smile on his face transformed into a smirk.

"And you can wipe the smug look off your face. Do ghosts have faces? Yes, you were right."

Judy glanced at her watch. *Time to go.*

***

Accepted as part of the family, as though she and Myron had married, Judy opened the door to the Myerson home and walked in. She went directly to the kitchen and kissed Ruth on the cheek.

"Some brownies from Rebekah for tomorrow," she said, as she placed them in the refrigerator.

"Thank her for me, sweetheart."

"What can I do to help Mama Ruth?"

"All under control here, waiting for stuff to finish cooking. I'll join you in the living room shortly."

Entering the living room, Judy kissed both Myron and Art hello before sitting next to Myron on the sofa.

"Much to discuss today," Myron said.

"Okay, darling."

He handed Judy a sheet of paper, containing a summary of all her Frank related earnings. "This is what you wanted."

Judy looked at the numbers. "Wow," was all she said as she digested the information.

"Wow, indeed!" Art echoed.

"Is this enough money to finish repaying Frank's investors?"

"More than enough."

"I want to repay them all, Myron. I owe it to Frank, and I need an ending for my book."

Despite all that had transpired between them, and despite having acknowledged, each could feel the other's emotion, the words hadn't been spoken directly. Perhaps, in fear of breaking the spell.

"I love you, Judy," Myron said, and flushed.

Judy hadn't exchanged those words with anyone for more than a decade. Not wanting to admit, even to herself, what the words meant to her, she kissed his cheek. "I know, darling."

"Everybody knows," Art said.

"Everyone knows what?" Ruth asked as she entered the room.

"That Myron loves Judy."

"Of course he does. We all do."

Judy buried her head into Myron's shoulder to cover the tears escaping from her eyes. She couldn't recall feeling such deep love and affection, and Myron's acceptance of Ali had somehow made her love him more.

"I love you too, Myron," she whispered in his ear.

Myron smiled. "I know, sweetheart."

"We all know Judy." Ruth said, even though Judy was sure Ruth couldn't have heard her whisper.

Judy was trying to understand how her falling in love with Ali could have increased, not diminished, her love for Myron. *Frank knew.*

She raised her head from Myron's shoulder and contemplated Art and Ruth. *They're open, honest, accepting, and non-judgmental. Everything my parents weren't.* Judy had been a lesbian from puberty for more than a decade and had never mentioned her preference to her parents. Myron's parents knew she was bisexual and dated Ali Friday nights. *They accept me, exactly as I am.*

She needed to refocus herself when Myron returned to the matter at hand.

"Legally, we don't have the list of investors or the financial records, but we can fix that. Myriam's claim was thrown out and Frank's business will be auctioned next Tuesday."

"Myriam knew she had no chance, but wanted to mess with Susie."

"The owner of the auction house owes me a favor."

Judy smiled. *It seems half of the city owes Myron a favor.* "Of course he does."

"No one is interested in the company. They only want the stock from the warehouse, so won't bid anything close to the value of the business."

"Are we supposed to know it's value?"

"We are now. The books are open for inspection, but the only records people have asked for are the stock records."

"Okay."

"I think we should buy Phoenix Imports."

"Oh, umm… Together? Can we afford it? How could we run it? I don't think you'll be happy driving a forklift all day."

"Yes. Equal partners. I've arranged funding. Initially, we won't make much because the first thing is to repay the funding."

"Important not to carry debt," Art said. "Funding can help a business grow in the boom times, but debt sends the business broke during difficult times. Being debt free can make a company, or a person recession proof."

"Two brothers," Myron explained. "Clients of mine, now bankrupt, because their major customer went out of business. They imported air conditioners, air purifiers and dehumidifiers from China, and ended up doing most of their business with a property developer, who ran into financial trouble and stopped paying them."

"Never trust a property developer," Art opined.

"Being bankrupt means they can't own a business for seven years. Having lost their houses, they took their families back to their parents' farm. Their father had retired and was planning to sell the farm, but he let his sons take it over. It's not a big farm, so supporting two families and their parents is a stretch.

"They can run the business for us. Keeping the name Phoenix Imports will make it easier to maintain relationships with the international suppliers."

"I'd like that," Judy said. "Frank didn't choose that name by accident."

"One brother can handle imports and the other distribution, maintaining Frank's system of one week in and one week out, because it's efficient. They can stay in the apartment at the warehouse and switch on Sundays. One brother will attend to the farm while the other looks after our business.

"We'll pay them a fair market wage and give them twenty percent of the profits. If they're still with us in seven years, we can replace profit share with a percentage of the company, and we'll retain eighty."

Judy said, "Sounds like a good deal. You said it was an excellent business after Frank died." Frank's eyes appeared in her mind. "Frank's happy knowing we'll keep his business alive, and I like the idea of helping those brothers. I don't have business knowledge, but I trust you. I'm excited…"

Myron gave her a suggestive look. She squeezed his leg to tell him to behave himself.

She continued, "I'm a little concerned about how the family will feel if we buy the business cheaply."

"They don't know its value, which is why they're auctioning it. Anything is worth whatever someone will pay for it. By buying it at public auction, we're paying the market value."

Ruth said, "Time for dinner."

"I'll help Mama Ruth," Judy said. "We can finish talking about this later."

"Yes," Myron agreed. "There's more."

"Really?"

Judy kissed Myron's cheek and followed Ruth into the kitchen.

***

After dinner, they returned to the living room.

Judy smiled. "My head's still spinning from *everything* you've told me today."

"Before the day is over, your head'll be more than spinning. I need a bigger warehouse and workshop for the vending machine business. I don't see any value in paying rent, so I'm buying the warehouse complex. The owners think Frank's business will close and are offloading the property."

"Nothing wrong with paying rent," Art said. "As long as you're the landlord."

"I plan to run Phoenix Imports on one side and Reliable Vending on the other. I'll need two warehouses for that. There are tenants in the three remaining warehouses. You may have noticed there used to be a convenience store in front of warehouse six, opposite Frank's warehouse. Been closed for years. Going to reopen it as a laundromat and automat."

"Automat?"

"When we converted our guest laundries to public laundromats, we installed vending machines, coffee, snacks, including sandwiches and cakes, not just chips and chocolate bars, and cold drinks.

"We track sales electronically. The street level laundromats were popular overnight, mainly for snacks and coffee. Taxi drivers use them. We added more tables and chairs where we could. Did some research and opened a few more outlets in the areas where taxi drivers do their change of shift. It's proven successful."

"You're very smart Myron," Judy said.

"I'm not. I didn't think taxi drivers needed somewhere to get a coffee and snack overnight. They're using them during the day now too. I wanted to maximize the income from the guest laundries in our hotels. I got lucky."

"No," said Art. "Not lucky. You paid attention to your business, noted a pattern, saw an opportunity, and reacted. Not everyone would do that. Don't sell yourself short."

"I don't know how you find the time for all that you do," Judy said.

"Capable and dedicated staff."

"I agree with Papa. You shouldn't sell yourself short. You have uncommon vision to see how everything fits together."

"I like how we fit together…." Myron began.

Judy flushed and looked at Ruth, who was pretending not to have heard or understood.

"Behave yourself," Judy whispered.

"There's more. You know Dorothy is retiring."

"She's been talking about retirement more lately."

"We'll take over the lease on the shop and the apartment upstairs. Agreed to buy Kansas Café. We'll own it equally like Frank's business, with Rebekah managing it and getting a twenty percent profit share.

"After five years, she'll get twenty percent of the business. I want her to have an incentive to keep her life on track and a goal to work towards. It shouldn't come too easy, or she won't value it."

"You're right," Judy said.

"You'll get to keep your café. I'm sure Rebekah will want to update it, but I don't think she'll go ultra-modern."

"She seems to like the old-world charm of the café as it is. Fantastic news Myron. Appreciate you doing this for me. Been worried about finding somewhere else to work. Atmosphere is important, and there's Frank's err… memory. I'm guessing we can afford it."

Myron smiled. "All part of the funding I arranged. A few more customers like you would be nice. We'll talk to Rebekah, tomorrow. Need to find her some help, too. She should finish her courses, if she's going to run a café."

Ruth said, "The way you have adopted Rebekah and given her the chance of a future makes us proud of the pair of you."

"I've been looking into the building." Art explained. "Heritage protected, so not of interest to developers. Exactly the type of building we like. I'm making some enquiries. Early days yet, but we might buy it."

Judy was trying to come to terms with all she learned that day. She wouldn't have considered any of this before she met Frank.

There were implications, and she wanted to discuss them with Frank. He always helped her get things straight in her head.

Rebekah's Opportunity

Judy was enjoying her cappuccino at Kansas Café, listening to Nina Simone's *Feeling Good.* She frowned. "Oh, this was playing the day you died, Frank. Do you remember? Of course, you don't. You were standing outside shouting at Myriam. Guess she got the last word.

"Good news, Frank. We're going to finish your work and repay your investors the last of what they lost. Going to buy your business too, we'll keep the name and your model. And we're going to buy this café. Never would've believed I'd have business interests."

Frank remained silent, but he was beaming.

"What does it mean that Myron wants us to own the business fifty-fifty? He *never* does that. Equal partners. Is that significant? Is this a trial for becoming partners in life? Does he already see us as partners? Do you think he'll propose? If he does, should I accept? I like the way our life is now… Do I want to change that?"

Frank wasn't forthcoming with any answers, but Judy continued asking questions.

"If we were to marry, would I have to become Jewish? Would I need to spend the whole sabbath with Ruth and Art? If I did, would I resent it? What of our Farrington Girl's nights out? Don't want to give them up."

Judy savored the coffee and studied her friend.

"Where would we live? Prefer to stay in my apartment. The location is convenient for my life. Probably imagining problems where none exist. Perhaps I should wait until I have all the information." *Just the facts, ma'am.*

Why do people create problems in their minds before they exist? May be a feature in that. I'll write a feature about Dorothy and her life in Kansas Café. Call it Dorothy's Not in Kansas Anymore.

If Myron proposes, I'll say yes. The only way my life will remain as it is now. If I say no, because I want my life to stay as it is, everything will change. My life will be lost. Before long, the magic between us will be gone. My answer will be a definite yes.

"He said the words yesterday, Frank. We've both known he loves me, but he never voiced it. Neither did I. Maybe neither of us wanted to be first. Yes, I did, Frank. Been difficult for me not to. I think now it's said, the next step may be marriage or cohabitation… Yes, I suppose they're the same thing these days."

Myron called to confirm his taxi would arrive soon.

Rebekah would join them for brunch at Bait & Switch. Judy gathered her belongings into her shoulder bag, still her constant companion.

"Goodbye Frank, see you tomorrow."

She rang the counter bell and paid Dorothy. "May I interview you this week about your life here in Kansas?"

"I'd like that. So many memories."

"I'll enjoy hearing about them. Can you tell Becky it's time to leave?"

Judy and Rebekah said their goodbyes to Dorothy and headed outside to meet Myron's taxi, which arrived almost as they left the café.

Myron sat in the front. They climbed into the back. *Doesn't feel right, Myron sitting in the front. Can't snuggle into him for our ride down to the docks. Don't like this at all. If we marry, I won't allow the little things, like snuggling in the back of a taxi on the way to Sunday brunch, to stop.*

Myron had dropped his bag home to Judy's on the way.

***

The taxi arrived at the Fisherman's wharf, which housed Bait & Switch. Myron had changed their reservation to three people, but they still ordered the seafood platter for two.

Before the platter arrived, Myron said, "Rebekah, Dorothy is planning to retire."

"She's been talking about it since I started. I'm hoping she hangs on long enough so I can finish my culinary course. They'll do a job placement for me."

"If you had the opportunity, what would you do with the café?"

"That's easy. Been thinking about it because I spend most of my time there and it's often quiet. It'll need a facelift, but I wouldn't turn it into one of those modern clone cafes with no character.

"I'd turn it into a nineteen fifties style diner, with an authentic menu, updated to modern culinary style. The food and beverages they had back then, with a modern twist. We had a lesson where we needed to choose a dish from a fifties menu and modernize it. They gave us a menu they found online from Murphy's Diner. Thought about many of the dishes and how they could be modernized, so I think that'd work.

"Replace the sofas with booths and add stools in front of the counter. Keep tables and chairs in the middle. The kitchen would need to be updated.

"I'd want to be busier than now, but not too busy. Steady enough to make a decent living would be perfect. This is my dream now… to own a café, with a fifties theme, but not that over-the-top burger joint that's almost a caricature. You know the type… a *Happy Days* version of the nineteen fifties. I'd want it to have some class, be authentic with authentic food."

Judy smiled. "I know what you mean, but I'm a little surprised you know *Happy Days*, way before your time, I think."

"I didn't, did some research," Rebekah said. "Didn't know Ron Howard used to be an actor. Anyway, just a dream, but it's good to have a dream… to see a future. When I was inside, and even when I first got out, I never saw a future. Never had a dream. I didn't care about tomorrow or even if I had a tomorrow. I do now."

The seafood platter arrived. Rebekah said, "Wow! Look at that."

They ate in silence, as both Judy and Myron preferred.

After they finished eating, Myron said, "Rebekah, Judy and I are going to buy the café from Dorothy. Would you be interested in running it for us?"

Is this real? "Of course I would, but I don't know enough to run it. I'd hate to fuck it up."

"You'll be fine," Myron said. "You'll finish your courses and my people will monitor things and guide you."

"Will it be possible to finish the courses and run the café at the same time? What about somewhere to stay? If Dorothy goes, where will I live?"

"We're taking over the lease of the café and the apartment upstairs. You'll need some help. We'll hire someone."

"Oh wow, Uncle Myron. I can't believe this." Rebekah was crying a little. "This is my dream come true."

"Do some research and find some examples of how you'd like the new café to look, and we'll get some shop fitters in. Also, work out what equipment you need in the kitchen. You'll need to design a menu, decide on opening hours, that sort of thing."

So much to do. So exciting. "Can we hire Darnell?"

"Darnell?"

"Darnell Williams. He's amazing with flavors. In my culinary class, but one of us can change to the other class. It runs twice each day because of people's work schedules. Darnell's in the same program as me. Had some trouble too, but he's trying to get away from his past. Like me."

"Up to you, but as this is your first hire, Judy and I would like to meet him. Given this is a new venture, you'll also need to determine what you think will be a fair wage both for yourself and Darnell.

"On top of your wages, you'll receive a yearly bonus of twenty percent of the profits. I think we could meet Darnell tomorrow. We'll want him to prepare a sample platter of his cooking. So, let's say lunch time?"

"I'll talk to Darnell, but I think it'll be fine. It's his day off."

***

After brunch, the three took a taxi to the Gourmet District, where Judy bought sour dough bread and white chocolate, mandarin and macadamia cookies. They stopped at Soup Master for broccoli and blue cheese soup for dinner. Judy bought a large and small soup, and she had bought a second sourdough loaf so Rebekah could take her dinner home with her.

Next, they went to Lexington Deli for salad and Exquisite Jams for the honey, mustard and macadamia salad dressing. Judy purchased a large and a small of each.

They returned to Judy's apartment for coffee and cookies.

Rebekah tried the coffee. "Wonderful coffee. What is it?"

"The John Farrington Blend, from Coffee Roasters," Judy said. "People can make their own blend, or choose any blend they want. John's blend has become popular."

"Do you know John Farrington?"

"A friend of mine."

Myron said, "Judy's almost part of the Farrington family now, ever since Frank died at the café. The John Farrington Blend is Coffee Roasters' best seller because Judy wrote about it. Judy knows John and Coffee Roasters very well."

"Frank? That guy who died outside the café. John's his brother?"

"Yes."

"Interesting."

After coffee and cookies, Rebekah took the dinner items and walked home, glancing at her watch every few minutes. It would soon be time for Darnell's break.

She stopped outside a bookstore and called Darnell, hoping he could take his break on time. Her head was spinning with ideas, and she couldn't wait until he finished work to share them.

Darnell

Nineteen-year-old Darnell knew it was only a matter of time before he ended up inside. Occupational hazard. *Won't make much difference. Still be working. Do my time, and when I get out, get my corner back.*

He didn't know his incarceration would coincide with the aftermath of a violent confrontation between the Aryans and the Brothers, which had left three inmates dead, a dozen in hospital and a white corrections officer dead, shanked by a black inmate.

He arrived during lock down. The corrections officers—especially those with white supremacist leanings—were angry, many looking for retribution. The murdered officer had been one of their own. It was the usual prison policy to put new inmates with their own kind, less trouble that way. These were not usual times.

"Right, boy. Let's get you to your cell," the white officer said as he escorted Darnell after processing.

Despite the eerie silence of the prison, the air crackled with tension.

Stopping in front of a cell, the officer opened the door and shoved Darnell inside. "Present for you, Hamlet," he said.

A loud clunk as the door locked behind him. Hamlet was a large biker who, shirtless, stood to greet his new cellmate. If any part of his body wasn't tattooed, Darnell couldn't see it. *What the fuck?*

"Got me a nigger to play with," was Hamlet's welcome speech.

Darnell dropped the few prison issue items he carried and landed a punch on the side of Hamlet's jaw.

Hamlet seemed unaffected. His retaliation sent Darnell across the cell. Darnell flung his arm out to stop from crashing into the wall, but dislocated a finger. Hamlet was on him immediately, and a second blow smashed Darnell's head into the wall, hard.

The third had a similar result, and Darnell sank to the floor. Hamlet rained blows on him until Darnell was bloody, beaten senseless, and drifting in and out of consciousness.

He was vaguely aware of being dragged and thrown face down half on the bed. Darnell felt Hamlet loosen his trousers and drag them and his underwear down to his ankles; he couldn't grasp what was happening. He hurt everywhere. As he blacked out again, he thought he heard Hamlet say, "Hamlet's mother fucked her brother. Always wanted to fuck me a brother."

Excruciating pain as Hamlet penetrated him brought him back to consciousness. He tried to move, to escape the pain, but Hamlet was on top of him, pinning him down. He drifted into unconsciousness again.

***

Darnell came to in the night. Realizing his trousers were around his ankles, he moved to pull them up. He winced. Everything hurt. It felt like a piece of two by four was still shoved up his ass. He remembered what happened. *If I had a blade, or a razor, or anything I could use, I'd slit the motherfucker's throat.*

He gingerly swung his legs off the bed and shuffled to the toilet to relieve himself. Walking made his ass hurt. Despite not having eaten that night, his hunger was only for revenge. He shuffled back to his bunk, sat on the edge, and stifled his cry as he manipulated his dislocated finger back into place.

He winced as he lay down, staring at the bottom of Hamlet's bunk, consumed by a mixture of shame and self-pity, and imagining various ways he could exact his revenge.

***

Morning. Hamlet, naked, climbed down two steps from the top bunk and jumped to the floor. His limp cock, still bouncing when Darnell—who hadn't undressed and still wore his prison-issue boots—seized his opportunity. Darnell's right boot slammed into its target, and Hamlet screamed.

As Hamlet sank to his knees, his hands instinctively moved to protect his genitals from further attack. Darnell's left boot connected with Hamlet's head. Off-balance, he fell backwards, and without his hands to cushion his landing, his head hit the floor hard.

Moving through his own pain, Darnell launched himself towards the prone Hamlet.

Hamlet was no stranger to brawling. Being Sergeant-at-arms of the Nomad Motorcycle Club, he handled club discipline. A hard man, among hard men.

Hamlet anticipated Darnell's move, and used his momentum against him, propelling him into the wall. Crumpled on the floor, Darnell grabbed the chair to haul himself up and launch a second attack. He hadn't expected Hamlet to be on his feet so quickly.

Seeing his opportunity, Hamlet launched himself, elbow cocked like a professional wrestler, onto Darnell's arm. Not a choreographed move to entertain the fans, real life. The sharp crack of Darnell's arm breaking echoed through the cell, followed by Darnell's scream.

Job done, Hamlet moved to the toilet to relieve himself, fondling his testicles in the process to make sure they were intact.

Hamlet sat at the table, nursing his genitals. After twenty minutes, he returned to Darnell, still on the floor, cradling his arm, and straddled him. "Okay bitch, kiss it better."

Darnell glared at him through the pain, but made no move to comply.

Hamlet reached down and squeezed Darnell's broken arm. The pain was excruciating. Darnell screamed again.

"Open your mouth, boy, or I'll crush those bone fragments."

Fearing more pain, Darnell complied, and Hamlet inserted his hardening penis into Darnell's mouth. Darnell's eyes were fixed on Hamlet's hand, still hovering above his arm.

"Suck it hard, boy, and don't try anything cute."

Before long, Hamlet tensed. Darnell gagged as Hamlet's load shot into his mouth.

Hamlet stood. "You need to learn your place, boy, and we'll get along fine. No one likes an uppity nigger."

Darnell remained on the floor, nursing his broken arm and broken pride. He glared at Hamlet through pain and disgrace. *When I get a shank motherfucker, you'll feel my place.*

The door unlocked. A trustee—an older man with a deep scar running down the left of his lined face, with the appearance of someone who'd spent the better part of his life locked up—shuffled in with their breakfast, which he placed on the table. The trustee glanced at the naked Hamlet, and then at Darnell crumpled on the floor, trying to support his broken arm.

"Please…" Darnell said. "Tell the guard I need a doctor."

The trustee looked at Hamlet, who said "He's fine, don't need no doctor."

The trustee nodded, gave Darnell one more glance, eyes full of pity, then shrugged and left the cell.

Hamlet, still naked, sat at the table and began eating. "No breakfast for you, boy, until you earn it."

Darnell didn't care, his appetite did not extend beyond ending Hamlet.

***

Darnell was lying on his bunk, feeling sorry for himself and hating his cellmate, when Hamlet climbed down.

"Roll over, boy, I need to use that tight pussy."

"Fuck you."

Hamlet leaned into Darnell's bunk and reached for him. Darnell swung his good arm at Hamlet's head. It connected, but there was no power behind the punch.

"You want foreplay, boy?"

He dragged Darnell from the bed and threw him on the floor. Darnell cried out in pain as he landed on his broken arm. Hamlet stomped on his head several times, pounded it into the concrete floor. He aimed a kick at Darnell's broken arm, and then another. Darnell screamed in pain.

Hamlet reached down, opened Darnell's trousers, and pulled them down. He rolled him over onto his broken arm, causing Darnell to scream again.

If anyone heard Darnell's screams, they ignored them. Hamlet dropped his own trousers and climbed on top of Darnell, who screamed one more time, as Hamlet penetrated him. Each thrust from Hamlet drove Darnell's broken arm into the concrete under the weight of their two bodies. Darnell's screams became whimpers.

***

Dark now. Hamlet had finished with him hours ago. Darnell still lay on the floor, trousers around his ankles like a badge of shame. He sobbed for hours, like the day his father left when Darnell was a child.

He slowly and painfully drew his trousers up. His head ached, throbbing from being repeatedly stomped into the concrete. Every time he moved the wrong way, his arm sent shooting pain into his body. His stretched and torn asshole pulsated almost in unison with his head, creating a feeling that his body was palpitating in stereo.

He dragged himself up and onto the bed, a process that took his pain to a new level. He could not endure any more punishment. Hamlet had broken more than his arm.

***

The next morning, Hamlet cautiously climbed down from his bunk. Darnell didn't look at him. He heard Hamlet relieve himself. Moments later, Hamlet was beside him.

"Alright boy, open your mouth."

Darnell positioned himself, opened his mouth, closed his eyes, and complied.

***

Darnell heard the door open, and the trustee bring their breakfast in, deposit two trays on the table and leave.

Hamlet sat at the table. "Okay, boy, you've learned your place. Come, eat."

Darnell slowly left his bunk and made his way to the table. It was the first time Hamlet had allowed him to eat since he'd entered the cell. Despite this, he ate without enthusiasm. He didn't taste the food. He ate not because he was hungry; he ate because Hamlet told him to.

***

Lockdown ended. Darnell had surgery on his arm, now pinned in several places, plastered and immobilized. He was recuperating in the prison hospital.

“Hey bro,” Darnell addressed an inmate working as an orderly.

The orderly looked at him, but didn’t respond.

“I need a shank.”

“Sorry, bro, can’t help. Not even supposed to be talking to you.”

“What?”

“You don’t exist. You a sissified nigga. Shouldn’t be fucking that white piece of shit.”

“I ain’t sissified. He raped me. Look at what he did to me. I was barely conscious.”

“Maybe the first time.”

“I fought back, but he was too big and strong.”

“Word is you Hamlet’s bitch now.”

“I ain’t no bitch.”

“Sorry man, ain’t no brother gonna help you.”

“Get me a shank, and I’ll prove I ain’t no bitch.”

The orderly shook his head and walked away.

Darnell knew how things worked. He was on his own.

***

Recovered and back in his cell and in his place, Darnell still harbored an intention to end Hamlet. Normally, he’d have transferred to the vulnerable prisoner’s unit, but that would have led to many awkward questions being asked of the corrections officers. They recorded his broken arm as accidental.

He visited the cell of the leader of the Hispanic faction.

“El Jefe, I need a shank.”

“You want to finish Hamlet, ese?”

"Yeah."

"Ain't gonna happen."

"I'll owe you. Shank anyone you want me to."

"Even one of your own niggers?"

"Ain't got no niggas."

"I'd like to see that motherfucker dead, but I can't help you."

"Why not?"

"Another nigger killing an Aryan, especially one like Hamlet, would see us back in lockdown. Bad for business. Ain't no one gonna thank you for that."

"I'll get a shank from somewhere."

"Suicide ese. The brotherhood'll make it slow and painful an' leave your body hanging somewhere as a warning. Better use that shank on yourself, and save yourself a whole lotta pain."

Darnell knew El Jefe was right.

***

He was on his own. The only group that would accept him were the sissies, and Darnell wasn't no sissy.

For the remainder of his time inside, Darnell kept to himself. Usually eating alone and spending most of his time—when he wasn't working—in his cell. He kept his head down and looked at nobody.

Dorothy's Not in Kansas Anymore

Judy sat in her usual place at Kansas Café, talking with Frank, and listening to *Yesterday Once More.*

Beautiful voice. Don't know the singer. Must ask Dorothy.

Judy wore tight blue jeans and a dandelion-colored cotton blouse. That morning, as she was dressing, she'd studied her body in the mirror. *Seem to be getting younger.* Six months earlier, she'd resigned herself to getting older. *Certainly feel younger.*

She opened her iPad and added an item to her features file. *Does Regular Sex Keep Us Young?*

Judy was more intrigued by Frank's appearance. Now, the young, slim, handsome version of himself in his prime. The angry, fat man she'd first encountered had long gone.

Frank's ghost, or essence, or memory, or whatever he is, hasn't changed. My perception of him has changed. "Guess I helped you lose weight, Frank. Weight loss has a lot to do with perception."

Could be a feature in that, How People's Perception of Themselves Influences Their Weight.

She removed her digital recorder from her bag and placed it on the table. Dorothy was on her way.

"This should be an interesting history lesson, Frank."

Dorothy sat opposite Judy, and beside the unseen Frank. "Hi Judy."

"Hello Dot. I'm going to record this interview to save taking notes."

"Okay."

"Before we start, who was that singer? *Yesterday Once More.*"

"Dami Im. Australian or Korean or something. Beautiful voice."

"Lately, you've been playing unusual singers from other countries. How do you find that music?"

"I have a music site I listen to… online. Don't watch television, I listen to music and read at night. Been using it for years; about the only technology I use. If I like a song, I add it to the café playlist. A few months ago, I changed the umm…. What's that called? Filters. Changed the filters to global. Now I listen to music from all over the world."

"Can you give me the site later?"

"Sure."

"Let's begin, shall we?"

"Where should I start?"

"Wherever you want, and we'll see where it goes."

"Married young. Not a good marriage, not a bad marriage either. It was a nothing marriage. No kids, but it lasted over ten years."

A nothing marriage, many marriages like that, could be a feature.

"He came home late every day, ate dinner, and went to bed. Up early in the morning and back to work. I had friends and my parents, but I was lonely. Ron didn't talk to me. Turned out he'd been having an affair for years. Finally, divorced me. Pretty big news then in a small town. Not like today, where divorce is part of marriage."

Divorce is part of marriage, could be a feature in that too.

"Did all right in the divorce. Got about seventy percent when we sold the house and a small alimony. I never remarried. He still pays after all these years, don't know for how much longer. Never heard from him again. Not surprising, never heard from him much when we were married.

"My father—he's gone now, both of them are, within a year of each other, fifteen years ago—said not to worry about buying another house. I'll always have the family home to come back to. I love that house. Rented now, a little extra income, and it's still waiting for me. Looking forward to going home.

"Dad told me to follow my dreams. I always dreamed of owning a café, so I came to the city and made Kansas Café. I loved it, still do. Been my home for three decades. Living my dream. I feel sad to be leaving so many memories. I'll miss it, but it's time to go."

Suppose I'm living my dream, too.

"When we first opened, we were busy. Had two girls working for me, Milly and Joana. We had fun, like a small family. Lots of regulars. Over time, more cafes opened, the city expanded, and people moved away. Regulars stopped being so regular, they drifted away, but called in occasionally. Some people would come every six months to remember. They lived too far away to visit regularly. The world changes. We were doing okay, but not as busy as we were.

"Milly was first to leave. She got married, became pregnant and moved out to the suburbs. She came back to visit for years, but I haven't seen her for around five years. People move on with their lives. I didn't replace Milly because we didn't need two waitresses.

"Joana left a few years later. To be honest, I hadn't needed her for more than a year before she left, but times were different then. Employers felt responsibility for their employees. Joana was part of our family, so I kept her on. These days people only care about how much money they make, they don't care about employees or tradition or loyalty. I hear people complaining about employees not being loyal anymore, but I think it's because companies stopped being loyal to their employees.

"Seen so much over the years. Made friends who later drifted away, watched people falling in love, saw people breaking up. Always sad. Well, usually sad, sometimes I thought it was for the best. Witnessed people grow up, change, and develop over the years. Shared in people's successes and consoled people after failures. It was like a big extended family. I loved this place. Still do.

"On that sofa over there," Dorothy said, indicating a red sofa on the opposite side of the café. "Silvia was born. Mary went into labor unexpectedly. Called EMS, but when they arrived, Silvia was on her way, so they had to deliver her here. It was exciting. For years afterward, Mary would bring Silvia to visit me, but the visits became less frequent, and they moved to another city. They came back after a few years, just to visit one more time.

"Thought I'd seen it all, but I hadn't. That friend of yours, Frank, died there," she said, indicating the pavement outside the window.

Judy glanced at Frank, sitting on the sofa beside Dorothy. He smiled and shrugged.

"Seen everything here, a birth, a death, love starting and ending, success, failure.... Life playing out in this café. Love this place. It's been my world, but it's time to go home.

"We used to sell a lot of takeout coffee in the mornings, people on their way to work, but when Starbucks came to the city that stopped. Not overnight, but it didn't take long. People still come in for a takeout slice of cheesecake, and orders for whole cheesecakes. People do like my cheesecake. Sometimes it seems like a cheesecake shop with a café on the side.

"Business has become slow, but I don't mind. Slowed down with me over the years. I'm as worn and threadbare on the edges as this sofa of yours. Called it *Judy's sofa* for years now.

"Make enough to cover the rent on the café and the apartment, plus the costs of the business. That's all I need. Why I've been able to stay open when others in my position would have closed long ago. Eat in the café.

"My father took some of the money from my divorce and established a pension fund for me because 'you don't have a husband to rely on.' Been paying half the alimony into my pension fund too. So, I'll be doing all right when I retire. Pension for life.

"There are a couple of cafes in my hometown. Hoping one of them will take my cheesecakes and maybe promote orders for whole cheesecakes too. Give me something to do.

"Used to listen to some of my customers talking about a cruise they took. I never had the time. Haven't been away from here since I opened, except when my parents died. Doesn't matter because it's never felt like work to me. Always dreamed of taking a cruise. Suppose they'll be different now, but I still want to go on a cruise. Who knows, if it's what I hope, I may take one every year."

"Have you ever thought about marrying again?" Judy asked.

"No. Not that I wouldn't. Don't have a strong feeling about not being married; haven't met somebody I wanted to spend the rest of my life with. You never know, I might meet someone on my cruise. Dated a few times, more than a few, when I was younger. Sometimes for a long time. Tony and I dated for several years, and I had a couple of years with Simon. Good company, but not for marriage.

"Sylas proposed after dating for a few weeks, but I declined, and he lost interest. He wanted a wife. *Who* wasn't important. Besides, I've been married to this place, I guess."

"You've had an interesting life."

"Well, the café used to be interesting," Dorothy said. "Anyway, I must get back to the kitchen to see how those kids are doing. Maybe Darnell needs me to keep an eye on something while he's talking to you. Good kid that Darnell, like him a lot."

Dorothy returned to the kitchen. Judy turned her digital recorder off and returned it to her bag. "You know, Frank, this place must've been interesting in its day. I can understand why Dot loves it so much."

Judy entered her two new feature ideas into her iPad and glanced at her watch. *Time to meet Darnell.* Myron would come later. He thought Darnell would be more open if it was only Judy because Judy had "a magic that made people open up."

"No Myron," she said. "I just get out of people's way and let them talk."

Darnell and Rebekah

"What'll we make of Darnell, Frank?" Judy asked.

Rebekah accompanied Darnell from the kitchen. "Aunt Judy, this is Darnell," she said.

Handsome. Short hair, smallish ears. His nose, a little broad, but not dominant. Thickish lips, straight white teeth and a firm chin. *Fit and strong.* Eyes guarded, in defensive mode. *An intensity, a depth to his gaze despite the guarded stance.* Judy suspected when he relaxed, his smile would light up the room. *I like him.*

"Hello, Darnell. Myron's running a little late, but we can chat while we're waiting."

"Hello, Ma'am. Pleased to meet you. Bec's told me a lot about you."

Rebekah squeezed Darnell's shoulder. "I'd better keep an eye on the food."

Darnell nodded. Rebekah returned to the kitchen.

Good. Best talk to Darnell one on one. "Why don't you start by telling me a little about yourself?"

"My full name is Darnell Luther Williams, to honor Dr. King. If I'm gonna work here, I gotta tell ya I'm on parole and will be for another two years."

She could see Darnell was nervous, waiting for her to respond, but Judy remained silent. *Let people talk, and they relax.*

"I grew up slinging drugs in the projects. Nothing special, just a stereotypical black kid, according to my P. O… Parole Officer. He's probably right. Every time one of us gets killed or put inside, another one takes his place. Caught with drugs and got five years, non-parole period of three."

Darnell was quiet for a while, then continued. "Funny y'know. Somethin' can happen, and we think it's the worst, but it turns out to be the best… Timing is everything."

"What do you mean by the worst thing, becoming the best thing that could've happened?"

Darnell hesitated. "Bec says I can trust you, says she told you everything, so I'll just tell you."

Judy smiled and waited for Darnell to collect his thoughts.

"When I went in, the prison was on lockdown. They put me in a cell with Hamlet, a big mean biker. No way to get help… Took 'im three days to break me, but he broke me. I became his bitch.

"When lockdown ended, the gangstas disowned me. Wouldn't acknowledge me. On my own and Hamlet's bitch, not really a bitch, because there was no relationship. Nothin' more than a human wanking sock. Sorry, I…"

Judy interrupted, "I didn't realize it was so common. Three people have told me about their experience on the inside. They've basically been the same."

"Guess one is Bec. Did the other one have a crew?"

"No, he didn't."

"When someone isn't part of a crew, they're unprotected, easy targets. I was different. It was the lockdown. Hamlet constantly beat me and raped me, broke me." Darnell stared out the window, took a deep breath, then resumed. "Tried to fight back, but he was bigger and stronger. Left me sobbing like a little girl."

He looked Judy in the eye. "If not for the lockdown, it would've been different. Could've got a shank from my crew on the first day and protected myself. If I hadda shank, one of us wudda ended up dead. If they put me in with the gangstas, I wudda dun what I know. Wouldn't a got parole. If I got out, wudda gone back to my crew until I got put inside again or killed. A nothing life, with no future.

"Kept to myself because I had no choice. Did the work assigned but usually stayed in my cell. Kept my head down and didn't look anyone in the eye. This gave me a chance for parole. No trouble, no attitude, no rule breaking.

"My P.O. got me into the culinary school. Turns out I'm good at cooking. Who knew? Besides, can't go back to the projects. They'd kill me. Culinary school was the only option. Got lucky. Talk to my Moms and Grams on the phone, but can't visit. When I'm settled, they can visit me.

"Met Bec at culinary school. Recognized each other. Y'know, similar experience so we understand each other. If Hamlet didn't make me his bitch, I'd be waiting to die, inside or outside. Now I have the chance of a life. I'm skilled at flavors. Love creating food, and I met Bec. Hamlet gave me something I didn't have, a future.

"Bec too. We understand what it's like to be powerless and alone, so we can talk about it. Talkin' about bad things helps. Didn't believe it. Didn't want to think about it. My P.O. wanted me to join a support group, but I couldn't do it. Bec and I became each other's support group. What happened to us—she had it worse than me—isn't who we are, it doesn't define us… been researching it…

"Learned what I felt was powerless and alone. They say being powerless is the most stressful thing a person can experience. The rapes didn't fuck me up. It was being powerless, of having no control. Bec said you're easy to talk to. She's right."

Darnell glanced at his watch. "I'm sorry. I need to get back to the kitchen."

"Okay, Darnell. Thank you for being open with me."

***

"Well Frank, I think that young man has given himself a future… assuming he can cook. One thing's for sure, this place won't be the same. I agree with Dot and Becky. I like him."

The bell rang as the door opened. "Here's Myron now," Judy said.

"Hello, sweetheart."

"Hi, darling." She kissed him. "Darnell will be fine. Similar background to Becky. They can understand each other, accept each other's past and provide support and understanding we can't."

"Let's hope he can cook."

Dorothy joined them for the tasting, again sitting beside the smiling Frank.

Judy said. "Not long now and you can relax."

"I'll store most of my stuff here for now and enjoy a cruise holiday. After my tenants move out at the end of their lease, I'll go home. Always planned to go home," Dorothy said. "I like a quiet life. May even marry again, many single old men around. Maybe I'll find an interesting, clean one who wants some company in his old age. Funny how this has all come together so quickly."

"You've been talking about retiring for a long time."

"Didn't know if I would, but I can now. Glad this place is going to friends. It'll change, but it'll still be here, just wearing a new set of clothes." Dorothy looked around, "and about time too. I think Rebekah will do a wonderful job and that young man of hers sure can cook."

Rebekah brought a tray with the first of the dishes for them to try, along with cutlery and three small tasting plates. Scrambled eggs made with cream, butter, and grated parmesan cheese, a French influence. An herb salad dressed with the honey, mustard and macadamia dressing from Exquisite Jams Judy liked, and a small crispy garlic and parmesan flat bread on the side.

"My God," said Judy. "I can see myself changing my breakfast routine."

Next, cream of vegetable soup made with carrots, peas and tomatoes, a delicate balance of herbs and spices with cream and three cheeses, blended into a thick smooth soup, accompanied by a warm sour dough roll from Alice's.

The third dish, a starter of marinated eggplant with beetroot and goats' cheese stuffed mushrooms. The eggplant had been skinned and cubed before being marinated in soy and ginger with a hint of chili. Then baked, along with the mushrooms filled with goat's cheese and topped with beetroot, squared using a tall square cookie cutter. The dish comprised four cubes of varying sizes and looked amazing.

"Delicious," Myron said. "A modern take on a traditional Greek vegetarian dish."

The first meat dish, lamb shank, braised in Beaujolais, with mini hasselback potatoes and brussels sprouts roasted in the remains of the braising wine and lamb juices. A reinvention of roast lamb with roast potatoes.

Judy said, "If they produce food like this, they'll do well."

"Yes," Myron agreed, "and so will we."

Next, meat loaf cooked in a round ramekin. Seasoned with basil, thyme and finely diced caramelized onions with Panko breadcrumbs. A demiglace topped the meatloaf, giving it a shimmer and adding a depth of flavor. Served with creamy mashed potatoes and honeyed Julien carrots, both placed in circular cookie cutters before serving. Three circles in contrast to the four cubes of the earlier dish.

"Best meat loaf I ever tasted," Judy said. "They can add Susie's mac and cheese to their menu, too."

Dorothy said, "With food of this quality, your diner will be a success."

Frank smiled.

The last item. A triple chocolate cheesecake. Milk chocolate crumb base made from intense chocolate cookies, a thin layer of dark chocolate studded with fresh raspberry pieces, and a white chocolate cream cheese filling topped with raspberry dust.

"Oh, my," Dorothy exclaimed. "This is exceptional cheesecake."

"Yes," Myron agreed. "The tasting menu was excellent. I expected a tasting platter just to see if Darnell can cook, but this was much better. It's given us a sense of what the diner will be."

Dorothy said, "Thank you for including me. A wonderful tasting. I'll help clean up. Got to sing for my supper."

Judy said. "Can you ask Becky and Darnell to come out for a chat?"

"Sure."

As Rebekah and Darnell approached, Judy glanced across the table. Frank was now standing beside the sofa. Slim and handsome in his fitted brown suit. Judy smiled at him, then realized Myron was watching her. He gently squeezed her hand but didn't comment.

Rebekah and Darnell appeared happy and natural together. *Excited but apprehensive, to be expected.*

Myron said, "If you guys produce food like that, you'll be very successful. Judy has a recipe for the best mac and cheese you ever tasted that will fit well with your menu."

Judy said, "I'm guessing you guys will live together?"

Rebekah responded, "Yes Aunt Judy, that's our plan."

Judy said, "That mac and cheese is wonderful, but it's not my recipe. I got it from my friend Susie who found it online. It belongs to a chef, Marco Pierre White."

"Wow, cool," said Darnell. "He's a legend."

"Some people find living and working together too much," said Myron. "Do you think you'll be able to get along spending so much time together?"

"Uncle Myron," Rebekah explained. "We spent the last few years sharing a small cell with somebody we hated. Sharing an apartment and working with someone we like will be easy."

"Thing is," Darnell expanded. "Spending so long in the company of another person, even someone you don't like, conditions people so they feel lonely if they live alone. Most hate the loneliness of solitary, which is why it's a punishment."

Myron continued. "Sometimes when people try to get their life together, their past reaches out and drags them back in. Have you thought about this possibility?"

"Frank Dunn said that," Darnell explained. "Unlikely in my circumstances, because they disowned me. Haven't had any contact with them, and I won't go back to the projects. Not even to see my family."

"Between Judy and I we have a lot of contacts in this city. If anyone approaches you, please talk to us before you do anything."

"Okay," Darnell committed, "and thank you."

Myron continued, "We want you both to finish the culinary course, but how will you be able to do that if you're both working here?"

Rebekah explained, "We both want to finish it, too. Besides, finishing the course is a parole condition, as is working. We both do evenings, which is how we met. Darnell will transfer to the afternoon class and work evenings. We'll need to hire a part-time waitress, and we're hoping we'll be busy enough to need her full-time."

Darnell confirmed. "Spoke with Frank Dunn. He'll approve my change of class, and my change of employer and residence, but he wants to meet you guys before signing off on everything."

Judy reached into her bag for a card. Myron took one from his wallet, passing them both to Darnell.

"Happy to talk with him," Judy said. "Either together or separately. I might write a feature about the program."

Glancing at Myron, she asked. "Are there any more formalities we need to deal with?"

"Not at the moment. We need you guys to put your heads together and outline your ideas. I think Dorothy will move out in around ten days, but she'll store some stuff here for a few weeks."

"We were up all night talking about it," Rebekah explained. "We need to finalize our menu, but we don't want too many items, so it remains manageable. Include a few vegetarian options because any group of friends and family will have at least one vegetarian among them. That Gordon Ramsay show about bad restaurants…"

"*Kitchen Nightmares*," Darnell said. "Been watching to learn what *not* to do. Want to make fewer mistakes."

Rebekah continued. "We've been thinking about a name. There isn't a landmark around here. Something like Rebekah's Diner or Darnell's Diner wouldn't be authentic. Dorothy's Diner is too much and Kansas Diner…. Most diners back then had a strong white male name. We want to call it Frank's Diner. Authentic and honors your friend who died here. We can put up a memorial plaque, too."

Judy glanced at Frank, who was beaming. "That's a wonderful idea."

Myron nodded. "And appropriate, the diner wouldn't be happening without Frank's influence."

Judy thought for a moment. "You're absolutely right, Myron." *Thank you, Frank.*

Darnell hesitated. "Plus, we thought your book about him might create some interest in the diner, too."

"Quite right Darnell," Myron agreed. "What are your thoughts about the diners' customers and design?"

Darnell explained. "We won't get a liquor license, so we'll focus on fifties style sodas and milkshakes and coffee. Without alcohol, best be family friendly, with a kid's menu. Open for breakfast, sit down, but a pre-made take out selection too. People can grab breakfast on their way to work. Lunch will include a set menu option, three choices for people who need a quick lunch. An afternoon tea special, to use up any leftover sandwiches from lunchtime, and of course, dinner."

Rebekah continued. "We plan to open 7.00am to 10.00pm Monday to Saturday and have Sunday Brunch from 10.00am to 3.00pm. Booths around the windows and the wall where the sofas are. Tables in the middle like now, and stools at the counter, diner style. Moveable stools will be better. More flexibility. Sunday Brunch will be buffet style and we'll use the counter for the buffet. Sunday buffet will use up the previous week's produce while it's still fresh enough. Common way for restaurants to cut wastage."

"Seems well thought out, and appears sound to me, but I'm concerned it'll be too many hours, too much work," Myron said.

"Never had days off inside," Darnell said. "So that won't bother us. Important to put the time in to learn our business and make sure it works. We need it to be successful enough to live a comfortable life doing what we love.

"This is an opportunity we never thought we'd have, not for many years. If you're prepared to put up the money, we're more than prepared to put in the time. This is a chance at a real life for us, a normal life. Few people in our situations have such an opportunity."

"We won't let you down, Uncle Myron. We'll make it work." Rebekah promised.

Myron said, "We believe in both of you. My accounting office will contact you next week and help you prepare a business plan, and my property management company will arrange for a designer to work with you. They'll do some drawings and make a model to help you envision the diner."

Phoenix Rising

The next day, Judy sat on her sofa in Kansas Café, listening to Ella Fitzgerald singing *Someone to Watch Over Me*. She was sad Kansas was closing, her sofa replaced with a booth. A plaque commemorating Frank Farrington placed on the wall above their booth. *Wonder what will happen to Frank.*

She was enjoying her cappuccino and New York style cheesecake, one of the last made by Dorothy. *End of an era.*

"Well Frank, all being well, we'll buy your business today. Never thought I'd be a business owner, but now I'll own two businesses. Didn't imagine my life would change so much because I met you, or that I'd meet you… after you died.

"When I first saw you, I didn't think 'look at that fat angry man, I'll buy his business and this café which I'll turn into a diner in his memory.' Interesting. We think we know how our life will play out, but we haven't got a clue. If you asked me when we met what would happen in my life in the next six months, I'd have gotten very little right.

"What about you, my friend? Did you know your story would continue after you died? If we buy your business today, Frank, letters will go out to those who lost money from your investment company, and the last of their losses will be repaid. Your dying wish fulfilled. How is this possible, Frank?"

Rebekah sat beside Frank, unaware of his presence.

"Aunt Judy, do you think I could do a deal with Coffee Roasters to use that John Farrington Blend as our house blend?"

"A wonderful idea. I can arrange an introduction, but I'm not sure how cheap it'll be."

"It'll be more expensive than a coffee supply company, but if it's much better, people will be happy to pay a little more. What about Alice's Bakery and Exquisite Jams? Do you have contacts there?"

"Yes, Becky. I'll introduce you. I like the way you're thinking."

"Thank you, Aunt Judy," Rebekah said, and headed back to the kitchen to tell Darnell.

Myron called. "Be there soon."

She gathered her belongings into her ever-present shoulder bag.

"Well, Frank, heading off to buy your business. Wish me luck!"

Frank smiled and nodded, giving Judy the impression he knew the outcome.

***

Excited, Judy snuggled against Myron in the back of the taxi on their way across town to Frank's warehouse. *Myron's warehouse now.*

When they arrived, Mike Eagleton was inside the security office, but he didn't look bored, and he wasn't watching TV.

"Will there be a job for Mike?" Judy asked.

"There will. I like him, and I like the way his uniform is always clean and pressed. It shows pride. A lot of guys in his position wouldn't bother."

"That'll be down to his wife."

"Yes, of course, his generation, but if his clothes weren't clean and pressed, he couldn't bear it, I can tell."

"Hello Mike," Judy said.

"Oh… Hello Judy Vernon. I didn't expect to see you again. Hello Myron."

Judy smiled. Men always remembered her.

"Hello Mike," Myron said. "Many people here?"

"Around fifteen."

They entered the warehouse. Myron had a quiet word with the auctioneer. Judy looked around, still in awe at the volume of Frank's stock.

Returning to Judy, he said, "Good news, sweetheart. The other bidders are only trying to get their hands on cheap stock. I have some papers for you to sign for the purchase of the warehouse."

"Oh… I didn't realize you meant the warehouse, too."

"I wasn't clear."

Judy found the auction quite exciting. The auctioneer opened at with a broad description of what was being offered.

"We'll start the bidding at fifty thousand dollars. Do I hear fifty?"

A dozen men held up paddles, but not Myron.

"Sixty, Seventy… Do I hear one hundred?"

It was noisy, between the auctioneer shouting and men talking. Myron still hadn't bid.

"Why aren't we bidding?" Judy asked.

"Too early. We'll wait and see who's serious. They'll start dropping out now."

"One-ten, one-twenty… one-fifty."

Myron was right, maybe half the bidders had stopped raising their paddles.

"This tells us who's done their homework."

Judy gave Myron a quizzical look.

"Stock didn't stop arriving when Frank died. There's more stock in the bonded warehouse than here."

Given the amount of stock in the Phoenix warehouse, Judy had difficulty conceiving this. The auction continued.

"One-seventy…. One-ninety. Do I hear two hundred?"

By the time it reached two hundred and fifty, there were three bidders left.

"The stock in the bond store still needs to be paid for, so it's worth less than what's here."

Myron's first bid was two hundred and fifty-five thousand.

"Two-sixty… two-eighty… three hundred."

Another bidder dropped out.

"Three-thirty… three-fifty."

Two bidders remained, including Myron.

"This is ours. Only a matter of how much we need to pay."

Judy noticed Myron paying close attention to the other bidders.

"He's at his limit, and rightly so because we're at the approximate value on the stock. We're well under ours because we want the business. He'll push on a little in the heat of the moment, but not too far."

"Going once at three hundred and seventy-five thousand, going twice.... Sold!"

Judy was half owner of a business and a warehouse.

After the auction concluded, they adjourned to Frank's office to attend to the paperwork. Apparently, it would happen quickly and within a few days, Phoenix Imports would rise, without the ashes, thanks to Myron.

Myron handed over the check, and the auctioneer handed Judy the keys to the warehouse. *The keys to my kingdom.* Judy didn't know what she expected, but it was anti-climactic.

Myron disconnected Frank's laptop and put it into his bag. "We need to analyze any more business information that may be on here, besides those files you borrowed. After my people are finished, you can give the laptop with his personal information to Frank's family. This week—now we legally have the investor list—your letters with a check from my trust account will go out to Frank's investors."

"Everything's happening so quickly."

"We've been here nearly all day." Myron toyed with her.

"You know what I mean."

"Sometimes it's like that. After weeks or months of preparation, the deal's done in minutes. I need you to sign a few more documents, so we can close everything this week. The first batch is for our purchase of the warehouse. The second batch formalizes the new leases on the café space and the apartment. Then there's the registration of the business name and the change of name documentation for Frank's Diner."

A few signatures and I've acquired an empire... of sorts. Her head was spinning.

"Thank you for including me. I never considered being involved in any of this. I don't say it enough, but I *do* love you."

Myron smiled. “I wouldn’t have done this without you.”

He leaned in, his lips found hers, and he kissed her, long and slow.

When she finally released him, he said, “The brothers will come down in a few days.”

“I doubt I’ll contribute anything, but I want to be involved.”

“You don’t need to know about business. We have people for that. But it’ll be good for you to understand the big picture. If we’re going to be partners… Well, we are partners, but if we… It’s like my parents, even though Papa runs the business, Mama understands it because we talk about everything. They include you too now. It’ll help you feel a part of things if you know what’s happening… Mama and Papa, including you in our discussions about our family business, is huge, by the way. It means they’ve accepted you as an equal part of our family.”

“They make me feel part of your family.”

“*Our* family sweetheart.”

***

They settled into the back of the taxi.

“The day after Kansas Café closes, I want to hold a function in the café. A family meeting with Frank’s family. I want to announce we bought Phoenix Imports and introduce them to Frank’s Diner.”

“A wonderful idea. Rebekah and Darnell can cater it, and I’ll make sure the plans and model of the diner are ready. Talking about catering, Franco’s for dinner?”

“Yes, please, and an early night. I’m quite excited after today.”

Myron smiled that cheeky smile of his. “Sweetheart, you’re always excited.”

“Your fault.”

A few months earlier, Judy recalled, Myron would’ve flushed.

“And I’m permanently hard, which is your fault. You have a *very* sexy ass. Not only me who thinks so. I see the way men—and some women—look at it.”

She snuggled closer to Myron, smiling contentedly.

***

The next morning, Judy sat in Kansas Café as usual. They'd settled into a routine which suited them both. They seldom had morning sex now. Myron would get up early and either play squash or have a run and then go to work. He showered in the ensuite bathroom of his private office. He often spent much of his day in meetings, so an early start enabled him to finish his work prior to the meetings.

Judy got up shortly after Myron left, did her own exercise routine at home, showered, had breakfast and worked on her features and mini features before walking to Kansas Café. Both were happy with the arrangement, which suited their working styles.

Myron had been even more vigorous than usual the previous night and Judy was a little sore, not that she was complaining her orgasms had been intense.

"Did I mention Myron has incredible stamina, Frank? Congratulate me. You're looking at the new owner of Phoenix Imports. You should thank Myron, without him your company would have died yesterday, with those vultures picking its carcass clean."

Rebekah brought Judy's cappuccino and cheesecake to the table. Judy smiled and thanked her.

"I'm so excited, Aunt Judy. Darnell and I can hardly believe it… Since we learned we'll be able to run our own place, the sex has been amazing." Rebekah flushed. "I'm sorry, I just had to tell somebody."

"Oh, I know what you mean. We bought Phoenix Imports yesterday and I'm a little sore this morning. Business success makes men more, umm… vigorous."

They laughed and felt a little closer after their shared confidence. *Could be a feature or two in there somewhere.*

Rebekah returned to whatever she was doing.

Judy settled back to enjoy her morning coffee and cheesecake, listening to Perry Como's version of *And I Love You So.*

"What's it like, Frank, having employees? I'll be adopting Dorothy's approach and treating them like family, more important than profit margins. That's what Myron does too. Helps broken people put themselves together. Between everything, I'll have six or seven employees by the end of the month. Six or seven people I'll be responsible for.

"You were so close to being able to rebuild a life for yourself. Guess you know that. Quite sad. Sorry you died, Frank, but I'm glad I've gotten to know you.

"No reason to reach out to Myron. Wouldn't have met Ali or your family, nor would I have written a book, or half the features and mini features I have lately. Certainly wouldn't have businesses and property. And Frank Farrington, I wouldn't have known what an amazing man you were."

Frank remained silent, communicating with his smile, now a sheepish grin, and still pleading eyes.

"A man of rare character and integrity and that, my friend, would've been my loss. If I remembered you at all, you would have been a fat, angry man shouting into your phone."

Judy's phone rang, interrupting her dialogue, or perhaps monologue, with Frank. She glanced at caller ID. "Hello darling."

"Hello sweetheart, I have some more paperwork for you to sign."

"More?"

"Yes, formalizing the ownership of the Bitcoin app."

"I own an app now, too?" Judy struggled to get her head around everything that had happened in the last few days.

"Yes, we acquired all Frank's business interests, even those under development. Frank gave you that BC file for a reason."

"I own an app?"

"Well, thirty-five percent of one. I have the same, and the other thirty percent will go to the app company."

After Myron rang off, Judy sat staring at Frank, who was beaming, like a man who'd given his lover a puppy.

The Rookie

Darnell sat at a table in Kansas Café. The bell jangled when the door opened, but he was too engaged studying recipes online to look up.

A familiar voice unexpectedly beside him. "What up, D?"

Fuck! Darnell's head jerked up as a young man sat opposite him.

"Worm!"

"Nobody calls me that anymore. It's Notches."

Darnell said nothing. He closed the laptop. His body tensed.

"Because of all the notches I got on Nina Ross."

His eyes hardened as he glared at Worm. "What the fuck do you want, Worm?"

"Your Moms says you gonna be runnin' this place."

"I'm just a cook."

"Whatever. You're gonna distribute product to suits."

"Ain't gonna happen." Darnell, hands flat on the table, remained rigid, recoiled, and ready to react.

"It is." Worm lifted his shirt enough to reveal the gun tucked into his jeans. "Or you'll find out why they call me Notches."

Darnell didn't flinch. He maintained his cold, hard stare until Worm looked away.

Worm continued. "You'll be working for *me* now. I'm givin' you a chance to get back in… even though you went sissy inside."

"I ain't no sissy."

"Your chance to man up."

"I held out for days. I know you, Worm. Without that biscuit to hide behind, you would've lasted three minutes."

"Dis me agin and you'll be eating my biscuit."

"The owner's got connections. You don't want the kinda heat they'll throw your way. Tellin' you, Cuz. It ain't gonna happen."

"You got until tomorrow." Worm lifted his shirt to reveal his gun again. "I'll be back for your answer."

"Answer's no, Worm."

Brow furrowed, and eyes blazing, Worm left the café.

Darnell walked to the window and watched his cousin climb into the back of a black Jeep Liberty. He stood for a long time, body stiff, eyes hard, staring out the window. *Can't bring this down on Bec, I gotta leave.*

Knew everything was goin' too well. Never gonna have a normal life. He shuddered. The hardness left him. His shoulders drooped, his head bowed, and he felt the familiar wetness on his cheeks. For the third time, life as he knew it was over. He sobbed silently, his head buried in his hands.

***

After placing two cheesecakes in the oven, Rebekah left the kitchen and stepped into the café proper. Darnell was standing by the window, his shoulders shaking with silent sobs.

"Darnell!" She ran to him. "What is it? What's happened?"

Darnell wiped his eyes with the back of his hand and turned to face her. He accepted her embrace and said through his tears, "They reached out Bec. They're gonna fuck everything up. I gotta leave so they don't fuck it up for you, too."

Rebekah led him to Judy's sofa. They sat together, opposite the unseen Frank.

"Okay, Darnell, tell me everything."

When Darnell finished, Rebekah wanted to scream. *Please God, don't let them fuck this up.* Darnell was fragile, so she forced herself to remain calm. She took the phone from her pocket.

"We promised Uncle Myron we'd tell him if this happened."

"Don't imagine he can help. Better for everyone if I leave."

Myron was in a meeting.

She called Judy. "Aunt Judy, we have a problem."

***

Judy had been with Harry White all day; it was almost the end of tour. He talked about his life as a beat cop, which Judy recorded. However, he hadn't given her the answer she wanted.

"So Harry, have you decided to hang up your spurs or ride a desk?"

"Can't see myself riding a desk. I've put in my papers. I'll get a full pension, so I'll be fine."

Judy smiled. "Thought you would. What'll you do?"

Harry shrugged. "Don't know. Probably keep walking my beat as a civilian for a while…"

Judy's phone rang, interrupting him.

"Hello Becky."

"Aunt Judy, we've got a problem."

"I'm sure it's nothing we can't handle. Tell me what's up."

Rebekah explained.

"Okay. Don't worry, Frank says there's a solution to every problem. We'll find it. I'll be there in about half an hour."

Judy ended the call.

Harry asked, "What is it?"

Judy relayed what Rebekah had told her.

"Young Rebekah is one of my success stories," Harry said. "Hate to see it turn to shit now. I'll go back to the station, sign out and change. Better I don't go in uniform. Meet you at the café."

***

Judy sat on her sofa at Kansas Café. Darnell and Rebekah opposite. Frank sat beside Judy, which was unusual. *Wish I could hold his hand, feel him just once.*

Darnell's eyes told her he was devastated. She smiled to ease the tension.

"Harry White will be here soon. We'll put our heads together and see if we can't find a solution."

"If I go to the police, they'll kill me," Darnell said.

"Unofficial, he's off duty," Judy clarified.

"He's a good guy, Darnell. Helped me a lot," Rebekah explained.

The bell jangled, and Darnell's head spun round. Harry arrived as if on cue.

Frank stood beside the table.

Rebekah said, "Hello Mr. White. Thank you for all you've done for me."

Harry smiled and shrugged. "I told the truth."

Darnell said, "Hello, sir. Thank you for coming, but I don't know…"

"It's no trouble." Harry interrupted. "One more good deed before I retire. One of my former rookies is now with Organized Crime. Called him. He can help you, but you'll need to wear a wire. Don't know if you'll want to do that to your old crew."

Darnell shrugged. "Owe them nothing. Turned their back on me when I needed them, but if they suspect I'm wired…"

"They'll execute you. I know."

"Not worried about me. Always gonna end that way for me. Worried about Bec." He placed his hand on Rebekah's arm. "Best I leave."

Judy reached across the table and rested her hand on Darnell's. "Let's not decide now. There must be another way. With his contacts, I'm sure Myron will think of a solution," *or Frank.*

"Judy's right. Sleep on it and tell me tomorrow what you want to do." Harry said.

Rebekah and Darnell went to prepare coffee and cheesecake for Judy and Harry. Frank took his usual seat opposite Judy.

Harry said, "One thing about being old, I've trained a lot of rookies in my time. Some of them are in very senior positions now. Nearly every cop in the station was my rookie at one time…."

Harry stopped talking. Unaware he was staring at Frank, who was staring back, smiling.

He shook his head and refocused when Rebekah arrived with their coffees and cheesecake.

"On the house Mr. White," Rebekah said.

He took a forkful of cheesecake. "Damn, that's good."

"Best in the city," Judy said.

"I think I might have a solution. *The Rookie*. I'll attempt to arrange it at roll call tomorrow morning. I'll let you know."

***

At the end of roll call the next morning, Sarge said, "That's about it. Harry would like a few words before you head out."

Harry stood. "Guys, some friends of mine have a problem. Young couple, trying to get their lives together. The past is reaching out, wanting to deal from their café. Darnell's willing to wear a wire, but they'll execute him when they work it out. Kansas Café, best cheesecake in the city. Thinking if some of you guys could slip in for coffee and cheesecake on your break, it might discourage the gang."

One officer said, "You stole that from *The Rookie.* I saw that episode."

Harry shrugged. "Sometimes TV gets it right."

A second officer said, "Know what people do and know when they do it."

The officers, most having been trained by Harry, had all heard that speech. They met the comment with laughter.

Another officer said, "*NYPD Blue*."

Sarge said, "Okay, that's it. If it's quiet, take an extra break, lets see if we can help these friends of Harry's and… Hey, let's be careful out there!"

Two older officers said, almost in unison, "*Hill Street Blues*."

The officers left to begin their tour in good humor.

Sarge squeezed Harry's shoulder. "You're gonna be missed around here, Harry."

***

Two officers pulled up outside Kansas Café.

They nodded and smiled at Darnell when they entered. Rebekah took their orders.

Darnell stiffened when he saw Worm's black car park across the road.

As soon as the officers left, Worm slipped out the back of the Jeep and crossed the road.

Darnell was waiting for him.

Worm entered and placed his hand on his gun. "You call fuckin' five-O, D? I'll end you right now."

Darnell, eyes hardened, stepped inches away from Worm. He couldn't show any weakness.

"I ain't no rat."

Worm was easing his gun out. Darnell noticed another police car pulling up. He placed his hand over Worm's. "Suicide, Cuz."

"What the fuck D?"

"Told you ain't gonna happen. Owners got connections and you don't want the heat."

"What's with all the five-O?"

"Dunno. Think they like the old woman's cheesecake or something."

Worm turned to leave. "I'll be back."

He left as the officers entered. One officer rested his hand on his gun as he looked at Worm. His partner squeezed his arm. "Not here. I got his plate. We'll run it later."

The officers sat at a table, and Darnell approached to take their order. "Thank you for doing this, officers. What can I get you?"

"Coffee and cheesecake." They answered in unison.

***

Two days later, Worm was pulled over in a traffic stop. He was charged with carrying a concealed weapon. A routine ballistics examination revealed nine bodies on his gun.

Frank's Diner

Kansas Café had closed the previous day. Judy sat on her sofa for the last time, drinking cappuccino and eating her New York style cheesecake. The café was silent, no music playing. Frank was sitting opposite as usual, smiling with a twinkle in his eye. The pleading had gone.

Dorothy had left for her cruise. Judy smiled, remembering the last thing she said to Dorothy as she climbed into her taxi. "You're not in Kansas anymore, Dorothy."

That morning, she'd finished a feature, the first of a series, about becoming a business owner. This afternoon, she'd host a get together for *her* Farrington family.

"How do you feel Frank? Do you feel? About your first family reunion in a decade?"

The next day, the workers would arrive and begin gutting Kansas Café, a part of her life, her daily routine for a decade. Mournful tears built behind Judy's eyes, held back by a dam of exhilaration at the birth of Frank's Diner. *Emotions are fickle. Fleeting and lingering, exciting and sorrowful, at the same time.*

Judy opened her iPad and added *Keeping Track of Our Contradictory Emotions* to her list of features. Judy's features continued to reflect her random thoughts, but her mini features were based on her observations. She was unaware of the distinction.

"Our last quiet moment together on this sofa. Not sure if you'll stick around, but I hope you do. I'll miss you if you go. You've been a good friend."

Wish he'd speak to me.

"Yes, Frank. We've been good friends to each other."

Judy stared out the window, remembering Frank on the day they met.

"My life's changed so much since that day, and look at you… No longer that angry fat man I met. Younger, slim. The way you were in your prime when you were going to be anything. A man of rare character and integrity."

She drank the last of her coffee and glanced around the empty café. A solitary tear made its way down her cheek.

My life's full of people now. Before I met Frank, spent most of my time alone. Not lonely or unhappy. Enjoyed my life. People drift out of our lives, and we don't notice.

Judy looked up when she heard the doorbell. *Must ask Becky if we can keep the bell. I like to hear it as people enter and leave.*

"Here's Myron now, Frank."

She stood to greet Myron with a powerful hug and a long kiss.

"Wow. That's a greeting. You look amazing, sweetheart. My God, I see you for a minute, and my cock is hard as steel. Feel it." Myron positioned Judy's hand on the bulge in his trousers.

Judy caressed it a little, feeling herself become moist. "Behave yourself."

"Not my fault you have a sexy ass. I'm a lucky man. Better check on Rebekah and Darnell."

"Better get that bulge under control first, I think." She smiled as she returned to the sofa, and Frank.

The door brushed the bell again. John, Ali, and their children. *I really must ask Becky to keep that bell.*

"The family is arriving, Frank. How long since you've seen them all together?"

She stood and went to greet them.

Judy greeted the children first, "Hi kids."

They replied in unison, "Hello, Aunt Judy."

I've acquired so many nieces and nephews. "Find yourselves somewhere to sit. Hello John." She hugged him and kissed his cheek.

Ali held her tight and kissed her lightly on the lips, whispering, "You look amazing, darling. I see you for a minute and I'm almost dripping. You wanna feel it?"

"Behave yourself," Judy whispered back.

John asked, "Are we the first to arrive?"

"Myron is in the back with Becky and Darnell."

"Assumed Susie would be first," Ali commented.

"Yes, me too," Judy agreed.

"Said she needed to collect a letter or something on the way," John explained.

"Make yourselves comfortable. I'll let Myron know you're here. You guys wanna coffee?"

"Of course, John'll have one," Ali said. "I will too."

"Okay."

"John and Ali have arrived," she said as she entered the kitchen.

"I'll go say hello," Myron said.

I like how he always goes out of his way to say hello to people. He liked *her family*, and he genuinely liked Ali. No hint of jealousy. As Myron passed her, she stopped him for a moment and kissed him.

"I love you, darling. You're an amazing man."

Rebekah squeezed Judy's arm. "I think you guys are both amazing."

Darnell added, "Me too. Few people would've warmly accepted someone with my history."

Judy swallowed back her tears.

"Becky, I want us to keep that bell on the door. Do you think we can?"

"Of course, Aunt Judy. I love hearing that bell."

"Becky, would you mind making some coffee for John and Ali?"

"Sure. I'm trying our flat white made with The John Farrington Blend today. Works better with the blend than a latte. Those macadamia, mandarin and white chocolate cookies from Alice's pair well with the coffee. Been talking to them about selling them in the diner. They're being very agreeable, seems your blog about those cookies has made them famous."

"If any cookie deserves a blog, it's those cookies," Darnell suggested.

Rebekah added, "I want to meet John Farrington and compliment him on his blend."

The doorbell sounded as somebody else arrived.

"Love that sound," Judy repeated as she went to greet whoever it was. "Maybe some sodas for the kids too, Becky."

Jenny, Dave, and their kids.

"Hi Aunt Judy," the kids said.

"Hi kids. Becky will bring you guys some sodas."

Judy joined Myron in welcoming Jenny and Dave.

"Susie, not here yet?" asked Jenny.

"No, she said something about collecting a letter on the way," John explained.

"Oh… hello John," Jenny said. "Hi Ali."

"Take a seat," Judy said. "Becky's organizing some coffees."

"Hi everyone," Rebekah said. "Won't be a moment." She placed a selection of sodas on the counter. "Help yourself to sodas, guys."

Myron said to John and Dave, "Give me a hand and we'll rearrange these sofas a little so we can all sit together."

As the men were moving sofas creating a square with four sofas and two tables in the middle, Jenny motioned to the sheet that was covering a table and something on the wall. "What's under that Judy?"

"The reason we're having this get together here. Myron and I have two announcements to make."

"Two?" questioned Ali quietly, so only Judy and Jenny could hear. "Pregnant and getting married?" she asked.

"No… On both counts," answered Judy with a smile.

"Would you like a coffee too, Uncle Myron?" Rebekah asked.

"Yes, please Rebekah."

"Me too," said Judy.

"Guessed that." Rebekah smiled.

Darnell placed plates of cookies on the table and on the kids' table. Then helped Rebekah bring the coffees to the table.

John took a sip of his coffee and smiled. "My blend!"

Rebekah said, "It's wonderful."

Susie arrived with her children, who joined their cousins.

Judy stood to greet her. Susie hugged Judy hard, and for a long time. It seemed she didn't want to let go. "You're a remarkable lady," she said.

Releasing Judy, she said, "Hello everyone." And unable to resist her dig at her brother, "Hello junior," who rolled his eyes and grimaced.

"He'll never learn," said Ali.

Susie couldn't contain herself. "You won't believe what this remarkable lady has done. She's finished repaying Frank's investors. I can't believe it."

Susie reached into her bag and retrieved one of Judy's letters to an investor. "You see… Look at this letter," she said, as she passed it to John. "I'm so proud of our Judy."

John stared at the letter. "Unbelievable. Thank you, Judy," and gave it to Ali, who read it before handing it to Jenny.

"You really *are* amazing, Judy," Ali said.

When Jenny read the letter, she said, "Frank can rest in peace now. He would've been so proud of you. Thank you." She showed it to Dave, who shook his head as he looked at Judy with admiration.

"Has Susie stolen your thunder?" Jenny asked. "Is that what you were going to announce?"

"No. I didn't plan on mentioning it." Judy replied. *What Frank wanted.*

Susie squeezed her hand and sat down. Taking a sip of her coffee, she said, "Junior's coffee."

John grimaced.

Ali said, "Never."

"I have more news," Susie said. "Frank's business sold for more than expected. Apparently, someone wanted the business, not just the stock."

John said, "Good news, Suse."

Jenny said, "I like the idea of his business carrying on. He spent so many years developing it. Would've been a shame if it died with him."

"That brings us to our first announcement," Judy, who had remained standing, said. All eyes focused on her. "Myron and I bought Frank's business. Jenny's right, Frank put so much of himself into that business, we couldn't let it die. Plus, being honest, we believe it'll be profitable."

"Fantastic news. Of course, you'll want it to be profitable," Susie said. "I had no idea you were thinking about it."

"It happened quickly. An auction. Weren't sure if we'd be able to afford it… You never know about these things."

John said, "Thought of it, but wouldn't know where to start with running it."

Judy explained, "We'll hire two brothers, clients of Myron's whose business went bankrupt. They're trying to survive and support their families. Myron helps people like that, gives people second chances. Frank would like to know his business is helping the brothers get back on their feet."

"He would," Jenny agreed. "Frank always helped people when he could. John's correct, any of us could've bid. This way, it gets to stay in the family and Frank helps those brothers. Plus, we'll get more than we expected from Frank's estate. Susie's right, it's fantastic."

Darnell and Rebekah began bringing the food out, and placing it on the counter buffet style.

Judy said, "Lunch is almost ready. So, I'd better tell you our other news. This place closed yesterday."

Susie said, "That's sad. I like this place. It's like a home to you."

"Been a big week for us. Myron and I bought this place too. Rebekah and Darnell will run it. Myron giving people a second chance."

Judy looked at Myron. Her eyes filled with love and admiration.

Myron flushed as he stood and walked to the covered display. He removed the cover and revealed the model and the drawings for the design of Frank's Diner.

"May I present Frank's Diner?"

Judy said, "We'll replace the café with a diner which we're naming in memory of Frank."

Susie jumped up and almost ran to the model. "I can't believe this."

The others followed.

Myron said, "There'll be a plaque on the wall adjacent to where Frank passed away."

Susie read the plaque.

In memory of Frank Farrington: A man of rare integrity and character.

She gasped. Tears were running down her cheeks as she turned and embraced Judy tightly. "Thank you, thank you, thank you," she sobbed. "I can't believe this, can't take it all in."

John stared in disbelief.

Rebekah said, "The John Farrington Blend will be our house coffee."

John looked at her, stunned. "Really?"

Jenny said little, but stared at Frank's memorial plaque. Like Susie, tears fell from her eyes. Susie hugged her and they gazed at the plaque commemorating their brother.

Dave was talking with Myron, discussing the plans.

Ali hugged Judy. "You're a *special lady*, Judy."

Jenny and Susie looked at each other, and despite their emotion, rolled their eyes. Ali was constantly singing Judy's praises.

The children crowded around the model, talking excitedly.

"Lunch is ready, everybody," Darnell said. "Take a plate and help yourselves. If you need anything, just ask."

"You kids go first," Susie said. "Don't be wasteful and take too much."

Meatloaf and mashed potato, fish and chips, stuffed mushroom caps, Susie's mac and cheese, some grilled vegetables, and a seafood spaghetti dish.

"These are samples of the food we'll be serving at the diner," Rebekah said.

Judy said to Susie, "Your mac and cheese. I gave Darnell the recipe. John's coffee and your mac and cheese seemed appropriate."

"A real Farrington Family connection." Susie agreed.

"This is damn fine food." Dave said.

"Agreed," said John. "If this is the quality of the food, we'll be regulars. Won't we Ali?"

"Oh yes. Those chips are unbelievable, and the meatloaf is to die for, not dry at all."

"I add bone marrow," Darnell explained. "It keeps the meatloaf moist and adds depth to the flavor."

Jenny said, "We'll be regulars too. I think that mac and cheese is better than Susie's."

Myron was standing with Rebekah and Darnell. He squeezed each of their shoulders.

"We're going to do well here, I think."

***

After the meal, Rebekah brought out another round of coffees and slices of Dorothy's New York style cheesecake.

"This is Dorothy's cheesecake," she said. "We'll be keeping it on the menu, but will rename it Kansas Cheesecake as a tribute to Kansas Café."

Judy said, "Becky, could I have mine in my usual seat? One last time." *Frank seems so lonely sitting there by himself.*

Judy sat opposite Frank, enjoying her cheesecake and coffee. Quietly talking with him so no one would notice. Nobody disturbed her.

Frank was looking at his family, smiling. He surprised Judy when he stood and indicated she should stand as well. The only time he'd communicated with her, outside of her mind, beyond his eyes and his smile.

Frank stepped towards Judy and hugged her warmly. Judy was confused. *How can I feel him?* Her confusion didn't stop her from relishing Frank's hug.

Judy was wide eyed and slack jawed when Frank spoke to her for the first time, living or dead.

"Thank you, Judy… for everything."

He released her, turned and walked away, leaving the Café, through the door.

***

Myron was standing with Susie, discussing the model of Frank's Diner, when they heard the doorbell. They both glanced at the door, but nobody was there.

"Strange," said Susie.

"Maybe not," replied Myron, who was looking at Judy, standing by herself, smiling with a tear running down her cheek.

He sensed, rather than heard Judy say, "Goodbye, Frank."

Sonny Kohet

Sonny began writing fiction late in life.

During the 2020 Covid lockdown in Beijing, Sonny completed the Start Writing Fiction course from Future Learn. Two exercises from week two were to describe a writing space, and to imagine a character.

These two exercises became the first chapter of this book, as Sonny continued writing. The simple exercise in a writing course became a series of five character-driven stories focused around the life of the main character, Judy Vernon.

Experiential travel, living in different countries, and working in remote and unusual locations, through seven different careers, has introduced Sonny to a range of unusual characters, broken people, and misfits who fuel the characters he brings to life in his writing.

Any feedback, comments, suggestions, observations, or questions can be directed to Sonny at sonnykohet.com.

www.ingramcontent.com/pod-product-compliance
Lightning Source LLC
Chambersburg PA
CBHW072109250626
47159CB00007B/2363